Bert Leston Taylor, Alvin T. Thoits

Under Three Flags

A Story of Mystery

Bert Leston Taylor, Alvin T. Thoits

Under Three Flags
A Story of Mystery

ISBN/EAN: 9783744747622

Printed in Europe, USA, Canada, Australia, Japan

Cover: Foto ©Andreas Hilbeck / pixelio.de

More available books at **www.hansebooks.com**

Under Three Flags

A Story of Mystery

BY

B. L. TAYLOR AND A. T. THOITS.

CHICAGO AND NEW YORK:
RAND, McNALLY & COMPANY.
MDCCCXCVI.

In The Chicago Record's series of "Stories of Mystery."

UNDER THREE FLAGS

BY

B. L. TAYLOR AND A. T. THOITS.

(This story — out of 816 competing — was awarded the THIRD PRIZE in THE CHICAGO RECORD'S "$30,000 to Authors" competition.)

UNDER THREE FLAGS.

CHAPTER I.

"OVER THE HILLS AND FAR AWAY."

"No; I am not tired of life. Who could be on such a day? I am weary simply of this way of living. I want to get away—away from this stagnant hole. It is the same dull story over and over again, day after day, world without end, amen!"

"Would you be a bit more contented in any other spot?"

"I think so. I cannot believe that mankind in general is so selfish, so hypocritical, and, worst crime of all, so hopelessly stupid as it is here. The world is 25,000 miles in circumference. Why spend all one's days in this split in the mountains?"

"But, tell me, what is your ambition, then? Have you one?"

"You would smile pityingly if I told it you."

"No; I'll be as serious as—as you."

"Then incline thine ear. I would I were the ruler of a savage tribe, in the heart of far-away New Zealand, shut in by towering mountains from the outer world."

"But why spend all one's days in a valley?"

"Oh, well, if you're going in for a valley, why not have a good one?"

She throws herself down beside him on the grass and clasps her arms about his neck. "You foolish boy; you don't know what you want."

"Don't I?" He draws the glowing face to his and kisses it.

The two are idling in a grassy nook on the slope of one of Vermont's green hills, sheltered by a clump of spruce from observation and the slanting rays of the sun.

There is an infinite calm in the late spring air, and the golden afternoon drifts by on lazy pinions. Away in the west, across the vale, the main spur of the Green Mountain range awaits the last pencilings of the low-descending sun. Southward Wild River sings its way through buttercup and daisy flecked meadows; to the north the smoke from the chimneys of Raymond blurs the lines of as fair a landscape as earth can boast.

Derrick Ames pulls his hat over his eyes, stretches himself on the greensward and gazes long and lovingly at his companion. The fair face, browned by many rambles among the hills; the rippling hair, tumbled in confusion about mischievous and laughter-laden brown eyes; the rounded arms; the slim, girlish figure, about which even the coarse dress donned for mountain climbing falls in graceful lines; the dainty feet and the perfectly turned ankles, make a picture for an artist.

She picked up the book which lies open upon the grass and glances over its pages, dreamily.

The sun goes down in a golden haze, and still the lovers tarry in their sylvan trysting-place.

"It is getting late and damp; we had better be moving," he says, finally.

They arise and take their way across the pasture, their arms clasped about each other's waist. Derrick is talking in low, earnest tones, with an infrequent interruption by his companion.

"It's no use," he exclaims, impatiently, in reply to a protest on her part. "Twice I have spoken to your father, with the same result. I have been refused and insulted. He is selfish, overbearing—"

She places one hand upon his lips. "But will you not make a third trial—for my sake," she pleads.

"For your sake I would do anything," he answers, pressing the soft hand to his lips. "There is no time like the present. Will you wait for me here?" She nods. "Where will I find your father?"

"At the bank.　I think he said he would be there all the evening."

"I will return shortly, for I know what the answer will be."

She watches the erect form of her lover as he strides down the road leading into the village.

The shadows deepen in the valley.　The opalescent light that hangs over the range fades into the darkening gray.　The moon rises in full, round splendor and transforms the river into a silver torrent.

The clanging of the Raymond town clock, as it hammers out the hour of 8, rouses the girl.　"Derrick should be here soon," she murmurs.　Then she clutches her heart with an exclamation of pain and terror.

It is a swift, sharp spasm, that passes away as quickly as it came, and which leaves the girl for several minutes afterward somewhat dazed.　Footsteps echo in the road.

"The result?" eagerly, anxiously queries the girl as Derrick reaches her side.

He must have walked swiftly.　He is breathing hard and his face is pale as the moonlight.　Or is it the reflection of that light?

"Come away from here, for God's sake!" he exclaims in a harsh, unnatural voice, half-dragging her into the road.　"I beg your pardon; I did not mean to be rough," he adds, as the astonished eyes of the girl look into his. "Will you come for a walk, dear?"　And as she follows, mechanically, wonderingly, he walks swiftly away from the village.

"I am all out of breath," she protests, after a few moments of the fierce pace he has set.　And they stop to rest at a spring beside the road.

"You have quarreled with father," asserts the girl, half questioningly; but Derrick remains silent.

He stops suddenly, and, holding her in his arms, smooths back the dark ringlets from her moist brow. "Helen, darling, do not press me for an answer to-night. Let us be happy in the present.　God knows it may not be for long."　He presses a passionate kiss upon the girl's unresisting and unresponsive lips, and then lifts to the moonlight a face as troubled as the tossing river behind the dusky willows. As he releases her he extends his arm toward the ball of silver that is wheeling up the heavens. "See!" he cries. "The moon is up and it is a glorious night. Shall we follow that pathway of silver over the hills and far away?"

A loving look is her willing assent.

The witchery that the moon is said to exert o'er mortals must be more than a poet's myth. A strange peace has come upon the girl. Her senses are exalted. She seems to be walking on air. Nor does she now break upon the silence of her companion, whose agitation has been replaced by a singular calm.

What a stillness, yet what a busy world claims the woods they are crossing to-night! The crawling of a beetle through the dead leaves is distinctly heard, and a thousand small noises that the day never hears fill the forest with a strange music.

A short distance farther and the wanderers emerge into the open and pause to marvel at the picture spread before them.

It is a wondrous night. Bathed in a radiance that tips with silver every dew-laden spear of grass, the pasture slopes down to a highway, and the brawling of the brook beside it comes to their ears as a strain of music.

Silently the lovers take their way through this fairyland, clamber over the wall into the road, and continue on.

"I am cold," complains the girl, with a little shiver. Derrick wraps his light overcoat about her shoulders.

*   *   *   *   *   *   *

The striking of a town clock causes them both to start.

"Where are we?" asks the girl, looking about her in bewilderment. The moon passes behind a cloud. The spell is over.

"Why, this is Ashfield, isn't it? There is the station, and the church and the—Derrick! Derrick, where have we been wandering? Five miles from home and midnight! What will Louise and father say? We must go home at once."

"Home," he repeats, bitterly, pointing to the north. "There is no home yonder for me. Listen, Helen!" He draws her to him fiercely. "If we part now it must be forever. I shall never go back. I cannot go back! Will you not come away with me—somewhere—any-where? Hark!"

The whistle of the Montreal express sounds from the north.

The girl seems not to hear him. The long whistle of the express again echoes through the night.

"Helen, darling!" There is a world of yearning and entreaty in his voice.

She throws her arms about him and kisses him. "Yes, Derrick; I will go with you—to the end of the world."

The station agent regards the pair suspiciously. In the dim light of the kerosene lamps of the waiting-room their features are only partially discernible.

"Sorry," he says, "but this train don't stop except for through passengers to New York."

"But we are going to New York," almost shouts Derrick. "Quick, man!" The train has swept around the curve above the village and is thundering down the stretch.

"Wall, I guess I kin accommerdate ye," drawls the station master. He seizes his lantern and swings it about his head and No. 51 draws up panting in the station.

"Elopement, I guess," confides the station agent to the conductor, as Derrick and the girl clamber aboard the train.

The latter growls something about being twenty minutes late out of St. Albans, swings his lantern and No. 51 rumbles away in the mist and moonlight.

CHAPTER II.

THE PRISONER OF WINDSOR—THE TRAGEDY OF A NIGHT.

"Stanley, I have good news for you."

"All news is alike to me, sir."

Warden Chase of the Vermont state prison regards the young man before him with a kindly eye.

"Your sentence of three years has been shortened by a year, as the governor has granted you an unconditional pardon," he announces.

"His excellency is kind," replied the young man in a voice that expresses no gratitude and may contain a faint shade of irony.

He is a striking-looking young fellow, even in his prison garb, his dark hair cropped close and his eyes cast down in the passive manner enjoined by the prison regulations. His height is about five feet ten inches and his figure is rather slender and graceful. His face is singularly handsome. His eyes are dark brown, almost black, and the two long years of prison life have dimmed but little of the fire that flashes from their depths. A square jaw bespeaks a strong will. The rather hard lines about the firm mouth were not there two years before. He has suffered mentally since then. There are too many gray hairs for a man of 28.

Warden Chase touches a bell. "Get Stanley's things," he orders the attendant, who responds.

"Sit down, Stanley." The young man obeys and the warden wheels about to his desk.

"I am authorized to purchase you a railroad ticket to any station you may designate—within reason, of course," amends Mr. Chase. "Which shall it be?" A bitter smile flits across Stanley's face and he remains silent.

"North, east, south or west?" questions Mr. Chase, poising his pen in air.

"I have no home to go to," finally responds Stanley, lifting his eyes for the first time since his entrance to the room.

"No home?" repeats the warden, sympathetically. "But surely you must want to go somewhere. You can't stay in Windsor."

Stanley is thoughtful. "Perhaps you had better make the station Raymond," he decides, and he meets squarely the surprised and questioning look of the warden.

"But that is the place you were sent from."

"Yes."

"It is not your home? No; I believe you just stated that you had no home."

"I have none."

"And you wish to revisit the scene of your—your trouble?"

Stanley's gaze wanders to the open window and across the valley.

"Well, it's your own affair," says the warden, turning to his desk. "The fare to Raymond is $2.50. I am also authorized to give you $5 cash, to which I have added $10. You have assisted me about the books of the institution and have been in every respect a model prisoner. In fact," supplements Mr. Chase, with a smile, "under different circumstances I should be sorry to part with you."

"Thank you," acknowledges Stanley, in the same impassive tones.

"And now, my boy," counsels the warden, laying one hand kindly on the young man's shoulder, "try to make your future life such that you will never be compelled to see the inside of another house of this kind. I am something of a judge of character. I am confident that you have the making of a man in you. Here are your things," as the attendant arrives with Stanley's effects.

Mr. Chase resumes his writing and Stanley withdraws. Once within the familiar cell, which is soon to know him no more, his whole mood changes.

"Free!" he breathes, exultingly, raising his clasped hands to heaven. "What matter it if my freedom be of a few days only, of a few hours? It will be enough for my purpose. Heavens! Two years in this hole, caged like a wild beast, the companion of worse than beasts—a life wrecked at 28. But I'll be revenged! As surely as there is a heaven above me, I'll be repaid for my months of misery. An eye for an eye, and a tooth for a tooth!"

He throws his prison suit from him with loathing. Then he sinks back into his apathy and the simple toilet is completed in silence.

A suit of light gray, of stylish cut, a pair of well-made boots, a neglige shirt and a straw hat, make considerable change in his appearance. He smiles faintly as he dons them.

He ties his personal effects in a small package. They are few—half a dozen letters, all with long-ago postmarks, a couple of photographs, and a small volume of Shakespeare given him by the warden, who is an admirer of Avon's bard.

"Off?" asks Mr. Chase, as he shakes hands. "Well, you look about the same as when I received you. A little older, perhaps"—surveying him critically—"and minus what I remember to have been a handsome mustache. Good-by, my boy, and good luck. And, I say," as Stanley strides toward the door, "take my advice and the afternoon train for New York. Get some honest employment and make a name for yourself. You've got the right stuff in you. By the way, do you know what day it is?"

"I have not followed the calendar with reference to any particular days."

"The 30th day of May—Memorial day," says Mr. Chase.

"It will be a memorial day for me," responds Stanley. "Good-by, Mr. Chase, and thank you for your many kindnesses."

"I'm rather sorry to have him go," soliloquizes the warden, as his late charge walks slowly away from the institution. "Bright fellow, but peculiar—very peculiar."

Stanley proceeds leisurely along the road leading to

the station. His eyes are bent down, and he seemingly takes no note of the glories of the May day, of the throbbings of the busy life about him. A procession of Grand Army men, headed by a brass band that makes music more mournful than the occasion seems to call for, passes by on the dusty highway.

"Homage for the dead; contumely for the living," he murmurs, bitterly.

The train for the north leaves at 4:30. Stanley spends the time between in making some small purchases at the village.

"At what hour do we arrive at Raymond?" he asks the conductor, as the train pulls out.

"Seven forty-five, if we are on time."

"Thank you," returns the young man. He draws his hat over his eyes, and turns his face to the window.

*　　*　　*　　*　　*　　*　　*　　*　　*

At 7:45 o'clock in the evening Sarah, the pretty house-maid at the residence of Cyrus Felton, answers a sharp ring at the door bell. In the semi-darkness of the vine-shaded porch she distinguishes only the outlines of a man who stands well back from the door. The gas has not yet been lighted in the hall.

"Is Mr. Felton at home?" inquires the visitor.

"The young or the old Mr. Felton?"

"The young or the old?" repeats the man to himself. Sarah twists the door-knob impatiently. "Well?" she says.

"I beg your pardon; I was not aware that there were two Mr. Feltons. I believe the elder is the person I wish to see.

"He is not at home."

"He is in town?"

"Oh, yes. He went down-street about 7 o'clock, but we expect him back before long."

"Would he be likely to be at his office?"

Sarah does not know. Mr. Felton rarely goes to the office evenings. Still, he may be there.

"And the office is where?"

"In the bank block." Sarah peers out at her questioner, but, with a "thank you," he has already stepped from the porch. As he strides away in the dusk and the house door slams behind him, a second figure leaves the shadow of the trellis, moves across the lawn and pauses at the gate.

"In the bank building," he muses. "One visitor ahead of me. Well, there is no need of my hurrying," and he saunters toward the village, the electric lamps of which have begun to flash.

At 8:05, as Sarah afterwards remembers, Cyrus Felton arrives home. Sarah comes into the hall to receive him.

"A gentleman called to see you, sir, about ten minutes ago. Did you meet him on your way?"

"Probably not. I have been over to Mr. Goodenough's. Did he leave any name?"

"No, sir. Oh, and here is a letter that a boy brought a little while ago." Sarah produces a note from the hall table and disappears upstairs.

Mr. Felton opens the note, glances at its contents and utters an exclamation of impatience. He crumples the paper in his hand, seizes his hat and hurries from the house and down the street.

In the brightly lighted room of Prof. George Black, directly over the quarters of the Raymond National Bank, a party of young men are whiling away a few pleasant hours. The professor is lounging in an easy-chair, his feet in another, and is lost in a "meditation" for violin, to which Ed Knapp is furnishing a piano accompaniment. Suddenly the professor rests his violin across his knees.

"Hark!" he exclaims and bends his head toward the open window. "Wasn't that a shot downstairs?"

"Probably," assents one of the group. "The boys in the bank have been plugging water rats in the river all the afternoon."

"But it's too dark to shoot rats."

"Oh, one can aim pretty straight by electric light. Go ahead with your fiddling, George. Get away from that piano, Knapp, and let the professor give us the cavatina.

That's my favorite, and your accompaniment would ruin it. Let 'er go, professor."

As the strains of the Raff cavatina die away, a man comes out of the entrance of the Raymond National Bank. He glances swiftly up, then down the street. Then he crosses the road in the shadow of a tall building and hurries toward the station.

"There is no train, north or south, before 11:50," says the telegraph operator, in response to a query at the window. He is clicking off a message and does not turn his head. His questioner vanishes.

*　　*　　*　　*　　*　　*　　*

"Jim, Mr. Felton wants to see you," the clerk of the Raymond Hotel informs the sheriff of Mansfield County, who is playing cards in a room off the office. Sheriff Wilson is a man with a game leg, a war record, and a wild mania for the diversion of sancho pedro. When he sits in for an evening of that fascinating pastime he dislikes to be disturbed.

"What's he want?" he asks absent-mindedly, for he has only two more points to make to win the game.

"Dunno. He seems to be worked up about something."

"High, low, pede!" announces the sheriff triumphantly. "Gentlemen, make mine a cigar." He throws his cards down and goes out into the office. Cyrus Felton is pacing up and down excitedly. He grasps the officer by the arm and half drags him from the hotel. When they are out of hearing of the loungers he exclaims, in a voice that trembles with every syllable:

"Mr. Wilson, a fearful crime has been committed. Mr. Hathaway has been murdered!"

"Murdered!" The sheriff's excitement transcends that of his companion, who is making a desperate effort to regain his composure.

"He is at the bank. I discovered him only a few moments ago. Come, see for yourself."

They soon reach the bank, which is only a stone's throw from the hotel. After passing the ·threshold of the cashier's office in the rear of the banking-room the two men stop and look silently upon the grewsome sight before them.

Lying upon the floor, one arm extended toward and almost touching the wide-open doors of the vault, is the body of Cashier Roger Hathaway. His life has ebbed in the crimson pool that stains the polished floor.

CHAPTER III.

JACK ASHLEY, JOURNALIST.

A loud pounding on the door of his room in the tavern at South Ashfield awakens Mr. Jack Ashley from a dream of piscatorial conquest.

"Four o'clock!" announces the disturber of his slumbers, with a parting thump. Ashley rolls out of bed and plunges his face into a brimming bowl of spring water.

It is early dawn. A cool breeze, laden with the scent of apple blossoms, drifts through the window.

"God made the country and man made the town," quotes the young man, as he descends to the hotel office.

"Ain't used to gittin' up at this hour, be ye?" grins the proprietary genius of the tavern.

"The habit, worthy host, has not fastened upon me seriously. This is usually my hour for going to bed. Hast aught to eat?"

"Breakfas' all ready," with a nod toward what is known as the dining-room.

Ashley shudders as he gazes at the spread. It is the usual Vermont breakfast—weak coffee, two kinds of pie on one plate, and a tier of doughnuts.

"Gad! This country is a howling wilderness of pie!" he mutters, surveying the repast in comical despair. "And to flash it on a man at 4 a. m.! It is simply barbarous!"

During his short vacation sojourn Mr. Ashley's epicurean tastes have suffered a number of distinct shocks. But the ozone of the Green Mountains has contributed toward the generation of an appetite that needs little tempting to expend its energies. He makes a hearty breakfast on this particular morning, drowns the memories of the menu in a bowl of milk, and announces to Landlord Howe that he is ready to be directed to the best trout brook in central Vermont.

Mr. Howe surveys the eight-ounce bamboo with mild disdain. "Them fancy rigs ain't much good on our brooks," he declares. "Ketch more with a 75-cent rod."

"I am rather inclined to agree with you on that point, most genial boniface; but it's the only rod I happen to have with me, and I expect to return with some fish unless the myriad denizens of the brook which you enthusiastically described last night exist only in your imagination. By the way, what do you think of the bait?" passing over a flask.

Mr. Howe's faded blue eyes moisten and a kindly smile plays over a countenance browned by many summers in the hay field.

"Didn't buy that in Vermont," he ventures.

"Hardly. I'm not lined with asbestos."

The landlord grins. It is a habit he has.

"I keeps a little suthin' on hand myself," he confides in a cautious undertone, although only the cattle are listening. "But fact is, there ain't no use er keepin' better'n dollar'n a half a gallon liquor. The boys want suthin' that'll scratch when it goes down. Now that, I opine," with an affectionate glance at the flask which Ashley files away for future reference, "must a cost nigh onter $3 a gallon."

"As much as that," smiles Ashley. "That, most appreciative of bonifaces, "is the best whisky to be found on Fulton street, New York. Well, I must be 'driving along.' Where's this wonderful brook of yours?"

"Follow that road round through the barnyard and 'cross the basin to the woods. Good fishin' for four miles. And mind," as Ashley saunters away, "don't bring back any trouts that ain't six inches long, or the fish warden will light on ye."

"Thanks. If I should run across the warden——" and Ashley holds up the flask.

"That'd fetch him, I reckon," chuckles Mr. Howe. Ashley vaults over the bars and strides across the meadows.

Ashley is in high feather. "This air rather discounts an absinthe frappe for stimulative purposes," he soliloquizes. "Ah, here's the wood, there's the brook, and if I mistake not, yonder pool hides a whopper just aching for a go at the early worm." But it doesn't and Ashley enters the forest.

The farther he plunges into the spice-laden wilderness the more is he enchanted with his surroundings. Picture a cleft in the mountain whose sides drop almost sheer to a gorge barely wide enough to accommodate a wood road and a brook that parallels and often encroaches upon it. Tall pines interlace and shut out the direct rays of the sun and every now and then a cascade comes tumbling somewhere aloft and plunges into a broad, pebble-lined basin.

As Ashley sits by one of these pools, his wading boots plunged deep in the crystal liquid, and pulls lazily on a briar pipe, the reader is offered the opportunity of becoming better acquainted with him.

He is a prepossessing young fellow of something like 27, medium height and rather well built. Blue eyes and an aggressive nose, on which gold-bowed eyeglasses are airily perched, are characteristics of a face which has always been a passport for its owner into all society worth cultivating. A well-shaped head is adorned with a profusion of blond curls, supplemented by a mustache of silken texture and golden hue, which its possessor is fond of twisting when he is in a blithesome humor, which is often, and of tugging at savagely when in a reflective mood, which is infrequent.

Ashley is noted among his friends for chronic good humor and unbounded confidence in his own abilities. He is one of the brightest all-round writers on the New York Hemisphere, and he knows it. The best of it is, City Editor Ricker also knows it. All the office sings of his exploits and "beats" and does their author reverence. Jack always calls himself a newspaper man. That is the sensible title. Yet he might wear the name of journalist much more worthily.

Ashley is in Vermont for his health. Five years of continuous hustling on a big New York daily has necessitated a breathing spell. He was telling Mr. Ricker that his "wheels were all run down and needed repairing," and that he believed he would take his vacation early this year.

"I'll tell you where you want to go," volunteered the city editor, who was "raised" among the Green Mountains and served his apprenticeship gathering locals on a Burlington weekly.

"All right; let's have it."

"Take three weeks off and go up into Vermont."

"Vermont—Vermont—where's Vermont? O, yes, that green daub on the map of New England. Railroad run through there?"

"Now, see here, Jack," retorted Ricker, "you're not so confoundedly ignorant as you imply. That's the trouble with you New Yorkers who were born and bred here. You consider everything above the Harlem River a jay community. You're a sight more provincial than half the inhabitants of rural New England."

Jack laughed. "Come to think of it, you hailed from there."

"Yes, and it's a mighty good State to hail from. Now, you run up to Raymond—it's a little town about in the Y of the Green Mountain range. You'll not have Broadway, with its theaters, and restaurants, and bars, but you'll get a big room, with a clean, airy bed to sleep in—none of your narrow hall-chamber cots—and good, plain, wholesome food to eat. Those necessities of life which Vermont does not supply, good tobacco and good whisky, you can take with you. You'll come back feeling like a fighting cock." And before his chief finished painting the attractions of the Green Mountain State, with incidental references to John Stark and Ethan Allen,

Ashley was willing to compromise and two days later found him en route for Raymond.

Jack fishes the brook as he does everything else—without any waste of mental or physical exertion.

Landlord Howe did not deceive him. It is an excellent trout brook, and by the time the sun is well up he has acquired a well-filled creel. He is sauntering along to what he has decided shall be the last pool, when, as he turns a bend in the road, he runs upon a man lying beside the path, with one arm shading his face and clutching in the other hand a package.

"Hello!" sings out Ashley, stopping short in surprise. The man arises and passes his hand over his eyes in bewilderment.

"Off the main road, aren't you?" queries Ashley. The stranger makes no reply. He bestows upon Ashley a single searching glance and hurries down the road in the direction of the village.

"He'll be likely to know me again," is Jack's comment. "Gad! What eyes! They went through me like a stiletto. What the deuce is he prowling around here for at this time o' day? He isn't a fisherman and he can't be farming it with those store clothes on. Well, here goes for the last trout."

The last trout is not forthcoming, however, so the fisherman unjoints his rod, reloads and fires his pipe and strolls slowly back to the hotel. Landlord Howe sees him as he comes swinging across the basin and waits with some impatience until the young man gets within hailing distance, when he informs him dramatically:

"Big murder at Raymond last night."

"How big?" asks Ashley, with lazy interest. Murders are frequent episodes in his line of business.

Well, it is the largest affair that Mr. Howe has known of "round these parts since dad was a kid." Roger Hathaway, cashier of the Raymond National bank, has been found murdered and the bank robbed of a large sum of money, and there is no clew to the murderer. The details of the tragedy have come over the telephone wires early this morning, and the whole county is in a fever of excitement.

"No clew?" muses Ashley, and his interest in the affair grows. Then he thinks of the man he encountered on the brook an hour ago. "Seen any strangers around here?" he inquires of Mr. Howe.

"No one 'cept you," replies that worthy, contributing a broad grin.

"Oh, but I can prove an alibi," laughs Jack. "I came down from Raymond on the early evening train, and everyone was alive in the town then, I guess. Are the police of this village on the lookout?"

"Well, rather. The local deputy sheriff is on the alert as never before in his life."

"It is not impossible that my early morning friend on the brook was mixed up in last night's affair," thinks Ashley. But he says nothing of the meeting. What is the use? If the unknown was fleeing he must be pretty well into the next county by this time. But in what direction?"

The Raymond murder is the one topic of the day at South Ashfield. The villagers are gathered in force about the hotel veranda and Ashley fancies that they regard him a trifle askance as he hunts up a chair and kills an hour while waiting for the up-train, in listening to the rural persiflage of the group and the ingenious theories of the local oracle.

"At what time did the killing occur?" he inquires of one of the loungers. Somewhere around 8 o'clock the night before, he is informed.

"And no clew to the murderer," he meditates. "Now, if this was New York I'd take hold of the affair and work it for all it was worth."

'He little dreams what effect the "affair" is to have on his future. Yet as the train bears him to Raymond the instinct of the newspaper man tells him that it is a cast possessing phases of peculiar interest. And he is not wholly unprepared for the telegram that is thrust into his hands when he leaves the train.

"One of the disadvantages of telling your paper where

you intend spending your vacation," he remarks as he glances at the dispatch. Then to the telegraph operator: "I'll have a story for you after supper."

CHAPTER IV.

THE STORY OF A CRIME.

The following dispatch appeared in the columns of the New York Hemisphere, under the usual sensational head-lines:

"Raymond, Vt., May 31.—This quiet town among the Green Mountains had cause indeed to mourn upon this year's occurrence of the nation's Memorial Day. Last evening, at the close of the most general observance of the solemn holiday yet undertaken in Raymond, the community was horror-stricken by the discovery of the foulest crime ever committed within the limits of the state.

"Roger Hathaway, cashier of the Raymond National Bank and treasurer of the Wild River Savings Bank, was found murdered at the entrance of the joint vault of the two institutions, which had been rifled of money and securities aggregating, it is thought, not less than $75,000. The crime had apparently been most carefully planned and evidenced not only thorough familiarity with the town and the interior arrangements of the banks, but also the possession of the fact that the national bank had on hand at the time an unusual amount of ready money. The position of the murdered cashier and the conditions of the rooms indicated also that the official had met his death while endeavoring to protect the funds entrusted to his care, his lifeless body, in fact, barring the entrance to the rifled vault, a mute witness to his faithfulness even unto death.

"The Raymond National and Wild River Savings Banks occupy commodious quarters on the ground floor of Bank Block, a three-story brick structure on Main

Street, the principal business thoroughfare of the town. The banking rooms are in the northern portion of the block, occupying the entire depth of the building, the only entrance being from Main Street. The north wall of the block is parallel with a tributary of the Wild River, which joins that stream, about 300 yards distant. The interiors of the banking-rooms are plainly but conveniently arranged. A steel wire cage extends east and west, separating the officials of the institutions from the public, with the customary counter and two windows for the savings and national bank, respectively. At the rear of the room is the private office of the cashier, separated from the main room in part by the vault, an old-fashioned brick affair, built into the partition in such a manner as to be partly in both rooms. The iron doors to the vault open into the cashier's private office, although originally designed to be entirely within the main office. Some years prior the office of the cashier was enlarged to accommodate the meetings of the directors, and the partition was moved east, bringing the major portion of the vault within the enlarged room. Two doors communicate with the cashier's room, one opening from the public office, the other from the interior of the main banking-room. Two large windows, looking respectively west and north, afford light for the cashier's office. Both these windows are heavily barred, as indeed are the two windows on the north side of the main office. A dark closet, four by six feet, in the southwest corner of the cashier's room, serves in part as a storage-room for old ledgers, account-books and supplies, and as a wardrobe for employes.

"It was in the cashier's room that the tragedy that has so sadly marred the evening of Memorial Day took place, that witnessed the awful struggle between the assassin and the white-haired custodian of the bank's funds. The details of that struggle may never be known, but the circumstances tell plainly that Cashier Hathaway either surprised the assassin in the dark closet, where he had perhaps concealed himself to await an opportunity to work upon the combination of the safe, or had himself been surprised while about to close the door of the vault.

"The crime was committed in the vicinity of 8 p. m., and its early discovery—within less than half an hour thereafter, indeed—singularly enough was due to a letter which the murdered cashier had previously sent to the president of the bank, requesting his immediate presence to confer on a business matter. The president, the Hon. Cyrus Felton, upon returning to his residence shortly after 8 o'clock, found a note from Cashier Hathaway asking him to call at the bank at once. The note had been left by a messenger, the servant stated, about fifteen minutes before. Mr. Felton hastily repaired to the bank, about ten minutes' walk. He found the outer door ajar, but the door to the cashier's private office was locked. This was not unusual, and, presuming that the cashier was busy within, Mr. Felton used his own key and opened the door without knocking. Then the awful discovery of the murder was made.

"Cashier Hathaway lay face downward in front of the open safe door, his right arm partially drawn up beneath the body and his heavy oaken desk chair overturned near by. His first thought being that the cashier had fallen in a shock, Mr. Felton hastened to raise the recumbent form. As he turned the body over, the soft rays from the argand lamp on the cashier's desk revealed an ominous pool upon the polished floor, even now augmented by the slight moving of the body. Roger Hathaway lay weltering in his own blood, slowly oozing from a bullet hole directly over the heart.

"It was several moments before Mr. Felton could pull himself together to take cognizance of the circumstances. He then noted the unmistakable evidences of a desperate struggle. As stated, the cashier's own chair lay overturned near the body; one of the side drawers in the desk was partially drawn out, and the orderly row of directors' chairs were now disarranged as if a heavy body had been flung violently against them. The door of the dark closet was wide open and a lot of old ledgers that had been piled upon its floor were toppled over into the room. The doors of the safe were open, and a glance within revealed the principal money drawer half-withdrawn, and empty save of two canvas bags of specie and nickels; a goodly bunch of keys with chain attached hanging in the lock. The story was told. Cashier Hathaway had been murdered and the bank robbed.

"Mr. Felton immediately notified Sheriff Wilson, and the legal machinery of the town was at once set in motion to encompass the capture of the murderer and robber. It was thought that with the short start obtained the feat would be a comparatively easy matter.

"Nearly $50,000 in available cash, and half as much more in securities, part negotiable and part worthless to the robber, were secured by the murderer. The presence of this unusually large amount of ready money was due to the fact that $50,000 of Mansfield County bonds matured to-day and were payable at the Raymond National Bank.

"The presence of Cashier Hathaway in the bank at that particular time was by the merest chance, and the conclusion is therefore irresistible that the murder was not premeditated. The savings and national banks, though both among the most prosperous and stable fiduciary institutions in the state, are comparatively small, the capital of the national bank being $50,000 and employing but a small clerical force. The latter comprise, besides the cashier, the teller of the bank, Frederick Sibley; the bookkeeper of the savings bank, Ralph Felton, son of the president, and one clerk, a youth named Edward Maxwell. For the last two weeks the teller, Mr. Sibley, has been confined to his residence by illness, and considerable extra labor has necessarily devolved upon the cashier. Memorial Day, a legal holiday in Vermont, the bank had been closed, and on returning from the services at the cemetery, in which he had taken part—for Mr. Hathaway had been a gallant soldier in the famous Vermont brigade—the cashier had dropped into the bank, apparently to complete some work upon the books. It is possible that the robber—the opinion is general that there was but one engaged in the enterprise—had previously entered the bank, and upon the entrance of the cashier concealed himself in the only place available, the dark closet. He may have remained an unobserved spectator of the cashier through the partly opened door and as the latter finished his work and prepared to close the safe, the robber may have concluded, by a coup de main, to save himself the trouble of attempting to solve the combination, and, noiselessly stepping from the closet, have sought to surprise the cashier. On this hypothesis the presumption is that Mr. Hathaway became aware of his danger, and turning sought to ward off the blow, when the struggle ensued that was ended with his death. Or the cashier may have discovered the presence of some intruder in the closet, and seizing his revolver, which he kept in a drawer of his desk, he may have approached the closet, when the robber sprung upon him and, wresting the weapon from the feeble hands of the old banker, turned it against the latter's breast.

"The fatal shot was fired at so close range that the clothing of the victim was scorched by the explosion. No weapon was found in the room; the revolver which, as noted above, the cashier was known to have kept in his desk, is also missing. The wound was made, the physicians state, by a 32-caliber bullet, which penetrated the breast directly above the vital organ, and death must have been instantaneous. The shot was fired at about 8 o'clock. Prof. Black, who occupies rooms directly over the cashier's office, heard a shot at that time, as did several friends who were in the room with him, but they attributed it to boys shooting water rats from the bridge beneath the professor's window.

"Thus far the tragedy possesses few extraordinary features. But what has become of the murderer? Raymond is not so populous that the presence of a stranger would be unnoted. Yet no one has volunteered information of any suspicious characters in town. Within fifty minutes of the commission of a daring crime the perpetrator disappeared, leaving not a trace for the local sleuths. The last seen of Mr. Hathaway alive, so far as known, was about 7:45 o'clock, when he stepped to the door of the bank, and, calling a boy who was standing on the bridge, throwing stones into the stream, asked him to take a letter to President Felton at his house. Half an hour later he was found shot through the heart in his office.

"President Felton was seen by the Hemisphere representative to-day, and told the story of the finding of the dead cashier substantially as outlined above. He was terribly affected by the tragedy and could hardly be induced to converse regarding it.

"Roger Hathaway was one of the best known and highly esteemed residents of Raymond. He was 63 years of age and had been identified with the national and savings banks ever since their organization, the last twenty years as cashier and treasurer respectively. He was prominent in Grand Army and church circles; a deacon in the Congregational Church. Of a severely stern but eminently just disposition, it was not known that Deacon Hathaway possessed an enemy in the world. He lived in a plain but substantial mansion, the family homestead of several generations of Hathaways, with his two daughters, his wife having died some ten years before. He was one of the founders of both the savings and national banks, which under his management had prospered to an unusual degree and stood high among the banking institutions of the state. He had held several important positions in the gift of his townspeople, and as town treasurer his rugged honesty, economic conservatism and strict observance of the letter of the law in the handling of the town's funds, had earned for him the sobriquet of 'watchdog of the treasury,' a title which he sealed even with his life blood.

"Up to a late hour this evening no clew to the murderer has been discovered. The theory is held by the local police that the deed was clearly that of an expert bank robber, and they are inclined to think that he may be a member of the same gang that has broken into numerous postoffices in New Hampshire and Vermont within the last few months. The officials cite the fact that the local papers had advertised that $50,000 in Mansfield

County bonds were to be redeemed at the Raymond National Bank upon this particular date, and the natural presumption that the bank would have on hand a large amount of currency, with the knowledge that yesterday was a holiday, when the bank would be closed and afford an unusual opportunity to work upon the safe, would form a strong inducement to a daring burglar."

CHAPTER V.

A STRANGE DISAPPEARANCE.

(By telegraph to tne New York Hemisphere.)

"Raymond, Vt., June 1.—A startling sequel to the murder of Cashier Hathaway and the robbery of the Raymond National and Wild River Savings Banks was developed to-day in the mysterious disappearance of Miss Helen Hathaway, the younger daughter of the dead banker, and Derrick Ames, a well-known young man of Raymond.

"Ames is about 27 years old, and occupied a responsible and lucrative position in the local office of the Vermont Life Insurance Company. While not possessing a positive reputation for evil, Ames was regarded askance by the more staid and conservative residents of the town, and his position socially was somewhat anomalous. He had resided in Raymond some five or six years and was known to have been a warm admirer of Miss Hathaway. But it was equally apparent to the gossip-loving townspeople that Deacon Hathaway regarded the young insurance clerk with distinct disfavor, and had forbidden his daughter's continuing the intimacy. It was likewise well known that the missing girl had frequently met Ames clandestinely.

"Neither Miss Hathaway nor Derrick Ames was seen after the discovery of the bank tragedy. Ames was at his boarding house at noon on the day of the murder, but did not return to supper. His room, with all his effects, was left as usual and gave no indication that he contemplated a hasty departure. Even at the office where he was employed he left some personal effects and half a month's salary was to his credit.

"In the case of Miss Hathaway, also, there are absolutely no indications of premeditated departure. Her sister states that she has taken not even a wrap, only the clothes she wore that afternoon as she left the house. Neither man nor maiden was seen by any person to leave Raymond. No vehicle was secured for either of them, and no one answering their description boarded the train at the Raymond Station. They have disappeared as completely, as suddenly and as mysteriously as did the murderer of Cashier Hathaway.

"The knowledge of these circumstances has intensified the excitement occasioned by the murder and robbery. The coincidence, if it be but a coincidence, of the unpremeditated elopement of Helen Hathaway upon the very day, nay, perhaps the very hour, that her aged father was stricken by the bullet of the assassin, is sufficiently startling of itself to cause the most intense excitement.

"Is there any connection between the disappearance of Derrick Ames and Helen Hathaway and the shooting of Cashier Hathaway and the subsequent looting of the bank vault? Why did the couple, if they simply ran away to get married without the parental sanction, do so manifestly on the spur of the moment, without any prearranged plans, without notification to even their intimate friends? And why, if they went innocently away, have they failed to acquaint any one with their present whereabouts, when they must be aware of the cruel murder of Miss Hathaway's good father, the details of which have been published far and wide, not only in the provincial newspapers, but throughout the metropolitan press?

"There is not a resident of Raymond who will hint at even the possibility of any guilty knowledge of the taking-off of her father by Helen Hathaway, before or during her hurried flight. For although regarded as unusually high-spirited and impetuous, she was loving and lovable to a degree and the idol of her sister. The only indiscretion that can be attributed to the missing girl was her occasional meetings with Derrick Ames without the sanction of her father.

"Her companion in flight, on the other hand, was not especially favorably known in Raymond. While he came to the town with excellent credentials, he was not a favorite in any particular set or society. Handsome in face and figure, an athlete of considerable local repute, with alternate moods of extreme depression and satirical good humor, he was such a one as might be expected to turn the head of a romantic young girl like the absent Miss Hathaway. Ames was free with his money, and while not a drinking man, in the sense of the term in this part of the country, he occasionally wooed the wine cup with great energy and originality. He had enemies in plenty and but a week before the tragedy had abruptly resigned the lieutenancy of the Raymond Rifles because of a trifling disagreement with the captain. It must be stated, however, that no mean or ignoble act or petty crime had ever been attributed to him, the chief cause of his unpopularity proceeding from his reserve, the sharpness of his tongue and the irascibility of his temper.

"Had Derrick Ames disappeared alone, on the evening of the murder, there would have been but one opinion as to his guilt or innocence. But the unaccountable flight of Miss Hathaway—this is the one flaw in the chain of circumstantial evidence. Some people will explain this away on the universal theory for every inexplicable action of the human mind—hypnotism. It is said that Ames placed Miss Hathaway within the spell of his own powerful will, and unknowingly, unwittingly, blindly obedient, beautiful Helen Hathaway accompanied the cold-blooded slayer of her own father in his flight from the scene of his crime.

"Did Ames and Miss Hathaway leave Raymond together? While there is no evidence that they did, the presumption is so strong as to compel the inference. In any event Raymond has practically convicted Derrick

Ames of complicity, if not actual participation, in the murder of Roger Hathaway.

"It is possible that the murder was not premeditated, as was intimated in these dispatches yesterday. Ames may have called upon the cashier at the bank, to plead again his suit for the hand of Helen Hathaway. A blunt refusal, hasty words, a bitter quarrel, Ames' temper, quick and ungovernable, a brief struggle, the fatal shot and the older man lay dead upon the floor. What more natural than that the young murderer, fully appreciating his terrible situation, and cognizant of the large amount of ready money in the safe, should wrench the familiar bunch of keys from the pocket of the dead cashier and possess himself of the treasure? It requires something of a stretch of the imagination to fancy the assassin, his hand yet reeking with the blood of her father, inducing the young girl to accompany him in his flight for life and liberty, yet it is not impossible—and in the belief of many it is just what Derrick Ames did do.

"There is but the faintest possible clew as yet to connect any one else with the crime. Besides a few hotel arrivals—commercial men comparatively well known— one stranger, and one only, is believed to have been in Raymond on the day of the murder. No one saw him come, no one saw him leave the town. Inquiry was made at the depot, the telegraph operator states, shortly after 8 o'clock, as to the time of departure of the next train south. The operator did not notice the questioner particularly, although he is positive he was a stranger in Raymond.

"The theory of a prearranged plot to rob the bank on the night the cashier was shot has been assiduously worked by the local authorities. It was known that there would be a large amount of money in the bank on the night preceding the paying off of the. matured county bonds. Was it not worth while for an organized gang of bank robbers to plan a descent on the Raymond institution? Was it not possible that they did so plan; that they had already secured access to the banking-room while the populace was watching the parade in the afternoon; that they were awaiting the cover of darkness to begin work upon the safe, when all unexpectedly the cashier arrived and entered the bank; that the robbers retreated to the dark closet; that here they remained hidden while Mr. Hathaway performed some pressing work upon the books, meanwhile sending the note requesting the presence of the president; that while he stepped to the front door to secure a messenger for the letter the robbers may have conceived the daring scheme of seizing the cash drawer from the vault; that the cashier returned while they were in the very act of executing their design; that he rushed to his desk and had already possessed himself of his revolver, when he was seized by the robbers and shot dead before he could succeed in making use of his own weapon, which was subsequently picked up and carried off by the robbers?

"More careful investigations of the scene of the murder developed the fact that the struggle between the cashier and his assailant, or assailants, must have been not only a severe one, but of several minutes' duration. There were marks of violence on the body of the dead banker, the physicians report, which must have been made by an exceptionally strong man. The right wrist showed quite severe abrasions, as if it had been grasped fiercely by a strong hand, and on the other side of the wrist was a purple mark that was evidently made by a seal ring pressed into the flesh by the tremendous force with which the hand had been seized. The snow-white and abundant hair of Mr. Hathaway was also disheveled, when the body was first discovered, and the chain to which his bunch of keys had been attached was snapped off, only about two inches remaining upon his person. No signs of a weapon or any burglarious tools were discovered in or about the bank premises, but evidence of the extreme coolness and sang-froid of the murderer is afforded by the fact that, apparently in searching for suitable paper in which to wrap the big package of bills two or three full pages of the big bank ledger were torn out and used for the purpose.

"Nothing was missing from the person of the dead

man, except, singularly enough, a curiously fashioned locket which Mr. Hathaway wore as a watch charm. It contained miniatures of his two daughters, Louise and Helen. No reason for its being carried off is apparent. The link which held it to the watch-chain was broken as if the locket had been violently removed.

"The exact amount of money stolen cannot as yet be stated. President Felton alleges that, until the trial balance is drawn off, it will be impossible to give figures. Certainly not less than $40,000 in greenbacks was secured, and probably half as much more in securities, which, however, are not negotiable and are therefore worthless to the robbers. The bank is perfectly solvent, President Felton states, and will resume business at an early date.

"Mr. Felton is well-nigh prostrated by the shock of his awful discovery on the evening of Memorial Day and has aged visibly in the last two days. He does not attach so much importance to the dual disappearance of Derrick Ames and Helen Hathaway as do most of the citizens, and expresses the opinion that it is a simple elopement and that the couple will return shortly.

"The directors of the savings and national banks, at a meeting this morning, authorized the offer of a reward of $4,000 for the capture and conviction of the murderer or murderers, in addition to the purse of $1,000 'hung up' by the town.

"The coroner's inquest will be begun to-morrow."

CHAPTER VI.

THE CORONER'S INQUEST.

For a town the size of Raymond, 3,000-odd inhabitants, the Mansfield County court house is an unusually large and commodious structure. But the spacious room is not nearly adequate to the demands of the pushing crowd that seeks admittance to the inquest that has been summoned by Coroner Lord to sit upon the body of the dead cashier, Roger Hathaway. George Demeritt, the town's sole day police force, is literally swept off his feet by the surging assemblage, and in less than five minutes after the throwing open of the doors the room is a solid mass of perspiring humanity.

With much difficulty Sheriff Wilson makes a passage for the dozen witnesses under his charge, the crowd gazing, with the sympathetic impudence of an inquest audience, at the statuesque form of Miss Hathaway, heavily veiled, and the bowed figure of President Felton of the Raymond Bank.

The jury selected by Coroner Lord files in from the judges' room, and after the customary preliminaries the autopsy performed by Drs. Robinson and Dodge is read by the latter. The document, stripped of its verbiage and medical terms, alleges that Roger Hathaway died from a bullet wound, the leaden missile having entered the left breast almost directly over the heart, and that death must have been instantaneous. There were signs of violence on the person of the dead man, a severe contusion on the forehead that might have been inflicted by a blow or might have been caused by the fall to the floor. There were also slight abrasions on the right wrist.

Dr. Dodge states, in reply to an inquiry from the coroner, that Mr. Hathaway had probably been dead an hour when he reached his side. Rigor mortis had not begun.

"Mr. Cyrus Felton."

There is a craning of necks in the court room as the coroner calls to his feet the aged bank president. Jack Ashley, who is sitting at the lawyers' table, jotting down a few notes, begins to take a lively interest in the case.

Mr. Felton slowly walks to the witness stand. That he is greatly moved even the least observant in the throng can but notice, and his hand trembles visibly as he replaces his pince-nez and turns to face Coroner Lord.

The usual formal questions as to his acquaintance with the dead man, his connection with the bank, etc., are asked and answered.

"I visited the bank in response to a note which I found when I returned home from my—from the postoffice," Mr. Felton states.

"The note was from Mr. Hathaway?"

"It was."

"And its contents?"

"The note merely said: 'Come to the bank immediately.'"

"Have you the note with you?"

"No; I tore it up," replies Mr. Felton, and the expression which accompanies his words is noted by Ashley, who is scanning narrowly the countenance of the banker.

"The note had been left at my house a short while before I returned home, my servant tells me," proceeds Mr. Felton. "I went at once to the bank." The witness has grown so agitated that he is obliged to seat himself, and his voice is hardly audible in the stilled room.

"The front door was slightly ajar and I walked through the bank to the directors' room. The door to this apartment was locked; I unlocked it and entered. Mr. Hathaway lay face downward in the middle of the floor, I should think. I thought he might have fallen in a shock and went to lift him up, when I saw the blood. I felt for his pulse, but there was no motion." The voice of the witness breaks as he utters these words and he covers his face with his handkerchief.

"Were there any evidences of a struggle?" the coroner asks, after a moment.

"Yes. Mr. Hathaway's office chair was overturned and the directors' chairs were disarranged. One of the drawers in Mr. Hathaway's desk had been pulled so far out that it had dropped to the floor and the contents were spilled. A lot of old ledgers that had been piled in the closet were toppled over into the room. I glanced into the closet and then turned my attention to the open vault. I found the cash drawer in the safe withdrawn and empty except for a couple of canvas bags of silver and nickels. I then hastened to find Sheriff Wilson."

"What hour was it when you entered the bank?" asks Coroner Lord.

"About 8:20 o'clock."

"And at what time did you notify Sheriff Wilson?"

Mr. Felton hesitates a moment and glances inquiringly at that official. "It did not seem more than a minute that I spent in the bank. But I was so shocked—and I—and I stopped to gather up the papers on the floor— perhaps it was five minutes before I got to the hotel."

"Did you notice any weapons on the floor of the cashier's room?"

"No, sir."

"What amount of money do you estimate was stolen from the safe?"

President Felton debates a moment, as if making a mental calculation, and replies: "At least $37,000 in currency and gold, and some securities. The exact amount of the latter we cannot tell until we have listed our papers."

"That is all, Mr. Felton."

A suppressed murmur of intense interest runs around the crowded room as Louise Hathaway takes the witness stand. As she raises the veil that has concealed her features the townspeople marveled at the composure her marble countenance evinces. Ashley glances at her with interest and draws a long breath. "Gad! she's a beauty," he decides, and then drops his eyes as they encounter the calm gaze of the witness.

Her father left the house to go to the bank about 6:30 o'clock, Miss Hathaway testifies. Tea was served at 6 o'clock. Her sister Helen had not returned at that time, but at her father's request they had not waited the tea, because he said he had some work to do at the bank. It was an unusual thing for him to go to the bank evenings, but the illness of the teller had necessitated extra work.

"Miss Hathaway, do you know where your sister is?" The silence in the court room is intense as the coroner asks the question.

"My sister did not return that afternoon," declares Miss Hathaway, after a brief pause. "I have reason to think that she has gone with Mr. Ames to be married."

"And you do not know where they now are?"

Miss Hathaway shakes her head, as her fingers clasp and unclasp nervously in her lap. The ordeal is a trying one.

"When did you last see your sister?"

"About 2 o'clock in the afternoon."

"And when did you last see Mr. Ames?"

A slight flush replaces the pallor for a moment; then as suddenly recedes, leaving her paler than before.

"I have not seen Mr. Ames for a fortnight," she replies in a tone barely audible.

"Did your sister indicate to you her intention of eloping?" is the next question.

"I had no reason to think that she contemplated a clandestine marriage. But I should prefer not to discuss the matter further, Mr. Lord," says the witness, in evident agitation. "I am sure Helen's departure can have no possible connection with—with that awful deed. It was only an unfortunate coincidence that they went away on that afternoon. I—I am sure they will return in due time."

Coroner Lord glances irresolutely at the state's attorney, and after a moment's deliberation permits Miss Hathaway to retire.

Sheriff Wilson, the next witness, describes minutely the appearance of the bank and vault and of the body of the dead cashier.

Sarah Johnson, the maid at Mr. Felton's residence, testifies that the note referred to by Mr. Felton was left at the house shortly before 8 o'clock by a lad named Jimmie Howe. A few minutes later a stranger inquired for Mr. Felton at the house. There is a slight buzz of excitement among the audience at this first mention of the presence of a stranger in the village on the evening of the tragedy.

"How do you know he was a stranger?" sharply inquires the coroner.

"For the reason that when I asked him which Mr. Felton he wished to see he replied that he did not know there were two Mr. Feltons." That evidence is conclusive. It is, so far as the audience is concerned.

"He asked where he could find Mr. Felton, and I told him perhaps at his office in the bank building," continues Sarah.

Miss Johnson is closely questioned as to the demeanor of the stranger, but she knows little of importance, as she had not seen the visitor's face. He was of medium height, she says, and his voice was pleasant. Sheriff Wilson, who has first learned of this clew, smiles patronizingly upon Ashley and the other newspaper men.

A bright-faced lad of 12 is Jimmie Howe, whom Coroner Lord next calls to the stand. Jimmie was playing on the bridge when Mr. Hathaway called to him from the bank door and asked him to take a note to Mr. Felton and to hurry about it. After he delivered the note he went home.

Prof. George Black, Edward Knapp and three others, who were in Prof. Black's room in the bank building, testify to hearing a shot about 8 o'clock, but whether before or after that hour they cannot agree.

Alden Heath, the telegraph operator at the depot, stated that some one—he was busy at his key at the time —asked somewhere around 8 o'clock when the next train left. He answered without looking up, and when he did glance at the window the inquirer was gone. It was a strange voice; of that he was positive.

George Kenney, who states that he is the station agent at Ashfield, is next sworn. His testimony establishes the probable fact that Derrick Ames and Helen Hathaway boarded the midnight train for New York.

There is an involuntary but quickly suppressed exclamation from the witnesses. Miss Hathaway is trembling and Ralph Felton, who is sitting near her, is savagely biting his mustache.

As Coroner Lord calls the name of Richard Chase and the stalwart warden of the State prison at Windsor appears on the witness stand there is a hush of expectancy.

"Ernest Stanley, a convict in the Vermont State prison,

was released at noon of Memorial Day," Warden Chase says succinctly. "He asked for and was given a ticket to Raymond, and left on the north-bound afternoon train. He was five feet ten inches in height, of medium build, dark complexion, smooth face, and had closely cropped dark hair. He wore a light tweed suit and a straw hat."

As Mr. Chase concludes his testimony the coroner consults for a few moments with the state's attorney and then summons Ralph Felton, son of President Felton, and the bookkeeper of the Wild River Savings Bank.

As the young man steps to the stand Ashley glances at him interestedly, and after a good look decides that he does not like him. There is a certain shiftiness of eye that the New Yorker does not fancy, and the notes which he takes of the witness' testimony are nearly verbatim.

Young Felton answers in the briefest phrases the questions of the coroner. He had seen no strangers in the bank in the last few days. He had last seen Mr. Hathaway the afternoon before the tragedy, when the bank closed for the day. On the afternoon of Memorial Day——

The witness stops abruptly and a flush overspreads his features as he nervously bites his tawny mustache.

"On the afternoon of Memorial Day," invites the coroner.

"I was around town as usual," finishes Felton.

For some reason the momentary hesitation of the witness apparently impresses Mr. Lord, and he seems disposed to make minute inquiry.

"Where did you say you were on the afternoon of Memorial Day?" he again interrogates.

Ralph Felton looks straight at the coroner an instant, and then his gaze wanders over the stilled room and finally rests upon his father, who, roused from the impassive attitude in which he has sunk after completing his own testimony, casts a startled look upon his son.

The sudden hush that has involuntarily accompanied Mr. Lord's question is intensified, as father and son gaze at each other, apparently oblivious of the unanswered coroner.

CHAPTER VII.

FATHER AND SON.

An almost imperceptible raising of the eyebrows by the elder man, and Ralph Felton turns quickly to the coroner.

"Really, Mr. Lord, I cannot furnish a detailed statement of my every movement during the last week," he says, nonchalantly. "I witnessed the procession, or at least the local post, on its way to the depot to meet the Ruggbury contingent, and later went to the Exchange for dinner. In the afternoon I was in the billiard room of the hotel, and I believe I visited the postoffice in the evening."

"What time did you last see Mr. Hathaway?" The persistence of the coroner in questioning the bookkeeper is inexplicable to the audience, who have not observed the little slips of paper that State's Attorney Brown has passed along the table to Mr. Lord.

"About noon on the day of the murder."

"Where?"

Ralph Felton is for the first time manifesting signs of impatience. "He was in the bank. I went to get something which I had left there, and while I was there Mr. Hathaway came in. I left him there and a short time afterward saw him in the procession."

"Mr. Felton, where were you between 7:45 and 8:30 o'clock the evening of Tuesday?"

A dull red replaces the slight pallor on the face of the young man.

"Mr. Lord, I cannot say where I was during that particular time. I have my own personal reasons—not connected with this case, I assure you—for not desiring to answer your question."

The murmur which has begun to overspread the room is quickly but only temporarily hushed as the coroner announces:

"The inquest is adjourned until to-morrow morning at 9 o'clock."

*   *   *   *   *   *   *

"You know why I did not answer Coroner Lord's question. I am tired of this hypocrisy. I simply will not go on the stand again—and that settles it!"

Within the richly furnished library of Cyrus Felton's home the inquisition so abruptly broken off by Coroner Lord has been resumed.

The president of the Raymond National Bank now bears little resemblance to the bowed old man who, with trembling lips and pallid brow, testified regarding the murder of Cashier Hathaway a few hours before. There is an angry flush upon his face and a stern setting of the chin that causes one straight line to mark the location of his lips.

At the last defiant words of his son a spasm as of sudden pain for a moment distorts his patriarchal face, and his hand involuntarily presses his heart.

"I am going to leave Raymond—at once—to-night. Leave as Derrick Ames left," continued Ralph Felton, with an imprecation. "It's no use talking. My mind is made up and you should be the last man to urge me to remain. You know——"

"Ralph, this is madness," interrupts his father. "There can be no necessity for your leaving town, least of all while matters are as they are. The bank——"

"The bank needs both of us—I don't think," rejoins the younger man flippantly. "As the boodle is gone I guess you can get along without a bookkeeper for a time—maybe forever. But go I shall, and money I must have. Oh, I know what you are going to say," as Mr. Felton opens his lips. "It doesn't make any difference where it has gone. Suffice it to say, it is planted. If you have ever had any experience with—but here it is getting on toward 11 o'clock, and at 12:10 I must take the Montreal express. I don't propose to board it here. I shall drive to South Ashfield. Now, understand me, father," as Cyrus Felton again seeks to interrupt him, "it is just as much for your interest for me to be a couple of thousand miles from Raymond as it is mine. It is bound to come out—why, what's the matter?"

Once again that ashen pallor accompanies a spasm of severest pain, and this time Cyrus Felton emits a slight groan as his fingers sink into the heavily upholstered arms of the sleepy-hollow chair into which he has sunk.

"Nothing—nothing but a pleurisy attack," he faintly replies.

There is silence for a moment, broken only by the sonorous ticking of the mantel clock.

"Well, the money?"

"Ralph, you know that I can ill afford to spare any considerable amount just now. But your safety must, of course, be considered, and I will endeavor to send you funds later. What I can spare now ought to be sufficient to start life anew in some western city."

Ralph Felton smiles sardonically as his father steps to the little safe set in the wall, and, moving the screen from the front, turns the combination. He lounges toward the receptacle, and, leaning on the screen, gazes down at his father, who has withdrawn one of the two drawers which the safe boasts and is running over a package of bills. The contents of the lower drawer are exposed by the withdrawal of the upper one, and the light from the chandelier is reflected back from some shining substance in the till. It catches young Felton's eye and his long arm passes over the stooping figure of his father and picks the gleaming metal from the drawer. It is a loaded revolver of the bull-dog variety, 32 caliber, and one chamber has been discharged.

Cyrus Felton raises his head. The shining little engine of destruction in the clasp of his son is almost before and on a level with his eyes.

With a shudder the elder man turns his head and slowly and laboriously rises to his feet. He seems to have suddenly aged even in the last few moments.

Ralph Felton examines the revolver critically, looks at his father's averted face, and, without speaking, lays the weapon in the drawer. There is silence in the room, broken at last by the almost apologetic tones of the father. "How will you reach South Ashfield?" he asked.

"Oh, Sam must drive me over with the mare. I will start him up now."

As his son leaves the room Cyrus Felton sinks into an easy chair and his head drops upon his bosom. Who can tell the thoughts that surge through his troubled mind at the moment? The clatter of hoofs on the concrete driveway beside the window arouses him from his reverie, and a moment later Ralph Felton enters, a satchel in his hand.

"Well, father, Sam is ready and I must go. We shall have little more than an hour to make the ten miles and catch the express. Good-by; it is all right, sir; believe me, father," the younger man drops his disengaged hand not unkindly on the other's shoulder, "my sudden departure will do nobody here any harm, and least of all will it affect you. One thing I will say; I will find the scoundrel who took Helen Hathaway from Raymond, if he is above ground, and when we meet he will have occasion to remember that time." Ralph Felton's face is darkened by a savage scowl as he speaks, and he raises a clenched fist with a gesture so suggestive that his father involuntarily steps back. "Yes, I have two objects in cutting the town. One reason you know, the other is to seek and find the hound who has stolen Helen Hathaway from me. I cared for her as I shall never love another woman, and I meant to have her. Now——"

The musical chime of the clock begins to strike the hour. Ralph Felton seizes the package of bills that lies upon the table and places it in an inner pocket.

"I will return sometime, father, when this bank affair has ceased to be a subject of investigation," he says, with his hand on the door-knob. "Good-by. Just keep a stiff upper lip and you'll be all right. I'm off."

The outer door closes with a sharp click and a moment later the impatient stamping of hoofs is succeeded by the even footfalls of the fastest mare in Mansfield County.

As the sound grows fainter and fainter Cyrus Felton suddenly starts as if aroused from a stupor.

"Why did I let him go? Idiot that I am! It is madness—worse than madness. It is confession. Am I losing my senses, that I did not insist upon his remaining and completing his testimony? At the worst it could never be proved. The wages of sin! The wages of sin!" he groans, as he sinks back in his chair and buries his face in his hands.

* , * * * * * *

"Mr. Ralph Felton to the stand," orders Coroner Lord.

As on the preceding day, the court room is packed with the people of Raymond. There is a craning of necks toward the settees reserved for witnesses. Ralph Felton is not there, and there is a death-like stillness as Coroner Lord again calls this now most interesting of witnesses.

"Mr. Coroner!" The lank figure of the station agent at South Ashfield elevates itself above the crowd. "If it please your honor, Ralph Felton boarded the Montreal express at South Ashfield last night."

Of course there is a sensation, a murmur of voices that the coroner quickly checks. The few remaining witnesses are unimportant and the inquest is adjourned until afternoon.

CHAPTER VIII.

A PROPOSITION OF PARTNERSHIP.

The usual congress of village gossips is in session to-night at the Exchange Hotel. It is the fourth day since the Raymond Bank affair, and the details of the tragedy are discussed with an animation and a wealth of clew that brings a smile to the face of John Barker, the New York detective, who retreats to a quiet corner of the hotel veranda to finish his cigar and muse upon the affair with the calm contemplation characteristic of men in his calling.

The detective's face expresses a shade of annoyance as

Jack Ashley ascends the steps to the veranda, draws a chair opposite his, lights a cigar and tilts his seat back at a comfortable angle.

"You are John Barker, the detective," began Ashley. Barker assents with a nod.

"I haven't a card with me, but my name is Jack Ashley, and I am attached to the staff of the New York Hemisphere." Barker looks duly impressed.

"You are an ordinary detective, I presume?" Barker stares. "What I mean is, if you will pardon my frankness, you are not a Sherlock Holmes or a M. Lecocq?" It is apparent from his face that the detective is in doubt whether to laugh or express his displeasure. He compromises with a faint smile and accepts the proffered cigar.

"My reason for asking," goes on Ashley, "is that I have a proposition to offer you."

Barker strikes a match to touch off his weed. "That proposition is——"

"That we work this bank case together." Barker drops the lighted match and gazes at his new acquaintance in astonishment.

"Have another match," remarks the other, passing it over.

The detective lights his cigar and puffs away on it for some moments in silence. "I am not in the habit of taking in partners," he observes finally.

"I always take a deep interest in an affair like the Hathaway case," resumes Ashley, without reference to the other's remark. "In fact, my special line on the Hemisphere has been the running down of mysterious crimes. I have trailed quite a number of them, and you will pardon my egotism when I say I have been quite successful in my dual capacity of sleuth and newspaper man." Barker looks a trifle bored.

"To be candid, however, this case is a bit too big for me to handle alone. It spreads out too much. It is too much of a job for one man to look after."

"Indeed?" The irony in the detective's voice is thinly veiled. He says:

"Then on the strength of your intimation that you are a devilish clever fellow—you will pardon my frankness this time—I am asked to take in an assistant who will gladly share with me the $5,000 reward in the event of the murderer being apprehended."

"No; I sha'n't bother about the reward. I am simply looking for glory."

"You are young in the newspaper business?"

"About twelve years."

"And looking for glory?"

Ashley laughs. "For my paper; not for myself." He passes over a telegram received that day. It read as follows:

"Jack Ashley, Raymond, Vt.: Work up case at any expense, and discover murderer if possible.   Chambers."

"Now," says Ashley, as he replaces the dispatch in his pocket, "I will tell you why I think it would be to your advantage to join forces with me." Barker evinces some interest.

"I am in possession of some facts which you not only do not know, but are not likely to get hold of unless I enlighten you."

"Ah!" The detective draws his chair nearer his companion and glances about to make sure there are no outside listeners.

"When I finish, if you consider my information as valuable as I appraise it, you can do as you please about the partnership idea. At any rate you will be so much ahead. Come up to my room. We will not be disturbed there." When they are comfortably seated and fresh cigars lighted Ashley begins his story.

"I have run onto two clews. One of them I consider important; the other less so. By the way, how long have you been in town? Come in on the after-dinner train?"

"Yes, I have acquainted myself with the known facts in the case and the result of the coroner's inquest. Deceased came to his death at the hands of some person unknown.''

"But who will be known ere long. But to resume. As you know, a man called at the house of Cyrus Felton shortly before 8 o'clock of the night of the killing. To the inquiry of the housemaid as to which Mr. Felton was wanted the man replied that he 'did not know there were two.' Not long after 8 o'clock that same evening a man appeared at the ticket office of the railroad station and inquired when the next train left. These incidents, while not startling in themselves, seem to prove that in each case the questioner was a stranger to Raymond. Every one around these parts knows that there are two Feltons, father and son, and the natives are also presumed to know that there is no night train through the town before 11:50.''

"Very well reasoned,'' remarks Barker.

"As you also know, on the afternoon of Memorial Day a chap named Ernest Stanley was liberated from the State prison at Windsor, after serving two of a three years' sentence for forgery. Despite the fact that Raymond was not his home and that he had not, so far as known, a friend or acquaintance in the place, and contrary to the advice of the warden, who took an interest in the fellow, he bought a ticket to this town and started north on the afternoon train. That latter fact was proved by the ticket agent at Windsor, who sold him the ticket and saw him board the train. I went to Windsor this forenoon, after the inquest, saw a photograph of this Stanley, and secured a pretty accurate description of him.''

"But there is no evidence that he left the train at this station. Or if he did——''

"He could have been, as I believe he was, the visitor at Felton's house.''

"I am not so sure of that,'' contends the detective. "On the evening of Memorial Day the agent of a granite manufacturers' journal, published at Chicago, stopped at this hotel. He arrived on the afternoon train from the north, and after supper, the clerk told me when I quizzed him, he inquired where Cyrus Felton lived. Felton, you know, is the principal owner in the Wild River Granite Quarries. It is more than likely, is it not, that he was the visitor at the Felton residence?"

"Still he may not have called that night."

"True. Admitting the caller to have been Stanley, what then? A motive must be assigned."

"We will discuss that later. For the present suffice it to be known that Stanley was sentenced to State prison for forging the name of Cyrus Felton two years ago."

"Well, what of it? If Stanley's thoughts were of revenge they were apparently directed against Felton, not the man who was murdered."

"That is precisely the point that is not clear to me," confesses Ashley.

"Now, listen. Here's a proposition for you: If Stanley was not concerned in the bank affair, what was he doing at 6 o'clock next morning asleep in the bushes in a lonely gorge near South Ashfield village?"

"The devil!"

"With a package of papers clutched fast in his hands, about the size that a bundle of treasury notes and securities would make."

"You know he was there?"

"I met him."

Barker is thoughtful. "You said nothing to the authorities or in your dispatches about the incident?"

"No. I didn't consider it worth while. The authorities were already scouring the country round about, and I did not exploit it in my dispatches because I concluded to save it for a longer and better story when we run down the criminal—beg pardon, when the criminal is run down. But," continues Ashley, as Barker remains silent, "that is the clew to which I attach the less importance.

"I had heard from some source that Ralph Felton had been seen at this hotel a good share of Memorial Day, and I started in on a pumping expedition, beginning with John Thayer, the clerk. Thayer was noticeably uncommunicative; I thought I'd bluff him a bit, so I remarked: 'Well, you've concluded to tell me what you know, eh?' The bluff appeared to work, for he flushed a little and replied: 'I'll tell you all about it if you will agree to keep it out of the paper.' As I had suspended all dispatches to the Hemisphere pending the discovery of a story worth filing, I readily enough agreed to refrain from publishing his secret to the world. Then he extracted a promise that I should not divulge a word to any one in the village.

"'Ralph Felton is as innocent of that crime as you or I.' asserted Thayer when all the conditions for secrecy had been satisfactorily arranged.

"'That is possible, but why did he refuse to answer the coroner and why did he cut the town?' said I.

"'He had a good reason for wanting to keep dark, and I suppose he ran away to prevent being compelled to testify where he was Memorial Day afternoon and evening.'

"'You know where he was, then?'

"'Yes; he was here at the hotel. I tell you this because I want you to know that he is innocent. Felton is a good friend of mine, and I thought perhaps if you knew how the facts were you might see your way clear to letting him down as easy as possible in the paper.' I assured him that my specialty was setting folks right and then Thayer told off the following story:

"About 2 o'clock on the afternoon of Memorial Day a woman arrived at Raymond on the afternoon train from the south, came to this hotel and registered as 'Isabel Winthrop.' She was superbly dressed and displayed an abundance of jewels. According to Thayer, whose head was completely turned by her appearance, she was magnificently, phenomenally beautiful. You can take that for what it is worth. Thayer assigned her a room and showed her to it. As she passed in she requested him to send a messenger to acquaint Ralph Felton that a lady desired to see him. Finding him was an easy task, as he was at that moment playing poker in a room in the hotel. Felton appeared somewhat surprised when called out, but threw up the game and went to the woman's room. That was the last Thayer saw of him for an hour, when Felton left the hotel. His face was flushed and he seemed to be laboring under strong excitement. Before he left he called Thayer to one side. 'John,' said he, 'if you are a friend of mine say nothing about my caller to-day. You understand?'

"I remarked casually: 'Then he returned to the hotel that afternoon?'

" 'Oh, yes,' said he.

" 'And was there during the evening?'

" 'Yes, I noticed him in the office at the time the alarm over the bank affair was sounded. He left the hotel then and I did not see him again that night.'

" 'Well,' I asked pointedly, 'can you swear that Felton was in the hotel between 7:45 and 8:30 the evening of Memorial Day?' I never saw a chap so taken back as was Thayer. He could not locate Felton at any particular time during the evening; moreover, he could not say positively that the Winthrop woman spent the evening in her room. He supposed she did. The only point that Thayer was sure of was that the woman left for the south on the first train the next morning.

" 'Thayer,' said I, consolingly, 'the only way I see to clear your absent friend is to find this Winthrop woman. Describe her to me as accurately as you can.' He did so and I have a pretty good pen portrait of the unknown in my memorandum-book, marked 'Exhibit A.'

" 'Oh, by the way,' said Thayer, 'she left a handkerchief in the room.'

" 'The deuce she did! I must have that,' said I. And here it is," said Ashley, passing over a dainty lace creation for Barker's inspection. In one corner is the letter "I" curiously embroidered in silk.

"There are thousands of such handkerchiefs," comments the detective.

"Yes, but not scented with that variety of perfume." The detective sniffs it. "Did you ever smell anything just like that?" queries Ashley. Barker allows that he never did and his acquaintance with scents is an extended one.

"If Isabel Winthrop is found," declares Ashley, "that handkerchief, and especially that perfume, may play an important part in her discovery." Barker smiles.

"Truth is stranger than fiction, my boy," retorts Ashley. "Well, what do you think of my clews?"

The detective wraps himself in cigar smoke and thought for several minutes. Then he extends his hand.

"I believe I'll accept your proposition." Ashley returns the pressure warmly.

"I think we'll make a strong pair to draw to," he says.

"But," adds Barker, "you will see that I am more or less disinterested when I tell you that I incline to the belief that neither of your clews, good as they are, is the correct one."

"No? Whom do you suspect?"

Barker rises. "Ashley," says he, "you are young, enthusiastic and clever. How are you fixed for patience?"

"Job was a chronic kicker in comparison," is the prompt reply.

"Well, then, about to-morrow evening I shall be ready to talk with you and lay out the campaign. Satisfactory?"

"Perfectly. Let's go down to the billiard room and knock the balls around for an hour."

CHAPTER IX.

LOUISE HATHAWAY.

"Good afternoon. Will you walk in?"

"Thank you. I will detain you but a short time." Jack Ashley follows Miss Hathaway into the half-lighted drawing room, accepts the offered chair and seats himself beside the big bay window. She sinks quietly into a chair opposite him and glances at the bit of pasteboard in her hand.

Ashley has seen Louise Hathaway at the inquest and

has remarked that she is an unusually attractive woman. And now, as his glance for an instant sweeps over her, he votes her superb.

Brief as is his admiring gaze, it is critical. It rests upon the twined mass of golden hair, drifts over the face to the long white throat and the strong shoulders, thence to the faultless figure and sweep of limb. She is as different from her sister Helen as the placid morning is unlike the beauteous night. Louise is the morning. There is a strong sunlight in her glorious blue eyes, but now they are shadowed by the grief of the last few days.

She lifts her eyes from the visiting card. "You are a reporter," she says, with a shade of weariness in her voice.

"I have the honor of representing the New York Hemisphere. I do not desire to cause you any annoyance, but there were some matters not brought out in the inquest which I wish to investigate."

"And you have come all the way from New York for this?"

"No; I have been spending my vacation in Raymond, and, of course, when the news of the tragedy reached our paper I was instructed to look after it. I know that the errand on which I have come must be a painful one for you to discuss, but I assure you that I have more than a reportorial interest in the case."

"Yes?" She looks at him inquiringly.

"You must be aware that the case is an unusual one," he goes on. "My interest in it has grown into a determination to run down and bring to justice the slayer of your father."

He tries to read in the glance she gives him a trace of gratitude, of approval. Failing, he decides that Louise Hathaway is an extraordinary young woman.

"Have you discovered anything—anything that the local authorities—they are so stupid—have overlooked?" she asks, and he fancies there is something of anxiety in the calm, slow tones of a very musical voice.

"Yes," he replies. "We, the detective and myself, are engaged on several clews. But it is necessary that we should be in possession of every bit of knowledge obtainable concerning all the persons who have any bearing, near or remote, upon the case."

Miss Hathaway turns upon Ashley a pair of blue eyes in whose depths he can read naught but purity and honesty. "I fear I can tell you little," she says.

"Derrick Ames——"

"Is innocent," she interrupts.

"I am of the same opinion. Derrick Ames and your sister were lovers?" She nods.

"Your father, I am told, strongly opposed the young man's attentions. There was a more favored suitor."

Miss Hathaway regards him with mild surprise. "You knew then——"

"What I have come to ask you about more particularly," finishes Ashley, unblushingly, regarding his digression from the truth as a bit of diplomacy.

"I was not very well acquainted with him," avers Miss Hathaway, "although we have lived in the same town nearly all our lives. But father regarded him as a model young man, and until lately encouraged his attentions to Helen in every way."

"Now, who the deuce is she talking about?" wonders Ashley, who has simply chanced it in his assertion that there was a more favored suitor than Derrick Ames.

"I never fancied him, and Helen disliked him exceedingly," continues Miss Hathaway. "But the more she discouraged him the more persistent he became. One night Helen came to my room in tears. They had had a fearful scene, she stated. She should marry him or none, he had declared, and had made all sorts of wild threats."

"I did not know he was such a desperate character," remarks Ashley tentatively.

"I do not believe the people of this town knew what his true character was. Helen said he seemed to have torn off the mask that night and that his face was that of a demon. He was wild with rage and left the house with curses. I sometimes think——" Miss Hathaway pauses and her face wears a troubled expression.

"What on earth does she think?" meditates Ashley, who is becoming a trifle bewildered.

"I sometimes think it was his hand that struck down our poor father. But then he could have had no motive, and there was in my eyes a reason for his action which other people could not surmise."

"And yet that action seemed unexplainable?" hazards Ashley.

"To others, yes. It seemed perhaps a confession of guilt. But after what Helen told me I firmly believe that he has gone to search for her. And when he and Derrick Ames meet, I shudder to think of what may happen."

Ashley sees the light at last. So Ralph Felton was the favored suitor—Ralph Felton, whom nearly every one in Raymond regarded as a model young man, and who, despite his unaccountable flight, found plenty of people willing to explain it in a dozen charitable ways.

"You say that until lately Mr. Hathaway regarded Felton's attentions to your sister with favor. Had he any reason for suspending his approval?"

"I imagine so. During the last month or so he rarely spoke of him, and once, when his name was mentioned at table, he frowned."

"I suppose you know that the case looks black against Ames; that not half a dozen people in the town have a good word to say for him?"

"I do not care what is said against Derrick Ames. I am sure that he is innocent of any connection with my father's death. What he was to others I cannot say, but in the eyes of Helen and myself he was a noble-hearted young man, incapable of an unworthy thought or act."

"She pleads for him as if for a lover," thinks Ashley, regarding with admiration the girl before him. The flash in the blue eyes and the flush in the cheeks tell of warm sympathies and a loyal heart.

"Your sister never intimated to you the likelihood of an elopement?" Ashley inquires.

"Never. Had she a thought of such a thing I should have known it. We kept nothing from each other."

"You knew that they met clandestinely?"

"I did."

Ashley shifts the line of questioning to return to it at a more favorable opportunity. It is apparent that it is becoming painful to the girl.

"What were the relations between your father and Mr. Felton—the elder Felton?"

"Almost wholly of a business nature."

"They were friends?"

"Yes. I had noticed, however, that during the last few weeks they did not meet as often as before."

"Was Mr. Felton at your house within a short time previous to the murder?"

"He was here the evening before it."

"Anything out of the ordinary in the visit?"

"Nothing, except that Mr. Felton appeared to be angry."

"Will you make an effort to recall what happened on that particular evening?" Louise is thoughtful for a few moments.

"I fear I can recall but little," she replies slowly. "I was passing through the hall on my way upstairs, and as I stepped by the library door I glanced in. Father was sitting in his desk chair and Mr. Felton was standing near the door, with his hat in his hand."

"Did you hear any of the conversation?" queries Ashley, with the keenest interest in the new scent.

"Let me see—yes; I remember Mr. Felton said: 'I can't and I won't!' I think those were his words."

"Did he appear to be excited?"

"Perhaps so. He spoke very loudly."

"And your father's reply—did you hear that?"

"Yes: I remember I paused an instant from curiosity. Father said, and I recall that his voice sounded rather harsh: 'Then there is but one alternative.' Then I went upstairs to my room. A few minutes afterward I heard the front door slam. Father did not retire until several hours afterward."

"It was not his practice to do so?"

"No; he usually retired early. I don't see what this

has to do with the mystery—but then I am not a detective or a newspaper man."

"It may have much to do with it," murmurs Ashley. Miss Hathaway looks at him inquiringly.

"What do you think?" she asks.

"Candidly, I don't know what to think," he confesses.

"Will you permit me to turn inquisitor for a few moments?" Miss Hathaway requests. "There are one or two questions I should like to have answered."

"I will answer a thousand," replies Ashley cheerfully, as he meets the direct gaze of the young lady.

"Is there any evidence against Derrick Ames, other than was brought out at the coroner's inquest?"

Ashley notes the anxiety in the voice and hesitates. It may be cruel, but it also may be profitable, so he replies slowly to Miss Hathaway:

"I regret to say that there are a great many things about Ames' movements that will have to be explained away."

Miss Hathaway covers her face with her hands. A less keen observer than Ashley could note the hopelessness in the face that she finally lifts.

"But you said that you believe him innocent," she exclaims, almost eagerly.

"I said so, surely," admits Ashley. "But in order to prove his innocence it will be necessary to produce him."

A silence. Miss Hathaway's troubled gaze is fixed upon him. His quick brain has been working and he has arrived at a conclusion. "This woman believes in the possibility of Ames' guilt and she has some reason other than the evidence that has been produced. Ah, why didn't I think of that before?"

"Miss Hathaway," says Ashley, speaking deliberately, "you said a moment ago that you would do anything to assist me in tracing the slayer of your father." She nods.

"Then will you show me the letter which you received from your sister upon her arrival in New York?"

If Ashley expects any result from this haphazard question he is assuredly not prepared for what really happens. Miss Hathaway's face turns ashen and a great fear springs into her eyes. She rises to her feet, her hands clenched.

"Who told you I received a letter?" she demands in a trembling voice.

"We newspaper men have many means of obtaining information," replies Ashley.

"Mr. Ashley," the girl says—she is quite calm now—"I appreciate your efforts fully and thank you for them. God grant that they may be crowned with success. As for my sister's letter, I cannot show it to you, as I have destroyed it. Its contents I shall never reveal."

"I shall hope to see you again before I leave Raymond," remarks Ashley, as he rises to take his leave; for the interview has reached its natural limits.

"I am at home to you at any time," responds Miss Hathaway, acknowledging gravely his pleasant adieu.

As Ashley saunters back to the hotel his mind is in a more bewildered condition than at any other time since he has begun work on the Hathaway case.

"Now that I am in it, I shall stay, if it occupies the rest of my natural life," he determines. "What a magnificent young woman! Fortunate that I am not susceptible, else I should already be idiotically in love with this queen of the morning, whose sad blue eyes haunt me still, in the words of the old song."

Oh, the self-sufficiency of youth!

CHAPTER X.

MR. BARKER'S DISCOVERIES.

After supper Ashley retreats to the most secluded corner of the veranda and amuses himself blowing smoke rings over the railing. Barker has been gone ever since morning. He must have struck a warm trail. Twilight gathers ere Ashley beholds the familiar figure swinging down the street toward the hotel.

The detective draws a chair beside that of Ashley, and, after making certain that no listeners are about, remarks complacently: "My boy, I believe we are on the trail of Roger Hathaway's murderer."

"Indeed! I confess that I am deeper in the woods of speculation than ever."

"Ah, but when I give you the result of my day's work I think you will find yourself out of the forest and on the broad highway of conviction."

"Then you must have put in a more profitable afternoon than I spent, and I accomplished considerable. Had your supper?"

"No. Guess I'll run in and have supper and then we'll adjourn to my room for a smoke talk."

Half an hour later finds the New Yorkers comfortably settled in Barker's second-floor.

"I may as well state at the outset that, as you intimated when you introduced yourself last evening, I am not a Sherlock Holmes," begins Barker. "But I have had considerable experience in ferreting out criminals. A good memory for faces, an extensive acquaintance with the brilliants and lesser lights of the crook world, a knack of putting two and two together with a view to obtaining four as a result, more or less analytical abilities, an excellent physique, a fair amount of sand and an unlimited stock of patience are my qualifications for the profession upon which I have thus far brought no discredit."

"Pretty good stock in trade, I should say," comments Ashley.

"Thank you. Now, every detective waits patiently for what he regards as his big case. I think this Hathaway affair is mine—or ours, as we are working together. Now, I'll get down to business and tell you what I have discovered to-day. We may as well begin with a comprehensive study of the cast of characters. Unfortunately, three of the leading ones are beyond our reach."

"Then you figure Derrick Ames extensively in the case?"

"Rather. We will begin with him and consider his

probable relation to what is destined to be a celebrated case.

"It is unfortunate that the people in the world whose photographs one is likely to want at some time or another are the very people who seldom run to pictures," resumes Barker. "There isn't a picture of Ames in existence. So far as known he never had one taken. Nor are there any photos of Helen Hathaway to be had. The only portraits of her in existence are the miniature in the locket missing from the dead cashier's watch-chain and a crayon portrait which, I am informed, hangs in a room at her late home.

"I find that Ames was regarded as an odd stick by the discriminating inhabitants of Raymond—principally because he did not associate with them more than was absolutely necessary. He is said to be well educated and is of a high-strung, poetic temperament. Heaven knows how he came to locate in such a prosy town as Raymond, but the explanation of his remaining here as long as he did is simpler; he was apparently devoted to Helen Hathaway. I say apparently for want of knowledge of what his exact sentiments were. Of his early history I learned little, save that he came here some three years ago from New York State, studied law with a local counsellor, and finally took an excellent position with the Vermont Life Insurance Company.

"Oddly enough, the one male companion that Ames chose was a chap about as opposite in temperament and every other way as one can imagine. Sam Brockway is the name of the fellow, and he is employed as a cutter in the sheds of the Wild River Granite Company. And Ames hunted him up only when he got into one of his periodical fits of the blues, and the two would start off on a racket that would last several days. It was this habit of drinking, combined with a cynical skepticism upon matters and things dear to the heart of a deacon, that made Ames objectionable to Mr. Hathaway, and the antipathy was cordially returned. Helen, however, was a loyal little woman, and despite her father's commands she continued her intimacy with Ames. An elopement was a logical sequence of such a companionship, and were it not for certain damning evidence that I extracted from this Brockway and discovered myself, I should dismiss Ames, temporarily at least, as having no connection with the bank case."

"Yet you say Brockway is a friend of Ames'," remarks Ashley.

"He is. But while a good-hearted chap and loyalty itself, he is not especially astute and by shrewd questioning and judicious bluffing I discovered that he was probably the last man who saw Ames before he disappeared from Raymond, Roger Hathaway excepted."

"You mean——"

"I mean that Derrick Ames was seen to enter the Raymond National Bank about 8 o'clock on the evening of Memorial Day."

"H'm! That is serious. Yet his mission may have been an innocent one."

"True. But to continue. This forenoon I visited the station at Ashfield, where Ames and the girl—there can be no question that they were the pair—boarded the night express south. While I was lounging about the station, waiting for the train back to Raymond, my eye caught the glitter of an object lying between the inside rail of the track and the south end of the platform, and partly under the latter. It was a revolver, 32 caliber, and one chamber was empty. With that for a basis, I questioned the station agent on another tack, and he finally succeeded in remembering that just as the train pulled into the station that memorable night the girl handed Ames his coat, and as he threw it over his arm an object dropped from one of the pockets, which Ames quickly recovered and replaced in the coat as he and his companion clambered aboard the train. Might not this revolver have been the object dropped by Ames, and might he not when he put it back in his coat have slipped it into the sleeve, through which it dropped as he stepped upon the train?"

"Well, the theory is ingenious, even if wrong," muses Ashley.

"I clinched it a bit more," continues Barker. "Where

had Ames and the girl boarded the train? The station agent remembered that it was at the south end of the platform, as the New York sleeper was made up next behind the engine and baggage car."

"I beg to remark," puts in Ashley, "that the fact of one chamber in a revolver being empty is not at all unusual. I have in my pocket a gun in that condition, but as it is a 38 caliber, that lets me out of any connection with the tragedy."

"Of course," smiles Barker, "I take all these bits of evidence for what they are worth. While waiting for my train I argued in this wise: Derrick Ames was in love with Helen Hathaway, and the attachment resulted in an elopement. Neither was seen after 2 o'clock of Memorial Day, and the inference is that they were together somewhere all the afternoon and evening. The elopement was apparently unpremeditated, as they took nothing with them, so far as known, except the clothes they wore. There must have been some cause for such an impromptu exit. People do not elope that way no matter how love-mad they may be. Where was Helen when Ames was seen going into the bank? Waiting for him somewhere. What was his errand? To make a final appeal for the girl's hand, with an elopement in mind as the last resort, perhaps. But even failing in that, why elope that particular night? There must have been a cause for hurrying him away. But if you assume that Ames committed the crime, even as the upshot of a fierce quarrel, even perhaps in self-defense, you must figure him a moral monstrosity, for only such could strike down a father and elope subsequently with the daughter. And then there is the missing money. You see it argues a villainy more despicable than a man like Ames could have been guilty of."

"Yet pathology records even more singular instances of moral distortion."

"Even so. But is it not more reasonable to believe that Ames may have been only a witness to the murder, or a spectator on the scene of the tragedy after it had occurred, and that he was hurried away by the horror of the affair? But in either event would he not have argued that to fly would be the worst possible thing he could do? I confess that when I arrived at Raymond I was in doubt as to Ames' possible guilt, but my afternoon's investigations have about convinced me that Derrick Ames had nothing to do with the death of Cashier Hathaway."

"Then you must have substituted some other person as the object of your suspicion."

"Yes; but the substitution is not especially recent. Before I give you the result of my afternoon labors let me tell you of a discovery that I made yesterday, not three hours after my arrival in town.

"After I had posted myself from the stenographic notes of the inquest I dropped into the bank to have a talk with the officials. President Felton took me into the directors' room, where the tragedy occurred, and I sat in the cashier's chair and glanced around to get a few bearings. While Felton was retelling his story of the finding of Hathaway's body I toyed with a blotter on the desk. It was the ordinary blotter, larger than the average, with the advertisement of an insurance company on one side. As I glanced carelessly at it I noticed that it had taken up the ink of some unusually plain characters.

"Felton was called out of the room for a moment and I slipped the blotter in my pocket to examine it at my leisure. When I returned to the hotel I made an investigation, and I discovered—but I will let you see for yourself. Hand me that small mirror on the wall."

Ashley does so. The detective takes his prize from a bundle of papers in his pocket, smooths it flat on the table, and places the mirror perpendicularly before it. Then he draws the lamp over and remarks complacently: "Look here upon this picture!"

And this is what Ashley sees as he gazes upon the reflecting surface. There are three groups of characters. The first group reads:

"Come to the bank immediately——"

The second:

"Your personal account overdrawn——"

And the third:

· "These things I charge you fail not, Cyrus Felton, at the peril of your good name.   Roger Hathaway."

"Jove! It reads like an accusation!" cries Ashley, dropping back into his chair.

"It is an accusation!" declares the detective, with the ring of triumph in his voice.

CHAPTER XI.

A SIFTING OF EVIDENCE.

Both men smoke on in a brief silence that Ashley breaks with an inquiring "Well?"

"Much," is Barker's smiling response. "Now, my boy," he adds briskly, as he extracts a bunch of writing paper from his grip and sharpens his pencil, "tell me everything you know concerning the dramatis personae in this drama. We will get our facts together, and then I'll give you my theories—for I have more than one. Go ahead."

·When Ashley has exhausted his stock of information and has hazarded one or two ingenious theories, the detective leans back in his chair and for the space of five minutes says not a word. Finally he turns to Ashley.

"This Hathaway mystery," he begins, "is either simplicity itself or it is shrouded in a veil that only the patient search and unceasing effort of months will lift. My first glance at the case led me to believe that the murder was the work of a professional, so swiftly had it been accomplished and so completely had the work of the operator been covered up. But the most earnest search has failed to discover the presence in town on Memorial Day of any person who could possibly be regarded as a suspicious character, except Ernest Stanley, of whom more anon.

"Then the deed must have been committed by some

one in Raymond. Thus far we have evidence affecting four men—Derrick Ames, Cyrus Felton, Ralph Felton, and Ernest Stanley. If two of the four were implicated it could have been only the Feltons, father and son. I do not say that any of the four is the guilty man. But a chain of evidence must be forged about the slayer of Roger Hathaway, and in order that this chain shall be complete, minus not a single link, it becomes necessary for us to establish the innocence of these four men, if they are innocent, as well as the presumptive guilt of a fifth party, if a fifth party committed the crime."

"In other words, we are hampered by a superabundance of clews."

"Exactly. I will pardon your interruption, but no more of them, unless they are good ones. Now, your attention."

"Roger Hathaway was killed in his office in the bank on the evening of Memorial Day, some time between 7:45 and 8:30 o'clock. No definite minute or five minutes can be fixed. Two of our characters were, we know, and the other two may have been, at the bank between 7:45 and 8:30. To begin with Ames. Sam Brockway tells me that he saw Ames enter the bank after Hathaway had handed a note to the boy, Jimmie Howe. Brockway did not stay to see Ames come out; when the latter did emerge he was unseen. It is not unreasonable to assume that Ames killed Hathaway as the climax of a bitter quarrel over the latter's daughter, and that, to facilitate his escape, he helped himself to the bank's funds. But it is unreasonable to assume that subsequently he induced the daughter to elope with him. That is the weak link in that chain."

"But suppose that the elopement was already under way; that everything had been arranged for, hour of departure, route and conveyance," debates Ashley. "Would not Ames argue that solitary flight, and a failure to carry out the prearranged plans must weigh heavily against him? An elopement is an excellent excuse for leaving town hurriedly, you know."

"Possible," returns the detective. "Now, the letter

which you say Louise Hathaway received from her sister, but the contents of which she refuses to reveal, must have contained some reference to Ames which Miss Hathaway has reasons for concealing. At any rate, there is good ground for suspecting that Ames knows something of the murder of Roger Hathaway, whether or no his own hand was stained with the cashier's blood. Now," says Barker, turning to the blotter and the mirror on the table, and propping up the reflector with the water pitcher, look that over carefully, Ashley, and tell me what you find."

Ashley draws his chair up to the table and examines critically the characters on the blotter as reflected in the mirror.

"All of the words which are distinguishable were not, when blotted, on the same sheet of paper," he asserts. "At least two and perhaps three sheets of paper were used. The words, 'your personal account overdrawn,' must have been at the bottom of one sheet and those with the signature attached upon another, but whether top, middle, or bottom of the page is of no consequence."

"Very good," approves Barker. "That was the first conclusion I arrived at when I examined the blotter. Now, how about those words, 'Come to the bank immediately'?"

"Their position is not so clear to me. Their nature would indicate that they began the letter, but if so I cannot see why they should blot and the words following them should not appear."

"But if they were part of another letter—what then?"

"Ah," remarks Ashley, thoughtfully.

"I am assuming, and I think reasonably, that the blotter was first used upon the letter or letters whose contents we are attempting to guess," says Barker. "There are many faint marks around the legible words, but naturally only the words concluding each page would be distinguishable. Those above would be either dry or in process of drying. But what else do you deduce, Ashley?"

"Well, the writing does not display, in my opinion,

undue haste or agitation. I am not an expert in handwriting, but I should say that this letter was written at a normal speed and by a man in a comparatively calm condition of mind. The signature is bold and firm, as are all the legible characters. I should also say that this letter was the one which Roger Hathaway sent to Cyrus Felton half an hour or so before he was found dead in his office."

"You remember Felton's testimony at the inquest?"

"Perfectly. He stated that the note he received contained the simple request: 'Come to the bank immediately.'"

"Then you think he lied to the coroner?"

"It would seem so. Unless——"

"Unless the note he received at his house on the evening of Memorial Day did contain only that brief summons, which is contained in the five words at the top of the blotter."

"Precisely," agrees Ashley. "That brings us to the question, when was the other letter written? It must have been previous to the note referred to at the inquest, but how many hours or days before? Let me have your theory, Barker. My mind is already shaping a shadowy one."

The detective chews his cigar reflectively. "Suppose that Roger Hathaway discovered, some time ago—within a few weeks, we will say—that the affairs of the bank were not in the condition that they should be?" he hazards. "An examination of the books showed not only that the president's personal account was overdrawn, but that certain operations of the latter had jeopardized the soundness of the institution. The knowledge might have been expected or unexpected. In either case the cashier realized that something had to be done, and at once. So on the day before Memorial Day, or even earlier, he wrote a letter to the president and couched it in plain English. He instanced the overdrawal of the president's personal account and a number of other unpleasant conditions, and urged upon that gentleman the necessity for an immediate adjustment of the critical affairs, closing

with the admonition, 'Fail not, Cyrus Felton, at the peril of your good name.'

"Having dispatched his letter to the president, the cashier waited anxiously for a reply. It came in the form of a call by Felton at the residence of Hathaway the evening before Memorial Day. The interview was a stormy one. At least we know it was not harmonious. The cashier again set forth the necessity for immediate action. Ways and means were discussed, but no way out of the tangle seemed clear. In desperation the cashier suggested some unpleasant but safe method of salvation. The president responded angrily, 'I can't and I won't!' and the cashier answered decisively, 'Then there is only one alternative.' Without waiting to discuss this alternative, the president left the house in a temper and the cashier sat up in his library for hours afterward, meditating on the crisis.

"Now, what was this 'one alternative' indicated by the cashier? Clearly publicity of the bank's condition and its subsequent wreck. The next day was Memorial Day. The cashier took part in the solemn services and in the evening he went to the bank to perform some necessary work upon the books, the teller being ill. No word had come from the president, no intimation that he was prepared to follow out the course pointed out the night before, and avoid the disgrace which the wreck of the bank would entail. Again the desperation of the situation flashed upon the cashier. The president must act, and at once. So the cashier indited a brief but peremptory note to the president: 'Come to the bank immediately.' This he delivered to Jimmy Howe, whom he found on the bridge tossing pebbles into the stream.

"The president answered the summons. Within the cashier's office the accusation, apparently so plainly indicated on this blotter, was repeated verbally. A sharp dispute followed. Hot words led to blows. The drawer of the cashier's desk was open and his revolver lay in view. Can you supply the rest?"

"But the open vault and the missing money and securities?" contends Ashley.

"The vault may have been, probably was, already open. The missing funds—had been missing for some little time," replies Barker, with a significant smile. Then he resumes:

"Felton testified that on the night of the tragedy he reached the bank about 8:20. As he left his house about 8:05 he must have got to the bank not far from 8:15. It is not more than ten minutes' walk, even at an ordinary pace. He told Sheriff Wilson, when he found the latter at the hotel, that he discovered Hathaway 'only a few moments ago.' Yet the sheriff stated to me that he was positive it was 8:35 when he was informed of the affair. He looked at his watch when he was accompanying Felton to the bank. Again, Felton told the coroner that 'it did not seem more than a minute that I spent in the bank,' so that here we have a hiatus of fully a quarter of an hour. Now, where was Felton during that fifteen minutes if not in the company of Roger Hathaway? If Hathaway was dead when Felton reached the bank, why was not the sheriff informed earlier? You see there is an apparent discrepancy that might be explained on the theory that Hathaway was alive when Felton entered the bank, and that an interview of ten or fifteen minutes was ended by the death of the cashier."

<hr>

CHAPTER XII.

FURTHER CONSIDERATION OF CLEWS.

Having allowed Ashley to digest the food for thought furnished by the detective, the latter resumes his story:

"Upon my return from Ashfield I called upon Cyrus Felton, found him at his residence and interviewed him in his library for fully an hour. When I introduced myself as a detective he started visibly. In place of the extreme agitation which characterized his testimony at the inquest, he betrayed a nervousness rather peculiar, to say the least, in one whose knowledge of the crime embraced only what he related to the coroner.

"I questioned him minutely, avoiding any direct query that would be likely to arouse his suspicions. To my question, 'When did you last see Mr. Hathaway?' he replied that it was on the afternoon of Memorial Day, when the Grand Army post marched to the cemetery.

"'And before that—when?'

"He hesitated a few moments and answered that he had last talked with the cashier several days, probably a week, before the tragedy.

"'Your relations with Mr. Hathaway were always of a friendly nature?'

"'Eminently so.'

"The answer was straightforward and the look that accompanied it was open and direct, the only one, by the way, during the entire interview. Of course I was not at the time aware of the unharmonious interview which, as Miss Hathaway reported to you, occurred at her father's house on the evening preceding Memorial Day. Lie No. 1, conceding that he told the truth about the note which he received from the cashier on the evening of the tragedy.

"'Now, this revolver of Mr. Hathaway's, what sort of a weapon was it, Mr. Felton?' I asked. He gave me a half-startled look and I fancied that his gaze strayed for an instant to the safe set in the wall of his library. It flashed upon me that the lost gun was concealed behind the steel door of that same safe.

"'The revolver,' he said, in an absent sort of way; 'oh, it was an ordinary affair, 32 caliber, I believe they called it, nickeled and with a pearl handle. I had often seen it lying in Mr. Hathaway's drawer, but so far as I know it was never used.'

"'Would you recognize that revolver if you should see it again, Mr. Felton?'

"'I don't know as I could positively identify it. Revolvers are so much alike, are they not?' I nodded, and again his eyes shifted toward the door of his safe.

"Well, as I say, I talked with him for about an hour,

most of the interview dealing with the forgery case of two years ago, in which our mysterious friend, Ernest Stanley, figured as the principal. But of that more later.

"It was about 5 o'clock when I called at Felton's house, and the supper bells of the neighborhood were ringing when I left. Instead of going to the hotel I struck down a side street to the river road, for a smoke and a stroll, and a chance to run the Hathaway case over in my mind.

"Half a mile below the village there is quite a stretch of road without any houses along it. The cemetery is on one side, the river on the other. I was sprawling on the stone wall that skirts the city of the dead and looking toward the village, when I saw a figure rapidly approaching. 'Cyrus Felton or I'm a goat!' I exclaimed, and rolled out of sight behind the wall. My eyesight is keen and I could not mistake the tall, lank form of the bank president. 'What the deuce is he doing down this road at an hour when he should be peacefully eating his supper?' I wondered.

"When Felton passed around the bend in the road I sprung over the wall and followed at a cautious distance. He looked around once or twice, and I had to dodge behind a tree each time. Suddenly he stopped and walked out upon the bank of the river, while I again took up a position behind my friendly stone wall.

"Our banker walked to the edge of the river, and, with his hands clasped behind him, stared at the water, now and then casting a look up and down the road.

"'Heavens! Is he going to commit suicide?' I thought. Surely my mild catechism had not driven him to such an extremity. My fears were shortly allayed. He suddenly thrust his hand into his coat pocket, and, withdrawing some object, hurled it into the stream. It sunk with a small splash. I was too far away to more than guess what the object was. Felton remained on the bank for several minutes, gazing at the surface of the river, then suddenly wheeled and started toward the village. As he passed me I fancied he looked a bit more relieved in mind.

"After he was out of sight I walked over to the river

and marked as near as possible the spot where he had stood. The river at that point is deep, and I fear that the bottom is muddy, as the stream makes a sharp bend and spreads into a broad lagoon, with little or no current."

"You intend to go a-fishing?" queries Ashley.

"At daylight, if we can get a boat of some sort."

"And if our search is rewarded by the finding of a revolver—the revolver—what then?"

"Then I think we shall have a case against Cyrus Felton stronger than we shall make out against any one else. I can see by your face that you are only half convinced of that fact," continues Barker. "You are more inclined to suspect the younger Felton than the elder. eh?"

"Well," argues the newspaper man, "in the case of Ralph Felton there is a motive, an evil temper, and what is usually regarded as confession of guilt—flight."

"Good. Let us look over young Felton's case." says the detective. "Ralph Felton, we know, is possessed of an evil temper and a disposition to bullyrag a young lady who is sensible enough not to love him. We know also that he gambles with traveling men who put up here, and drinks more or less. As the good people of this town regard Ralph as a model young man, his indulgence in cards and wine on the quiet shows a broad streak of deception in his character.

"His inclinations toward gayety were not cultivated in his native town. Previous to a twelvemonth ago four or five years of his life were spent in New York, Chicago and other cities. His occupation during a share of that time was that of representative and selling agent for the granite company in which his father is the principal stock owner. He was apparently wild and reckless, for a year ago he returned to Raymond and through the efforts of his father was given the position of bookkeeper in the bank, a position which does not usually pay much. It would appear that the elder Felton had enacted the role of the prodigal's father.

"While Ralph Felton was 'down country' he fell in

love with a pretty face, and upon its possessor he squandered all his means and more. When Ralph returned to Raymond the woman wrote to him demanding money and a fulfillment of pledges. The former he had not; of the latter he had no thought, as he had become desperately enamored of Helen Hathaway. Unable to obtain satisfaction by a correspondence, the woman visited Raymond the afternoon of Memorial Day, registered as 'Isabel Winthrop,' and sent word to Ralph that a lady desired to see him. He went to her. The interview between the pair was not harmonious. Sounds of a quarrel came from the room, and once or twice the word 'money' was used. Half an hour or so from the time he entered the hotel Ralph left with a flushed countenance, first pledging the clerk to say nothing of his feminine caller.

"He has essayed promises with her, but something substantial is demanded to back them up. He must have money, but where is it to be secured? No use to apply to his father, that he well knows. The more he racks his brain the more desperate becomes the situation. Then a wild thought comes to him. The bank! There must be a large amount of money in the safe. The county bonds mature the next day. He knows, we will assume—perhaps the knowledge is accidental—the combination of the safe.

"Ralph returns to the hotel, and, with a calmness born of a desperate resolve, informs 'Isabel Winthrop' that he has arranged for the needed funds, and reiterates his promises for the future. As dusk comes on he leaves the hotel unobserved by the clerk, goes to the bank, opens the front door and locks it behind him, and proceeds to the cashier's office in the rear, wherein open the doors to the vault.

"As with a trembling hand he twists the combination of the vault he hears the sound of a key in the outer door. He springs to his feet and casts a startled glance about him. There is no egress from the room save by the way he came. Ah! The closet! He secretes himself in the dark closet at the farther end of the room, and at that instant Roger Hathaway enters.

" 'The cashier,' murmurs the prisoner in the closet, as through the partially open door he watches Hathaway light his desk lamp. 'He has dropped in to get some papers and will soon be gone,' thinks Ralph. But to the latter's despair the cashier opens the vault, takes out the big ledger, and settles down apparently to an evening's work.

"Here is a nice predicament, but there is nothing to be done except wait until the cashier finishes his evening's work and goes home. Half an hour or more goes by. The closet is dusty and Ralph is seized with an irresistible desire to sneeze. The explosion, a half-smothered one, occurs, and the cashier looks about him in surprise and wonder. But he continues his work. Suddenly Felton sees him seize a pad of writing paper, scratch off a brief note and leave the room to find a messenger. Has the cashier suspected the presence of some person in the bank besides himself and has he taken this means to summon assistance? As this thought flashes upon him young Felton becomes desperate, but as he watches the face of the cashier, who returns calmly to his writing, he convinces himself that he is mistaken.

"Again that cursed inclination to sneeze, which in vain he attempts to smother. This time there is no mistake. The cashier rises to his feet and glances about the room in alarm. His eyes finally rest on the partly opened door of the dark closet. Hathaway is a man of nerve. He opens the right-hand drawer of his desk, takes out and cocks his revolver and walks deliberately toward the closet.

"All this is seen by Ralph, and his plan to rob the bank is succeeded by a desire to escape from the building unrecognized. To accomplish this the cashier must be overpowered. So when the latter flings open the closet door the man within reaches out, grasps the revolver arm and draws the cashier into the darkness of the closet. Then ensues a fierce struggle, for Roger Hathaway, though old, is still a powerful man. This would account for the old ledgers that were toppled over into the office, and for the marks on the body of the murdered man.

"During the struggle the revolver is discharged and the bullet enters the cashier's heart. The doctors in the case tell me that the course of the bullet was such that the leaden missile might have come from a pistol discharged during such a struggle as I have described. But to continue:

"Ralph Felton draws the limp form of the cashier out into the office and lays it upon the floor. A moment's examination shows him that the man is dead, and he realizes his frightful position. Then the thought occurs to him that, if he carries out his original plan of robbing the bank, the crime will be ascribed to burglars. So he fills his pockets with what money and securities are in the safe, closes the door to the cashier's office behind him and leaves the bank, with the front door unlocked or ajar."

"Unless——" interrupts Ashley.

"Unless what?"

"Unless," says the newspaper man, leaning back in his chair and blowing a cloud of smoke ceilingward—"unless Ralph Felton, when he rose from his examination of the body, was suddenly confronted by his father, who had come to the bank in response to the summons sent by the cashier!"

CHAPTER XIII.

THE KEY TO THE MYSTERY.

"Following along the lines of your theory," continues Ashley, "if Ralph Felton rose from the corpse of Roger Hathaway and confronted his father upon the threshold of the cashier's office, that dramatic meeting would explain many things. It would explain the startled glance that Cyrus Felton shot at his son—I was studying the faces of both—when the latter refused to state at the inquest where he had spent the time between 7:45 and

8:30 on the evening of Memorial Day. It would account for the carrying off of the cashier's revolver and its subsequent burial among the waters of Wild River; for young Felton's flight, and for the extreme agitation of the elder Felton ever since the night of the killing."

"And," adds Barker, "it would satisfactorily clear up the interim of fifteen minutes between the time Cyrus Felton should have reached the bank and the moment when the sheriff was notified. In fact, if the Felton family is responsible for the death of Roger Hathaway there must be some understanding between father and son. But we will now proceed to the consideration of an important character in our tragedy—Ernest Stanley.

"Two years ago, while the directors of the Raymond National Bank were holding their annual meeting, the teller stepped into the room and announced that a stranger had presented at the bank for payment a check for $1,000, signed by Cyrus Felton.

" 'Impossible!' exclaimed that individual, who was presiding over the directors' meeting. 'Let me see the check.' The teller produced it, and Felton at once declared it a forgery, and a bungling one at that. An officer was quickly summoned and Ernest Stanley, who had presented the check, was arrested.

"His trial in the Mansfield County Court was short. The forgery was proved and the young man was sentenced to three years in the state prison at Windsor. In his own defense—he had no money with which to employ a lawyer—Stanley stated that the check had been given to him two days before he presented it, by a casual acquaintance who claimed the name signed to the bit of paper. It was in payment of a gambling debt and the transaction occurred in Phil Clark's well-known lair of the tiger on Fifth Avenue, New York."

"Which, by the way, is no more," puts in Ashley. "The place was closed out six months ago and Phil is now in 'Frisco."

"It was in existence during Stanley's trial," resumes Barker, "and the trial was adjourned a couple of days while his improbable story was looked up. As was expected, neither Phil nor any of the habitues of his place knew of such a person as Ernest Stanley, much less such a transaction as he alleged to have occurred there.

"Stanley received his sentence calmly. Beyond stating that his age was 26 and his occupation that of a bookmaker he refused to furnish any details of his birth, early life or present residence. He served two years of his sentence and was pardoned by the governor this last Memorial Day. Strangely enough, the pardon was secured by the man whose name he was alleged to have forged—Cyrus Felton. Now, what feelings do you suppose actuated Felton in securing a remission of a year in the prisoner's sentence? Compassion?"

"What should you say were I to suggest the word 'remorse'?" replies Ashley.

"I should say," declares the detective, with a smile of approval, "that you had hit upon the very word. It is plain that you foresee what I am leading up to."

"To the theory that Stanley was innocent of the forgery and that the check was given to him by Ralph Felton?"

"Exactly. It will be difficult to prove, but if it can be proved it will have an important bearing on the Hathaway mystery. It will show Ralph Felton's capacity for wrongdoing and will enable us to surmise to what extent Cyrus Felton would shield his son from conviction of a crime. At the time the check was presented Ralph Felton was supposed to be in New York, and as he had been for some time more or less of a trial to the old man the latter doubtless suspected in an instant what we are assuming to have been the truth. He had to decide between his son and a stranger, and, as usual, the stranger suffered."

"What led Stanley to attempt to cash the check in Raymond?" debates Ashley.

"Well, if he was a stranger in New York he would find it impossible to cash it at any of the banks in that city. Why not run up to Raymond and cash it at the bank on which it was drawn? I forgot to say that at the trial Stanley alleged that his acquaintance of the gambling rooms claimed to be a Vermonter and appeared to have plenty of money."

"And he did not hazard the suggestion that this acquaintance was the son of the man whose name was forged?"

"He did not know that there was a son. To prove this, if the visitor at Cyrus Felton's house on the evening of Memorial Day was the released prisoner of Windsor, note his surprised reply to the housemaid, 'I did not know there were two Feltons.'"

"True," admits Ashley. "Keep along, old man."

"If Stanley was that visitor," pursues the detective, "his object in revisiting Raymond was to obtain revenge for the wrong that had been done him.

"When he arrived at Raymond, at 7:45, he went directly to Felton's house. Failing to find the bank president at home, he obtained directions as to where Felton's office was and proceeded to the bank block. The office, which is on the second story, at the south end of the block, was dark and Stanley returned to the street. As he stood in front of the bank and thought of the day, two long years before, when he stepped from its portals with a constable gripping his arm, he noticed a light in the rear. Perhaps Felton was within. So he pushed open the door and——"

"Hold on a bit. How does the bank door come to be open? You are assuming a great deal this time, Barker," laughs Ashley.

"I am assuming that he got into the bank some way or other," retorts the detective. "If not—and here I will quote your own words when you imparted to me your valuable discovery—'What was Stanley doing at 6 o'clock the next morning asleep in the bushes in a lonely gorge near South Ashfield village?"

Ashley laughs merrily. "I was expecting that," he says. "But I'll be hanged if I will believe that an Edmond Dantes sort of a chap like Ernest Stanley is capable of——"

"Permit me to suggest that Ernest Stanley may be

a cheap criminal instead of an Edmond Dantes," interrupts Barker, with a withering sarcasm that only increases Ashley's good humor. "We have given him a good character simply to suit our present theory. He may have really forged old Felton's name, and his visit to Raymond may have been actuated by a base desire for revenge upon a stern justice meted out to him. Alone in the bank with Roger Hathaway and the open vault, murder and robbery may have come natural to him. We know nothing that should lead us to decide that he was a much-abused young man."

"Yet you believe he is, I'll wager," asserts Ashley.

"I confess that I do. A man would be half a dozen kinds of a fool to forge the name of the president of a bank and present the check for payment at the latter's own bank. Still what evidence we have against Stanley is strong. We can account for the flight of Derrick Ames on the simple elopement theory. We can explain the levanting of Ralph Felton on the theory that he refused to establish an alibi because it would necessitate the confession of an acquaintance with 'Isabel Winthrop,' when he was an ardent suitor for the hand of Helen Hathaway, and on the further supposition that he has gone to hunt for the woman he insanely loved. We can explain the nervous condition of Cyrus Felton on the assumption that he fears his son was implicated in the bank robbery and trembles for his safety. But we cannot explain why Ernest Stanley fled from Raymond the night of Memorial Day and hurried over mountain and stream and through forest, chased like a wild beast, until he found a haven of refuge. The open bank door is the break in the chain of evidence against him, and that may be mended by assuming that the cashier forgot to lock the door behind him when he entered the bank.

"We must find Stanley," Ashley promptly declares.

"And there are others to be found," the detective rejoins dryly. "But especially must we run down Stanley. I am convinced that he is the key to the mystery, and when we have located his position in this puzzling case I believe that the rest of the race will be plain sailing."

"I fear it will be a long, stern chase."

'Such chases usually are," remarks Barker, composedly. "I have already set the machinery in motion, and the police of the entire country are on the lookout· for a chap answering Stanley's description. What makes our task the harder is the probable fact that Stanley is not a member of the criminal class, and so a comparatively easy channel of pursuit is closed. He presumably made for New York, and somewhere in that busy human hive we may run across him."

"Then our labors at this end of the road are about completed?"

"Nearly so. To-morrow morning, before the village is astir, we will go a-fishing. If we find what we expect the case may be precipitated a bit. Otherwise we will shift the scene of our operations to New York, after I have pumped the servants in the Felton family and inquired as far as is possible into the affairs of the bank. Is your vacation about wound up?"

"It will be in a day or so. I have nothing to keep me here longer except a pleasant duty that I owe to myself."

"And that is——"

"To make an unprofessional call upon Miss Louise Hathaway."

"Ho! Sits the wind in that quarter?" laughs the detective.

"Don't be absurd, my friend," smiles Ashley. "Miss Hathaway interests me only as would a statue of the Venus de Milo."

"Indeed? Still, men have lost their hearts to a statue."

"In books and plays. If we are to arise at daybreak I would suggest the advisability of retiring."

CHAPTER XIV.

A CHANGE OF BASE.

"I believe this is the exact spot; yes, I am sure it is. Drop your anchor, Ashley, so that the bow will point up-stream," says Barker, as he grasps a long pole with a hook at one end, and prepares to explore the bed of Wild River.

Ashley lets go the rock that does duty as an anchor and remarks ruefully, when all but a yard of the rope is run out: "This is deep-sea fishing. There is over twelve feet of water here."

"Thunder! And mud enough to bury a man-of-war," grunts the detective.

After fifteen minutes of earnest but ineffectual groping in the slimy bed of the stream Barker throws the pole from him and remarks: "No use."

"Can't the river be dredged?"

"Yes; with a force of men and a steam dredger, and the whole township looking on and asking questions. We can do nothing this morning. Up anchor and away! I could use a little breakfast."

"By the way," observes Ashley, as the two men walk back to the hotel, "in all your talk last night you said nothing of that locket, with the miniatures of the Hathaway sisters, which was stolen from the watch-chain of the murdered cashier the night of the killing."

"Do you know it was stolen on that night?" asks the detective.

"We must assume that it was until we know otherwise, I suppose," returns Ashley. "If the missing locket is found in the possession of any one of our suspects it would be a strong link, would it not?"

"Very likely, but we must find our man first. Shall you be ready to leave for New York to-night?"

"Sure thing."

"Good. We must strike the trail there and follow it, if need be, to the end of the world."

Ashley has been in Raymond only two weeks, but already he begins to sigh for the pleasures and palaces of gay, crowded and babel-voiced New York.

"Hang it!" he growls to Barker, as he packs his valise, "this Vermont country is all right, but the natives are atrocious. They know no literature except those provincial Boston dailies and the current paper-covered rot; no music except Sousa's marches, no art except the colored supplements to the Sunday newspapers and no conversation higher than horse, hay and village gossip."

"Your criticism is too sweeping," replies the detective. There is more culture in Raymond, in proportion to its population, than there is in New York, I'll wager. And where in that politics-ridden city will you find another woman rivaling your fervid description of Miss Louise Hathaway?"

"Ah, she is a rose in a wilderness. And that reminds me that I have promised myself the pleasure of a farewell call upon her," says Ashley.

"Farewell?" repeats the detective, skeptically. "You will not see the last of Miss Hathaway to-day unless I am much mistaken. I have known of more than one lover of statuary who failed to be content with the marble and warmed it into living, breathing womanhood."

"Nonsense!" laughs Ashley. "I shall live and die a bachelor."

But he spends fully ten minutes in tying his cravat, brushes his hair with unusual care, gives his mustache an extra twist, and saunters up to the Hathaway homestead in an expectant frame of mind. Foolish Jack Ashley! In after years he will smile at the recollection of the thoughts that flit through his busy mind to-day.

Just as he turns into the path leading to the Hathaway residence Miss Hathaway is stepping out upon the veranda. She sees him and smiles in her grave way.

"Good afternoon," she says to her visitor. He answers, uncovering his head.

"I called to say au revoir. I leave for New York to-night."

She leads the way to the reception room. After they

have taken their seats near the open window she answers:

"You will return? Your work here on—on the case is not yet finished?"

"No; we shall have occasion to visit Raymond more than once before the mystery which shrouds the bank case is dispelled. It is going to be a long chase, I fear, Miss Hathaway. But I hope to come to you some day and tell you of its successful end."

"I hope so," she replies dreamily, her thoughts far away.

"You have heard nothing more from your sister?"

"Nothing." Her look is frank.

"I can tell you nothing of our plans," says Ashley, "further than that our principal endeavor will be to discover Ernest Stanley."

"Ernest Stanley?" repeats Miss Hathaway. "Oh, the young man who was pardoned from State prison on Memorial Day. Do you think he committed the crime?"

"Frankly, no. But we believe that he knows something of its perpetration. In other words, we regard him as the key to the mystery."

"And Derrick Ames?" questions Miss Hathaway, with the anxious expression of yesterday in her gaze.

"Derrick Ames must be found, also. If you could give me any information——"

"I can tell you nothing," she replies hurriedly.

"Ralph Felton is another absentee whose presence is earnestly desired," he resumes.

"You say you do not believe that Stanley is the guilty man. Does it, then, lie between Ralph Felton and——"

"And Derrick Ames?" finishes Ashley. "Not necessarily. There is another, but for excellent reasons I should prefer not to mention the name. Have you any plans for the future?"

"No definite plans. Mr. Cyrus Felton has been appointed executor of the estate and after that has been settled I shall probably make my home at his house."

"At Cyrus Felton's?" murmurs Ashley, in such a peculiar voice that Miss Hathaway looks at him in surprise.

"Yes; that is the only place I can go to at present. He has long been a friend of the family."

"Have you no relatives—in Boston, New York, or elsewhere?"

"No near relatives. It will not be very long ere I shall have to make a home for myself. I am told that the estate will settle for very little," confesses Miss Hathaway, with a red spot in each pale cheek. Ashley understands and regards her sympathetically.

There is a short, somewhat embarrassing silence. Then Ashley rises regretfully. He says:

"I am afraid it must be good-bye—or, perhaps, au revoir. I shall hope to see you again before the summer is gone."

"I trust so," Miss Hathaway responds, this time quite cordially, as she gives him her hand at parting, and Ashley holds it an instant longer than ordinary courtesy calls for. And as he walks slowly away from the house he carries with him the vision of a tall girl, with a pure white face and sad blue eyes, into which the sunlight will some day come again.

At night he and Barker take the Montreal express for New York.

*   *   *   *   *   *   *

Summer drifts into autumn and autumn into winter. Life goes on much the same in Raymond. The Hathaway mystery gradually fades from public interest, and it is set down as a crime that will never be explained.

The Raymond National Bank has closed its doors. The robbery of its vault was a blow from which it found it impossible to recover.

No tidings are received of Derrick Ames and Helen Hathaway or of Ralph Felton. None, unless they are in the keeping of the silent, stern-faced Cyrus Felton or the beautiful girl with the sad blue eyes who abides under his roof.

Every Sunday, in rain or in sunshine, mid heat or cold, Louise Hathaway may be seen ascending the hill in the little cemetery by which Wild River sings its way, her mission of love to deposit a basket of flowers upon a grave at the head of which stands a plain white shaft bearing, besides the name and dates, the simple inscription, "Faithful Unto Death."

CHAPTER XV.

SHADOWS OF COMING EVENTS.

It is early in the evening. Jack Ashley is seated at his desk in the Hemisphere office enjoying his pipe preliminary to setting forth on an assignment.

The month is March. Nearly a year has elapsed since Ashley's first visit to the Vermont town which, for a brief space, came into the world's eye as the scene of the mysterious death of Cashier Roger Hathaway in the Raymond National Bank. During this time no further light has been shed on the mystery, which has gradually dropped from the thoughts of all save a few persons, two of whom are Ashley and John Barker, the detective.

Jack hears from Barker occasionally. The latter is busy on other work, but he still keeps a live interest in what he regards as the case of his life, and both he and his newspaper colaborer hope some day to astonish Vermont, and incidentally the country, by solving the Hathaway mystery, one of the most remarkable in the criminal annals of New England.

But as the months slipped by Ashley's stock of confidence decreased slightly and to-night finds him wondering whether he will ever have the privilege of handing the news editor a bundle of "copy," with the remark "There is an exclusive that is worth while."

"I have helped run down a number of crimes and fasten them upon the guilty persons," he soliloquizes, "and have flattered myself that I was something of a detective. But in each of those cases the trembling villain was on or about the scene of his crime and when you had your case made out all there was to do was to clap a heavy hand upon his shoulder. But in this Hathaway drama about all of the leading characters have disappeared, and the man whom we regard as the key to the mystery, Ernest Stanley, is the very man we are least likely to find.

"But is Stanley the key?" continues Jack, stretching himself in his chair. "I don't think Barker and I have attached sufficient importance to that blotter found on Hathaway's desk. These fragments of sentences keep haunting me, even amid my daily duties. Something tells me that if we had the imprint of an entire page of that letter to Felton we could solve the mystery without finding our men. 'These things I charge you, Cyrus Felton, fail not at the peril of your good name.' 'These things——' "

Ashley is slowly scratching a match to relight his pipe, when he suddenly stops and his thought-wrinkled forehead smooths.

"Hello! Here's an idea, perhaps a valuable one. It is possible that Barker and I have been all wrong in regarding that letter as an accusation. The English language is elastic. 'I charge you, Cyrus Felton,'—'I charge you, I charge you, I charge you.' Now, instead of 'I accuse you,' read 'I adjure you.' But 'I adjure you,' what? To 'fail not.' To 'fail not' in what? Ay, there's the rub. I am as much in the dark as before. Still the idea is worth considering, and I'll spring it on Barker."

Ashley finishes his smoke in silence and when the last flake of tobacco has yielded its solace he draws on his coat and boards an uptown car.

In that brilliantly lighted section of Broadway where stands the Hoffman House, Jack stops a moment to chat with an acquaintance.

"Say," remarks the latter, "there's a chap yonder staring hard at you. Know him?"

At his friend's suggestion Ashley turns suddenly and catches the searching gaze of a tall, handsome man with a dark-brown beard trimmed to a point. He is richly but simply attired, and his appearance is unmistakably that of a gentleman. As Ashley returns his stare with interest the stranger turns and enters the hotel.

The incident is trivial, but it awakens curious emotions in Ashley, and absently overlooking his acquaintance's suggestion of a visit to the cafe, he says an au revoir and continues up Broadway.

"I have seen those eyes somewhere," he muses, "but hang me if I can recall where."

As, late in the evening, his assignment covered, Ashley is sauntering down Broadway, he is haunted by the vision of a bearded face surrounding a pair of piercing eyes. He even drops in at the Hoffman House and looks through the bar room, cafe and reading rooms, but the handsome stranger is not in view.

Ashley has been in Raymond once since he left it, the spring before, and he was kindly received by Miss Hathaway. But that was all. Not all his engaging manners and clever conversation could penetrate the reserve with which she surrounded herself, and he almost decided that she was indeed the marble which he professed to Barker to have solely interested him. Still, that pure white face, with its matchless blue eyes and the sad smile that occasionally lighted it, lingers vividly in his memory and will continue to linger until——

He is at the Hemisphere office now. A very short time suffices to write and hand in his "copy" and then he lounges into the cable editor's room, with the inquiry: "What news from over the sea, Chance?"

"Nothing special except the insurrection in Cuba," Chance tells him. "Affairs are getting hot down there. You can judge of the magnitude of to-day's battle at Cienfuegos when you read that thirty Spaniards were killed and fifty captured."

"I should say so," laughs Ashley. "The average mortality per battle is three men killed and four wounded, is it not?"

The cable editor throws a handful of "copy" from him. with a sniff of disgust. "One can never tell how far to trust this rot we are getting from Madrid and Key West," he says. "I wish the Hemisphere had a live man such as you down in Cuba to give us some straight information on the conflict."

"Thank you. I have no desire to run up against Yellow Jack."

"Hang Yellow Jack! He is only dangerous to those half-fed raw recruits that the government is sending over from Spain. I have talked with Mr. Hone about the advantage of sending a representative to Havana or Santiago, and he is seriously considering it. "Hold on! Here's something coming now," and Chance turns to his table.

Ashley waits until the dispatch has been received, and then reads with interest the following special from Madrid:

"Ten thousand additional troops will be dispatched to Cuba within a week, in response to the demand of Gen. Martinez de Truenos, the new captain-general of the island. Gen. Truenos has had experience in fighting Cuban insurgents, and a speedy termination of the uprising is looked for."

"Same old bluff," comments Ashley, and then, awakened to an interest in Cuban affairs by the words of the cable editor, he visits the night-editor's den in search of further information.

The longest story is from Key West, and a portion of it runs in this wise:

"The insurgents are winning victories every day. The Cuban patriots do not need more men. All they want is arms and ammunition.

"It is whispered that the greatest difficulty with which the present captain-general has to contend is the conspiring among his own alleged supporters and advisers. One or two Spanish generals and a number of influential residents and land-owners at Havana, Santiago and other important points are suspected of active sympathy with the insurgents, but no proof of such complicity can be obtained. It is even said that the chosen president of the provisional republic is at present in Cuba, and that under the very nose of the hated oppressor he directs the movements of the patriot armies. It is thought that this condition of affairs is responsible for the change in captain-generals, as Truenos is reputed to be a clever diplomat as well as a tried soldier. The next few months will probably decide the fate of the republic. The Cubans must win this year or never."

What do you think?" Ashley asks the night editor. "Has the island any chance of liberty?"

"The prospects were never rosier," is Chambers' reply. "It is evident that the Castilian has an enormous job on his hands in the present insurrection. We received a dispatch a short while ago which has a local reference. I sent it up to Hone, and perhaps Ricker has it by this time. It states that the insurgents count upon valuable assistance from New York and that an expedition is being fitted out here. This wire came from Washington and the Spanish minister there has asked our government to prohibit the assistance I speak of. Hello!" as a bunch of copy is thrown upon his table, "the president has issued a proclamation bearing on the matter."

The proclamation is brief but significant. It sets forth that, without a violation of the friendly relations existing between Spain and the United States, this government cannot countenance the fitting out of expeditions designed to assist the insurrectionists in Cuba. A number of United States vessels have been ordered to patrol duty, and a rigid surveillance of the coast will be maintained.

"That may be good government, but it is confoundedly un-American in sentiment," remarks Ashley, scornfully, for he is an American through and through.

"The government's course was clear," Chambers mildly observes. "The President could do nothing less. I do not imagine, however, that the patrol will be much more than perfunctory."

When Ashley reports at the Hemisphere office the next day he finds in his letter box two yellow envelopes. One is from the city editor and contains an assignment to interview Senor Rafael Manada of the Cuban revolutionary society in the United States. The senor is stopping at the Fifth Avenue and a full story on Cuban affairs from the New York end is wanted.

"Well this is something new, at any rate," thinks Jack, and he tears open the second envelope. This contains a dispatch dated from Raymond, Vt., the night before, and Ashley whistles softly as he comprehends the concise but thoroughly interesting contents:

"See you to-morrow afternoon at your office. I have found Hathaway's revolver.   Barker."

CHAPTER XVI.

THE BEGINNING OF THE TRAIL.

"Don Rafael Manada? Yes, sir! Front, show the gentleman to No. 48."

A few minutes later Ashley is ushered into one of the most sumptuous and expensive suites in the big hotel.

He bows gracefully to the tall gentleman who advances to meet his visitor, bearing in his hand the card that has preceded him. Don Rafael is a man at whom even the least observant would be likely to take a second glance. Of perhaps 40 years of age, his hair of raven hue and unusual abundance is still unflecked by gray. The face is of olive hue, cleanly shaven save as to heavy mustachios, which by an odd freak of nature are snow white; heavy eyebrows of the same hue as the hair surmount eyes of piercing brilliancy; a long, aquiline nose, lips and mouth a trifle too sensuous for the rest of the features, complete a singularly interesting countenance.

"You came from the Hemisphere?" queries Don Manada, in melodious tones, with hardly a trace of the Castilian accent. "I am pleased to greet a representative of that great journal, whose influence is always cast on the side of right and justice. I read with the deepest emotions of gratitude this morning an editorial in your journal protesting against the proclamation which the administration has issued against the fitting out of expeditions designed to aid the insurrection in Cuba. Your paper properly urged that the United States government should recognize the Cubans as belligerents. Ah, my dear sir, could that be done, Cuba would be a free republic within the twelvemonth," finishes Manada, enthusiastically.

"It was to secure an expression of opinion from you on the outlook in Cuba and the preparations being made in this country that I have been commissioned to interview you, Don Rafael," says Jack Ashley.

"Anything that it would be proper for me to say, as the

agent of the Cuban revolutionary party, I shall be glad to give," continues Manada, smilingly.

And now the Cuban patriot becomes imbued with nervous energy as he reverts to the absorbing hope and ambition of his life—the freedom of Cuba. He paces the floor with erect, military tread, as he speaks rapidly:

"This war is not a capricious attempt to found an independence more to be feared than useful. It is the cordial congregation of Cubans of various origin, who are convinced that, in the conquest of liberty, rather than abject abasement, are acquired the virtues necessary to maintain our freedom. This is no race war.

"In the Spanish inhabitants of Cuba the revolutionists expect to find such affectionate neutrality or material aid, that through them the war will be shorter, its disasters less and the subsequent peace more easy and friendly. We Cubans began the war; the Cubans and Spanish together will terminate it. If they do not ill-treat us, we will not ill-treat them. Let them respect and they will be respected. Steel will answer to steel and friendship to friendship. In the bosom of the son of the Antilles there is no hatred, and the Cuban salutes in death the Spaniard whom the cruelty of a conscript army tore from his home and hearth and brought over to assassinate in many bosoms the freedom to which he himself aspires. But rather than salute him in death the revolutionists would like to welcome him in life."

"Very good, indeed, Don Manada," comments Ashley as he hastily jots down a skeleton of the impassioned words of the Cuban.

"Now, to leave generalities," says Jack, "upon what specific elements of strength, or of weakness on your opponents' part do you base your hopes of ultimate success?"

Manada smiles. "All our elements of strength, nor all the Spanish sources of weakness, we may not divulge yet, First, and of this I believe you newspaper men need not be assured, the information that comes from Cuba or from Madrid is entirely untrustworthy, distorted, colored and manufactured to suit Spanish ideas and hopes. It tells you that the insurrection is limited to three or four provinces. Yet you will notice to-day's dispatches from Madrid state that a blockade of every port of Cuba is imminent, large and small, and an additional squadron of ten Spanish gunboats has been dispatched from Cadiz to aid the big fleet now patrolling Cuban waters. Think you that the Madrid government would declare that blockade if the insurrection were limited to three or four paltry provinces? Bah! I can assure you, while they may not now be ready or willing to declare themselves, yet touch every Cuban in the heart, let him whisper to you his sentiments, and you will find them to a man praying for the success of the revolution. You Americans, in the full enjoyment of true liberty, can form but a faint idea of the real situation in Cuba. Imagine a land where no one is free to write or say anything except what the government judges deem proper! Imagine a government ever ready to throw you into prison, confiscate your property, bring ruin to everything that is dear to you on earth, and to set over you a Spaniard to watch your acts, almost your thoughts! That is the way we live in Cuba. Of late the number of these spies has been increased by hordes. They are not all men. Some of them—and the shrewdest and most harmful to our cause—are women, who ingratiate themselves with prominent revolutionists, sometimes becoming possessed of invaluable plans, which they promptly reveal to the Spanish government. It is believed that some of these women are located in cities in the United States, where it is thought their presence may be useful to spy upon the movements of the friends of Cuba in this country. But of course that is a game two can play at, and we ourselves are not wholly unaware of the secret plans of the enemy."

"Reference has been made in some of the dispatches from Key West, Don Manada, to the fact that the revolutionists have become possessed of a steamer which has been remarkably successful in evading the Spanish cruisers and landing men and ammunition from the Dominican and Florida coasts?"

Manada's lip curls scornfully at Ashley's use of the word "evading." Then he smiles.

"Did you happen to read in any of the press dispatches an account of the loss of the Spanish man-of-war Mercedes?"

Ashley has seen a casual reference to the disaster. "She ran on a reef near the Great Exuma, while pursuing a suspected filibustering steamer, did she not?"

"The Mercedes was sunk in forty fathoms of water in fair and open fight with the Cuban cruiser Pearl of the Antilles," in slow and measured tones responds Manada, his black eyes glittering. "The Spanish government has strenuously sought to conceal that fact, but it has leaked out, and only yesterday I received from Le Director de la Guerra a copy of El Terredo's report of the battle. Ah, that was glorious! The Mercedes went down in less than seven minutes, while the Pearl was unharmed. Senor Ashley, we have to thank the inventive genius of your countrymen for the success of our gallant cruiser, for El Terredo states that it was the wonderful effectiveness of the new dynamite cannon and the Yankee gunner that accomplished the feat."

Ashley's unfailing scent for news assures him that this interview is good for at least a two-column leader in the Hemisphere. Here is information that will make a sensation in the morning. The American public has been wholly in the dark as to this new element in the insurrection, this Cuban cruiser, with her patent dynamite gun and Yankee gunner, that has destroyed one of the most powerful of Spain's cruisers.

"El Terredo? Is he the captain of the Pearl of the Antilles, Don Manada?"

"He is, and one of the bravest and most successful of our commanders on land as well as sea. Why, there is not a cruiser of the Spanish navy now in Cuban waters that alone would dare engage the Pearl! They are well aware of her prowess and the skill and bravery of her commander, whom they have rightly named 'El Terredo,' 'the terror.'

"Then we have other plans the details of which cannot be revealed. Do you remember how the sinking of De

Gama's Brazilian ironclad was effected in the revolution in that country? It did not require another man-of-war to destroy her. Only a little instrument less than five feet in length—whish! boom!—and the resistless water is gushing in a torrent through the sides of the ironclad. Ah, warfare is different in these modern days, Senor Ashley, and victory does not always rest on the side of the heaviest guns."

"It is said in a Washington dispatch, Don Manada, that the Spanish minister has received information that a formidable filibustering expedition is about to leave this city for Cuba. Have you any knowledge of the fact?"

Manada shrugs his shoulders. "Quien sabe? Are not all vessels clearing for any port obliged to obtain papers stating their destination? And does not the President's proclamation warn against the shipping of arms and ammunition to Cuba from American ports? But of this be assured—Cuban patriots will not be without arms and ammunition to bring this war to a successful conclusion. It is true that is what we most need now. Ammunition especially is not as plentiful as we could wish, but had we none at all, with his trusty machete a Cuban patriot is more than a match for a brace of the puny, boyish conscripts Spain is sending to find early graves on Cuban soil. In the battle of Siguanoa, of which also I have just received an authentic account, our comrades finally charged with their machetes, which they handle with wonderful skill, and completely routed the Spanish troops. The actual fighting masses of the revolutionists, senor, the soldados raso, are no mean soldiers, even from a northerner's point of view. And they are not all Cuban born or Spanish born who have settled in Cuba and become identified with the island. You would be surprised, I doubt not, to learn that not a few of your own nationality are fighting for human liberty on the side of the revolutionists."

"And the character of the Spanish officers?" inquires Ashley, getting more and more interested.

Manada frowns. "Gen. Truenos, the new captain-general, we know as yet only by reputation. His chief of staff, the Madrid papers state, is to be Gen. Murillo, who is now in this country—in this city, if I mistake not. He poses as a diplomat and is the head of the spy bureau. Of the other leading Spanish officers in Cuba, they are of the usual foreign-service character. Some veterans, some young and inexperienced, seeking to win laurels in this war, a few Spanish noblemen, whom the exigencies of the family purse have forced into the army. By the way, attached to the new captain-general's staff, I learn there is a young American, a sugar planter. His name, I am told, was Felton, but he changed it to Alvarez. More Spanish, you see."

Felton! A question is on Ashley's tongue, when the utter absurdity of connecting Ralph Felton's identity with that of a young Cuban planter occurs to him and he refrains.

"Well, Don Manada, I am obliged to you for the half-hour you have accorded me, and I only hope your words will have as convincing an effect on the readers of the Hemisphere as they have had on me."

"Thank you, Senor Ashley. I shall ever be pleased to meet you when your duties may oblige you to seek one of the Cuban revolutionary party. Adios."

"Well," remarks the interviewer to himself, as he stops a moment to strengthen his memory by a fresh Havana, "if my friend of the bleached mustachios is not a rainbow chaser of the latest approved political character, Gen. Truenos and the Spanish army—and navy, too—have considerable work cut out for them in the vicinity of the Caribbean Sea. Hello!" he exclaims, staring at a graceful figure that is crossing Twenty-third Street in his direction. "If that isn't Miss Louise Hathaway of Raymond, Vt., my memory for faces is entirely destroyed."

CHAPTER XVII.

A CUP OF CHOCOLATE AT MAILLARD'S.

"It is Miss Hathaway!"

"Why, Mr. Ashley!"

"Then I am not quite forgotten," smiles Jack, as he takes the little black-gloved hand.

"Forgotten? Ah, no, indeed. I was only startled to meet one familiar face amid this never-ending procession of strangers. But this, I presume, is your native heath, Mr. Ashley? How do you carry the memory of so many faces?" as Ashley bows for the dozenth time toward the stream of pedestrians.

"That is a part of our business, Miss Hathaway. A newspaper man acquires a passing acquaintance with all classes of society. But to drop shop talk, tell me of Raymond and of yourself. I feel quite an interest in the quaint old town. Here is Maillard's close by. Suppose we drop in and have a cup of chocolate. Oh, it is quite the thing," smiles Jack, as Miss Hathaway hesitates a moment. "Everybody goes to Maillard's after a shopping tour."

"Then, as we are in Rome, we must imitate the Romans," she acquiesces. "For surely these bundles must be quite sufficient to convict me of having been shopping."

When she is snugly ensconced in an alcove, with a steaming cup of the beverage so dear to the feminine heart before her, Jack studies her face across the tiny table.

More beautiful if that were possible, than ever, he decides, watching the shifting color in the rounded cheek; with more animation—yes, decidedly more animation; quite a different being from the doubly bereaved daughter of the dead cashier of nearly a year ago. But what is she doing in New York? thinks Jack, with a sudden twinge in the cardiac region that astonishes even himself. It cannot be that she has heard from Derrick Ames, and besides, her sister—— What rot, he mentally concludes, as the subject of his thoughts suddenly looks up and catches his puzzled expression.

Miss Hathaway's eyes twinkle. "Has it just occurred to you that you have left your pocketbook at home?" she asks. "Your expression was just such as the humorous artists attach to the subjects of such unfortunate contretemps."

"Ah, but that seldom does happen in real life, Miss Hathaway. No; my sole earthly possessions are at this moment resting securely in the bottom of one small pocket. But what lucky chance brought you within range of my defective vision on Broadway this afternoon?"

"Oh, I have been a dweller in the metropolis since last Saturday. We, that is Mr. Felton and myself, are en route to Cuba."

"To Cuba! Pardon me, but why to that war-racked isle? You see, I have just returned from interviewing a native of Cuba on the situation there, and his description hardly makes it out as a desirable watering-place just at present."

Miss Hathaway laughs, a trifle nervously. "Perhaps it is rather an odd place to go this spring, and while I had a great desire to visit the country I really had no serious idea of gratifying the wish. But one evening while I was thinking of the matter, Mr. Felton suddenly asked me how I would like to go to Cuba. I said I would be delighted to go to escape the chill winds of March, and to my great surprise he suggested that we make preparations and start at once for New York. So here we are, and on Saturday we sail for tropic climes. But do you think there is any danger to Americans traveling in Cuba? I thought—I had read—that the disturbances were limited to some of the far inland districts and that there was no trouble in Havana and the larger cities."

Ashley pulls his mustache thoughtfully. "No, I do not see how there can be possible danger for you," he says at last. "Be sure, to avoid any possible annoyance, to get your passports before leaving New York. By Jove," he murmurs under his breath, "if the Hemisphere should send a man to Cuba, and I that man—well, that wouldn't be half-bad."

"But why should Mr. Felton desire to go to Cuba?" Ashley asks. "I fancied all his interests were in Vermont."

"He says that he has some property that requires his attention there, a sugar plantation, I fancy, or something of the sort. Anyway, he is quite anxious to go."

A sugar plantation in Cuba! Jack draws a long breath and his active mind reverts to his interview with Don Manada. Felton-Alvarez of the captain-general's staff, a young American planter! The son has evidently forsworn his country and by joining the Spanish army has become a Spanish citizen. Therefore he undoubtedly cannot be extradited. But the father?

"How long does Mr. Felton contemplate remaining in Cuba?" Ashley asks, carelessly.

"That will depend upon his inclinations and the condition of his business affairs."

"That means indefinitely," Jack thinks. "Cyrus Felton must not go to Cuba!" Then aloud: "Miss Hathaway, pardon me if I revive unpleasant memories, but the deep personal interest I took in the case must be my apology. Have you head from your sister—since—since the tragedy?"

For a moment Miss Hathaway is silent, her face clouding with the sad thoughts of that last fateful Memorial Day. "Mr. Ashley," she says at last, looking him full in the face, "I have received two letters from my sister Helen. She is well, and I trust happy. She was married in this city the day after they—she—left Raymond."

"To Derrick Ames?"

Louise nods.

"Are they now residing in the city?"

"No; they are not now in this country—I should say this part of the country," she adds, hastily.

For a moment a silence falls and both absently sip their chocolate, busy with their thoughts. Then Ashley remarks, smilingly:

"Apropos of nothing, Miss Hathaway, did you ever hear of the great French ball, the annual terpsichorean revel of Gotham?"

"Certainly, I have read about it. I gather that it is not always strictly—well, not exactly in the same category with the patriarchs' ball."

"No—not precisely," admits Ashley. "What I was leading up to is this: I suppose I shall be assigned to do the ball for the Hemisphere to-morrow evening—I have done it for the last two years—and a friend of mine kindly presented to me a pocketful of tickets. Now, I know you would enjoy looking in on the brilliant scene for an hour or two in the early part of the evening."

"Why, Mr. Ashley, I really do not see how we could. It would hardly be proper."

"Not perhaps to mingle with the rush, but as a casual looker-on in Verona the propriety could scarcely be questioned. A mask, a box where you could sit and listen to the really good music and watch the glitter and gayety, I believe you would recall the hour whiled away as one of thorough enjoyment. Besides—and here is the selfish part of my proposition—it would render the affair less of an old story to me. You must really say 'yes,'" persists Ashley, as Miss Hathaway hesitates, with the inevitable result.

"Well, if Mr. Felton is willing to pose as a 'chaperon' for a brief space, perhaps I may consent to assist the Hemisphere."

"I assure you that that appreciative journal will be deeply grateful. Where shall I call for your ultimatum?"

"We are stopping at the St. James. And now I must hurry home to examine my purchases. Thank you so much for your kindness, Mr. Ashley. I am so glad to have met you again. Good-by."

"Au revoir—until the morrow," Jack responds, as Miss Hathaway's elegant figure threads its way through the throng. "I wonder what the straight-laced Vermont maiden would say if she could look into the wine-room of the garden about an hour before the French ball makes its last kick. But she won't, though. The first hour or two of the function is as decorous as an afternoon tea on Fifth Avenue—rather more so, I fancy. And now to the office to fire the Cuban heart with Don Manada's screed."

But seated at his desk at the Hemisphere office, Ashley's thoughts persist in straying away from the yellow sheets he is rapidly covering with the Manada interview.

The Raymond tragedy mingles with thoughts of Cuba. His previously conceived ideas are undergoing a decided metamorphosis. The knowledge that the elder Felton is going to Cuba, where his son, according to the description of Manada, is apparently settled, and for a long period, if not forever, suggests to the newspaper man the conclusion that Mr. Felton must have been aware of his son's movements since the sudden departure from Raymond; may even have counseled that flight. Nay, more, that father and son are jointly implicated in the death of Cashier Hathaway. The theory just evolved grows stronger the more Jack considers the circumstances. On Cyrus Felton, then, depends the unraveling of the mystery. And he left Raymond suddenly, according to Miss Hathaway's admission. Barker, judging from his message on the finding of the revolver, must have been in Raymond before or during the departure of Cyrus Felton. Is it not possible, then, that the ex-bank president became possessed of the knowledge that Barker is again actively at work on the case; that he further became aware that Barker had, or was likely to get, some important clew, such as the discovery of the revolver, for instance; that he considered discretion the better part of valor and determined to flee the country and join his son in Cuba?

Ashley's busy pen ceases to skim over the paper for a moment, as he rears this dazzling edifice.

"I believe I have struck the bull's-eye," he reflects. "If only Barker has a little more evidence to back up the finding of the revolver, Miss Hathaway may not take that trip to Cuba after all—at least, not with her present amiable traveling companion."

A few moments later the big batch of copy, the result of Ashley's visit to Don Manada, is tossed upon the desk of the city editor. Then, still preoccupied and unusually untalkative for jovial Jack Ashley, the interviewer has again drawn on overcoat and gloves and is leaving the entrance to the Hemisphere office when a hand is dropped on his shoulder, as Detective Barker earnestly greets him:

"You're just the man I want to see. Where can we indulge in a quiet talk for half an hour?"

"Come right up to the cable editor's room. He won't be in for an hour or two."

CHAPTER XVIII.

BARKER DECIDES TO STRIKE.

"Well, my boy," begins Barker, "it's a long lane that has no turn, and I think we have reached the beginning of the end of this Hathaway mystery. There is the weapon that sent Roger Hathaway to eternity Memorial Day of last year," handing it to Ashley, with a complacent air. "I am not a betting man, or I would wager a reasonable sum that, ere the anniversary of the crime rolls around, the murderer will be safely incarcerated in the Mansfield County jail in Vermont."

Ashley examines curiously the weapon Barker has produced. It is an ordinary 32-caliber Smith & Wesson revolver, of the bull-dog variety, covered with rust, and all of the five chambers, with possibly one exception, contain unused cartridges.

"Yes, there is one empty chamber," responds Barker, as Ashley attempts ineffectually to turn the rusty cylinder, "and that sent poor old Hathaway out of the world. And now I will tell you of some important clews that I have succeeded in running down since I saw you last.

"You know I subscribed for the Raymond local newspaper, and a mighty good investment that $1.25 proved. Week before last the paper contained a local item about a boy's finding a revolver on the bank of Wild River. It was only a ten-to-one shot that the revolver picked up by the river bank was Hathaway's missing gun, but I took the short end and posted off to Raymond. The result of my trip you now hold in your hand.

"The little chap who found the revolver had picked it up close to the opposite bank from which it had been thrown. It was quite a stretch beyond the deep pool that we explored. You see I was fully a hundred yards from Felton when he hurled the revolver into the stream, and I miscalculated the force he put into the throw. His feeling of loathing for the hateful weapon was such that he hurled it nearly across the river. Even then, it would have been covered by two or three feet of water had not the river been dammed last ·fall, a few rods above the place, to furnish power for a sawmill. That left only an inch or two of water over the revolver, and little Jimmy Jones, or whatever his name was, found it there while prowling about the river bank. It is Roger Hathaway's revolver, too, beyond a doubt. I had Sibley, who was teller of the bank, and who has seen it in Hathaway's desk a thousand times, examine it, and he positively identifies it.

"So far, so good. That revolver rivets a mighty strong link, I take it, to the chain we have already forged about Cyrus Felton. But the situation had become somewhat complicated, I found after I secured possession of the revolver. Felton has skipped from Raymond, taking the Hathaway girl with him, and evidently does not intend to return for some time, if indeed at all. Consequently our next and most imperative duty is to find where he now is and see that he does not get beyond our reach."

"I can do that in five minutes," Ashley quietly assures the detective. "Cyrus Felton and Miss Louise Hathaway are now at the St. James Hotel in this city. They sail for Cuba next Saturday."

"Good," remarks the phlegmatic Barker. "That is luck on a par with finding the revolver. But when Cyrus Felton leaves New York it will be to go back to Vermont. Bound for Cuba, eh? Why did he select that country instead of Europe, I wonder?"

"Because his son is in Cuba. Barker, I opine that it will be necessary for both of us to revise our theories of the murder," continues Ashley. "In the judgment of the undersigned, both Feltons, father and son, are equally implicated in that crime. As to which actually fired the fatal shot, I am not prepared to say. But I am confident that both were in the bank when Hathaway was shot. I learned to-day that there is a young American, a planter, in Cuba who has joined the Spanish army as an officer on the staff of the captain-general. His name is, or was, Felton. Now comes the senior Felton, en route to Cuba. Why should he go to Cuba just at this time while the island is in the throes of insurrection? He tells Miss Hathaway that he has business interests there—a sugar plantation. Isn't it clear that he is going to join his son?"

Barker taps his forehead reflectively. "The idea is plausible," he admits. "But what in the name of the great hornspoon is he taking Miss Hathaway there for? It isn't possible that he is so cold-blooded, so absolutely devoid of conscience, that he would wed the daughter of the man he had slain?"

"Decidedly not," returns Ashley, with very like a snort of disgust at the suggestion of the possibility of Louise Hathaway becoming Cyrus Felton's wife. "Miss Hathaway is Felton's ward, and of course he is obliged to take her with him. Besides she herself is anxious to go to Cuba. She told me so this afternoon."

"Anxious to go herself, eh?" repeats Barker. "Well, there is no accounting for tastes. I think if I were going on a pleasure trip, however, I should select some other spot than that home of Yellow Jack and the machete. But"—the detective's forehead is wrinkled in thought—"you don't suppose she has any friends in Cuba whom she is anxious to see—her sister or Derrick Ames?"

Ashley considers this possibility a moment. "It is possible," he exclaims. "She admitted she had received letters from her sister, who was well and happy—but not in this country, she said at first, and then changed it to 'not in this section of the country.' Ames and her sister may be in Cuba, as well as Ralph Felton; but not, I will wager a good deal, in the same vicinity—not, at least, if Ames knows it. Barker, it seems to me that instead of this matter becoming simplified it is daily growing more complicated. The thing for us to do is to cut the Gordian knot at once and bring matters to a climax."

"There is only one way to do it."

"Exactly. Arrest Cyrus Felton, and charge him with being the murderer of Roger Hathaway, or an accomplice before or after the act."

Barker picks up the revolver again.

"We have got a good deal of strong evidence against him," he says, slowly; "yet I should like to get the son in the same net. With the two of them jointly accused and jointly tried I am certain we could unravel the mystery. I have evidence against the elder Felton that I have not yet told you; in fact, what I consider as a sufficient motive for the crime. The absence of a good, healthy motive, you know, was the weak link in our chain.

"The president of those two banks, I am convinced, was short in his accounts with both institutions. In other words, he had used the bank's securities to tide over his own financial affairs, which I have discovered, were not in the flourishing condition supposed. Although he was aware that Felton's accounts were overdrawn, as was evidenced by the writing on the blotter, Hathaway was apparently ignorant of the fact that the president had taken many of the bank's securities and hypothecated them for his own account. That was done by the president through the connivance of his son, the bookkeeper. Get the idea?"

Ashley nods.

"Now then: You will recall that Cyrus Felton told you, after the murder, that nearly $50,000 in available cash and about half as much more in securities had been stolen. He testified at the inquest that some securities had been taken. My theory is that not one single one of those securities was taken from the bank that night. 'Cause why? Because they had previously been extracted by Cyrus Felton and his son. And the cash? That, I believe was Ralph Felton's share for his part in the tragedy. Perhaps father and son had planned for the latter to rob the bank that night—the former anxious for the covering up of the loss of the securities, the latter covetous of the money. The time was drawing near when the annual examination of the savings bank was due. It was to have taken place in June. Then the discovery that many of the 'jackets' that should contain securities were empty was inevitable. But Cashier Hathaway was at the bank that night. The son may have been concealed in that closet, awaiting his opportunity. The cashier, no longer willing to permit the president's overdrafts, wrote that imperative note to Cyrus Felton. The latter visited the bank. An altercation ensued. Heated words were uttered. Hathaway may have discovered the loss of the securities. The president and cashier, old men both, engaged in a scuffle. Perhaps the president sought to wrest the key to the vault from the cashier's hands. At any rate, a struggle. Ralph Felton leaped from his hiding-place, and seizing the cashier's revolver, which he knew was kept in the desk, rushed to the assistance of his father. The fatal shot, and—father and son gazed in dismay at each other across the dead body of the faithful cashier. The rest is simple of explanation—the rifling of the vault and the subsequent flight of the son. Ashley, that is my revised theory of the murder of Roger Hathaway. What do you think of it?"

"It is worthy of your perspecuity, Barker, and in some respects it appears flawless. Yet—well, sometimes I have a sort of intuition that we are off the right track altogether. Ah, Barker, if we could but find that chap I saw in the bushes that morning, Ernest Stanley. Now that you have revised your theory, and in the light of recent developments, I feel more than ever that Stanley possesses the key that will unlock the inner doors of the mystery.

"However, that is neither here nor there, for Ernest Stanley has as completely vanished as though the earth had opened and swallowed him up. It is almost inexplicable."

"No stranger than the fading away of Derrick Ames and Helen Hathaway. You know we traced them to this city, and the most searching investigation by both the metropolitan police and our own men could not find them or ascertain for a certainty whether they went west or east.

"But to return to the Feltons. Those two missing leaves from the bank ledger could a tale unfold, I fancy, in relation to Cyrus Felton's precise relations with the bank. Yes, on the whole, I believe we have sufficient evidence to strike. He is at the St. James, you say? I guess I had better arrest him at once, and then, if he declines to go back to Vermont without extradition papers, I can proceed to Montpelier to-morrow and get the necessary documents in season to start back to Raymond by Friday—unlucky day for him, I fancy. Well, old man, you will have to spill a whole bottle of ink on this, I suppose. Will you spring the full story in the morning?"

Jack starts suddenly. "By Jove!" he exclaims, looking at the detective, with a rueful glance, "it seems like a brutally cold-blooded thing to say, but do you know, I have invited Felton and Miss Hathaway to look in on the French ball to-morrow evening, and now—if the deed wasn't an apparent refinement of cruelty, I would ask you to postpone the arrest of Felton till day after to-morrow."

"You are positive he does not contemplate sailing for Cuba till Saturday?" inquires Barker.

"So Miss Hathaway said. And, yes." Jack's eye has run hastily down the advertised dates of sailings in the Hemisphere. "The Mallory Line steamer, City of Callao, sails for Havana and the West Indies on Saturday. That is the steamer they are evidently booked for. But to make assurance doubly sure I will telephone to the office of the steamship line and ascertain if staterooms have been secured for them."

Barker nods approvingly at the precaution.

"Yes," the reply comes over the wire, "Mr. Cyrus Felton and Miss Hathaway are booked for the Callao."

"For Havana?"

"Yes; for Havana."

"That settles that, then," observes Barker, cheerfully. "Felton can enjoy his little fling at the garden, and subsequently have something to think about while he awaits the action of the grand jury."

Inured as he is to tragic scenes and happenings, Jack winces slightly at thought of the part he expects to play in acting as the "guide, philosopher and friend" of Cyrus Felton on probably his last night of liberty.

"By the way," he remarks, "you said Felton had made preparations for an extended absence from Raymond. Did he cause that to become generally known in the town?"

"Per contra, as the lawyers say, no one in Raymond had any idea that he contemplated a trip to Cuba, understanding that he is off on a business trip to New York. A little judicious investigation revealed the fact that he had quietly severed every business tie that should connect him with Raymond. Even his house, I found, he has mortgaged to the chimneys, and then leased for a period of ten years to a western man, to whom, by the way, he has disposed of his interest in the quarries. His share in the bank block he sold two months ago, taking a mortgage for two-thirds the purchase price, but this mortgage he last week transferred to the Vermont Life Insurance Company, receiving cash therefor. Even his horses have been shipped to Boston and sold. All this Felton has accomplished so quietly that, as I said before, no one in Raymond suspects that he is not as deeply interested financially in the town as ever.

"Well, on the whole," finishes Barker, "I am glad we have concluded to postpone the arrest a couple of days, for I have some personal matters I must attend to. What have you on hand to-night?"

"Just an hour or so at the Madison Square Garden. Come to dinner with me and we'll go to the Garden together. I want to talk this matter over further," says Ashley.

Barker acquiesces, and as the newspaper man leads the way to the street he murmurs to himself:

"So the blow falls on Wednesday. Well, it will make one of the most interesting 'beats' in the history of the Hemisphere and I guess I had better begin on the story to-night."

CHAPTER XIX.

PHILLIP VAN ZANDT.

"What are they playing now, Phillip?" Isabel Harding draws the program to her and scans the musical numbers listed thereon.

"Is it possible that you do not recognize the immortal unfinished Schubert symphony?" her companion asks, with good-natured sarcasm.

"You know I cannot tell one symphony from another," Mrs. Harding remarks, pettishly. "I wish you would pay less attention to the music and more to me."

Phillip Van Zandt smiles, but makes no reply to this reproach. And while he listens intently to the divine music which the orchestra is making, his companion sips her claret punch with a pretty frown upon her face.

The place is Madison Square Garden; the occasion, one of a series of classical concerts which Mr. Walter Damrosch and his orchestra are furnishing New York.

The two—Mrs. Harding and Mr. Van Zandt—are sitting by the wall in a comparatively uncrowded section of the Garden and more than one person who glances at them remarks that they are a handsome couple.

Phillip Van Zandt is not far from 30 years of age. There is nothing effeminate about his singularly handsome face; the closely trimmed brown beard does not conceal the firm, almost hard lines about the mouth. A mass of dark-brown curls cluster about a noble forehead that fronts a well-shaped head. But the striking features of the face are the eyes. Something inscrutable lurks in their dark-brown depths, now dreamy and tender, and again cold and glittering.

Who he is and what he is are points upon which his nearest acquaintances—he has no intimate friends—have never succeeded in satisfying themselves. He came somewhere out of the West less than a year ago. He occupies luxurious quarters at the Wyoming apartment

house, spends money ireely, and seems to be drifting
through existence with the insouciance of a man who
has lived his life and who looks forward to nothing this
side of Charon's ferry—or perhaps beyond.

He plays at cards and plunges at the track and wins
or loses with the inevitable composure which character-
izes his every action. To men he is cold, often insolent;
to women he is indifferent, although infinitely courteous.
Handsome, distingue, wealthy, witty in a dry, cynical
sort of way, he is a man who could be immensely popular
with his fellows and fascinating to the other sex. That
he is neither one nor the other is his peculiarity.

His companion of this evening, Isabel Harding, is a
personage, who would attract instant attention in a crowd
of attractive women. She is magnificently proportioned
—a splendid animal, as Van Zandt remarked when first
his careless gaze rested upon her. Her hair is black as
midnight; her eyes, large and lustrous, can either flash
with the fury of the tiger or beam with the softness of
the dove. Her mouth is somewhat large, but it is firm,
and between full, scarlet lips gleam two arcs of strong,
milk-white teeth.

She has known occasions when propriety was not
finically insisted upon, but on this night she is as demure
as innocence at 16. For she knows Van Zandt well
enough to understand that, while virtue and worth may
not interest him, viciousness and unworthiness decidedly
do not. And the least discerning student of human
nature can see that she loves him—loves him blindly,
madly, and—hopelessly.

Van Zandt cares nothing for her, save in his indifferent
way, and she knows it. But she does not despair. She
is a woman.

Somewhere in Bohemia, Van Zandt met Isabel Harding. She interested him, she was so unlike the other
women at the little French restaurant where he had
dropped in to get lunch and a bottle of really good wine.
Some small service by him rendered sufficed to establish between the two a camaraderie that continued until
the present. It witnessed no alteration of sentiment on

the part of Van Zandt. But Isabel—she began by admiring and finished by worshiping.

He never asked who or what she was, although she was obviously a woman with a story to tell. She was a widow, she said. Widows are many in Bohemia.

"Some day I will give you my history," she told him. But Van Zandt only laughed and asked, "Shall we go to the play to-night?"

"He cares no more for me than for the glass he is holding," Mrs. Harding now thinks, as she watches his face, turned again toward the orchestra. "Don't you ever think of anything except music?" she demands, a little impatiently.

"Oh, yes; of a great many other things. For instance, I was this minute thinking of you."

"Oh, indeed?" ironically. "Something vastly complimentary, no doubt."

Van Zandt smiles emphatically. "I was thinking that I should like to set you to music, if I possessed the faculty," he says, as he glances humorously at his companion's pouting face.

"What should you write, a waltz refrain or a dancehall ditty?" asks Mrs. Harding.

"Neither; I should write a symphony, a wild sort of affair," he smiles. "It would begin quietly and run along for bars and bars in a theme that would suggest days when the heart was young and life seemed a pathway of roses. This would give place to scherzo and the whole movement would be light and playful and singing. Then the music would begin to grow troublous, anon turbulent, and would finally burst into uncontrollable tumult. This would gradually pass away, and the third movement would be capriccio, the music now flashing fire, again singing on like a mountain brook, on and on, and on."

"You are very discerning, Mr. Van Zandt," says Isabel, biting her lip. "What name should you bestow on this remarkable symphony?"

"I should call it 'Isabel.'"

"And the last movement, what would that be?"

"Oh, that would be unfinished, like Schubert's," Van Zandt replies, with a provoking smile.

"Fortunately. For if you design to complete it you will have to do so from memory. I am going away," declares Isabel, with a flush in each cheek.

"Going away? Where?"

"Ah, mon ami, that is for you to find out. Besides, what do you care? I have had an offer—diplomatic service, I believe it is politely called. I leave in two days."

"By Jove! You would do well in diplomatic circles," exclaims Van Zandt, glancing at her in frank admiration. "You said nothing of this before."

"I have only just made up my mind. Your symphony decided me," Isabel avers with some bitterness.

"The Garden is filling up," Van Zandt remarks abruptly. About all the tables around them are beginning to be taken. "Hello! There's that chap again," he adds, as two men seat themselves at an adjoining table and fall to chatting.

"Didn't know I was a musical critic, did you, Barker? Well, you see our regular music expert is off duty sick to-night, so they put me on the job. It's a short one."

"Your duties, friend Ashley, appear to be beautifully, diversified."

"They are that. Anything from a murder to a concert. I suppose Raymond is about the same as when we left it, about a year ago?"

"To a dot. Same crowd on the hotel veranda. Same symposium of hay, horse and village gossip."

"Just the same it is a great country. I'd give several good iron dollars to be back for one morning in that gorge near South Ashfield, on the old wood road where I ran upon Ernest Stanley."

"Push over a bit. Here's another party," says Barker, as a jolly quartet approach.

"Plenty of room," they declare, as they find chairs and seat themselves close by. The man nearest to the detective and the newspaper man is a stout, florid-faced party, whose clean-cut visage and smooth bearing betoken the sporting man. His companions are well-dressed young men about town.

"Hold on, major," remarks one of the latter, interrupting the stout party in the act of giving an order to the waiter. "I'll buy this round, gentlemen, and we will make it wine. I played in luck to-day."

"So? Cards run well, eh?"

"Never saw them come easier. I had a bit of luck, major, which does not materialize often enough to render poker a continuously profitable employment. I sat between two men who raised the pot four times before the draw, and I filled up a straight flush."

"You stood the raises on a bob flush?"

"I had to. It was open at both ends. Basket of wine, waiter, and fetch it in a hurry," adds the young man, whom his friends call Chauncey, and he gives the waiter a tip that sends him a-flying.

The major smiles as the reminiscences of innumerable interesting jack-pots are stirred up by the story of his young friend's good luck.

"Speaking of straight flushes," he observes, "I never saw a hand fill more neatly or appropriately than during a little game in which I was sitting three or four years ago."

"Story by the major, gentlemen," cries Chauncey, rapping the table to order and receiving the angry glances of a number of people about him who are trying to hear the music. "Here comes the wine. We will drink a toast to all straight flushes, high or low, and then the major shall have the floor."

——— ———

CHAPTER XX.

A SUPPOSITION BECOMES A FACT.

"You remember when Phil Clark was running up on Fifth Avenue," begins the major, after the wine has been brought and pronounced only half-iced.

"Rather," responds Chauncey, dryly. "I dropped five hundred there one night and it wasn't much of a game at that."

"Well, I drifted into Phil's one night three years ago, more or less, and found the place as quiet as a country village. There was no big game going on, and mighty few small ones. In one of the rooms I found Col. Dunnett. You remember Dunnett. We were chatting and commenting on the dullness of the evening, when two young men came into the room and, after a glance at us, one of them suggested a hand at poker.

"I knew one of the young men slightly. His name was Stanley, I believe. Quiet, reserved sort of a chap. He hadn't been in New York long, he said. Made books out at the Sheepshead races. I did not fancy his friend, who had been drinking some and was inclined to be a bit noisy. His name—let me see—Fenton, or Fallon; no, Felton, that was what Stanley called him.

"We began the game and it broke up after the hand I started in to tell you about. The betting simmered down to Felton and Stanley. Felton held four aces and bet all the cash he had. 'I ought to raise you,' said Stanley; 'still,' he added, 'if that is all the cash you have——'

" 'You needn't worry about me,' sneered Felton, as he took a check-book from his pocket. 'I said that was all the change I had with me, but my check is good.' He scratched off a check and threw it on the table. 'You can see that, or call my previous bet, as you please.'

"Stanley was as calm as I am now. He leaned over to me, and, spreading his cards, asked: 'Major, will you loan me a thousand a moment to bet this hand?' I glanced at it and had a trifle of difficulty in restraining my surprise. He had filled, as he told me afterward, the middle of a straight flush, king up!

" 'Cert, my boy,' I replied, cheerfully, to his request, and I passed over two $500 bills. Stanley tossed them on the table, and looked inquiringly at Felton. The latter, with a smile of sublime confidence, spread out four aces. 'No good,' was Stanley's calm announcement. He exhibited his hand, and then pocketing the stakes, after returning me my thousand, he remarked: 'Thank you, gentlemen, for your entertainment. I don't believe I'll play any more to-night.' And putting on his coat and hat, he left the room.

"Felton sat like one dazed for some moments. Then he walked to the bar and after a stiff drink hurried off. I never saw either of them after that night."·

Ashley and Barker have been silent and interested listeners to this yarn by the major. As the latter and his friends rise Ashley rises also and taps the major on the shoulder. "Pardon the intrusion," he says, with an engaging smile. "I have been vastly interested in your poker story, sir, for the reason that I think I know one of the players—Felton, I believe you called him. Do you happen to recall what sort of a looking chap he was?"

"Hanged if I remember," replies the major, wondering at the other's earnestness.

"Was he a rather tall, good-looking young fellow, with light-brown hair and eyes and a tawny mustache?" persists Ashley.

"Now that you speak of the mustache, I believe that your description fits him. He had a heavy, yellowish mustache, which he was in the habit of biting, as though his dinner did not suit him."

"Thank you," says Ashley. "Will you have something more to drink, gentlemen?"

But the major and his party take themselves off and Ashley resumes his seat with a satisfied smile.

"So, Barker, we hit it about right after all, eh?"

"It would appear so," returns the detective complacently. "We now know what we have assumed to have been the case—that Ernest Stanley suffered imprisonment two years for another's crime, and that the real criminal, the man who forged Cyrus Felton's name, was none other than his son, Ralph Felton."

As Barker pronounces these words Ashley hears a smothered exclamation behind him and turns quickly. But all he sees is a gentleman and lady gathering their wraps preparatory to taking their departure. The man's back is toward Ashley, but the latter waits until the party faces his way and then for the space of a second their eyes meet.

"There is only one more selection, and it does not amount to much," Van Zandt tells Mrs. Harding, and they join the crowd that is leaving the garden.

"Do you know those two men who sat at the next table to us? The younger looked at you as though he knew you and was waiting to be recognized."

"Your imagination, cara mia. I know neither of them," replies Van Zandt, lightly. Then, as he hands her into a carriage at the corner and says "Kensington" to the driver, he holds Isabel's hand a moment at parting and inquires gravely: "So you are really going away then?"

"In two days," she answers, and searches his face for some evidence of regret. It is as impassive as the sphinx.

"Well, I suppose I shall see you at the French ball to-morrow evening?"

"You may, if you care to look for a Russian court lady, attired wholly in black."

"Rest assured that the festivities will be robed in sables until I find her. Good-night." Van Zandt closes the carriage door, watches it a moment as it rattles up the avenue and then saunters toward Broadway.

Ashley and Barker have remained at their table in the garden and Jack is telling the detective that for the second time within twenty-four hours he has caught the stare of the man with the brown beard and piercing eyes. "I have seen that face somewhere," he mutters, as he wrinkles his brow in a desperate effort to burst the memory cell that prisons the secret. Suddenly he smites the table a blow that sets the glasses jingling and invites the disapprobation of the waiter. "Oh, memory! Memory, thou sleepy, shiftless warder of the brain!" he cries.

"What is the matter now?" asks Barker.

"Keep calm, old chap," returns Ashley, gripping the detective's wrist. "Keep calm while I confess to you that we have let slip through our hands the key to the Hatha-way mystery!"

"What!" almost shouts the detective, starting to his feet. "You mean——"

"I mean that the man with the brown beard and stiletto optics who just left us is my friend of the mountain gorge. He is Ernest Stanley!"

"Well, he has slipped us this time," says the detective, disconsolately, as they stand outside the garden and sweep the street with anxious gaze.

"Not yet," Ashley rejoins cheerfully. "See! There he is beyond that third light, handing his magnificent companion into a carriage."

"Call a cab and follow them," says the detective, starting toward the line of conveyances pulled up at the curb.

"No need of that," Ashley interrupts. "He is not going to ride." At that moment it was that Van Zandt closed the door to the carriage which bore Mrs. Harding to the Kensington, and as he starts toward Broadway the detective and the newspaper man follow at a cautious distance.

Unconscious of the espionage Van Zandt starts uptown at a swinging gait. At Thirty-second Street he branches into Sixth Avenue, and the two men behind him wonder that he does not ride. At the park he turns down Fifty-ninth Street and finally enters the Wyoming apartment house, leaving Ashley and Barker staring up at the brownstone elevation.

The former waits five minutes and then pulls the bell. "The name of the gentleman who has just gone upstairs?" he asks the colored attendant who responds.

"Mr. Phillip Van Zandt," replies the sable youth, as he slips a half-dollar into his pocket.

"Van Zandt—is that his name?" queries Ashley, a trifle disappointed, although he might have expected a strange name. Then the porter tells him that the gentleman with the brown beard has been a resident of the Wyoming for several months; that he is a wealthy bachelor, and a variety of other equally important information.

"Well, what do you think now?" asks Barker, as they walk over to the elevated road.

"I haven't changed my opinion," is Ashley's response. "I believe that Phillip Van Zandt is or was Ernest Stanley."

"Well, we have him located, at any rate," remarks the detective. "See you at the French ball to-morrow night? I am on the lookout for a couple of gentry whom I expect to be there. This is my station. Good-night."

CHAPTER XXI.

"DON CAESAR DE BAZAN."

The big French ball, that annual revel at the metropolis, brings together a motley assemblage of the devotees of folly. The scene at the entrance to Madison Square Garden to-night is the same scene witnessed at this function the year preceding, and the year before that. A mass of cabs and carriages in apparently inextricable confusion fill the street. They struggle up and deposit their fares and escorts and chaperons fight their way through the mob that blocks the brilliantly lighted entrance, and not always without an unpleasant encounter.

Upon the threshold of the gay interior Louise Hathaway pauses diffidently and thanks fortune that a mask hides her face from the inquisitive stares around her. But led by Jack Ashley, Louise and Mr. Felton proceed to a box and once within its shelter the young girl gives herself up to an unmixed enjoyment of the brilliant spectacle before her.

The scene is decorous, even sedate. Few acquaintances have been made, and when the strains of "Loin du Bal" arise in voluptuous swell only a small number of dancers respond.

"Why this is as proper as one of our country dances, and far less noisy," Louise whispers to Ashley, but that knowing young man winks mysteriously behind his mask and remarks: "Wait!"

"Oh, but I shan't wait," is the young lady's response.

"You remember what I emphatically declared—only an hour or two and then we return to the hotel."

"Then you need fear nothing that would shock you in the least degree," Ashley assures her. "The rioting does not begin until after midnight, and does not amount to much then. But see. The floor is filling up, the reserve is wearing off, and it would need only the eruption of some reckless spirit to bring on a pandemonium."

It is apparent that only a desire to humor the wishes of Miss Hathaway has led Cyrus Felton to the garden. And yet it is all so novel, all so bright and full of color, that he becomes interested in spite of himself, and when Ashley proposes a tour of the floor with a peep at the wine-room, Mr. Felton glances irresolutely at Louise. The young lady nods an assent.

"Do not be gone long," she enjoins, "although I could listen to the music and watch the picture half the night."

When they are gone she leans back in her chair, partly draws the box draperies, and watches dreamily the ever-changing panorama on the vast floor.' Suddenly there is borne to her ears a melody strangely sweet, yet filled with a subtle melancholy. Louise catches her breath and listens. It is the andante of the Beethoven Sonata Pathetique she played so often in her old Raymond home. It has always been her favorite, and she is really an artist in soul and execution. Some one is whistling softly the divine first theme, and with a tenderness she has often felt yet could not satisfactorily express through the medium of an unsympathetic pianoforte.

She leans over the box and her eyes rest upon the figure of a man attired in the costume of Don Caesar de Bazan. He is leaning carelessly against the pillar of the box in which she is sitting, not a dozen feet from her. So closely does his costume fit him and so bravely does he bear it that he looks a veritable Don Caesar who has stepped for an hour from a bygone century. A brown beard covers the lower part of his face; all above is hidden by a black silk mask.

While Louise is taking note of this interesting personality she hears the door open behind her, and turns expecting to greet Mr. Felton or Ashley. Instead a stranger steps rather shakily into the box and closes the door with an affable "Good-evening, mademoiselle." Louise makes no reply, and her unwelcome visitor drops into a seat with easy familiarity.

"I have been more enthusiastically received to-night, but I will let that pass," he remarks, with cheerful impudence.

"I do not know you, sir," says Louise frigidly, as she rises and casts a wildly anxious look over the ball-room.

"Oh, well, I am not so hard to get acquainted with," offers the insolent mask. "Will you drink a bottle of wine with me?"

"Leave me at once!" commands Louise, pointing to the door with trembling finger.

"By George! That's an attitude worthy of Lady Macbeth," remarks his insolence, in frank admiration. "I will go," he adds, in mock humility, "but I must at least have a kiss to solace me for the loss of your society."

"You would not dare!" gasps Louise, retreating to the box rail.

"Dare?" laughs his insolence; "I would dare anything for such a prize," and he approaches her unsteadily.

Louise's frightened gaze is turned toward the ball-room and again rests upon Don Caesar de Bazan, who, attracted by the colloquy, has stepped a pace out upon the floor and is an interested spectator of the encounter.

"Save me!" she whispers, and sinks upon one knee.

But the entreaty is superfluous. Already Don Caesar's hands are on the rail and with a vault he is in the box. His arm shoots out and his insolence goes down with a crash. He struggles to his feet with an oath and makes for Don Caesar; but the latter's threatening attitude, clenched fist and eyes that flash fire through the black mask, cause him to stop, and muttering, "You will hear from me again," he leaves the box.

Don Caesar lifts his cap and is about to follow, when Louise interrupts him. "Do not go," she says gratefully, "until I have thanked you a thousand times for the service you have rendered me."

Don Caesar bows. "As for the service," he remarks lightly, "it was nothing. The fellow has been drinking, and seeing you alone——"

"My friends have left me only for a few moments," Louise hastens to explain, as she glances over the floor and bites her lips in vexation.

"Then I may remain until they return?" Don Caesar observes inquiringly, dropping into a chair. "Some other graceless scamp may blunder in here."

Louise's eyes express a timid assent to the proposition.

"This is the first of these balls that you have attended?" asks Don Caesar, noting that she is ill at ease.

"Yes; and it will be the last. I had read much of them, how brilliant they were, and all that, and I naturally acquiesced when I was tempted with an invitation. For I was told that if one went masked there was no harm in looking on for an hour."

"Nor is there. The wickedness will not begin for some time, and it is at best, or worst, a cheap, tawdry wickedness, wholly unattractive to saint or sinner. It is all inexpressibly stupid. A lot of tinsel-decked people rushing hither and thither in the dance, with little regard for the rhythm of the music and less for the etiquette of the ball-room, and a line of weary clubmen, bankers, men-about-town, butchers and bakers and candlestick-makers looking on."

"Yet you attend, though your remark indicates familiarity with the function."

"Oh, yes, I attend. For in spite of it all there are flowers and music, light and color and a certain brilliancy that enables one to forget for the nonce the even deadlier stupidity of the outside world."

"Don Caesar de Bazan of old was not a cynic," remarks Louise, smilingly.

"Had he been he would not have maintained our ever-green regard. When we sit down to a book or a play we like to leave our cynicism behind us; to live with men who have not a care beyond the morrow; men who mount horse and ride away from their troubles; whose swords leap from their sheaths at the breath of an insult; good, hearty, whole-souled fellows whose fortunes one delights to follow, but whom, alas, we seldom meet in the flesh."

"Perhaps it is as well. You might grow awfully tired of them."

"Perhaps. I sometimes think that, outside of the lasting friendships with the people in books and plays, the only satisfactory acquaintances are the chance ones."

"True," murmurs Louise, dreamily. She wonders whether the face behind the black mask matches the melody of the voice. A similar thought flits through Don Caesar's mind, as his eyes take in the graceful figure of the girl, clad all in black, a single ornament fastened at the long white throat.

"I, too, have few friends," says Louise. "But there is one friend who never fails me, through joy or sadness —my music."

"Ah, there is naught like it to drive away that enemy to life, dull care," put in the Don. "It is my one passion. And I have cultivated it only lately. But now I give myself up to it entirely, attending every concert of any repute, and bewailing fate a thousand times that I cannot play, or sing, or write."

"I think I can guess your favorite melody—one of them, at least."

"Can you, indeed?" asked Don Caesar, in interested surprise.

"The Sonata Pathetique."

"Ah, is it not beautiful? You have guessed correctly, but how?"

"You were whistling it softly as you stood near yonder pillar, a moment before the occasion for your presence here arose."

"Very probably. It is continually running through my head. Do you know, the melody has two meanings to me. When I am out of patience with the world and myself it seems tinged with an inexpressible melancholy. And when I am in good spirits the refrain becomes singing, joyous, triumphant. Has it ever seemed so to you?"

"I do not know. It has always seemed beautiful. It is my favorite."

"And mine. You are not a New Yorker," ventures Don Caesar.

"So? It is now my turn, Don Caesar, to marvel at your guessing powers."

Don Caesar laughs softly. "It does not demand an extraordinary acute discernment. Your accent and manner betoken the New Englander."

"Are we then so provincial that we so easily betray ourselves? But you are right. I am a Vermonter."

"I thought so. Odd, is it not, how dominos conduce to confidences, even among strangers?"

"Yes. And yet I think they would prove unsatisfactory for conversational purposes among people who——" Louise pauses.

"People who have been formally introduced, eh?" finishes Don Caesar. "Are you in the city for any length of time?"

"Only until Saturday. We sail for Cuba then."

"Cuba? That is a long way off," muses Don Caesar. "I came very near forgetting that I had not been formally introduced and expressing the regret that I should not see you again before you sail."

"You said a moment ago that the only satisfactory acquaintances were the transitory ones," Louise reminds him.

"True. But that rule has its exceptions, like all others."

"Consistency is no more a man's attribute than a woman's," moralizes Miss Hathaway. "My friends approach, Don Caesar," she adds, as she catches a glimpse of Mr. Felton and Ashley threading their way over the crowded floor.

"That is the signal for my departure, then," says Don Caesar. "Before I go I would crave one small boon."

"I owe you some return for your timely assistance. Speak, Don Caesar."

"Just a glimpse of the face that your mask so jealously veils."

"Oh!" cries Louise, somewhat disturbed.

"Remember," urges Don Caesar, "we shall never meet again—— But 'twould be ungenerous to press my request," he adds, rising. "I must say farewell, then, with only the memory of a sweet voice to recall one of the few pleasant quarter-hours that I have known."

Some impulse, she can hardly explain what, seizes Louise. With trembling fingers she detaches her mask and uncovers a face suffused with blushes.

"I thought so!" murmurs Don Caesar, as his eyes take in the glory of that face, which is almost immediately veiled again.

"Thank you," he says, simply, and presses to his lips for an instant the hand she timidly gives him in parting.

He is gone, and Louise sinks back into her chair with beating heart, wondering whether she has been foolish, or unmaidenly, or indiscreet. She forgets to administer to Ashley the scolding he deserves for his long absence and receives abstractedly his explanation of a row in the wine-room and their detention by the crowd. Her gaze wanders about the ball-room in search of the graceful figure of Don Caesar de Bazan, but he has vanished.

CHAPTER XXII.

A FAIRY TALE THAT CAME TRUE.

Toward 10 o'clock Louise Hathaway decides that she has witnessed enough of the brilliant panorama to warrant her in returning to the hotel, and as Cyrus Felton is plainly bored by a scene not attuned to his temperament, Ashley hunts up their wraps, hails a carriage and they are driven to the St. James.

"You will make a night of it, I suppose," Miss Hathaway remarks, as Ashley prepares to say good-night.

"No; I shall remain only long enough to finish my story for the paper. I wrote the introduction this afternoon. One year's ball is much the same as another's. Have you any plans for the morrow?"

"None, except mild sightseeing. Will you not lunch with us?"

"I shall be delighted," murmurs Ashley. To be near Miss Hathaway is pleasure unalloyed; incidentally he desires an opportunity to quietly study Cyrus Felton. "At 1 o'clock, say?" he asks.

"At 1 o'clock. We must thank you again, Mr. Ashley, for your escort this evening."

"Don't mention it—again," smiles Ashley. "I am sorry I cannot ask you to assist in my work to-morrow. It would be fully as interesting and more to your taste, likely, than the French ball."

"Then it cannot be a political meeting."

"Hardly. It is the trial trip of the new United States cruiser America, probably the fastest vessel of any size afloat in the world to-day."

"That will be delightful. You must tell me all about it when you return. Your description will be much more interesting, I am sure, than the newspaper accounts."

"Fully as interesting as the Hemisphere's story, perhaps. Good-night, Miss Hathaway. Oh, by the way, Mr. Felton," as Louise trips upstairs, "did you know that Roger Hathaway's revolver has been found?"

Ashley asks the question in the most casual of tones, but his keen eyes are riveted on the elder man's face. The result is not wholly what the questioner expected. Mr. Felton simply stares at Ashley and repeats: "Hathaway's revolver found? Where? When?"

"It was fished out of Wild River about opposite the cemetery a day or two ago. But perhaps it was after you had started for New York. Odd, is it not, that the weapon with which the crime was perhaps committed should be brought to light within a stone's throw of the grave of the murdered man? But pardon me. Perhaps, I have awakened painful reflections; so I will say no more. Good night."

Cyrus Felton stands like a stone upon the threshold to the reading-room for fully a minute after Ashley has left the hotel. Then he turns and goes slowly upstairs to his room.

WhenAshley reaches the Garden he hunts up Barker and rescues that amiable gentleman from the importunities of a brace of masks who are gayly informing him that they are "just beginning to like him." Ashley drags him away and asks: "Have you located the gentry for whom you were looking to-night?"

"No, but I have chanced upon one or two choice incidents in society life which the chief may find useful some day."

"Good. Let me in early when they materialize. Now, old chap, if you will kill time here for half an hour or so, until I finish my story, I'll join you."

Ashley hunts up an out-of-the-way corner and the work is soon finished and dispatched by a district messenger boy. Then the newspaper man returns to the wine-room, but Barker has strayed.

While Jack is lounging about the edges of the ball-room, his cheek is brushed by a Jack rose tossed from a near-by box. He looks around and sees leaning over the box rail a woman attired in the costume of a lady of the Russian court. The eyes behind the mask twinkle invitingly, and as she is alone Ashley fastens the rose in his coat, tosses a kiss to the donor and proceeds to look for the door leading to that particular box.

"May I enter, lady fair?" he asks, as he stands upon the threshold.

"On one condition," the lady in black informs him.

"Name it," he smiles.

"That you do not ask me to drink a bottle of wine with you; that you talk of something interesting; and that you do not make love to me."

"And you call that one condition? But I accept," says Ashley, closing the door behind him. The next instant he suppresses an exclamation and a tendency toward mild protestation. For in closing the door he has caught one finger on a nail which some careless carpenter omitted to drive home, and the digit gets a painful tear.

The lady in black extends sympathy and lends her own dainty lace handkerchief to bind up his wound. As he bends to tie the knot with his teeth the perfume on the lace almost startles him.

"Your first condition, madam, was easily accepted," he smiles, as he throws himself into a chair and toys with the handkerchief about his finger. "The second is more difficult to live up to, and the third is cruel." He is carelessly unwrapping the handkerchief as though to re-bind it, and is looking for some initial.

"Oh, tell me a story—something I haven't heard," yawns the lady in black. "At the first sign of stupidity I shall send you away."

"A story?" drawls Ashley. Ah, he has found what he sought. In one corner of the handkerchief is the letter "I," curiously embroidered in silk.

"Very well," he says, in rare good humor, "I promise you a story that, while it may not be entirely new to you, will hold your interest to the end. But first, madam, I must beg of you to lay aside your domino, that I may know whether my tale is interesting you or I am courting the unhappy fate which you threatened should be meted out to stupidity."

The lady in black laughs musically and, partially drawing the box draperies, she tosses off her mask, and, to Ashley's intense amaze, reveals the face of the handsome woman whom he remembers to have seen with Phillip Van Zandt the preceding night at the Damrosch concert.

But Jack Ashley is not a young man who permits his face or voice to betray his emotions. So he knots the lace once more about his injured digit, settles himself comfortably in his chair and begins:

"Once upon a time——"

"Is this a fairy tale?" interrupts his handsome auditor.

"A fairy tale? Perhaps. But a fairy tale that came true. Once upon a time there lived in a small New England community a youth to whom the simple amusements and rustic pleasures of his native town became as tedious as a twice-told tale. As his father was engaged in a business whose interests extended over the country, the youth was given a roving commission, and soon after he was tasting the sweets of an existence in the great city. Metropolitan life suited him to a T. His only regret was that his means were not sufficient to keep pace with his luxurious tastes.

"In the course of time he met and loved a very pretty girl. She had hair of midnight, eyes like black diamonds, a superb figure and a thousand charms. Whether her heart was as true as her face was fair, I know not. The torrent which bore these two hearts was more or less turbulent. In the trouble which came between them I am charitable enough to believe that the man was to blame. The youth found that living beyond his means has an inevitable and unpleasant result, and it was not long ere his father, after palliating innumerable offenses, summoned him home. He was given a position in a bank in the town which he still despised, and he soon forgot his city love, being assisted in this forgetfulness by a passion which he had conceived for the beautiful daughter of the cashier of the bank in which he was employed.

"The neglected one wrote many letters, but could obtain no satisfaction of her faithless swain. Finally she decided to visit him in his New England home; so on a memorable afternoon she arrived in his town, went to a hotel and sent word to the youth that she desired to see him at once."

"Well?" demands the lady in black, as Ashley pauses. The flash in her eyes and the nervous fingers tell him that, while his story may not be enjoyed, it is being listened to with intense interest.

"The youth obeyed the summons," he resumes, "and there was a scene. Money was demanded, and money he had none. But perhaps it was to be had somewhere. That night a murder was committed in the town. It was an extremely mysterious affair, and the excitement which it caused was intensified a day or two later, when the young man of our story suddenly disappeared and was never after heard from. The detective employed on the case assumed that if he could find the mysterious woman who registered at the hotel the day of the tragedy some light might be thrown upon the affair and the whereabouts of the absent young man ascertained."

"Have you any object in telling me this story?" asks the lady in black, in a voice which she strives to render calm and unconcerned.

"Only your entertainment."

"Then you have not succeeded."

"I have succeeded in one thing," returns Ashley, in quiet triumph. "I have found the woman."

"Indeed? That is more interesting. But perhaps you are mistaken."

"Impossible. The beautiful unknown left in the hotel room a lace handkerchief scented with a most peculiar perfume." Ashley is slowly unwrapping the lace creation about his finger, and he sniffs it as he speaks. "A perfume which the finder of the handkerchief had never known before," he goes on, as he spreads the lace upon his knee. "Besides the perfume, which distinguished this from thousands of other handkerchiefs, there was in one corner the letter 'I,' curiously embroidered in silk."

As if he were alone and talking to himself, Ashley takes from a wallet in his pocket the handkerchief which for months he had carefully treasured, and spreading it upon his knee compares it with the one which lately wrapped his finger. They are identical. Then he looks up and catches the half-scornful, half-startled gaze of the lady in black.

"Is that all?" she inquires.

"No. But I expect you to furnish the last chapter."

The lady in black again adjusts her mask. "Not to-night," she says. "Come to my hotel to-morrow and I will endeavor to gratify your curiosity."

"Whom shall I inquire for?"

"I believe you have my name."

"Ah, yes. And the hotel, madam?"

"The Kensington."

"And the hour?"

"Ten in the morning."

"Thank you. I will be prompt."

Ashley leaves the box humming a lively air and proceeds to look up his friend Barker.

"Busy, old man?" he asks, when he has finally located the detective.

"Not especially? Why?"

"Do you see that woman in black in yonder box, talking with a swarthy-looking gentleman?"

"I do."

"That is 'Isabel Winthrop.'"

"The devil!"

"No; but perhaps one of his satanic highness' amiable representatives. I have an interview arranged with her for to-morrow at 10; place the Kensington. I want you to follow her when she leaves the Garden and keep an eye on her until 10 o'clock to-morrow morning. If I do not hear from you before that hour I shall consider that she has made the engagement in good faith. I have a big day's work to-morrow, and I believe I will go home and turn in."

"All right, Jack, my boy. I will keep her ladyship in view if she leads me to China. So long."

* * *

CHAPTER XXIII.

A REPRISAL OF TREACHERY.

"Don't be absurd, Don Manada."

"Absurd? Dios! I was never more thoroughly in earnest in my life."

"Nevertheless, you are absurd," Isabel Harding smiles tantalizingly over her champagne glass at the flushed face and glistening eyes of her companion.

This conversation occurs shortly after midnight at an

out-of-the-way table in the arcade at the east end of the
Garden.

For all it began so decorously, this year's ball is a particularly riotous affair and already the fantastic orgie is
well under way. Masks have been scattered to the pat-
chouli-laden winds. Yet there are a few discreet folks
who, though they mingle with the mad crowd, have re-
tained their masks. As Don Manada and his companion
are comparatively removed from observation, they have
laid aside their dominos for the moment and are conversing in earnest whispers.

Isabel Harding is so radiantly, magnificently, danger-
ously beautiful that it is a terrific strain for the gentleman at her side to maintain the least semblance of composure.

"In what does my absurdity consist?" he demands in a
passionate whisper.

"Can you ask? You tell me that you love me—which
I already know—and urge a suit which I have twice
before told you is hopeless. You profess to believe that I
could learn in time to honestly return your undoubtedly
sincere affection. It is impossible. I will be honest with
you. I am not one to whom love comes slowly. I love
only one man, and he—don't look so murderous, Don
Manada—he cares nothing for me," she finishes, bitterly.

"Come, a truce to lovemaking!" rallies Isabel. "Don't
look so fiercely downcast, Don Manada. Fill up the
glasses and we will drink a melancholy toast to unrequited love. We are alike unsuccessful lovers. But we
will continue to be good friends."

"Impossible," replies Don Manada, as he gloomily
pours out the wine. "I go to Cuba to-morrow."

"Indeed? I trust that I am not responsible for the
loss of your society to your New York friends."

"No, senora. I go because duty calls me, but I had
expected to wear a lighter heart than that which will
accompany me."

Don Manada is too much occupied with his despair to
note the peculiar look which Isabel darts at him from
between her half-dropped eyelids.

"Cuba?" she repeats, dreamily. "Ah, I should like to visit that country some day."

Don Manada looks up with swift hope. "You would, senora? Then you shall!" he cries. "We will leave to-morrow on my vessel. I will be your slave. You have but to speak and every wish will be gratified. You will do me this favor," he urges, and then, with the fervor and descriptive powers of a Claude Melnotte, he proceeds to paint a fascinating picture with a tropical background, his enthusiasm fired by ravishing glances from his companion.

"Quite an escapade you have outlined," smiled Isabel. "But it is too prosy. If the voyage promised a dash of adventure, if it were spiced with an element of danger, I——" she pauses and lifts the wineglass slowly to her lips.

"Danger?" echoes Don Manada, with a curious smile. "Dios! The voyage might not be without all the adventure your heart could desire, senora." He takes from his pocket a newspaper clipping and hands it to Isabel, after a glance about him to make certain that they are unobserved. The clipping is from the current edition of the Hemisphere. It is a dispatch from Key West, and a portion of it reads as follows:

"This city has been in a fever of excitement all day over the report that an important filibustering expedition is to leave New York this week to aid the Cuban insurgents. The report is backed by excellent authority, and there is no doubt that an effort will be made to send valuable assistance to the patriots of the Antilles some time during the week. In some way the United States authorities and the Spanish government have got wind of the proposed expedition and they are striving to nip it in the bud. The Spanish warship Infanta Isabel this morning steamed from this harbor for the purpose, one of her officers said, of intercepting the filibusters on the high seas.

"It is also stated that a prominent and gallant member of the Cuban revolutionary society will head the expedition, but his identity has not been disclosed."

Mrs. Harding glances through the clipping and hands it back with a quizzical smile.

"So you are the prominent and gallant member of the Cuban revolutionary society referred to?" she infers.

"Not so loud!" cautions Don Manada. "We may be overheard. What think you of the voyage now, senora?"

"I fear it is a bit too dangerous," replies Isabel, with a yawn. "We should never reach Cuba."

"Trust me," assents Don Manada, complacently. "Once on the high seas, the Isabel will lead the Spanish warships a pretty chase."

"Ah, the name of your schooner is the Isabel?"

"Of our yacht—yes. Is it not happily named?"

"Perhaps so," answers Mrs. Harding, with an enigmatic expression in her lustrous eyes. "And where should I find your yacht in case I should at the last moment decide to accept your offer of a merry voyage to the tropics?"

"My yacht? I should conduct you to it," says Don Manada in some surprise.

"Oh, no; that would not do," objects Isabel. "I should be driven to it veiled just preceding its departure."

Don Manada looks around the arcade, but there is no one within twenty feet of their table.

"North river, foot of 23d street," he whispers. "You will go?" as Isabel appears to be hesitating mid conflicting emotions.

"You will promise not to make love to me during the entire voyage?"

"I will promise anything, senora, though you have imposed an unhappy obligation."

"Then I think I will say—yes."

"Bueno!" cries the delighted Don Manada, and, seizing Isabel's hand, he covers it with passionate kisses.

"Oh, by the way, what time do you sail?"

"At 5 o'clock."

"Very well. I will send final word to your hotel in the morning. Now, leave me to dream over my folly," says Mrs. Harding, disengaging the hand which Don Manada still tenderly holds. .

Then, as the latter goes off to the wine-room to submerge his happiness in champagne, Isabel leans back in her chair and laughs softly. "The fool," she sneers. "Well, all men are fools—all but one."

"And that one?" inquires a voice behind her. She looks up startled, to meet the calm gaze of a man of perhaps 50, with dark hair and mustache slightly tinged with gray and the distinct air of a soldier.

"Ah, who but yourself?" returns Isabel composedly. "Sit down, Gen. Murillo. I have much to tell you."

The intelligence is plainly of a pleasing nature. Gen. Murillo murmurs "Bueno!" more than once as he listens, and when she finishes he remarks approvingly: "You have done well and may count on my gratitude."

"Gracias," responds Isabel. "That is about the extent of my Spanish, General."

"Ah, but you will learn readily. It is simple. Hist! a gentleman approaches. It were well if we be seen little together to-night. Until the morrow then, adios."

Gen. Murillo moves off toward the swirl of dancers and Isabel surveys with an air of recognition a gentleman in the costume of Don Caesar de Bazan, who has descended to the arcade by the north stairway and is coming slowly toward her. Don Caesar looks curiously after the departing form of the Spaniard; then, dropping into a chair beside Isabel, he tosses off his mask and asks carelessly: "Well, my dear Isabel, when do you leave for Cuba?"

"For Cuba?" repeats Mrs. Harding in simulated surprise.

"Exactly. After a glance at the gentleman who just left you I do not need to be enlightened as to the diplomatic duties to which you alluded last night."

"Well, Phillip, I have few secrets that you do not share," Isabel says sweetly; "I leave for Cuba to-morrow."

"So soon," he murmurs courteously.

"The sooner the better. Every day I am near you

makes eventual separation the harder. I know that you care nothing for me," she goes on, her cheeks flushed crimson. "Don't interrupt me," as Van Zandt seeks to interpose a protest. "I know that you care nothing for me, not in the way I would have you feel. I have your friendship, yes, beyond that I am nothing to you. And I—I love you, Phillip—love you as I never expected to love a man. I make the avowal without shame, for I know there is no possibility of a change in your sentiments toward me. And I am going away—to-morrow," half sobs the woman, as she covers her face with her hands.

Van Zandt lays his hand upon Isabel's head and smooths the dark tresses sympathetically. She pushes the hand away.

"Courage! Tears ill become a diplomat," declares Van Zandt. "This is a dreary world. We seldom attain our heart's desire, even though the object we seek be a lowly one. Will you have some wine?" Isabel shakes her head. She has dried her eyes and has relapsed into an apathetic melancholy.

Van Zandt signals to a waiter. "A little wine will help lighten our hearts," he tells Mrs. Harding; "for believe me, mine is not less heavy than yours. Cheer up and we will drink a toast to all unrequited love."

Isabel gives him a swift look of surprise. "You heard?" she demands.

"I heard nothing," he replies, smilingly. "What has given rise to your question?"

" 'Tis less than an hour since I offered that very toast. I have had a proposal to-night."

"Indeed? And you rejected it?"

"Can you ask such a question. The world is full of Don Manadas, but there is only one——"

"So? The swarthy gentleman, with the curious white mustachios?" interrupts Van Zandt. "I noticed you talking with him."

"I had rejected him twice before, but his persistence is worthy of a better cause. To-night I promised to accompany him on a filibustering expedition to Cuba. Think of it! The fool!" sneers Isabel.

"And you will not go."

"Most certainly not. I only half-promised. To-morrow I shall send word that I have changed my mind."

"And meanwhile you have accomplished something toward your new duties, eh?" remarks Van Zandt. If Isabel Harding could read the dark, handsome face that she loves so well, she would know that she has lost forever the esteem of Phillip Van Zandt.

"You have betrayed the man who trusted you," continues Van Zandt in the same quiet and impassive voice.

"Betrayed him? And what if I did?" flashes Isabel passionately. "Call it treachery if you will. I say it is only a reprisal of treachery. Take me out of here, Phillip. I am sick of these lights and the music and the scent of the flowers."

"I will see you to a carriage," says Van Zandt, quietly.

Ten minutes later he says good-by to her, as he prepares to close the carriage door.

"Some day, Phillip, you will realize how much I love you," Isabel whispers, as she presses to her lips the hand he mechanically gives her.

Words, words, words; but destined to have a tragic fulfillment!

Van Zandt looks after the retreating carriage with a darkening brow. "Call it treachery if you will," he repeats, grimly. "By George! I'll spike her ladyship's guns! The cause of liberty shall not be jeopardized by the indiscretion of its friends or the machinations of its enemies!"

As he turns and re-enters the garden a man steps to a waiting cab, and, indicating the carriage which is bearing off Isabel Harding, he whispers to his driver: "Keep that rig in view till it stops. Understand?"

CHAPTER XXIV.

FOR THE CAUSE OF LIBERTY.

"You proposed to a lady to-night."

"What is that to you, sir?" Don Manada turns fiercely upon the gentleman who has tapped him upon the shoulder and requested the pleasure of a few moments' conversation with him.

"Nothing to me, perhaps," returns Phillip Van Zandt, quietly; "to you much, possibly. Sit down. Or better, suppose we adjourn to the arcade. We shall be freer from interruption there."

"I must decline to accompany you, sir, until I have reason to believe that the matter on which you desire to talk is of more importance than your opening remark would indicate."

Van Zandt surveys the Cuban with a trifle of impatience. "As you please," he observes. "But permit me to say that upon your disposition to listen to what I have to impart depends the success or failure of the expedition which is to start for Cuba to-morrow—or, rather, to-day."

Manada starts violently and bends a searching look upon the other's face. "Nothing could be of greater importance to me, sir," he says, and without further remark he follows Van Zandt to the little table where an hour ago he for the third time offered Isabel Harding his hand and heart.

"Now, to business," remarks Van Zandt, glancing at his watch. "It is 1:30. Thirty minutes for talk, the rest of the night for action. You are Don Manada of the Cuban revolutionary society." That gentleman bows. "I am Phillip Van Zandt. That is all you need know concerning myself. Mrs. Isabel Harding, the lady to whom you made violent love to-night"—the Cuban scowls, but Van Zandt goes on relentlessly—"I have known for some months. She has honored me—shall I say?—with her deep regard. Perhaps she hinted as much to you."

Manada leans back in his chair and looks his new acquaintance over critically. This, then, was his rival; a negative one, to be sure, but a rival that any man might fear.

"If it will flatter your vanity to know that the lady in question confessed to me that she loved only one man in the world and that that happy individual was not myself, you are welcome to the information," Manada offers, sarcastically.

"Thank you. But I was already aware of the fact, and it is not to the point. You proposed to Mrs. Harding and were rejected. Stay," as the other colors and is about to make an angry retort: "I did not bring you here, sir, to refresh your mind one instance in which the usually discriminating Isabel displayed poor taste. But I repeat, she rejected you; hence subsequently something must have occurred between you to lead up to a rather peculiar agreement—Mrs. Harding's consent to accompany you on a filibustering expedition?"

"Caramba! She told you—you overheard——"

"I overheard nothing. Eavesdropping is not in my line. And she told me little more; but enough to warrant me in stating that you have been indiscreet, sir, to use no harsher term, and have jeopardized not only your own welfare but that of your fellow-countrymen."

"You seem to be pretty familiar with my affairs, senor."

"Not so familiar with them as the Spanish government and the United States authorities may be," responds Van Zandt, dryly. "All I know of your plans I have told you. What I do not know you will tell me now."

An angry rejoinder trembles on Manada's lips, but something in the stern, quiet air of the man before him checks his wrath.

"Mrs. Harding," resumes Van Zandt, "consented to go to Cuba with you, did she not?"

"Practically, yes."

"And you were to receive her final decision on the morrow?"

"Well, senor?"

"She will not go."

"Then you persuaded her—you interfered," cries Manada hotly.

"I did nothing of the sort. Still, I repeat, she will not go. But, stay, perhaps she will," murmurs Van Zandt, thoughtfully. "Perhaps her ladyship's plans lie deeper than I have supposed," he thinks. "But even if she does go, I tell you, my friend, it were far better that you burned your vessel where it now lies than that Isabel Harding sets foot upon its deck."

"Your meaning?" demands Manada in a hoarse whisper.

"Your face tells me that you have guessed the truth," Van Zandt says more kindly. "The woman has betrayed you. She is a spy—diplomat is the polite word—in the employ of the Spanish government."

"Caramba!" hisses Manada, sinking back into his chair with colorless cheeks. "But you can furnish proof of what you assert?" he cries almost eagerly.

Van Zandt's lip curls. "Had you watched the fair Isabel after you left her you would have seen join her a gentleman whose presence in itself would have been proof sufficient—Gen. Murillo. You know him?"

"Of the Spanish service," murmurs Manada in crushed tones.

"Precisely. I met him at the club the other day. And if I mistake not he has done an excellent bit of work for his government to-night."

"But I will find the woman," bursts out Manada, leaping to his feet. "Por Dios! I will search her out and——"

"You will do nothing of the kind," interrupts Van Zandt, drawing the excited man back into his chair. "Mrs. Harding left for her hotel half an hour ago. Even were she here it would avail you nothing to confront her with her—diplomacy. Gen. Murillo is already in possession of your plans. No, my friend; the mischief is done, but happily it is not irremediable."

"Ah!" cries Manada, with a flash of hope.

"Now, listen to me. We have wasted too much time already. What is the name of your vessel?"

"The Isabel."

"So? Pretty name, but have it changed at the first opportunity. Where does she now lie?"

'North River, foot of Twenty-third Street.

"Excellent," comments Van Zandt, his eyes lighting with satisfaction. "And at what time did you intend to sail?"

"At five in the afternoon."

"You are of course aware that both the Spanish and United States governments are on the keen lookout for filibustering craft?"

"Certainly," Manada replies, grimly. "But we were confident of slipping through unmolested. We had arranged to clear for the Bermudas, and once on the high seas we felt sure of running away from any warships that might lie in our course."

"Ah, your vessel is a yacht. And the cargo—of what does that consist?"

"Two thousand rifles and 200,000 rounds of cartridges."

"How is it loaded?"

"The ammunition is packed in kegs, ostensibly containing salt fish; the rifles are in bags and are hidden at the bottom of bins of potatoes in the hold."

"The cargo could be shifted before daybreak, do you think?"

"Two or three hours should suffice."

"Good. You must have noticed, lying in the neighborhood of your vessel, a rather trim article in the yacht line."

"The Semiramis? Yes. A magnificent vessel!" exclaims Manada.

Van Zandt nods. She is my property and I believe her to be the fastest vessel afloat in the world to-day. Now here is my plan—I consider it the only one that will extricate you from the dilemma in which you are placed: I will place the Semiramis at the service of the struggling patriots of the Antilles. We will shift the Isabel's cargo before the night is gone, and before the sun goes down on another day the Semiramis will be on her way to Cuba. Once without New York bay I defy anything short of a cannon ball to overhaul her. What say you, Don Manada?"

The Cuban's face expresses the astonishment and joy that he feels. To be raised suddenly from the depths of despair to the pinnacle of hope effects a remarkable change in one of his temperament.

"Santa Maria!" he cries, as he presses warmly Van Zandt's hands. "You have done me as great a service as one man can do another. Por Dios! We shall outwit them cleverly."

"Then let us be off," says Van Zandt. "It is after 2 o'clock and we have little time to spare."

The men secure their coats and hats and ten minutes later board a cross-town car.

"Senor Van Zandt, I owe you a debt of gratitude," declares Manada; "yet I find myself marveling that you, a stranger, and the one man to win Isabel Harding's affection, should interest yourself in me and the cause I represent."

"Oh, it promised an adventure; something I have long been in need of to stir my blood to action," replies Van Zandt, lightly. "Besides, am I not an American, and is not the cause of liberty a cause that appeals to every American with a spark of manhood in his soul? Only those who know what liberty is realize its priceless worth."

They are now walking along West Street. Manada silently reproaching himself with his recent folly, wraps his greatcoat more tightly about him, and breathes a shivering malediction on the cutting winds that sweep adown the Hudson.

The sky is overcast and a slight snow is falling. It is a good night for the work in hand.

The river front is black and silent and the outlines of the vessels about the pier are barely distinguishable through the driving storm.

West Street, though dimly lighted, is not deserted. From the grog-shops come echoes of many a brawl, and every now and then a drunken longshoreman reels or is thrown into the street and staggers off, heaven knows where. Every half-hour or so a ferry boat lumbers in and out of the slip, and there is a temporary bustle in the vicinage.

"A miserable night, senor," remarks Van Zandt, as they cross West Street and pick their way toward the pier where lies the vessel in which are centered now all of Don Manada's hopes. The latter has forgotten for the nonce his recent humiliation and is keenly alive to the adventurous undertaking in hand.

The men plunge through the gloom, muffled to the eyes and with heads bent before the biting blasts from the river, when their ears are suddenly assailed by the sound of a scuffle ahead of them and a half-choked cry for help. Quickening their steps, they run upon two men. One of them is prone upon the pier; the other, clearly his assailant, bends over him.

Before the scamp can rise Van Zandt deals him a blow with his heavy cane that stretches him beside his victim. He is not a courageous rogue, or if he is realizes that his chance for an argument is not especially good. So when he struggles to his feet he makes off without a word, without even an imprecation.

Van Zandt and Manada raise the prostrate form and bear it back to the street. As the lamplight falls upon the face of the unconscious man Van Zandt utters an ejaculation of astonishment.

"By heaven! it is Gen. Murillo! You see, my friend, that I was not mistaken. He probably came down here to have a look at the Isabel, and was set upon by one of the scum of the river front."

Manada nods a silent assent. "He must not see us," he mutters, uneasily.

"Don't be alarmed. He is not likely to recognize any one for a few minutes. I hope he is not badly hurt. Off with him to yonder saloon; or, better, to the ferryhouse. The man will be safer there, though we are more likely to find a policeman at the saloon."

A policeman is at the ferryhouse, however, and assist-

ance is summoned. Van Zandt and Manada wait until
Gen. Murillo is laid in the ambulance and the surgeon
in charge has assured them that the man is not fatally
hurt; then they tell their story to the policeman and go
about their business.

"A peculiar episode," remarks Van Zandt. "Our friend
will never know to whom he owes his rescue and perhaps
his life. Our affair must be hurried, nevertheless, for we
know what his first effort will be when he recovers consciousness."

"Yet some day, when Cuba is free, I shall have the
pleasure of recalling the incident to his mind."

"When Cuba is free," repeats Van Zandt. "Well, luck
favoring us, we shall fire a shot to-day that will ring
in the ears of the government at Madrid. Here we are
at the Semiramis. Where is the Isabel?"

"Just beyond. Not twenty feet away."

Van Zandt hails his yacht and ten minutes later he and
Manada are in the luxurious cabin, in consultation with
Capt. Beals, a bluff old Maine sea dog, who is prepared
for any caprice on the part of his employer and expresses
not the least surprise when informed that arrangements
for a cruise to Cuba must be instantly set afoot.

And that morning, while the wind howls around Man-
hattan Island, and drives the sleet into the eyes of belated
pedestrians; while Murillo awakens to consciousness in
Bellevue Hospital and tells the attending surgeon that,
head or no head, he leaves for Cuba within half a dozen
hours; and while the last carriage load of half-drunken
sports dashes away from the Madison Square Garden, a
work is in progress aboard the Semiramis that means
more to its owner than he dreams of as he stands with
folded arms in the dim light of the ship lanterns, watching
silently the transshipment of the insurgent's arms.

CHAPTER XXV.

TWO KINDS OF BLOCKADE.

About 9:30 of the morning following the French ball Phillip Van Zandt drops into his favorite seat in the dining-room of the St. James Hotel and picks up the morning paper.

Scarcely had he unfolded it when his attention was attracted by two persons seated at the table beyond him. They are Cyrus Felton and Louise Hathaway, and the latter never looked fairer than on this bright March morning.

"Ah, my divinity of the ball," he murmurs. "By Eros! She is superb. Hair, a mass of gold and the sunlight gives it just the right effect. Purity and innocence are in those blue eyes and in every line of the face. Knowing no evil and fearing none, and yet with the self-poise of a queen. It almost restores one's confidence in humanity to look upon such a face.

"I would be glad indeed to know her, but the opportunity for an introduction is not likely to arise. I could scarcely presume on last night's meeting, and besides, she would hold me to my word. What impulse possessed her to remove her mask at my request? I'll wager she regretted it an instant later. Well, she did not see my face, so I may devour her visually in perfect safety."

"And her companion?" Van Zandt goes on meditatively. "Not her husband, assuredly. Too old for that. More likely her father, or perhaps her guardian. They are going to Cuba, so she told me. Well, I am going to Cuba, too. I may meet her there. Friendships are easily cultivated in a foreign land. My dear Van Zandt, is it possible that you are becoming interested in a woman? Careful; you forget who you are," he concludes bitterly, and stares moodily out upon the crowded street.

Mr. Felton and Miss Hathaway are breakfasting leisurely, unconscious of the interest they have aroused in the gentleman at the next table. Mr. Felton is scanning the columns of the Hemisphere, with particular reference to the full dispatches from Cuba and Madrid. Suddenly he drops the paper with the exclamation: "This is very unfortunate!"

"What is unfortunate?" inquires Miss Hathaway, sipping her coffee.

"Here is a dispatch from Havana, stating that the government has ordered a complete blockade of the island and that all steamship engagements to and from Cuba have been canceled for an indefinite period."

Miss Hathaway looks up in mild dismay. "Then we cannot leave Saturday," she says.

"It would seem not. Ah, here is something more. The newspaper has looked up the report at the New York end and finds it to be true. The steamer City of Havana of the Red Star line, this paper says, will probably be the last passenger vessel to leave New York for Cuba until the blockade is raised."

"But can we not go on that?"

Mr. Felton reads on: "The City of Havana sails to-day at 11 o'clock." Then he glances at his watch. "It is now nearly 10. Perhaps we can make it. Wait, I will ascertain from the clerk."

Mr. Felton rises, and as he turns to leave the dining room Van Zandt gets a view of his face, and he starts as if from a nightmare.

"That face again!" he breathes. "That face, which has haunted my dreams and has been before me in my waking hours! And her father! Merciful heaven, it cannot be. There is a limit to fate's grotesquerie."

Miss Hathaway glances in Van Zandt's direction and their eyes meet. It is only an instant, but it leaves the girl somewhat confused and accentuates the young man's disorder.

At this juncture Mr. Felton returns with the information that they have little more than an hour to reach Barclay Street and the North River, from which point the steamer leaves.

"Then let us go at once. I am ready," Louise says,

"after I have scribbled a note of explanation to Mr. Ashley. He was to have lunched with us at 1 o'clock, you know."

After they have gone Van Zandt drops his head upon his hand, and for the space of ten minutes remains plunged in thought. Then, to the waiter's surprise, he leaves his breakfast untouched and quits the dining-room.

In the office he sees Mr. Felton settling his bill. Outside the hotel a line of "cabbies" are drawn up and these Van Zandt looks over critically, finally signaling to one of them, a jovial, red visaged Irishman.

"Riley, a lady and gentleman are going from this hotel to Barclay Street and North River within a few minutes. I want you to have the job of carrying them," says Van Zandt.

"I'm agreeable, sor."

"After you have secured the job, I want you to miss the steamer which sails for Cuba at 11 o'clock. Understand?"

Riley puckers up his mouth for a whistle which he decides to suppress.

"Sure that would not be hard, sor. It's tin o'clock now."

"Here they come now. Look to your job," says Van Zandt.

Mr. Felton and Miss Hathaway emerge from the hotel, followed by a porter with their trunks. Amid a chorus of "Keb, sir!" "Keb!" "Keb!" in which Riley sings a heavy bass, Mr. Felton looks about him in perplexity, and finally, as though annoyed by the importunities of Riley, who is rather overdoing his part, he selects a rival "cabbie."

Riley turns somewhat sheepishly to Van Zandt, who looks after the disappearing carriage in vexation.

"Shall I run them down, sor?" asks the Irishman, with a wink which means volumes.

"Can you prevent them reaching the pier?"

"Sure, I think so, your honor."

"I'll give you $50 if you do it."

"Be hivens! I'd murdther thim for that," exclaims Riley, as he leaps to his box.

The two cabs proceeded at a smart pace down Fifth Avenue, but as the congested trucking district is reached progress becomes slower.

"Can you make the pier in time?" Mr. Felton asks the driver anxiously, consulting his watch for the dozenth time.

"Sure thing," is the confident response.

Neither the driver nor his passengers see the cab behind them. Riley has his reins grasped tightly in one hand, his whip in the other, and the expression on his round red face indicates that he is preparing for something out of the ordinary.

They have now reached lower West Broadway, and before Mr. Felton's driver knows it-he has become entangled in a rapidly created blockade.

Progress now is snail-like. Mr. Felton becomes nervous, while Miss Hathaway finds much to interest her in the seemingly inextricable tangle of trucks, drays, horse cars, cabs, etc. Suddenly a space of a dozen feet or so opens before them, and the driver is about to take advantage of it when Riley gives his horse a cut with the whip and bumps by, nearly taking a wheel off the other cab.

Then ensues a duel of that picturesque profanity without which no truck blockade could possibly be disentangled.

Riley, who is ordinarily one of the most good-natured of mortals, becomes suddenly sensitive under the abuse heaped upon him and dragging the rival cabman from his box he proceeds to handle him in a manner that affords keen delight to the onlookers.

It is a snappy morning and Riley rather enjoys the exercise he is taking. But it is suddenly ended by a brace of policemen, who struggle upon the scene and pounce upon the combatants. Explanations are then in order and peace is restored. No one is arrested.

Riley is willing to break away, for as he looks around he notes with satisfaction that the blockade has increased to unusual proportions and he awaits serenely its slow unraveling.

Meanwhile Mr. Felton is invoking the vials of wrath upon all cabmen, past, present and to come. It is nearly 11:30 when they reach the pier and, as they expect, the steamer has gone.

"'Tain't my fault, mum," the "cabbie" explains apologetically. "Him's the chap what done it," indicating Riley, who has driven up to the pier with the triumphant flourish of a winner in a great race.

Mr. Felton casts a withering look upon the jolly Irishman. "We may as well return to the hotel," he tells Louise.

At this moment Van Zandt steps from his cab, and, raising his hat, remarks:

"I trust that the carelessness of my driver has not caused you serious annoyance."

"He has prevented our catching the last steamer that will sail for Cuba in probably some months," replies Mr. Felton, tartly.

"You blockhead!" cries Van Zandt sternly, turning to Riley, who averts his face.

"My dear sir, it is needless for me to assure you of my profound regret. It will not help matters. The mischief is done—and yet I think I can repair it."

"Repair it?" repeats Mr. Felton. "In what possible way, sir?"

"Very easily, if you desire. You were going to Havana, I presume?"

"Yes, sir."

"My yacht sails for Santiago this afternoon at 1 o'clock. I shall be happy to land you at that port, and you may thence proceed by rail to Havana."

Mr. Felton and Louise look at each other in surprise. "Really, sir," says the former, "you are very good, but I do not see how we can put you to such trouble."

"I assure you that you will not inconvenience me in the slightest. The yacht is large and you will be the only passengers, with one exception."

Mr. Felton hesitates. "How badly does he want to go

to Cuba?" wonders Van Zandt and he remarks: "This will probably be your only chance to reach Havana in some little time, if, as you say, there are no more steamers. Really, I almost feel like insisting on your accepting my offer, as some sort of reparation for the annoyance to which you have been put and for which I feel partly responsible."

"But a blockade has been declared about the island. Your yacht——"

"My yacht will land you at Santiago," supplies Van Zandt, with a peculiar smile. "We sail in about an hour, and we may as well proceed to the yacht at once. For I assume that you have decided to permit me to atone for the blackguardly behavior of my driver."

Mr. Felton consults Miss Hathaway and the matter is decided in the affirmative, and as Van Zandt hands them into their coupe, he tells the driver: "North River, foot of Twenty-third Street."

An hour later Miss Hathaway is expressing her admiration for the beautiful yacht that is soon to bear her to the tropics, and Capt. Beals is giving the last orders preparatory to getting under way.

As Van Zandt watches Mr. Felton cross from the pier to the deck of the Semiramis into his dark eyes comes a glitter of almost savage satisfaction, and he murmurs:

"I have you safe now, and by George! You will not soon escape me!"

CHAPTER XXVI.

THE PENALTY OF PROCRASTINATION.

A pencil of sunlight has struggled through the heavy draperies at the windows and laid a tiny straight line across the carpet in the comfortable apartments of Jack Ashley on West Thirty-fourth Street. The oriole timepiece on the mantel chimes the hour of 9 when that individual awakens with a series of prodigious yawns.

Fifteen minutes more and Ashley's toilet is complete, and with heels elevated to a comfortable angle, he proceeds to scan the pages of his morning paper. His own story of the French ball first claims his attention, and with a comment of satisfaction on the size of the headlines with which it is introduced, he runs his eye approvingly over the dozen or so illustrations with which the article is embellished.

A scare head of the largest size catches his eye, and with awakening interest he reads the sensational headlines. "Gaining Ground—Cuban Revolutionists Driving Spaniards Before Them—Hemisphere's Exclusive Interview with Senor Manada Creates Excitement in Washington—United States Man-of-War to Be Sent to Cuba to Protect American Interests," and much more of the same tenor. As Jack skims over the voluminous dispatches that follow the head, he reads with interest one brief item, dated Santiago de Cuba, via Nassau, N. P.   It is as follows:

The Government is redoubling its efforts to suppress the news, and is apparently determined that the press of the United States and elsewhere shall not learn the exact state of affairs on the island. Nine-tenths of the local newspaper men have been fined by the press censor. Several editions of the leading papers have been seized, and telegrams for transmission abroad from eastern Cuba are now absolutely forbidden. It is also a fact that foreign correspondents have been threatened with expulsion. The Spanish authorities allege that the mysterious steamer fired upon by the warship Galicia was not the American ward liner Santiago, but a rebel vessel which the insurrectionists have purchased in the United States and fitted up as a gunboat. A blockade of all the ports of the island, as previously intimated, has been formally announced."

"It looks as if the paper would be obliged to send a man down there," Ashley reflects, as he struggles into his topcoat. "What a superb day for the trial trip," as he opens the street door and steps into the sunlight. "And this is the day, too, that Barker is to arrest Felton. He didn't specify any time, probably not till afternoon, anyway. I almost wish I wasn't assigned to that trial trip. I should like to interview him after the arrest. However, my story is all written up and I can get the details of the arrest from Barker after I return from the America. I wonder how Miss Hathaway will take the affair," a softer light shining in his eyes as his thoughts revert to the beautiful ward of Cyrus Felton. "She treats him with the utmost deference and respect, but I cannot think that she cares especially for him. Heigho! Now for a cup of coffee and then for another tete-a-tete with the beautiful unknown of the Raymond Hotel."

It is on the stroke of 10 as Ashley saunters up to the clerk's desk in the Kensington and requests that his card, upon which he has penciled a few lines explaining his identity, be taken to Mrs. Winthrop.

"Mrs. Winthrop?" the urbane clerk repeats. "There is no such lady stopping here, to my knowledge."

Ashley is nonplused. So he has been duped, he thinks, by the fair unknown. But why has not Barker kept his agreement? A nice sort of a shadow if he cannot follow as striking-looking a woman as "Mrs. Winthrop." But stay! Perhaps she has given a fictitious name, but is actually stopping at the Kensington after all. Barker could not have slipped upon a simple matter like that.

Abstractedly twirling his glove, Jack leans over the desk and says in a low tone to the clerk, an old acquaintance: "Is there a rather striking-looking young woman, with dark eyes and midnight hair, stopping at the house?"

The clerk smiles.

"Sorry, Jack, but you are too late, I'm afraid. The beautiful Mrs. Harding left at 9 o'clock, bag and baggage."

Ashley turns thoughtfully away and repairs to the reading-room for a quiet think. So her name—for the present at least—is Mrs. Harding. But where is Barker? The detective is probably shadowing Mrs. Harding now. Ashley concludes that there is nothing for him to do but await Barker's return. He has been on the watch barely half an hour when the detective swings himself from a cable car in front of the hotel.

"Well?" is Jack's impatient salutation as he leads the way to a retired corner of the reading-room.

Barker is not in exuberant spirits; his brows are knitted in a frown and he is nervously biting his mustache.

"Well, she has gone—left town, and is apparently en route from the country—for Cuba, I believe."

"For Cuba!" and Jack stares at the detective in mild amaze. Verily, either a most remarkable series of coincidences or the tangled threads of the Raymond mystery are pointing unmistakably to the fair isle of the Antilles.

"Yes, for Cuba. Let me impress it upon your mind in the beginning that Mrs. Isabel Harding—that's the name she is sailing under—is no ordinary woman. Why —but to begin at the beginning. According to our understanding last night, I followed her to this hotel, where I found she was actually stopping. I naturally concluded that she made the engagement with you in good faith, else she would have given another hotel."

"She did give me a fictitious name," breaks in Jack. "Or, rather, she led me to believe that her name was still Winthrop."

"Did she? Well, that was useless. Anyhow, I decided to stop here last night, to be on guard early this morning. I found that my lady had breakfasted early. This made me suspicious and I kept close watch of her. Shortly after 9 o'clock she settled her bill at the hotel and with her trunks was driven to the Jersey City ferry. Of course I followed. At the Pennsylvania depot she was joined by a foreign-looking chap—Spaniard. Quite a distinguished-looking, duffer. If you should ever run across him you will know him by a small, crescent-shaped scar on his left cheek. I was successful in getting close enough to them to hear some of the conversation. It appeared from their talk, Ashley, that your Mrs. Harding is, in addition to her other accomplishments, a spy in the pay of the Spanish Government, and that she has been successful in learning some of the secret plans and plots of the Cuban filibusters in this city. She is now on her way to Port Tampa aboard the Florida limited, and I should judge it is their intention to proceed from Key West at once to Havana."

"Their intention? Did the Spanish officer accompany her?"

Barker nods. "He looked as if he was right out of the hospital; his head was bandaged. Perhaps some of the Cuban sympathizers had it out with him. However, that episode is closed, for the present at least. And now for Cyrus Felton. I shall take him directly to the Tombs, and according to our compact he will be invisible to any of the newspaper fraternity. Will you come with me to the St. James while I nab the bird?"

Ashley starts. He has for a moment forgotten the catastrophe that is about to overcome Cyrus Felton. He looks at his watch. "I am overdue at the office," he says. "But say, Barker, I had an engagement to lunch with Felton and Miss Hathaway at 1 o'clock. Can't you put off the arrest until to-morrow?"

Barker shakes his head. "Not a minute," he replies, emphatically. "I have delayed long enough. If you intended to lunch with the fair Miss Hathaway you will have an opportunity to do so just the same and your presence will doubtless be appreciated in her tremendous confusion. If you can't come with me I will drop round at the office and see you later."

"All right, then. Do the job in as gentlemanly a manner as possible," grins Ashley.

Barker nods and walks rapidly toward the St. James, while Ashley boards a Broadway car and rolls downtown.

The detective saunters up to the hotel office desk, writes the name "Cyrus Felton" on a bit of cardboard, and, passing it to the clerk, inquires: "Is that gentleman in?"

"No, sir; gone. Left an hour ago."

"When will he return?"

"Well, that's rather beyond me," smiles the clerk,

"Mr. Felton and a lady sailed this morning for Cuba, on the City of Havana. I assume that they did. They were driven from here to the pier."

"What time does the steamer sail?" asks Barker, taking out his watch.

"Eleven o'clock."

"Too late!" grits the detective. It is even now five minutes past the hour.

For a moment Barker permits his emotions to master his self-possession, and he startles even the debonair clerk, accustomed as the latter is to the strong terms sometimes employed by irritable guests.

His feelings relieved in a measure by this unusual outbreak, the detective sits down for a moment to consider the situation. Cyrus Felton, then, is on his way to Cuba, doubtless to join his son. Mrs. Harding, a valuable quantity in the mystery, is also headed for the Antilles. Everything seems to point to Cuba. Barker picks up a railroad timetable.

"Twelve m.; Florida express for Savannah, Jacksonville and Port Tampa," he reads.

"By the gods, I'll do it!" he exclaims, as he starts for the street. "First to the pier and make sure that the steamer has gone, and, if so, then to Key West. I shall be only two hours behind the woman, and I may reach Havana ahead of Felton. Hi, there, cabby!"

CHAPTER XXVII.

THE CRUISER AMERICA.

"Jack, Mr. Ricker wants to see you," is the information extended to Ashley when he reaches the office. He reports at the room of the city editor, and that gentleman informs him that he has not arrived any too soon.

"I know that I am an hour or so behind, but I have been working up a story that will make interesting reading," Ashley explains. "What's up? My trial-trip assignment isn't until 3, is it?"

"The start was set for 3, but it has been pushed forward to 1 o'clock," says Ricker.

"It is about noon now. I may as well start for Brooklyn at once. Good, snappy day for a run down the bay."

"Thunder!" says Ashley, when he reaches the street. "I had forgotten that I was booked for a consolatory lunch with Miss Hathaway at 1. I must send my regrets. Hang it, that will look as if I was on to the arrest and was afraid to show up."

But he sends the note, nevertheless, and feels better in mind. "If that cold-blooded Barker only handles the matter properly," he thinks.

Even as he reaches the Government dock Jack sees the pennant of Capt. Meade run up to the main truck of the cruiser whose initial trial in commission he is to report; he is none too soon for the gang-plank is being withdrawn by half a score of blue-clad sailors as he makes a flying leap and lands upon the deck of the newest and fastest acquisition to Uncle Sam's navy, the cruiser America.

Ere Jack has fully recovered his footing a youthful-appearing midshipman brusquely demands his business.

It takes sometime before Jack is permitted to tread the sacred precincts of the quarter-deck.

Capt. Meade is for the time being on the bridge, and, before making the acquaintance of the commander, Jack proceeds to look about the vessel.

The America has an air of being a ship made for getting there; an up-to-date cruiser, without frills and furbelows, but distinctively with an aspect of power. In the bright sunlight her snowy hull gleams like polished marble. Her four great smokestacks relieve in a measure the glaring effect of her big white bulk, while the polished brass and steel with which all the decks are gird-ironed suggest, without the presence of the murderous rapid-fire and revolving cannon stationed about the decks, that the vessel is designed for war.

Ashley is soon engaged in the collection of information

regarding the America for the benefit of Hemisphere readers. The cruiser is, the second officer informs him, of over 7,000 tons displacement. Her battery comprises two six-inch, 40-caliber rapid-fire guns, one on each side, forward of the superstructure; one eight-inch, 40-caliber on the center line, abaft the superstructure; eight four-inch rapid-fire guns in armored sponsons on the gun-deck, four on each side; six-pounder rapid-fire guns, four-pounders, one-pounders, Gatlings and torpedo tubes galore.

"There are three vertical, triple-expansion engines, each set driving a separate screw. The propellers are of manganese bronze and the ——"

"Thank you, that is sufficient, I guess," interrupts Jack. "The Hemisphere readers will have a very good idea of the offensive and defensive power of the America now, I am sure."

The cruiser is slowly backing out into the stream. There is a big throng on the pier to watch her departure, and a whole battery of cameras are leveled as she finally swings around.

Now the ship becomes indeed instinct with life and is pointing down the bay with a speed that augurs well for the shattering of records. The whistles of all the craft in sight screech a salute and the America's hoarse whistle bellows responsively. Past the Battery and Governor's Island she speeds and then, fairly by quarantine, the patent log is cast into the foamy wake and Capt. Meade rings "full speed."

The speed trial of the America has actually begun.

Jack is idly watching the rapidly receding island, when he becomes aware by the slight bustle on the quarterdeck that the commander of the America has returned from the bridge.

Capt. Meade, or "Fighting Dave," as he is affectionately designated in naval circles, is a man of about 60 years, but forty-five years of his eventful career have been spent in the navy. He has worked himself up, without political or social influence, from apprentice boy to commander of the. newest and best cruiser in the United States.

Jack has heard of "Fighting Dave," and he scans the famous naval officer with much interest. A figure slightly below the average, but stockily built; a cheerful visage, face weather-beaten and innocent of beard, surmounted by a shock of grizzly hair; eyes whose keen expression might well belie the jovial look upon the face —this is Capt. David Meade, U. S. N.

"Good face," thinks Ashley, as he completes his scrutiny. "I should like to know Capt. Meade personally, and I will."

With his customary assurance and easy grace Ashley approaches the autocrat of the quarterdeck and tenders his card.

Capt. Meade glances at the pasteboard and then his keen eyes wander to the newspaper man. Apparently the scrutiny is satisfactory, for the bronzed face wrinkles into the most benign of smiles and a tremendous fist grasps Jack's right hand with a grip which causes him to mentally question his ability to write up the trial trip, or anything else, for a week at least.

"So you are from the Hemisphere?" Capt. Meade observes. "Well, I like that paper and one of its representatives is heartily welcome to my ship. In these days of sentiment and gush and peace and good-will and brotherly love, and so forth, and so forth, it does my heart good to get hold of a paper which isn't afraid nor ashamed to speak right out in meetin' for the land we live in and the flag that floats above it. But come below, Mr. Ashley, and we'll clinch the sentiment with a toast." And the captain leads the way to his sumptuous quarters, where the "splicing of the main brace" is accomplished with alacrity and vigor by commander and newspaper man.

"Well, what do you think of the America?" asks the captain. "Did you ever see anything like that on a vessel going over twenty knots an hour?" setting his glass, filled to the brim, on the table. The surface of the liquid is scarce more ruffled than that of a mirror.

"No sign of vibration, eh? She stands up as steady as a house."

Jack is really surprised as he considers the circumstances. "From what little I have seen of her I should say she is a remarkable craft and one that Uncle Sam should feel proud of," he replies.

"Remarkable? She's a wonder! Why, she can walk away from anything that floats—anything, big or little, torpedo catchers or stilettos. I was on her when her first trial trip with the builders aboard took place, and while she made twenty-five knots then, she can do better. And she is going to do it to-day. Before we reach Sandy Hook, young man, you can just put it down in your log-book that the American flag is being borne over the water faster than any other flag is likely to be carried for some time. One more splice and then we'll show you how the trick is done."

As the captain and his guest return to the quarterdeck of the cruiser it is apparent that something unusual is attracting the attention of officers and crew. Those who are not actively engaged in the manipulation of the cruiser are gathered at the port rail watching intently a steamer that is running parallel with the America, about an eighth of a mile distant and about three lengths astern.

"What is it, Mr. Jones?" inquires Capt. Meade of the third officer, who has just removed the binocular glasses from his eyes.

"A strange craft, sir, evidently a yacht which is apparently using the America as a pacemaker. She pulled up astern of us fifteen minutes ago, and has since been steadily gaining. Very fast, sir, I should say, but she bears no ensign or pennant of any kind."

Capt. Meade takes the glasses from the hands of his subaltern and looks long and critically at the strange vessel. She is nearly the same length as the America, though manifestly of considerable less tonnage. And she is painted black, without a bit of gay color from stem to stern to relieve the somberness of her hull.

Two black smokestacks, that appear unusually large and are set at a decidedly rakish angle, are relieved by two narrow bands of white. Capt. Meade with a seaman's appreciative eye admires the shapely lines of the yacht, but as his practiced vision notices the comparative ease with which she is creeping up on the America his jovial face becomes slightly troubled.

"Mr. Jones, have the log taken and work out our speed at once," he orders.

"Twenty-four and a quarter knots," is the report.

For the next ten minutes the captain watches intently the strange yacht. Her course is apparently shaped precisely parallel with that of the America, and she still continues to gain, inch by inch, upon the white cruiser. Now she is amidships, and now the two vessels are on even terms.

A puff of white steam rises abaft the stranger's big smokestacks, and a long shrill whistle salutes the cruiser.

'Tis a challenge for a race and it stirs Capt. Meade's blood to fever heat. He sends for the chief engineer.

"How is the machinery working?" he inquires.

"Finely, sir; not the sign of the slightest trouble anywhere."

"Very well, sir; we will begin now to push her for a record. Put on every ounce of steam she will stand, first with natural and afterward with forced draught."

The chief engineer salutes, and returns to his domain, and a second later the hoarse whistle of the America sounds a defiant acceptance of the challenge of the black yacht.

<hr>

CHAPTER XXVIII.

GREAT RACE TO THE OCEAN.

"By Jove! I had no idea the captain had so much sporting blood in his veins," murmurs Jack Ashley to himself, as he watches alternately the challenging craft and the America. "It is a race fit for a king's delectation. I wonder whose yacht that is. I don't remember seeing her described in any of the papers, as she certainly would have been if she were owned in New York. She is a big one, and a beauty, too. And swift as the wind! But she doesn't seem to be gaining now. No, by Jupiter! We are gaining on her! The America has struck her gait at last! But that's a game craft there. She sticks to us like a leech and refuses to be shaken off. Ah!"

The impromptu race has been in progress nearly half an hour, and the two vessels, still less than an eighth of a mile apart, are gradually drawing nearer each other. It is apparent that the yacht is determined to continue the race at closer range, and has changed her course for that purpose. Meanwhile the big cruiser has held to her original course, and as the yacht straightens away for another parallel run she has lost her former advantage and the two vessels are practically on even terms.

It is a battle royal!

The white cruiser is cleaving the water with tremendous speed, her bow sending the spray curling nearly as high as her armored top, while the waves astern are churned by her triple screws into a foam that extends as far as the eye can reach. The roaring of her furnaces is audible above the whir of the machinery and the whistling of the wind through the rigging. From her three great smokestacks steadily increasing masses of inky smoke trail out above the snowy wake.

All eyes on the deck of the cruiser are riveted on the yacht. For a short space of time it looks as if both vessels might be propelled by the same power, so even are their relative positions. Then, to the practical eyes aboard the cruiser, it is apparent that the America is drawing ahead, slowly to be sure, and imperceptibly to the untrained eye, but still gaining.

A dozen yards, a quarter length, a half, a clear length ahead!

A hearty cheer is trembling on the lips of the crew of the cruiser, but it is not uttered. The race is still unfinished, the victory still hangs in the balance.

Like a thoroughbred that has been feeling her antagonist, the yacht now seems to respond to some undeveloped power. The cruiser gains no more—she is losing her advantage. The watchers on the quarter-deck of the America can see the black prow lessening the open water that separates the two craft. Now her bow laps the stern of the America, but not for long. She is overhauling the cruiser faster now, and in a few minutes—seconds, it seems to the anxious spectators on the latter vessel—she is abeam of the America.

Out beyond Sandy Hook, where the billows flash into curving crests like the manes of wild horses, a great fleet has gathered to watch the race against time of the famous warship. Instead it is their privilege to witness a race between two of the swiftest sea hounds ever unleashed on the trail of the wind.

Through the impromptu armada the racers speed over the toppling seas. A thousand glasses are upon them. What does it mean? The white cruiser all may recognize, but her sable-hulled consort, what is she? Straight out from staff and halyards the wind whips the flag and ensigns of the America, but neither ensign nor flag does the strange steamship show, and except for the great white wake that trails behind her she might be a phantom ship, another Flying Dutchman.

But ere the "reviewing stand" recovers from its first surprise, both craft are miles away, black bow and white bow piling over hills of foam like sleighs over snowdrifts and the surge that goes sobbing along the glistening sides of the cruiser, inaudible above the roar of her mighty engines, sounds like the weeping for a lost race.

For the black hull is bow and bow with the white, as, after a long and critical survey of the yacht from the bridge, Capt. Meade descends to the deck and summons the chief engineer.

"Everything is working finely, sir," that official reports. "We are steaming the extreme limit under natural draught. Shall we try the forced now, sir?"

Capt. Meade hesitates and again gazes long at the yacht. The latter has now a clear length of open water to the good and her stern is presented squarely in view for the first time.   The single word Semiramis is inscribed thereon in gold letters.   But no port is designated.

"The Semiramis," murmurs the commander of the America.   "I never heard of the craft before, but her name will be on every man's lips before long, I'll wager." Then to the chief engineer: "Yes, put on the forced draught."

Jack Ashley wipes the marine glasses with which the thoughtfulness of the second officer has provided him, and turns them again toward the afterdeck of the yacht.

"Well, may I be keelhauled, or some other equally condign nautical punishment," he mutters, after a long look.   "If that isn't Louise Hathaway, seated in a steamer chair, then do my optics play me strange pranks. But what is she doing on the deck of that yacht?   She appears to be alone;   at least there is no other lady passenger on deck.   Ah, there is Mr. Felton.   So Barker was too late.   Felton and Miss Hathaway must be the guests of the gay yachtsman who is making ducks and drakes of the America on her trial trip.

"Thunder and Mars!" cries the newspaper man, nearly dropping the glasses to the deck.   "Phillip Van Zandt! He is apparently the owner of the yacht.   Good heavens! What irony of fate brings together those two participants in the Raymond tragedy.   For Van Zandt is Ernest Stanley, I will swear it.

"Well, as the novelists say, the plot thickens.   How did Van Zandt ingratiate himself into the good graces of Cyrus Felton?   It must have been recently, for Miss Hathaway spoke as if they had no friends in the city. Hang it all!   I don't just fancy the situation.   How assiduously he is waiting upon her now!   Heigho, Jack! I think I would as soon have reported this trial trip from the deck of the Semiramis."   At which thought Ashley impatiently pitches over the rail the remains of one of Capt. Meade's favorite brand of cigars.

The black plumes of smoke that pour from the chimneys of the America are becoming denser and larger. The forced draught is now fully in operation, and in the boiler-rooms the half-naked stokers ceaselessly feed the greedy fires.

The cruiser has reached the limit of her speed.

How is it with the Semiramis?

For a time the America seems to hold her own and even to gain slightly. But the advantage is transitory. The yacht still apparently has speed in reserve. Once more she leaps forward and not again is opportunity afforded the America's people to view her gleaming sides.

For another hour both vessels are driven at their highest speed. The Semiramis continues to gain upon the America, and is now nearly a quarter of a mile ahead.

Half an hour later Capt. Meade sees a flag run up to the masthead of the vanishing yacht. He gives an order and the cruiser's forward gun booms a salute.

"What do you make of that ensign, Mr. Smith?" inquires the commander, turning to the second officer.

"A strange flag, sir, not the flag of any nation that I recall," is the reply.

"Ah, I have it," suddenly exclaims the captain. "Well, she is a great craft and magnificently handled. The America made a gallant fight against odds and lost; but you can say, Mr. Ashley," as that individual ascends the steps to the bridge, "that the America has broken all records in the navies of the world, and for two consecutive hours has exceeded twenty-seven knots an hour. Yonder craft has beaten that time, but she has not the heavy armament of the America."

"What was the ensign she ran up a moment ago, captain?" Ashley asks.

"That, sir," replies Capt. Meade, "was the flag of Cuba Libre, the emblem of the sometime republic of the Antilles!"

CHAPTER XXIX.

ASHLEY LAGS SUPERFLUOUS.

"If she is the property of the revolutionists, gentlemen, with her phenomenal speed she can run the strictest blockade the Spaniards can institute, can land arms, ammunition and re-enforcements at will, and practically snap her fingers at the whole Spanish navy."

The speaker is Capt. Meade and the place the officers' mess table on board the America. Naturally the one topic of conversation is the strange yacht and her remarkable performance.

"Yes," continues the captain, impressively, "I believe that the result of the insurrection may hang on the fate of that steamer. My sympathies as an individual, I do not hesitate to say, are with the rebels. But my duty as an officer impels me to notify the War Department of the departure of the Semiramis and the flaunting of the Cuban flag. However, I hardly think the warning will harm her, even if it should set the entire Spanish navy in pursuit."

"Do you think the yacht is bound for Cuba now?" inquires Ashley, with an unpleasant sensation in the vicinity of the fifth rib.

"Certainly. She is apparently coaled and equipped for a long voyage. She set low enough in the water to carry quite a cargo, too. Oh, yes; she is off for the West Indies sure enough."

Ashley relapses into a reverie and the burden of his thoughts is something like this: "Louise Hathaway, Cyrus Felton and this mysterious Van Zandt on the same steamer and bound for Cuba! How and why?" He mechanically pulls at his cigar. Finally, as the signal for breaking up of the dinner party is given by the commander, he murmurs: "What will John Barker say?"

The America has completed her run; and now, her officers and the naval experts aboard having expressed their satisfaction with her performance, the cruiser is steaming back to her dock. The shrill salutes of the many steam craft in the harbor greet the ears of Ashley as he accompanies the officers to the deck. The sun is shining in a haze of cold gray. The March air, a few hours ago so clear and warm, is dull and marrow-piercing. Ashley shivers and buttons his coat more closely about him.

A few moments more, and the cruiser is slowing down preparatory to making her pier, and Jack seeks Capt. Meade to express his thanks. The latter shakes his hand cordially and remarks: "Better come on our next cruise, my boy; we may have another try at the black yacht. The navy expert says it was rumored in official circles that if this trial was satisfactory the America is to be ordered immediately to Cuba to protect American interests. Good news, if true, eh?"

Ashley allows that if the captain says it is good news, good news it certainly must be; and a half-defined hope is forming in his mind as he steps once more on terra firma.

"After I turn in my story on the trial trip I shall proceed to hunt up some possible light on the latest twist in the Hathaway tangle," he meditates, as he sets his face toward the lights of Gotham town. "Felton and Miss Hathaway were booked to sail on the City of Callao on Saturday; yet I discover them to-day headed southward on the Semiramis. Miss Hathaway must have left some explanation, and it is barely possible that Barker may know something about the sudden departure. I should not be a particle surprised if John, too, were aboard the Semiramis. Nothing will ever surprise me again. But if Barker got left I shall probably find him sitting on the steps of the Hemisphere office, in a state of mind bordering on the profane."

But fate decrees that many days shall elapse ere the detective and his newspaper friend again clasp each other by the hand; days big with exciting events that the serene Ashley dreams not of as he saunters down Newspaper Row.

From his box in the office Ashley extracts a letter, evidently hastily written and sealed. The address is in Barker's handwriting, and Ashley tears it open. He reads:

"My Dear Ashley: I start for Cuba at 12 o'clock via Key West. Write this just before the train starts. Felton has eluded me—thanks to your infernal French ball—and sailed for Cuba on City of Havana at 11 o'clock. Don't know whether he got wind of contemplated arrest or not. If I have good luck at Key West will be in H. as soon as he. May trail him to the son and bag both at once. In any event, do not intend to lose sight of him again till he is safely landed in Vermont. I may run across your Mrs. Harding, and if I do will try my luck at making her tell what she knows of young Felton, on threat of exposing her as a Spanish spy. Good scheme, eh? Must close, train starting; will write from Cuba. Hastily,
                                        "Barker."

"So Cuba is to be the scene of the next act of the Raymond tragedy," Jack thinks. "How suddenly all the characters have betaken themselves to the southern isle, and how events have crowded on each other the last day or two! First, news that young Felton is in Cuba; then appear Cyrus Felton and Louise Hathaway in the city; then the mysterious woman of the Raymond Hotel, and the stranger of the mountain gorge—and all of these are at this moment en route to Cuba. Only Derrick Ames and Helen Hathaway remain to be accounted for, and if Barker's theory is correct, and they, too, are in Cuba, what a situation and what a complication! I must be there at the finish. The paper really needs a war correspondent in the ever-faithful isle, and I've half a mind to ask for the assignment."

From his desk Ashley takes a bulky package of manuscript, glances through it, and with a sigh replaces it within an inner compartment. "The Raymond mystery story, the newspaper beat of the year," is not to be used yet.

But the account of the trial trip of the America must be written, and soon the sheaves of yellow paper are being rapidly covered by Jack's flying pen.

At last it is finished, and with a grunt of satisfaction

Jack arranges the scattered sheets and proceeds to the desk of the city editor.

"Ah, Ashley," remarks that dignitary, glancing at the manuscript and without raising his eyes; "trial trip was a success, wasn't it? Yes; well, I have a little something here that I wish you would look up. You have done so much Cuban stuff lately that you are more familiar with the ground than any other man on the staff. The Washington wire states that a vessel, the Isabel, that was to have sailed from here to-day, has been detained at her moorings, foot of Twenty-third Street. She is suspected of having arms and ammunition for the Cuban rebels on board. The information was filed by the Spanish minister. Just look up the local end of the story, find out who fitted out the steamer, where she was ostensibly to clear for, etc. You had better see your filibuster friend, Manada. He might give you something on it."

"Blast Cuba!" mutters Jack, as he leaves the office. "Everything is Cuba now. Talk about Tantalus! His case wasn't a marker to mine. Here are all the characters in a drama in which I am interested gone to Cuba, while I lag superfluous on the stage, doomed to write up stuff about the confounded island and its affairs at long range. Besides, I haven't fairly got back my land legs, and now I must jaunt up the North River two or three miles. Well, there is no use kicking, I suppose. Guess I will look up Don Manada first, though."

Ashley's annoyance dissipates rapidly, however, and he has recovered his customary serenity when he tenders his card to the clerk at the Fifth Avenue Hotel, to be taken to Don Manada's rooms.

"Don Manada has left, sir" the clerk tells him. "He had his effects removed early this morning and stated that he might not return for some months."

"Where has he gone, do you know?"

"To Cuba, I think."

Jack turns away. "To Cuba, of course. Everybody with whom I have business to-day has gone to Cuba. If that filibustering vessel, the Isabel, has not eluded the officers and sailed for Cuba by the time I reach her wharf, I shall be mightily surprised. No; I have decided to be surprised at nothing hereafter. The Isabel! There's another coincidence—the first name of Mrs. Harding or Mrs. Winthrop or whatever it is—the woman of the Raymond Hotel. Well, here goes for the Isabel."

It is cold, foggy, dark and altogether disagreeable as Jack alights from the car at the foot of Twenty-third Street and picks his way down the long wharf to where he is informed the detained steamer is docked. She is still there; he sees her smokestacks and masts outlined against the sky. A single lantern is alight on the vessel, but the gang-plank has been hauled in.

"Steamer ahoy!" Ashley calls, and after several repetitions of the hail a gruff voice sounds from the gloom in the vicinity of the lantern.

"Ashore, there! What do you want?"

"Is this the Isabel?"

"Yes," is the brief reply.

"Well, I want to talk with you a moment. Can't you run out a plank and hold that lantern nearer, so I can see to come aboard? I am from the Hemisphere."

There is a moment's hesitation and then the lantern approaches the steamer's side and a plank is extended to the pier.

"Now, all I want to find out is about the alleged seizure of the vessel," begins Jack, thrusting a cigar into the fist that releases the lantern.

"There ain't much to say," is the reply. "I am a United States deputy marshal and was placed in charge of the vessel this noon. Whether her cargo contains arms and ammunition I can't say for sure, as she is not to be searched till tomorrow, but from the remarks dropped by some of the crew I'll bet a hat the cargo has been taken off. One of the crew was considerably under the weather when I came aboard and I gathered from his talk that some of the Isabel's cargo was shifted to another steamer, a long, black craft, some time after midnight or early this morning."

"What was the name of the other steamer?" inquires Ashley, a sudden suspicion entering his mind.

"Blessed if I know," replies the deputy marshal.

"The Semiramis, I'll wager $4 to a nickel," mutters Ashley, as he thanks the marshal and goes ashore.

CHAPTER XXX.

ON TO FAIR CUBA.

"There are only two bits of evidence needed to complete my moral conviction that I am the only person connected with the Raymond tragedy who is not in Cuba or on his way thither," remarks Ashley, loquitur, as he boards a cross-town car. "One is the assurance that Cyrus Felton and Miss Hathaway have left the St. James Hotel with no intention of an immediate return; the other, the knowledge that Phillip Van Zandt has closed his quarters in the Wyoming flats for an indefinite period. I believe I will try the St. James first."

He does. The clerk smiles benignly upon him when he inquires for the Vermonters. "Gone, Jack; but you were not forgotten," he says. "The day clerk turned this over to me," extracting a note from the letter rack.

"Thank you, Ed," acknowledges Ashley. He tears open the note and reads:

"Dear Mr. Ashley: I regret very much that circumstances have made it necessary to postpone indefinitely the luncheon for this afternoon at 1, to which I had looked forward with much pleasure. We have just learned that in order to reach Cuba we must sail on the City of Havana, which leaves New York at 11 o'clock to-day. With many thanks for your kindnesses, believe me, sincerely yours,   Louise Hathaway."

"Far from enlightening me, this note only plunges me deeper in the fog," thinks Ashley, sniffing the faint odor of violet that clings to the dainty stationery. "She asserts here that she is going to Cuba on the City of Havana, yet I discover her aboard the Semiramis. At any rate they have gone to Cuba, and there is no particular reason for my visiting Van Zandt's apartments. It is getting late, anyway, and I believe I will return to the office. If Ricker is in a good-humored mood I will attempt to convince him that the only feature which the paper at present lacks is a live man at Havana who can tell the difference between an overwhelming Spanish or Cuban victory and a fifth-rate scrimmage that a dozen New York policemen could quell in ten minutes."

Ashley swings himself upon a Broadway car and lapses into a meditation. "How the deuce do Miss Hathaway and Cyrus Felton come to be aboard the Semiramis?" And if Ernest Stanley is Phillip Van Zandt, where did he get the money to own such a yacht? Forty or fifty thousand dollars of Raymond National Bank funds wouldn't pay for one side of the Semiramis. But it may not be his yacht. I have simply assumed so because he looked as if he owned the ocean as well. Good gracious, I should be inclined to regard Miss Hathaway's disappearance as a clear case of abduction but for the fact that the fair Louise appeared entirely satisfied with her surroundings when I focused the America's glasses upon her graceful self. I am beginning to believe that I am clear off my reckoning on Van Zandt. The Semiramis may be owned by the Cubans and he may simply be one of the leaders of the expedition. And he may not be Ernest Stanley at all, although I think—hang it! I don't know what I think. I shall quit thinking from now on. It is too hard work."

Much relieved by this determination, Ashley sits at his desk, lights his briar and dashes off a short sketch of the detained filibustering vessel. This he tosses over to the night-desk men, and strolls into the city editor's den.

"When you are at leisure, Mr. Ricker, I should like to bore you for five or ten minutes," he announces.

"I am at leisure now, Jack. Sit down. It has been a rather light night and there is an unusual lull just at present. What is on your mind?"

"It is something like half a dozen years since I began work on the paper, is it not?"

"Just about, my son."

"And during that time I have never kicked on an assignment or asked for any particular job."

"Yes; if I recollect rightly, that is about the size of it," remarks Ricker dryly. "Now, what can I do for you?"

"I should like the assignment of war correspondent at Havana."

The city editor is silent for a moment.

"I am sorry you did not speak of this Havana business before," he says, encircling the pastepot with a ring of smoke. "Unfortunately I have mapped out two or three months' work for you at a place a good many miles from the capital of Cuba."

Ashley's face does not reveal the disappointment he feels.

"All right, Mr. Ricker, I have no kick coming. I will break another one of my rules and ask what the assignment is before I have been notified of it."

"It is an important mission, my son, and the selection of the man to fill the place does not come within my department. But as a good man was needed I urged the desirability of putting you on the job."

"You are very kind," murmurs Ashley.

"I intended to communicate to you his wishes tonight," resumes Ricker. "In fact, I received the assignment for you an hour ago and you would have found it in your box in the morning." The city editor tosses over a yellow envelope and Ashley finds therein the brief notification:

"Beginning March 18, Mr. Ashley will enter upon the duties as war correspondent at Santiago de Cuba."

Ashley looks up and catches the indulgent smile of his chief.

"Ricker, you're a jewel," he says, warmly, extending his hand. The friendship between the two men has long since leveled the wall of official dignity.

"I had no idea you wanted the job," smiles the city editor.

"Until to-day I had no desire to visit Cuba," replies

Ashley. "But at present I want to go the worst way—or the best way. And my wish to reach Cuban soil is not greatly influenced by personal reasons, either. I expect some day to turn over to you a story that will cover a good share of the first page and just now the trail is winding under the flags of three nations—Spain, Cuba and the United States. But why Santiago, instead of Havana?"

"For the reason that, as you may see by a look over to-night's telegrams, the eastern province of Cuba is likely to be the principal theater of the struggle for independence. You know the sort of stuff we want. Statements of fact, above all. You may have some difficulty in getting us the facts by wire, as the government controls the cables; but there are the mails, and in addition to the usual grind you might send a two or three column chatty letter every fortnight or so that would be interesting reading. Spend all the money that is necessary. Get right out into the fighting; there isn't one chance in a million of your being hurt. Above all, send us facts. We cannot pay too much for facts."

"Have you considered how I am to reach Santiago? You know there are no steamer lines running to the island."

"That has been arranged. The bulletin was received early this evening that the new cruiser America had been ordered to Santiago. The managing editor used his influence, and permission to send a representative on the vessel has kindly been granted. There is some value in being on the right side of an administration. The cruiser sails the day after to-morrow, the 18th."

Ashley and Ricker soon complete their talk and Jack starts for home in a complacent condition of mind. Arriving at his rooms he slips into a dressing-gown and stretches himself in an easy-chair for a smoke-lined night-cap, and as the rings curl upward he sees in fancy the various actors in the Raymond drama passing in review before a tropical background of hazy blue hills and palm-shaded groves.

Suddenly he utters an exclamation: "Jupiter! How

is Barker to get to Cuba? He must have shot off to
Key West without reading the morning paper, and he
probably was not aware that there are no steamers running from Key West any more than from New York or
other ports. When he does learn that fact his remarks
will not be fit for publication. Well, I suppose, he will
get there somehow, even if he has to swim. But in all
probability I shall reach the island before him.

"The trail is plain. It leads to Cuba, and somewhere
in the gem of the Antilles the threads of the Raymond
murder mystery will touch and cross and interweave."

CHAPTER XXXI.

THE FLAG OF CUBA.

"We shall have a race, Don Manada—a battle royal.
.he new United States cruiser America has just steamed
out of the bay ahead of us and we shall soon be abreast
of her."

"A race, Senor Van Zandt? Santissimo! We shall
have racing enough before we get to Cuba without challenging unsuspicious warships and courting investigation."

Van Zandt laughs at the Cuban gentleman's anxious
tones. "I told you, my friend, that once on the high seas
nothing short of a cannon ball can overhaul the Semiramis. Come on deck in an hour, senor, and I will
prove to you what may now seem an idle boast."

For excellent reasons Manada is keeping in the background as much as possible. But he finds the luxurious
cabin of the Semiramis much to his liking, and he smokes
and dreams of "Cuba Libre" while the Semiramis steams
down the bay and out upon the bosom of the Atlantic,
and when he goes on deck, wrapped in the long semi-
military cloak which effectually conceals his person, the

sight which greets his eyes fills him with apprehension, though challenging his liveliest interest.

The battle of steam is well under way. The America is less than a dozen lengths astern and presents a beautiful sight to the people on the Semiramis. The glistening white hull plows the water at a speed which dashes the spray high in air from the delicately carved cutwater, and the triple funnels vomit great clouds of inky smoke. Manada's eyes rove to the United States flag whipping out in the breeze and he mutters a favorite malediction as he thinks of the insurgent arms stored in the hold of the Semiramis.

But as he grows aware that the yacht of his strange friend is drawing away from the American man-of-war he becomes the incarnation of suppressed excitement. And when Van Zandt claps him on the shoulder and shouts in his ear, "Well, senor, what do you think of the Semiramis?" the Cuban shouts back enthusiastically: "El Semiramis es un diablo verdadero!"

Without the change of a muscle in his weather-beaten face, Capt. Sam Beals paces the bridge of the Semiramis, while the exciting duel of steam and steel continues, not a gesture or ejaculation indicating that the beautiful yacht is literally steaming away from the cruiser—a vessel heralded far and wide as the speediest craft among all the navies of the world.

But if the chief officer is apparently undisturbed, the same cannot be said of any other person on board. The excitement of the race has roused the owner of the yacht from his cold reserve, and as with sparkling eye and eager step he hurries from the engine-room to the quarterdeck, noting with each return the slowly but steadily lengthening space of open water that separates the two vessels, Louise Hathaway mentally retracts her decision that Phillip Van Zandt is cold and unsympathetic.

As for Miss Hathaway herself, she is thoroughly imbued with the spirit of the race. Securely sheltered from the fierce rush of wind which the tremendous speed of the Semiramis causes to sweep over the deck, she makes an attractive picture as she watches the race. The svelte form is outlined in a gown of navy blue; the beautiful face is framed in a golden aureole of wavy locks; the matchless blue eyes glisten with unwonted excitement, and a delicate color tints her cheek. It is not strange that Van Zandt divides his time between the race and his fair passenger.

Even pale, stern-faced Cyrus Felton has for the nonce became stirred by the infectious excitement, and with a zest that he has not manifested for years he watches the unavailing efforts of the warship to overhaul the pleasure craft.

"Isn't there more and blacker smoke pouring from the America's stacks?" inquires Miss Hathaway, as the owner of the Semiramis returns from a brief interview with the engineer, with the cheery assurance that the engines are running as smoothly as if the yacht were moving at quarter-speed.

"She is surely making more smoke and, if I mistake not, more speed," answers Van Zandt, a shade of anxiety replacing his almost boyish enthusiasm. "Mr. Beals, what think you of it?" turning to the executive officer; "is she gaining on us?"

"She has just put on her forced draught, sir, and is now running at her top speed. She is gaining, now, but——"

Without finishing the sentence the captain presses the electric bells which communicate with the engine-room. It is soon apparent that the yacht has not until now reached the limit of her speed. The regular vibrations that mark the revolutions of the twin shafts become one prolonged shiver, and the black hull is hurled through the water at incredible speed.

The effect becomes noticeable in short order. The white mass astern grows "fine by degrees and beautifully less," and as Capt. Beals closes his glass with a snap he remarks, complacently: "She'll be hull down in an hour or two if she doesn't blow out a cylinder head before that time."

Just about this time Van Zandt and Manada go below and reappear a few moments later with a closely rolled silken flag, which Van Zandt hands to the captain with the command that it be hoisted to the breeze. Without even examining the emblem, the imperturbable executive officer bends the silken roll upon the halyards. A few hearty pulls by a stalwart blue-jacket and the ensign reaches the masthead, where the stiff breeze quickly breaks it out.

As a singular flag, with a solitary star in a triangular field of blue, is revealed to the wondering gaze of passengers and crew, Don Manada reverently bares his head and his lips frame the words "Viva Cuba Libre!"

Suddenly there is borne to their ears, above the whistling of the wind and the mighty pulsations of the machinery, the sullen boom of cannon. All eyes instinctively seek the America. A puff of white issues from her forward barbette, and as Capt. Beals returns his glass to its socket, he tells Van Zandt:

"She has saluted the Semiramis and dipped her ensign. She is bearing off to windward and gives up the race."

"She saw the flag, do you think?"

"Doubtless," Mr. Beals replies, with a grim smile. "Shall we slacken speed, sir?"

"Only to natural draught. I wish to make our destination as soon as possible. And by the way, Mr. Beals, you may haul down the flag. It has served its purpose for the present," pointing to the enraptured Don Manada.

Then Van Zandt conducts his passengers below and is prepared for Miss Hathaway's question:

"Is that your personal emblem, Mr. Van Zandt?"

"No, Miss Hathaway," is the calm response. "That is the flag of the Cuban Republic. You are now under the protection of the provisional government of the gem of the Antilles. Permit me to introduce to you Don Rafael Manada, minister of war of the infant republic. Long may she wave!"

Manada bows low and looks vastly gratified by the official title jestingly conferred upon him. Cyrus Felton's face, however, is darkened by a frown and Miss Hathaway is not at all pleased.

"Will you not take seats and make yourselves entirely

easy?" Van Zandt proceeds, unruffled by the cold demeanor of his passengers.

"Perhaps I should have told you before you embarked," explains Van Zandt, with a glance at Miss Hathaway that does much toward reassuring her, "that although we are bound for Cuba, our primary destination is not Santiago. The Semiramis has a cargo of arms and ammunition which I have undertaken to deliver to the Cuban revolutionists. Senor Manada is the supercargo. Believe me," he adds, as Miss Hathaway pales at the word "revolutionists," "there is absolutely no danger, not the slightest—and least of all to you. Even if my yacht were apprehended—though I do not believe there is a vessel on the waters of the globe that can overtake her—you would be subject to no annoyance and but little inconvenience. After we have discharged our cargo we will proceed at once to Santiago, and you will be landed much earlier than if you had gone by a regular steamer. And I am sure this vessel is fully as comfortable as any of those stuffy, crowded craft."

"Then we are aboard a filibustering expedition," declares Mr. Felton, harshly.

"Hardly that. You are on board an American yacht, manned by American seamen, with just one Cuban patriot, a man as honorable and true as yourself, Mr. Felton." Van Zandt's voice is stern and dignified. "I am not a Cuban partisan, but liberty to me is as precious as the air of heaven. Until a few hours ago there was no thought of the cargo now beneath us. The arms were designed to go by another vessel. But at the last moment the plans of the patriots were betrayed. Then it was that I stepped in and offered the services of my yacht to convey the much-needed aid to the down-trodden men of the Antilles."

"And meanwhile you have jeopardized the safety of Miss Hathaway and myself," Mr. Felton sneers. "Suppose we are intercepted by a Spanish warship? Think you that they will not regard us—myself at least—as members of this expedition? What then, Mr. Van Zandt?"

The latter's lip curls slightly. "Again I assure you that there is absolutely no danger. I will answer for your safety on this voyage with my life." Then to Louise, with a look that brings a flush to her fair face: "Have you no faith in the yacht, if not in her owner, Miss Hathaway?"

"I think that Mr. Felton is needlessly alarmed," is that young lady's composed reply. "As for the yacht, I am quite carried away with it, figuratively as well as literally. This is my first voyage, Mr. Van Zandt, and if you will insure me against mal de mer, that dread bugbear of the voyageur, I will try to brave, with becoming equanimity, the perils of the Spanish main."

Cyrus Felton, however, is decidedly alarmed by Van Zandt's admission of the incidental errand of the Semiramis. A strong distrust of her owner begins to grow in his mind; this added to the qualms of seasickness, which have begun to make themselves felt, renders him thoroughly miserable in spirit and body, and without raising another objection he asks to be shown to his stateroom.

It must be confessed that Van Zandt does not manifest heartfelt regret at Mr. Felton's unhappy condition, and even Miss Hathaway is somewhat perfunctory in her expressions of sympathy. An unaccountable confidence in the handsome owner of the Semiramis has replaced her early distrust, and, happily exempt from the "dread bugbear of the voyageur," she accepts with pleasure Van Zandt's proposition that they explore the yacht.

The Semiramis is fair to look upon, from capstan to rudder, and from keelson to main truck. The Vermont maiden marvels at the comfort, convenience and luxury on every hand. The palatial saloon, with its unusually high ceiling, furnished in oriental magnificence and including a superb upright piano, Miss Hathaway's eye notes approvingly; the commodious staterooms, arranged en suite, with the respectable appearing stewardess in charge; the plain but ample and scrupulously neat quarters of the crew; the engineroom, with its masses of highly polished steel and brass—all possess elements of interest to the girl.

That night, as she lays her head on her pillow, "rocked in the cradle of the deep," she suddenly starts as if from a dream. For there comes to her ears again, from somewhere, that melody strangely sweet, yet filled with subtle melancholy, the andante of her beloved sonata.

Then a light goes up, as the Germans have the saying, and Miss Hathaway understands now her blindly placed confidence in the master of the Semiramis. For Don Caesar de Bazan is Phillip Van Zandt and—and—

But what Miss Hathaway thinks about as Atlantic's waves lull her to slumber would certainly interest the young man who sits up far into the night, chatting and smoking with the "minister of war of the Cuban republic" while the Semiramis rushes on her eventful voyage to the tropics.

CHAPTER XXXII.

THE FLAG OF CASTILE.

"Twelve hours from now, Miss Hathaway, you will have your first glimpse of Cuba. Then, our business transacted, a quick and uninterrupted run to Santiago, and tomorrow you will be on terra firma."

"It has been a remarkably short voyage, Mr. Van Zandt."

"Deplorably so. I never before regretted the speed of the Semiramis, but now—would that she were as snaillike as the old West Indian tub we overhauled yesterday. Can I prevail upon you, Miss Hathaway, to again favor me with my pet Chopin nocturne? The electric fans render the saloon as comfortable as the deck."

"My poor playing is always at your service, Mr. Van Zandt. I assure you that I never expected to enjoy a voyage, to Cuba or elsewhere, as I have this. Your kindness in granting us—"

"My kindness was purely selfish," interposes Van Zandt.

It is easy to see that for two people on board the yacht the last few days have swiftly sped. Van Zandt and Miss Hathaway have been much in each other's company. Confidences have been neither asked nor given, but a mutual sympathy has taken root that might prove destructive to the reserve of one and the "marble" of the other were the voyage to the tropics to last many days longer.

Cyrus Felton is restricted to his stateroom most of the time, a victim of the malady of the sea and a gnawing, indefinable distrust of the owner of the yacht. As for Don Manada, he divides his attention between the huge cigars from which his fingers or teeth are never free, and a careful outlook for any of the Spanish squadron that is supposed to blockade the coast of the isle of Cuba.

But the sensuous indolence of the tropic day and the glories of the tropic night lure Van Zandt and Miss Hathaway into dreams of peace and hope and fulfillment. The days spent on the quarterdeck, sheltered by an awning from the rays of the sun, the speed of the yacht providing a delightful breeze, glide gently into the brief twilight. The great stars shoot out of the blue with quivering points of fire, and the wind sighs musically through the rigging as the tireless steam drives the boat through the phosphorescent waves.

"Consider what the voyage would have been to me without your presence," continues Van Zandt, as he leads the way to the saloon. "With Don Manada there, engrossed in Quixotic schemes for achieving the independence of his beloved country, and Capt. Beals as communicative as a sphinx, your society has saved me from myself—a synonym for dreariness. And now for the nocturne."

While Van Zandt is telling Miss Hathaway that she is the only woman he has ever heard play Chopin intelligently, and the latter is modestly disclaiming such ability, the musical echo of the lookout's call is passed to the saloon:

"Sail ho!"

"Where away?" is the challenge.

"On the weather bow.   A large steamer, judging from her smoke!"

Don Manada casts his cherished cigar to the waves and glues his eyes to the telescope.

As announced, the unknown vessel is directly on the weather bow and will pass within half a mile of the Semiramis, if the two craft hold to their present courses.

The captain intently watches the approaching vessel. The Semiramis is far beyond the five-mile limit of the Cuban coast, but if the unknown is a Spanish cruiser she may become suspicious of the trim yacht.

It therefore behooves the American steamer to insure the stranger a wide berth if the latter displays the arms of Castile; to show a clean pair of heels, in the vernacular of the sailor, if flight is necessary.

Again are preparations made to force the Semiramis to her highest speed.   The awnings are removed, the boats once more unswung from the davits, the force of stokers in the engine-room augmented by half a score of sturdy seamen, and soon the roaring of the forced draught in the funnels again drowns the hum of the engines.

At rail or in rigging, from bridge or quarterdeck the people of the Semiramis watch intently the approaching vessel, whose funnels and upper works are now visible through the glass.

The Semiramis bears gradually to the westward, to afford the stranger at least three miles leeway.   Suddenly Capt. Beals lays aside his glasses and rubs his chin thoughtfully.

"Do you care to show your papers to the Don?" he asks Van Zandt.

"To the Don?   Is she a Spaniard, sure?   But we shall pass a comfortable distance to windward of her and she will not attempt to interrupt us."

"She has already changed her course and is bearing directly across our bows.   See!"

The unknown, now less than ten miles distant, seems to be steaming at full speed for a point directly in the course of the Semiramis. Her broadside is now visible to the anxious watchers on the yacht. She is apparently an armored cruiser of perhaps 5,000 tons, her hull painted a dull and featureless gray. No flag or emblem is as yet displayed from her taut and business-like rigging.

"She is painted and cleared for action. She is—ah! I thought so!"

A flag is broken from the cruiser's masthead, and Capt. Beals, as he focuses his binocular upon the streaming emblem, mutters between his teeth: "The flag of Castile!"

"'Tis a Spanish warship, Senor Van Zandt!" exclaims Manada, who has been studying the stranger. "Can your beautiful craft bear us from harm's way? I fear that yonder ship is the Infanta Isabel, the latest and most formidable accession to the navy of our hated oppressors. She has been detailed to intercept vessels supposed to bear arms and re-enforcements to our friends, and especially to watch for and destroy our gallant Pearl of the Antilles."

"Have no fears, Don Manada. Your cargo is safe. We will show the Spaniard a trick or two; eh, Beals?"

Capt. Beals does not reply in words to his employer's confident assertion, but an observant man might distinguish a slight relaxation of the muscles about his mouth.

The Semiramis holds steadily on her course. Only the increasing clouds of smoke that pour from her funnels indicate that anything out of the ordinary is expected of the yacht.

Only six miles distant! Five! Four!

A puff of white that rolls lazily from the forward deck of the cruiser is succeeded by a dull roar.

"Show the Don our colors," Capt. Beals orders the second officer.

While the smoke from the cannon yet lingers above the Spaniard's deck the glorious stars and stripes unfurl from the mainmast of the Semiramis, and snap gayly, defiantly, upon the breeze. And still the American yacht continues to steadily lessen the distance that separates the two craft.

Boom!

Another puff of white, followed a few seconds later by the report; and this time the watchers on the yacht can see the flash of the gun.

Only two miles distant now, and the Spanish warship, apparently convinced that the American understands and designs to obey the peremptory summons to heave to, has slowed her engines until the cruiser has barely headway on the long swells.

Calmly pacing the bridge, as if a thousand miles separated the vessels—nearly equal in size, but how dissimilar in destructive power!—Capt. Beals has not indicated a slowing of the yacht's engines, although the bow of the Semiramis points at the steep side of the Spaniard, directly amidship.

Not half a dozen lengths away!

·The officers and men on the man-of-war are clearly visible to those on the yacht. The captain and his sub-alterns are grouped on the quarterdeck, the marines amidship, the blue-jackets crowding the rail and adjacent rigging. The cruiser is stationary on the water.

But with no sensible diminution of speed the Semiramis bears upon the Spaniard, the white foam dashing high on either side of her bow. Capt. Beals is fingering the electric buttons that regulate the speed and course of the yacht.

The Spanish captain nearly drops his speaking trumpet. What is El Americano thinking of? He cannot stop in five times his own length at such a frightful speed! Is he mad? Ah! Dios! Caramba! And a dozen more Castilian expletives poured forth in a torrent of astonishment, rage and chagrin.

For with a sudden turn to the windward that causes the yacht to career until her white sides below the water line gleam for an instant in the sunlight, with an accession of speed that sends her forward as a whip would a nervous horse, the Semiramis darts by the stern of the Spanish man-of-war, the smoke from her furnaces enveloping for a moment the cruiser's afterdeck.

Two minutes later she is a mile astern of the warship, her long white trail sparkling in the sunlight, and the red, white and blue still snapping defiantly at the mast-head.

"I wonder if the Don can turn in five times his own length," observes the sententious Mr. Beals, as he watches the warship slowly getting under way.

Whether he can or cannot is not at this time to be demonstrated. The cruiser makes no attempt to about ship, but another report booms from the forward gun, followed a second or two later by one from the aft bar-bette, and a solid shot ricochets along the waves astern of the Semiramis and plunges beneath the water an eighth of a mile distant.

Van Zandt grows grave as he realizes the significance of this last shot, but a glance at the receding cruiser con-vinces him of the futility of the cannonade. The Span-iard, too, appears convinced, and the cruiser is soon lost to view in the expanse of ocean.

The rest of the day the Semiramis holds unmolested her course for the mountain-girth shores of Cuba. As night draws on the engines are slowed, and, with fires banked and double watch posted, the yacht quietly rocks on the bosom of the deep. A wavy outline on the horizon indicates the southern coast of the revolution-racked isle and somewhere on that outline is the sequestered little harbor of Cantero.

It is a weary, an unnerving vigil, for Don Manada at least. For hours his anxious gaze sweeps the horizon, while the Semiramis rides the breasting waves as grace-fully as a summer bird soars into the blue.

As the first shafts of light radiate from the emerging disk, Louise Hathaway, whom the unwonted excitement of the preceding day has driven early from her pillow, cries out with a girlish enthusiasm that brings a smile to the face of Capt. Beals: "Sail ho! Sail ho!"

Every one springs to rail or rigging. "Where away?" is the quick challenge of Mr. Beals.

"Right there, sir," is the unnautical response of Miss Hathaway, and she indicates a point not five degrees north of the rising orb of day.

With the glass at his eyes, the taciturn commander of

the Semiramis watches intently the speck on the glowing horizon that means much to the excited Manada at his elbow and to the latter's struggling fellow-patriots on the isle whose outlines are now bathed in the flood of sunlight.

Is it another Spanish warship, or is it the looked-for Cuban cruiser, the doughty Pearl of the Antilles?

CHAPTER XXXIII.

AN AFFRONT AND AN APOLOGY.

The Semiramis rests stationary upon the surface of the water, but there are scenes of activity in the engine room.   The columns of smoke from her stacks grow into thick black volumes, and the roar of escaping steam drowns ordinary conversation.

On deck, officers, passengers and crew are watching the rapidly growing spot upon the horizon.   That the approaching vessel is steaming very fast is apparent.   Her upper works are visible as Capt. Beals signals for the Semiramis to steam ahead at full speed.   The course of the latter is laid to pass the stranger a mile or two to windward, if she does not change her present course.

Don Manada has possessed himself of the captain's glasses and is earnestly scanning the distant steamer. Suddenly, in a very paroxyism of joy he embraces the owner of the yacht.

"It is the Pearl!" he cries; "the Pearl of the Antilles! Santisima!   Now will you display the flag of Cuba Libre?"   The English language fails to express the sentiments of the Cuban patriot at this juncture, and he launches a flood of Castilian that bewilders Van Zandt.

At a nod from the latter, however, Capt. Beals causes the fateful emblem of Cuba to be run up to the masthead. The silken banner is barely unfurled by the wind ere there are signs of excitement on board the strange steamship. A duplicate of the Semiramis' ensign is displayed, and then the course of the vessel is changed and she steams rapidly toward the yacht. Don Manada is not mistaken. The steamship is the famous Pearl of the Antilles.

The Semiramis has slowed down her engines, and awaits the approach of the insurgent cruiser. As the latters nears the yacht the resemblance of the two steamships becomes more striking. The Pearl is almost precisely the length of the Semiramis, and like her is rigged with two masts. Her two smokestacks are set at the same angle as those of the yacht and like the latter she is equipped with twin propellers. On deck, however, there is a decided difference. The engines of the Pearl are protected by heavy plates of steel, while on her forward deck a sort of turret has been improvised, within which, the people on the Semiramis can readily guess, is the famous "Yankee gun," the dynamite cannon whose well-aimed projectile sent the Spanish Mercedes to the bottom.

Five lengths away the Pearl becomes stationary on the waves, while through a speaking tube, the voluble Manada acquaints her commander with the character and mission of the yacht. A boat is lowered from the insurgent craft and is rowed to the side of the Semiramis, and a moment later a distinguished looking man in the undress uniform of an officer of the Spanish navy is clasped in the arms of Don Manada.

"Senor Van Zandt," the latter says, "permit me to present to you Capt. Gerardo Nunez, the commander of yonder vessel. Senor Van Zandt," he explains extravagantly to Capt. Nunez, "is the good angel who rendered it possible for us to convey the much-needed arms and ammunition in our hold to our struggling compatriots."

Capt. Nunez cordially grasps the hand of Van Zandt. "Senor," he says, "I am more than pleased to meet you, and join with Don Manada in expressing the gratitude of our people for your services in the cause of liberty."

Van Zandt waves his hand. " 'Tis nothing. My sympathies are with the insurgents and being in position to help Don Manada out of a box"—the Cuban flushes at the recollection of his last conversation with Mrs. Harding—"I was only too glad to do it. But what is the latest news from the seat of war?"

Capt. Nunez' eyes light up with enthusiasm. "Glorious!" he says. "Gen. Masso has just achieved a victory over 3,000 Spanish troops in the Puerto Principe District. El Terredo is receiving constant additions to his forces and the outlook was never brighter. It is to equip El Terredo's army that these arms and ammunition will be used."

"El Terredo?" inquires Van Zandt. "Is he not attached to the Pearl of the Antilles?"

"He has been up to within a week, but is now on shore duty. By the way, senor," remarks the Cuban commander, casting a glance over the deck of the Semiramis, "you have a magnificent yacht, and I doubt not she is as speedy as she is handsome."

"Speedy!" breaks in Don Manada. "She is as swift as the wind! She sailed away from the America, the fastest cruiser in the United States Navy, and as for the Infanta Isabel—poof! She snaps her fingers at her!"

Capt. Beals approaches the group at this moment and is introduced to the Cuban captain.

"I think, sir," he says to Van Zandt, "if we are to transfer our cargo it would be advisable to waste no time. There is no knowing when a Spanish gunboat will show up."

This advice is manifestly so timely that no time is lost in following it. The two hulls are laid side by side, the smoothness of the water permitting the operation in safety and hundreds of brawny arms are quickly at work transferring the cargo from the Semiramis to the Pearl.

At last the work is completed and Van Zandt looks inquiringly at Don Manada.

"Will you continue with the yacht or accompany the cargo on board the Pearl?" he asks.

The Cuban emissary hesitates. "If I might add to the already heavy debt of gratitude I owe you——"

"Oh, that's all right," interrupts Van Zandt. "So you will remain with us. I am glad of your company.

We sail for Santiago and afterward"—he hesitates a moment, his eyes wandering to Miss Hathaway, who is watching curiously the motley crew of the Pearl—"well, eventually back to New York."

Manada nods gratefully. "I am of more service to the cause in America than I could possibly be in Cuba," he says, apologetically.

The adieus are said, the lines cast off, and the Semiramis and Pearl move slowly apart. The latter shapes her coarse for the little harbor of Cantero, where the arms and ammunition are to be landed.

"'We are but ten hours' sail from Santiago, Miss Hathaway," Van Zandt remarks, as Louise idly watches the rapidly disappearing Pearl. "Then you will bid adieu to the Semiramis."

"Regretfully, indeed, Mr. Van Zandt. The last few days have sped all too quickly."

"'We take no heed of time but by its flight,'" quotes Van Zandt. "How long do you expect to remain in Cuba?"

Louise turns a troubled face toward the owner of the yacht. "That I cannot say. It depends upon Mr. Felton. He has business interests to look after, and if the climate agrees with him we may remain several months."

There is a silence for a little, the thoughts of both dwelling on the coming parting at even.

"Miss Hathaway," says Van Zandt, suddenly. "I am but an idle fellow, with nothing to call me hence but my own inclinations. Would it be distasteful to you if I should attach myself to your party while in Cuba? The country is necessarily unsettled during the war and perhaps I might be of service. I. am familiar with the Spanish language, which I believe Mr. Felton is not, and I should like to see something of the country. Please tell me frankly if for any reason I would be de trop?"

Van Zandt's luminous orbs are fixed on the fair face of Louise as he awaits the answer to his question. For a moment her blue eyes return his gaze. Then the golden-fringed lids fall and a soft blush mantles her face.

"I certainly should not be averse to your joining our party," she murmurs softly, "if—if it be your pleasure."

"Thank you," Van Zandt returns, simply, and a moment after Miss Hathaway retires to her stateroom.

"Well, Manada," remarks Van Zandt, slapping the Cuban upon the back, "your first engagement as supercargo must be rated a success, eh? The arms and ammunition—the biggest single consignment ever sent from the States, I think you said—have been safely delivered into the hands of the insurgents, without the loss of a single Winchester or cartridge.   Why this pensive look?"

"Only thoughts of the past, senor. I was——"

What were Don Manada's thoughts will never be known, for the people on the yacht are electrified by the hail from the bridge, "Ship ahoy!" followed a second later by the additional information, "Dead ahead and bearing this way!"

"There is no special necessity for evading her now, whoever she is, I presume, sir?" inquires Capt. Beals, removing his glasses from his eyes.

"None whatever," is Van Zandt's prompt reply. "Our papers are straight and we have nothing contraband, unless it be the Don there. Let them look us over if they wish."

"She's not a very large craft," comments the taciturn executive officer of the yacht, as the two vessels continue to lessen the distance between them.

"Probably one of the blockading fleet," is Van Zandt's surmise.

He is evidently right, for the stranger at this point displays the Spanish flag and at the same time the report of a cannon echoes across the water.

"Show our colors," orders Van Zandt, and the flag of the great republic is caressed by the soft southern breeze. Another shot is fired from the Spaniard, and as the Semiramis slows up a third cloud of white floats from the side of the war vessel, followed by the sudden boom of a heavier gun.

As the Semiramis steams slowly toward the Spaniard, now distant less than a mile, a forth report is heard.

"Shotted, by heaven!" ejaculates Capt. Beals, his eyes glued to the glass; "and the Don has changed her course and is standing off to pepper us. He is one of those tin-clad gunboats, only half our tonnage, and pays no attention to our flag." Still another shot is fired, and a solid shot skips over the waves, barely two lengths astern of the yacht.

"Shall we ram him, sir? We can send him to Davy Jones' locker in ten minutes, and not harm the yacht, either."

Van Zandt's eyes glance aloft at the Stars and Stripes standing out clear and free from the maintop, and then his eyes turn to the Spanish gunboat.

"Steam toward him full speed," he says at length, "and if he fires on the American flag again"—the white teeth shut with an ominous click—"ram him full amidship, let the consequences be what they may."

But the flag is not fired upon again. The Spaniard has once more laid a new course and is now bearing down full on the yacht. The two craft are quickly within hailing distance, and from the gunboat comes the inquiry in Spanish as to the name and character of the yacht.

"The Semiramis, pleasure craft, New York for Santiago," is Capt. Beals' reply.

The Spanish captain is profuse in apologies for firing on the yacht. She closely resembles a rebel craft, he explains, and the gunboat was sure she was that vessel, even if she did fly the American flag. Would the Semiramis accept his most humble apologies? His gunboat, La Pinta, was about to proceed to Santiago for orders, and if it please los Americanos they might sail thither in company, which would insure the stranger against the annoyance of being overhauled by some of the other numerous Spanish vessels blockading the ports.

Van Zandt consults with Capt. Beals.

"He wants to make sure we don't land anything," remarks the latter. "It might save some trouble to accompany him to Santiago."

Yes, the Spaniard is informed, the American accepts the apology and the escort of the gunboat to Santiago.

Before the brief southern twilight has drifted into night the Semiramis is lying at anchor in the harbor of Santiago, under the guns of the Spanish gunboat La Pinta.

CHAPTER XXXIV.

A SPANISH BILL OF FARE.

"I want some soft-boiled eggs, but I don't suppose you know a soft-boiled egg from a gas stove, eh?"

The waiter at the Hotel Royal, in Santiago, regards Jack Ashley with an expression as blank as a brick wall.

"Don't get the idea, I see," remarks Ashley. "Well, let me think. 'Huevos' means eggs, I know that much, but what the deuce is soft-boiled? I believe 'blondo' is soft, and soft eggs might express the idea. 'Blondo huevos,'" he tells the waiter, and the latter, though apparently puzzled, disappears.

For the next ten minutes Jack is occupied in receiving and sending back orders of eggs—eggs cooked in every conceivable style except soft-boiled. Finally in despair he selects a dish nearest to his wants, and gets along all right until he decides to have some chicken. An examination of the bill of fare fails to discover anything that looks like chicken, and the case appears hopeless.

"If I only had my phrase book with me I might do some business," he reflects. "As it is, I don't see any way out of it except to draw a picture of a chicken. Hold on; 'gallina' means hen, unless I have forgotten my studies, and if there is anything consistent in the linguistic diminutives of the Spanish language, 'gallinoso' must be the equivalent for chicken." So he orders "gallinoso" with a complacence born of a problem happily solved.

The waiter simply stares and waits patiently.

"'Gallinoso' doesn't go, then." Ashley looks the bill of fare over again. The most attractive item is "salchichas con aroz," but he does not dare risk that. Finally a happy thought occurs to him.

"Todos!" he orders. "Todos! Todos!" The waiter, with a grin of intelligence, hurries away and Ashley heaves a sigh of relief. "Great word, 'todos,'" he soliloquizes. "Most significant word in the language."

It is effective, at least, for the waiter arrives with a little of everything that the kitchen affords and Ashley manages to make out a meal.

Meanwhile he has noticed that his efforts at Spanish have vastly entertained a gentleman who sits at the table beyond and facing him. Particularly broad was his smile when the order for "gallinoso" was given. As Jack leisurely sorts out the most appetizing-looking of the array of greasy viands, he remarks: "If you were as hungry as I, senor, my attempts to secure a breakfast might strike you as being more tragic than humorous."

"I meant no offense," replies the senor. "You would yourself smile if you knew what 'gallinoso' is."

"So? What may it be, an octopus or a mule?"

"Almost as bad as either. It is a turkey buzzard."

"Ah, yes; they were probably just out of turkey buzzards. Oh, well, I'll get the hang of the language before I leave Cuba."

"Undoubtedly. It is easy of acquisition. You have, I assume, provided yourself with a phrase-book."

"A magnificent affair. It contains every possible phrase except the ones I have occasion to use."

The two finish their repast about the same time, and as they stroll out upon the veranda to enjoy the long, strong cigar that inevitably follows a Cuban breakfast the senor remarks:

"You are an American, I judge."

"New York," is the terse response.

"Have you been in Cuba long?"

"About two hours."

"Indeed? I was not aware that any steamers arrived to-day."

"Because of the blockade, eh? But I dropped in on the cruiser America."

"You are of the service?"

"No; I am just a plain American citizen."

"Well, senor, this is hardly a desirable time for Americans or others to visit Cuba."

"An eminently proper time for one in my line of business," replies Ashley. "I am a newspaper correspondent."

The senor looks the young man over critically. "Your profession is not regarded with especial favor at present by the Spanish Government," he says.

"I understand so," drawls Ashley. "Newspaper men have an unpleasant habit of stating facts, something the government is not particularly anxious to have abroad."

A flush of annoyance mounts the senor's face, and on the left cheek Ashley for the first time notices a small, crescent-shaped scar.

"Aha!" he thinks. "This gentleman rather answers my friend Barker's description of the party who left New York with the fair Mrs. Harding."

"The Government has no desire to conceal facts," asserts the senor, with some warmth, "but it naturally seeks to prevent the dissemination of false, exaggerated or malicious reports. What journal do you represent, senor?"

Ashley tenders his card. The senor glances at it and smiles half-derisively. "The Hemisphere! I had that very journal in mind," he says.

"My paper must be excused from feeling flattered, then."

"It was only a week or so ago," continues the senor, "that I read in your paper a sensational interview with a visionary enthusiast, which was a little more exaggerated and absurd than the average."

"That was before you left New York, probably," ventures Ashley, and the senor shoots a glance at him from a pair of keen black eyes. "You refer to the interview with Don Manada," goes on Ashley. "I had the pleasure of placing the distinguished Cuban's views before the public."

"I am not surprised," comments the senor, with quiet sarcasm.

"In other words you consider me a man who would deliberately put forth false, exaggerated or malicious reports."

"I did not say so, senor. I presume you are typical of your profession."

"And I believe I am. Our journal, like every other

decent paper, prints the news. If it were to investigate every dispatch that comes to it day by day there would be precious little information for the reader who turns to it each morning. If an injustice is occasionally done, the paper is ever willing to rectify its error and make all proper amends. You must naturally expect the American newspapers to favor the dispatches received from insurgent sources."

"Why, pray?"

"For the reason that little dependence can be placed upon the statements of the opposition. In fact," smiles Ashley, "the situation approximates somewhat the condition intimated in a joke now going the rounds of the press. A Spanish captain in surrendering to superior numbers or prowess, craves one boon at the hands of his conqueror. 'What is it?' asks the latter. 'Please announce the fact,' requests the Spanish captain, 'that I have won an overwhelming victory.'"

The senor fails to see anything amusing in the jest. "Do you intend to remain at Santiago?" he asks.

"For the present. The fighting appears to be principally at this end of the island. Later I may push on to Havana."

"There has been more than one instance of expulsion of foreign correspondents, senor."

"So I am told. Well, I shall do my duty, as well as I know how. I naturally sympathize with the Cubans, but I shall not permit my sympathies to lead me to color any reports of the war's progress. If a battle occurs to-morrow and the government forces are victorious, the simple facts in the case will be forwarded, without further comment than is required to make the story interesting. And if the Cubans win, the same impartiality will characterize my dispatch. I expect the same fair play that I extend. Is that not reasonable?"

"Well, at any. rate, I like your frankness," says the senor, with something approaching good humor. "I also like America and admire its people. Do your duty as you understand it, Senor Ashley, and should your zeal as a correspondent lead you into difficulty perhaps I may be of service to you."

"Thank you," acknowledges Jack. "But with my present limited means of identifying you, I should be more likely to be garroted or shot before I could send you word."

The senor smiles. "I am Gen. Murillo," he says. "Adios, Senor Ashley." And with a courtly bow the Spanish gentleman takes himself off.

"So," muses Ashley, looking after the retreating figure. "Gen. Juan Murillo, the chief of staff attached to the captain-general, is the patron of the beautiful Harding. I remember the Hemisphere noted his presence in New York. My lady's services must be booked for something out of the ordinary spy business. Murillo is in Santiago; so probably is she, but if this city is her base of operations she is likely to sail pretty close to the wind.

"Now, where on earth is Barker?" wonders Ashley. "Probably at the other end of the island, while the objects of his quest are at this end. The Semiramis rests serenely on the bosom of the bay, and Miss Hathaway and Messrs. Felton and Van Zandt are either aboard of her or are somewhere about the city. I believe I'll go out to the yacht and settle the question in my mind."

And he does. He is rowed out over the blazing sea by a sun-cured barquero and climbs to the deck of the Semiramis.

"Mr. Van Zandt?" repeats Capt. Beals, in response to Ashley's inquiry. "Left yesterday, sir: Where? Havana, I believe the destination was."

"And his passengers?" ventures Ashley. "I am a friend of theirs," he explains to Mr. Beals.

"His passengers went with him," the latter tells him.

Ashley is about to return to shore when he hears an exclamation and he sees coming toward him Don Rafael Manada, the distinguished member of the Cuban revolutionary society.

"Dios mio! Senor Ashley, I am delighted to see you," exclaims the volatile Manada, embracing him warmly. "What brings you here?"

"Business, my dear Don Manada. I am at present officiating as a war correspondent. Will you not come ashore and take dinner with me?"

"A thousand thanks, Senor Ashley; but," with a smile intended to be significant, "I believe it would be wise for me to remain here for the present."

"By the way," says Ashley, "you recollect that interview at the Fifth Avenue Hotel a week or so ago?" Manada nods smilingly. "Well, I met a gentleman to-day who spoke rather slightingly of the views which you therein expressed. Perhaps you know him. Gen. Murillo."

"Murillo!" cries the Cuban. "Ha! Is he in Santiago?"

"He was half an hour ago."

"Was he alone?   That is, was he not accompanied——"

"By the fair Mrs. Harding?" supplies Ashley.

Manada's face flushes. "Ah, you know her?" he says.

"Slightly," returns Jack. "No; Mrs. Harding was not with the general, though she may be in the neighborhood. They left New York together. Now, Don Manada, having imparted some information to you, I should esteem it a great favor if you would reciprocate." Ashley glances about and notices that they are out of hearing. "I will not ask you why you happen to be on the Semiramis, as I have no disposition to pry into your affairs, but I should like to know how Mr. Felton and Miss Hathaway came to be aboard of the yacht?"

Manada shrugs his shoulders. "I have not an idea," he says. "An hour before the Semiramis sailed they were driven to the pier in company with the owner of the yacht. Where they came from I cannot say."

"Did they appear to be well acquainted with one another?"

"Very nearly strangers, I should say. Senor Felton kept his stateroom during nearly all the voyage and seemed to avoid Senor Van Zandt."

Ashley is now getting some information of decided interest. "And Miss Hathaway? Did she appear to share the distrust or dislike?"

"Quite the contrary. They were together about all the time."

"Now, Don Manada, there is one query I should like to put to you."

"Come," smiles Manada, "I can guess what your question is to be."

"I will save you the trouble and ask it. As a man of years and experience, of keen discernment and calm conclusions, what should you say were the precise relations existing between Phillip Van Zandt and Louise Hathaway?"

Manada appears to reflect deeply. Then he says, with a gravity belied by the twinkle in his eyes: "Serious, my dear Senor Ashley; very serious."

"Thank you," responds Ashley. "Well, I believe I'll go ashore and get better acquainted with the natives. I hope to see you again, Don Manada."

"I shall probably be here until the yacht leaves, senor. Adios."

As Ashley is borne shoreward he digests the information extracted from his Cuban friend.

"So far as Miss Hathaway's tender regard is concerned, I appear to be a rank outsider," he soliloquizes. "But I have the consolation of knowing that I did not permit myself to fall in love with her. Rather a melancholy consolation, but philosophy was invented for just such cases as this.

"And Van Zandt. Well, Barker can doubt as much as he pleases, but I will stake my reputation as a soothsayer that Van Zandt and Ernest Stanley are one and the same man. And if Phillip Van Zandt is not a Nemesis, stalking on the trail of his prospective victim or victims, then I am indeed a prophet unworthy of honor in 'mine ain countree' or in the world at large."

CHAPTER XXXV.

A CAFE QUARREL.

"I suppose this is the Madison Square of Santiago," remarks Jack Ashley, as he notes approvingly the brilliant spectacle which the plaza affords, now that the tropic night is atoning for the enervating heat of the tropic afternoon. Santiago, like all Cuban cities, wakes up measurably early, bustles about for three hours or so, and then dozes or fans itself until the sun drops into the sea and night comes with scarcely a shadow of twilight.

And then Santiago wakes again with a start, and for a few more hours laughs and chatters, promenades and flirts until about 10 o'clock, when the curtain falls, not to rise again until the sun is well up the morning sky.

The nightly gathering on the plaza has been tersely described as "a scene of shoulders, arms, trains, jewels and cascarilla."

The women monopolize the plaza and the men the cafe, the latter a simple interior, a mere loafing-place for the Cuban, whose capacities as an idler are the result of many years' practice in the gentle art of doing nothing.

Into one of the cafés that border the panorama of gayety strolls Ashley. The place is crowded, but over in the farthest corner he sees a table at which only one person is seated. Toward this he threads his way, but when almost there his progress is impeded by a party of four who are taking up more space than the law of equality allows.

"Pardon me," remarks Jack, as he brushes past the chair of an unamiable-appearing individual in undress military attire. The latter moves reluctantly and growls something which Ashley suspects is not complimentary, and as he drops into a seat he asks the gentleman across the table: "Do you speak English, sir?"

"Occasionally," is the brief rejoinder.

"Then would you oblige me by translating the remark of the chap whose repose I just disturbed?"

"It's of no consequence," replies the other. "An impertinence upon Americans. The feeling against that people is very bitter in Santiago just now. The United States is suspected of encouraging practically as well as morally the present insurrection."

"Perhaps I had better go over and punch his head," observes Ashley. "His suspicions might be better grounded."

"It would be a waste of time and perhaps lead to a general row. He is only a Spanish captain who has invested his title with more importance than would suffice for the entire service. Spanish captains are as plentiful as Kentucky colonels."

"You speak by the card," laughs Ashley, as he orders a glass of jerez and a cigar. "Your English, too, is as pure as a New Yorker's—or perhaps I should say as unforeign. Pure English is not a drug in the New York market."

"I have resided in New York, as well as other parts of the United States. But after a short residence on this island a man drifts into the indolence and shiftlessness of the natives and loses much of his identity."

"He does not lose his Americanism, I hope."

"No; the same thrill comes over him when he sees the most beautiful of all flags streaming out on the breeze, and with it is increased his sense of the outrageous wrongs which the Cuban has suffered from generation to generation."

Ashley has been looking his acquaintance over with much interest, and the result of his "sizing up" is as follows:

Age, about Ashley's own; above the medium height, athletic of build, and straight as the proverbial arrow; general air denoting decision, dash, and a bit of recklessness. His garments are dark and somewhat travel-worn, and on his head, pulled down well over his eyes, he wears a soft hat that borders on the sombrero.

Just now he is scowling at the party of four near by, who are making merry apparently at the expense of the two young men.

"As I said before," observes Ashley, "if you will kindly translate the remarks of yonder chaps it will afford me considerable satisfaction to call them to order. Ah, if I could only tell them in Spanish what I think of them in English," he adds, recollecting an old opera-bouffe jest.

Ashley's acquaintance is evidently making an effort to keep his temper, but his resentment is apparent in the flash of his eyes and the red spot in each cheek.

"By Jove!" suddenly reflects Ashley, "perhaps our military friend understands English. I'll try him." Then to the apparent leading spirit of the quartet, who has just delivered himself of a sally that vastly amuses his companions, Ashley leans over and drawls: "Pardon me, senor, am I the subject of your mirth?"

The Spaniard may understand, but he makes no sign. The quartet set down their glasses and stare at the self-possessed young man who has risen and walked to their table and whose mild blue eyes run over the party in calm inquiry. And the young man notes that the time-killers for many tables around have ceased their chatter for the moment and are watching curiously the progress of the colloquy.

"I have reason to suspect," goes on Ashley, "that you are making a beastly nuisance of yourself, and unless you are anxious for a good American thrashing I would advise you to keep a civil tongue from now on. If you don't understand that I'll knock it through your head in short order."

The reply is a volley of red-hot Castilian, but Ashley is saved the trouble of attempting to comprehend it. For at this moment a long arm reaches by him and the Spanish captain is dealt a slap across the mouth that transforms his teeth for an instant into castanets.

Then there is confusion. The quartet spring to their feet and one of them seizes a bottle. But Ashley grips the uplifted arm with a wrist of steel and remarks in tones that carry conviction: "Easy, my friend, or I'll throw you through the side of the house."

The idlers in the cafe crowd about the combatants and the proprietor rushes up and protests against the disorder.

The Spanish captain and Ashley's friend glare at each other, and the latter, after pronouncing the words "Hotel Royal" with a significance appreciated by his antagonist, slips his arm through Ashley's and draws him from the cafe.

"Whither?" queries Jack, as they proceed down the street.

"To the Hotel Royal. I am stopping there for the night. And you?"

"Same cheerful hostelry. Is it the worst in Cuba?"

"The worst and the best. They are all off the same piece."

"Will you come up to my room?" asks he of the black eyes, when the hotel is reached. "We shall doubtless be waited upon presently."

"By our Spanish friend?"

"By his representative, more likely."

"But how is he to locate you?" questions Ashley. "No pasteboards were exchanged."

His companion smiles sardonically. "Capt. Raymon Huerta and I are not strangers," he says.

Even as he speaks there is a rap at the door and as it is thrown open in strides one of the Spanish quartet.

"Well, Senor Cardena," says the young man with the black eyes, glancing at the bit of pasteboard in his hand, "what is your pleasure?"

"What, Senor Navarro, you may expect," replies Cardena, declining stiffly the proffered chair. "Capt. Huerta demands satisfaction for the insult offered to him."

"Not only offered, but delivered," mutters Ashley, and he returns in kind Cardena's impertinent glance. "So my unknown friend's name is Navarro," he thinks.

"You may convey to Capt. Huerta my willingness to afford him the desired redress," says Navarro. "How will sunrise, on the beach below the city, answer?"

"I am authorized to make the necessary arrangements,

What you have proposed will be satisfactory. And the weapons?"

"Pistols, I suppose; I am provided with one."

"Hold on," puts in Ashley. "I have just the article. Excuse me a moment, gentlemen." Repairing to his room he extracts from his trunk two superb Smith & Wesson 38-caliber revolvers, and these he submits to Cardena and Navarro. Senor Cardena professes himself to be satisfied with the weapons and, with a perfunctory "Adios," he withdraws.

When he has gone Navarro tosses his arms impatiently and murmurs: "What a fool I am."

"All men are or have been at some period," Ashley assures him. "But what gives rise to your present self-accusation?"

"The thought that I permitted my temper to play the mischief with my judgment," is the gloomy reply. "A man has the right to risk his own life, but not the life, or what is dearer than life, of those whose interests he is intrusted with."

"See here," Ashley gently protests, "if there is any fighting to be done why not let me have the job? I began the row——"

"And I finished it. No, my friend, this affair must go on to the bitter end. Although, as you rightly suspected, you were the ostensible object of the remarks of the party at the cafe, they were in reality directed toward me. It was inevitable that Capt. Huerta and I should cross, though I might have to-night avoided a meeting which would better be left to the future. May I request you to second me in the meeting?"

"Assuredly, Senor Navarro. That is your name, I judge?"

"Yes; Emilio Navarro—quite Spanish, you see," with a peculiar smile. "And your name?"

"Jack Ashley; residence, New York; occupation, newspaper man; paper, the Hemisphere; ever heard of it?"

"The newspaper is not a stranger to me. Pardon me a few minutes," says Navarro, and he occupies himself in writing a somewhat lengthy letter, which he seals, without addressing, and hands to Ashley.

"Ashley, you are a man of honor," he says, laying one hand upon the newspaper man's shoulder. "Promise me that if anything happens to me to-morrow you will deliver that letter to a name I will whisper to you."

"I shall do so with profound regret, sir. The name?"

"Don Manuel de Quesada. He resides in the Pueblo de Olivet, on the edge of Santos, four miles west of Santiago."

Ashley places the letter in his pocket. "I will not fail you, if the occasion for my services should arise. But unless Huerta is more familiar with the American revolver than I believe him to be, I shall have the happiness of returning this document to you after you have filled him full of leaden satisfaction. How are you on the shoot, anyway?"

Navarro smiles grimly. "I have hit a playing card at fifty yards," he says.

"Oh, well; that's close enough markmanship. I am beginning to feel sorry for Huerta."

"Save your sympathy. I shall not kill him. And now, friend Ashley, I believe I'll go to bed. I have been riding all day and I am as tired as a dog. At daylight we start."

"At daylight it is. It is not too late to accept my offer to exchange places with you. I can't hit a playing card at fifty yards, but at least I am alone in the world, and, barring a few excellent friends, would not be especially missed. It is as much my quarrel as yours, you know."

"My dear Ashley," says Navarro, with much emotion, "I am deeply sensible of the goodness of heart that prompts your offer, but, I repeat, this affair must proceed as it has begun."

"Well, good-night to you, then," says Ashley, and he goes off to bed, wondering what manner of man is he who speaks of a thrill at the sight of the most beautiful of all flags streaming out upon the breeze, and yet claims the distinctly Spanish name of Emilio Navarro,

CHAPTER XXXVI.

JUANITA.

The sun is creeping up the range of hills when Ashley and Navarro leave the Hotel Royal and set forth at a smart pace for the meeting with Capt. Raymon Huerta. Ashley is in his usual good spirits, and the enlivening influence of his society is appreciated by Navarro, whose thoughts are plainly of a dejected nature.

Half a mile or more down the beach that stretches east of the city three men are in waiting. Two of them are Capt. Huerta and Senor Cardena; the third is evidently a surgeon.

The preliminaries for the exchange of shots are quickly arranged. Ashley, with the fifty-yards range in mind, proposes the comfortable distance of twenty-five paces, and Cardena assents. Then the revolvers are handed out and carefully scrutinized, and Huerta and Navarro face each other on the sands.

"How's your nerve, old man?" Ashley asks Navarro, as he gives the latter's hand an encouraging squeeze.

"Steady," is the response, in low tones.

"Good."

"Remember the letter," admonishes Navarro, and as Ashley nods and steps back the duelists signal that they are ready.

A minute later two shots startle into flight a flock of sea gulls that have been hovering along the shore.

With the echoes Capt. Huerta staggers and is immediately taken in charge by the watchful Cardena and the medico.

"Not scratched, eh?" Ashley inquires of Navarro.

"No; but the lead passed close enough for comfort. Unless my aim was poor, Huerta is not seriously hurt. To have killed him would have been to invite serious entanglement."

Nor is the Spanish captain in any immediate danger

of parting with existence. The bullet has plowed through the right shoulder, causing a ragged wound and a great flow of blood, but a few days will put him on his feet again, the surgeon reports to Cardena. Wounded honor is satisfied by the physical wound, and after a brief announcement of this fact and a stiff "Adios" the Spaniards drive away, and Navarro and his American friend are left upon the beach.

"Any trouble with the authorities likely?" Ashley queries, as the two turn cityward.

"I think not. Huerta is a thorough-paced scoundrel, but he has never been accused of being a coward or an informer."

A great change has come over Navarro. His eye is bright and his step elastic and he tells Ashley, as they stride along in the cool air of the morning, that he is terribly hungry and would appreciate a good breakfast.

As good a meal as Cuba affords is forthcoming, and as Ashley suddenly recollects the now happily unnecessary letter to Don Quesada, Navarro tears it into fragments and says abruptly:

"Ashley, amigo, have you ever seen the Pearl of the Antilles?"

"No; I haven't been in Santiago quite twenty-four hours yet. You mean the insurgent cruiser?"

"Ah, no; I mean the most beautiful girl in Cuba. She is the daughter of Don Manuel de Quesada, and is at once the joy and the despair of half the unmarried jeunesse doree of Santiago. Would you like to meet her?"

"By all means. Next to a good horse and a trim yacht, I know of nothing that interests me more than a beautiful woman."

"Good. I am going out to La Quinta de Quesada. Hunt up a horse and accompany me."

Navarro is already provided with a steed, a magnificent black animal that interests Ashley far more than the prospects of the acquaintance of the Pearl of the Antilles. "Came into my possession yesterday," Navarro tells him. "Isn't he a beauty?"

"He is that," is Jack's appreciative reply. "If you run across his mate put me in the way of acquiring him and I will do my war correspondence in the saddle."

Ashley succeeds in chartering a fairly presentable beast for the day, and the two young men set out for Santos in the best of spirits. They are in no hurry and the ride of something over four miles through El Valle de Bosque Cillos, the wooded valley, occupies an hour.

Passing through Santos, which is one of the smallest of villages, embracing only a jail, a church and a score of dwellings, the travelers take the road to La Quinta de Quesada, which is located in the center of the Pueblo de Olivet.

The Quinta is a square, two-storied affair and the principal material in its construction is coral stone. The inevitable and grateful veranda stretches around three sides and an air of quiet luxury is evident in the spacious house and its attractive surroundings.

As Navarro and Ashley ride slowly up the shaded carriage way and turn suddenly in sight of the quinta, the first objects that greet Jack's vision are two young people in one of the hammocks on the veranda. A young man's arm encircles a young lady's waist and the attitude of the pair suggests either the relations of lovers or of brother and sister. They start up in some confusion upon the advent of a stranger and come forward to greet Navarro. When the latter dismounts the young man embraces him warmly and Navarro, as he rests one arm affectionately about the youth's shoulders, says to Ashley: "My younger brother, Don Carlos." Then he turns to the young lady:

"Juanita, I want you to know my friend, Senor Jack Ashley of New York. Senor Ashley, La Senorita de Quesada."

Ashley has slid from his horse and his acknowledgment of the introduction is rather less debonair than usual; because, as he confesses afterward to himself, he is somewhat confused by the beauty of the young woman, who gives him her hand and tells him that the quinta has no friends more welcome than Don Emilio.

And here is an outline of Juanita de Quesada, the Pearl of the Antilles, as sketched rapidly but indelibly upon the tablets of Jack Ashley's memory:

She is 20 or thereabouts, and is considerably below the medium height. The proportions of her slender yet full form are as perfect as nature ever molds. Her face is oval, and her complexion a soft, creamy olive. Evidences of her race are in the lead-black hair, the dark, dreamy eyes of liquid fire, the rather large, tremulous mouth, with its scarlet lips, and the completing perfection of Cuban loveliness, the dainty little feet with the incomparable arches. All Cuban women are not beautiful, but as Ashley looks upon the present picture he decides that the imperfections of her sisters are amply compensated for by the dazzling loveliness of the Senorita de Quesada. "She is glorious," he thinks; and then: "I wonder if she knows anything."

Hardly less striking, though dissimilar in character, is the beauty of Don Carlos Navarro. He is a slender youth, with dark-brown eyes and curly hair, and if it were not for the effeminacy of his regular features he would receive the critical approval of the New Yorker. As it is, Ashley confesses that Juanita and Don Carlos are the handsomest young pair he ever set eyes upon, and he wonders what may be the relationship existing between them. For Carlos is no more Spanish in appearance than his brother Emilio.

"Where is Don Quesada?" asks Navarro, when the party have disposed themselves upon the veranda.

"With his books and papers, as usual," replies Carlos, with a significant glance at his brother. "Come, I will take you to him. He will be overjoyed to greet you. It is nearly two weeks, Emilio, since we last saw you."

"And it may be much longer than two weeks ere you see me again," says Navarro, as he follows Carlos into the house.

Ashley finds himself vastly interested in the young lady with whom he has been left tete-a-tete. He learns that she has not a near relative save her father (Carlos must then be her lover); that she is no stranger to the United

States, having resided in New York two years; that she
loves America and everything American; that, were it
not that her father's interests necessitated a residence in
Cuba, she would like to live always in America; and
much more information, imparted in a quiet, dignified
manner which Jack is positive was acquired by her short
stay in the land of the free and the home of the enterprising.

All too soon comes the interruption of luncheon, and
Ashley is presented to Don Manuel de Quesada. Jack
takes a good, square look at the tall, spare, elderly man
who grasps his hand warmly and tells him that he is
always proud and happy to meet an American.

Don Quesada is a typical Cuban in appearance; his
bearing is distinguished and his manner partakes of the
dignity and repose of his daughter. But there is a certain
weakness about the mouth that Ashley at once notes.

However, Don Quesada is cordiality itself, and after
lunch the three men adjourn to the library for a smoke,
Carlos and Juanita taking themselves off for a ramble
through the park.

The conversation drifts naturally to a discussion of the
patriotic uprising which has almost attained the proportions of a revolution that promises to be as successful as
the struggle for independence of the American colonists.
The talk is general, and Ashley surprises his companions
by remarking abruptly:

"By the way, Don Quesada, before I left America it
was hinted to me by an influential member of the Cuban
revolutionary society that the President of the Provisional
Republic of Cuba is a resident of Santiago."

"Ah?" says Quesada, inquiringly.

"That is, I suppose Santos may be considered a part of
Santiago."

Quesada and Navarro look at each other meaningly.

"In other words, that this President is none other than
yourself, Don Quesada," continues Ashley; and without
waiting for a reply to this direct speech he goes on:

"I tell you only what, as I say, was intimated to me in
the strictest confidence. I shall not ask for a confirmation

or a contradiction; I am not thinking of interviewing you. I am an American and the representative of an American newspaper. As such, I am supposed, while in Cuba, to maintain a neutrality. I had intended, before I met Don Navarro, to call upon you in a professional capacity, but now I find myself your guest. It is for you to say what is your pleasure in the matter."

Don Quesada studies keenly the face of the war correspondent, but reads only sincerity in the frank blue eyes. Then he looks at Navarro and the latter extends his hand to Jack.

"Ashley, I believe we understand one another," he says. "There is no need of further explanations. If there is any interviewing to be done, you can operate on me. I believe Don Quesada will willingly allow me to submit to the ordeal."

"I will be merciful," smiles Ashley. "But before I proceed further, permit me to present the vouchers for my discretion and reliability," and he passes over a letter which relieves Don Quesada of any possible distrust of his acquaintance of a few hours.

It is late in the afternoon when Navarro announces that he must depart. Ashley is courteously invited to enjoy for as long a time as he may care to the hospitality of the quinta, but duty demands his presence at Santiago until he gets his affairs into shape. However, he promises to call frequently while he is in this part of the country, a pledge he anticipates much pleasure in fulfilling. And as he rides away with ·Navarro his usually cool head is disturbed by speculations as to the probable relations between Don Carlos Navarro and Juanita de Quesada.

"By the way, Navarro," he says, suddenly to his companion, "is there any likelihood of my ever chancing upon El Terredo, the mysterious revolutionary leader whom we were discussing this afternoon?"

"Possibly," is the reply. The travelers have reached a fork in the road, about half-way between Santos and Santiago.

"My path lies yonder," says Navarro, pointing to the north. "We must part here."

"Well, take care of yourself," remarks Ashley, gripping the extended hand.

Navarro rides slowly away, but he has not gone five yards when he checks his horse and turns in his saddle.

"Would you like to see El Terredo?" he asks, with a smile.

"It would satisfy my curiosity," is Ashley's prompt response.

"Then, my friend, take your first look, and the last for many days, if not forever. For I am El Terredo!"

Waving his hat with a graceful sweep Navarro rides away to the mountains.

CHAPTER XXXVII.

ONE WAY TO GET TO CUBA.

"Whew!" For the nineteenth time John Barker gives utterance to the expressive exclamation, as he mops his perspiring forehead.

The detective is seated in the parlor car of the Florida express, which has just left Jacksonville, and is being whirled along toward Tampa Bay.

He soon indulges in a nap, while the train rumbles on, by the scattered negro huts, with their ebon-hued occupants drawn up in solemn array to watch the flying cars, through the dense forests of moss-entwined trees, across the trestle-spanned marshes and mud-colored rivers.

Barker is dreaming of a hand-to-hand encounter with Cyrus Felton, wherein the latter has succeeded in clasping the handcuffs about his (Barker's) neck and is slowly but surely rendering futile his breathing apparatus, when the porter's voice calling out "Tampa Bay" recalls him to his senses.

The single hotel at Tampa Bay, Barker subsequently finds, is not a half-bad institution, judged by the midnight inspection, and ascertaining from the clerk that the steamer for Key West does not sail until 3 o'clock the following afternoon, the detective retires in the confident belief that he has overtaken Mrs. Harding at least.

Barker is right in his surmise. He has nearly finished his breakfast the next morning, when the striking figure of Mrs. Harding enters the dining-room and is escorted by the obsequious waiter to the table at which the detective is seated. The latter lingers long over his coffee and muffins, while he improves the opportunity of studying his vis-a-vis.

"Handsome as a queen," is his conclusion, as the glorious black eyes glance idly into his. But there is a tinge of melancholy in her face, a preoccupation in her manner, that does not escape the observation of the detective, and at which he wonders.

"It cannot be that the military chap has given her the go-by," he thinks.

He has not, for at this moment the soldierly form of the Spaniard enters the room and he is directed to a seat beside Mrs. Harding.

"Nothing very lover-like in their greeting," ruminates Barker, as the two exchange salutations. "Since they are to be fellow-passengers on the boat to Key West and Havana I will postpone my interview until then." Barker strolls out upon the hotel veranda.

"How long does it take to run to Havana?" he inquires, casually, of the porter.

"About a ten hours' sail from Key West, when the steamers are running," he is told.

"When the steamers are running? Are they not running now?"

"No, sir; they run only as far as Key West now, since the blockade was declared."

Barker paces slowly up and down the veranda.

"Well, I must be hoodooed," he mutters; "that does settle it. Here I've raced 1,700 miles to head off my game, only to be foiled by a measly blockade. I can't stand it to charter a ship, and it looks mightily as if Cyrus Felton was going to slip through my hands. But how are my lady and the Spanish-looking chap to get there? I will go to Key West at any rate. There may be some way to cross the channel from there."

The detective is not in cheerful spirits as he boards the steamer, but he feels a shade of satisfaction while noting Mrs. Harding and her cavalier ascend the gang-plank just before the signal for departure is given.

"We will have a little tete-a-tete by and by, my lady," he murmurs. But, greatly to the detective's disappointment, Mrs. Harding does not emerge from her stateroom until the steamer has sighted the yellow stretch of sand that marks the entrance to the harbor of Key West.

"Well, we shall either be fellow-voyagers again, or 'on a tropical isle we'll sit and smile,' " reflects Barker, philosophically.

Determined that he will not lose sight of the charming Mrs. Harding again, Barker loiters about the steamer until she trips across the gang-plank, the last passenger to disembark. Her traveling companion has preceded her nearly half an hour, and Barker wonders again if they have parted company. Their baggage, he observes, is still on the pier, and even as Mrs. Harding steps ashore Barker sees the Spaniard coming rapidly toward her. He conducts her to the opposite side of the wharf, where is moored a neat little steam launch, manned by a number of sailors in the uniform of the Spanish navy. The baggage upon which Barker's watchful eyes are fixed is quickly conveyed aboard the launch, Mrs. Harding follows, still escorted by the military-appearing stranger, and a moment later the little craft shoots out from the dock and makes for a man-of-war lying at anchor in the harbor and flying the Spanish colors.

Mr. Barker's last opportunity for a tete-a-tete with "my lady" has vanished.

The detective watches the launch until it vanishes behind the bow of the warship, but words fail utterly to express his feelings. He mechanically picks up his grip and suffers himself to be conducted by an enterprising Bahaman to the American Hotel, picturesquely surrounded by tropical shrubs and plants.

"Well, Barker," the detective communes with himself,

"it looks decidedly as if my lady possessed a slight advantage in having a man-of-war at her call. But with all that fleet of boats in the harbor it does seem that there should be one bound for Cuba. How to hit that particular one is the question."

He strolls down the broad street to the harbor front, and from a wharf wistfully gazes at the Spanish man-of-war now nearly hull down on the horizon bearing away his fair fellow-voyager. A tanned and weather-beaten son of Neptune is making fast a small sloop, whose name Barker notes with idle curiosity is emblazoned in generous letters on her stern, "Cayo Hueso."

"Say, my good fellow," he says, "you don't happen to know of any way to reach Havana, do you? Are any of these vessels likely to sail for that port within a day or two?"

He of the weather-beaten face finishes making fast the little sloop without answering, and then slowly turns and looks at Barker. The gaze is a long and searching one, but apparently it is satisfactory.

"There's one way to reach Cuba, I reckon," he says, with a pronounced nasal twang. "That is, if you are sailor enough to stand that sloop and wise enough to keep your mouth shut on occasions."

Barker surveys the little craft doubtfully. She is of perhaps five tons' burden, and looks old and risky.

"I could stand the sail if the boat is seaworthy, and I am anxious to reach Havana," he finally says. "When do you sail?"

"At 6 o'clock. The Cayo don't go clear to Cuba, only about half-way across the channel. But we can put you aboard another craft that will land you in Havana. Got any baggage?"

Barker meditates a moment. "How long will it take to make the passage?" he inquires.

"Wall, if this wind holds you ought to be in Havana by to-morrow night. It will cost you—say, $25."

Barker's decision is made. "I'll chance it," he says. "I'll be here at 6 o'clock."

On his return to the Cayo Hueso, the detective finds

the crew of three already aboard and his sailor friend preparing to cast off. He ruefully surveys the small craft and thinks of the 120-mile trip, but there is no alternative, and he clambers aboard.

As the sails are hoisted Barker is amazed by the rate at which the little craft speeds out of the harbor. There is always a breeze on the keys, the captain of the Cayo tells him.

Soon the sea begins to growl a bit and Barker does not like it. As the breeze freshens, the commotion beneath his vest increases.

"Just the kind of a breeze for a run across, eh?" remarks the man at the tiller, with a voice that sounds to Barker like the rasp of a new saw.

"I dunno," replies the detective, whose face is rapidly becoming "sicklied o'er with the pale cast of thought."

But the little vessel continues to spin over the waters, as darkness settles upon the sea.

The stars are paling in the heavens and the gray dawn is creeping athwart the sloop, when Barker awakens from a troubled nap and struggles into a sitting posture. He sees only the bare horizon, the ocean lying black and leaden and wrinkled like an old man's face. There is no boat in sight, he thinks; they are not yet half-way to the Cuban shore.

But there is a boat in sight. Hull down to the east, imperceptible to his untrained eye, a delicate pearl shaft hangs like a pendant just on the horizon. For a time it seems dim and visionary; then even Barker, did he possess sufficient ambition to lift his head again, could see a duplicate of the sloop lazily crawling toward her, and, within half an hour, come alongside the Cayo Hueso.

At once certain mysterious boxes and casks, chiefly the latter, are transferred from one boat to the other. Then Barker laboriously and disconsolately steps from the Cayo Hueso to the strange boat, while his weather-beaten friend communes with the captain of the latter. His destination is a matter of supremest indifference to the detective. He manfully strives to hold up his head while

the exchange of salutations is made, fails and sinks
passively into the bottom of the boat.

The sun is gilding Maro castle as the little craft enters
the harbor of Havana.

"A remarkably quick passage," says the captain in
Spanish, as the sloop is being moored to a dilapidated
wharf in an obscure portion of the water front.

Barker struggles to his feet. "Are we in Havana?" he
inquires in Spanish, a trifle rusty, but still intelligible.

"Si, senor."

"Thank heaven!" is the pious ejaculation of the detective. "I'll live and die in Cuba before I'll every trust
myself in a cockleshell like that again."

CHAPTER XXXVIII.

A SOLDIER OF CASTILE.

"Heavens! They have just sized up my condition and
sent an ambulance," Barker grunts, as his eyes rest for
the first time on that marvel of vehicular construction, a
Cuban volante, which the good-natured captain of the
sloop has secured for his late passenger.

But before he clambers into the conveyance the detective, whose professional instincts are now awakening,
ascertains from the driver that the American steamer
City of Havana has not yet arrived, although due that
morning.

Barker begins to feel better. "Things seem to be
coming my way at last," he thinks complacently. "I'll
take no chances this time. John Barker, detective, will be
the first to greet Cyrus Felton when that gentleman steps
on Cuban soil. Now for the hotel and a bath, a visit to
the American consul and then to the wharf of the Red
Star Line, wherever that is."

It is a very different individual from the woebegone
passenger on the little smuggler that three hours later

lounges about the dimly lighted freight sheds of the American Steamship Line, awaiting the arrival of the overdue vessel. "Richard's himself again," he remarks; "or will be when his long-neglected appetite is appeased. I hope the City of Havana will not keep me up all night."

The night wears on—the longest, Barker assures himself, with one exception, that he ever knew, and the sun is well above the horizon ere his heart is cheered by the boom of a cannon on Moro castle, announcing the arrival of a foreign vessel. It is the American liner, and by the time the various custom officers, summoned by the signal gun, have arrived on the wharf, the steamer is being moored to the pier.

Barker has taken a position where he can command a view of the gang-plank, and with a grim smile he awaits the disembarking of the passengers. There are not many. A few Havana business men, a score or two of Cubans, three or four Spanish officers and half a dozen Americans cross the plank, and then there is a lull in the procession.

Barker's smile fades and there is a suspicion of anxiety in his expression as the tall, slim form of Cyrus Felton does not appear.

"Perhaps he is sick," the detective thinks. "I will go aboard and inquire of the purser."

No; there was no passenger on this trip named Felton, that officer states, running his eye down the rather abbreviated passenger list.

Barker stares vacantly at the purser. Rapidly there passes through his mind the circumstances preceding his interesting journey to Havana—the departure of Felton and Miss Hathaway from the St. James; his (Barker's) hurried trip to Key West; the unavailing effort to interview Mrs. Harding; the voyage in the smuggler to Havana; last night's long and weary vigil.

And Felton did not sail on the City of Havana after all!

Without a word of thanks to the courteous purser, the detective slowly turns and retraces his steps. He walks aimlessly from the wharf, his disappointment for the time being too bitter for expression.

But John Barker, whatever his errors of judgment, is

a clear-minded, persistent man, and after a half-hour's walk in the enervating atmosphere of a Havana midday he pulls himself up with a start.

"Well," he says as he wipes the perspiration from his face, "I'm euchred this time, it appears, and must make the best of it. But this is the deciding trick, and by heaven," the detective grinds his teeth, "I will track Cyrus Felton down if it takes the rest of my life! I have it! I'll see if the son, Ralph Felton, is actually here, as Ashley believes. If he is, I will at least have something to show for my trip to this awfully hot hole. Now for something to eat at the grand hotel Pasaje, if I can find the way. It's mighty lucky I know some Spanish."

The shadows are lengthening toward night when Barker awakens from the sound slumber into which his "siesta" after a comfortable meal has developed. He is feeling greatly refreshed and ready to pick up again the tangled threads of the trail that he has followed so far.

"Now for a little stroll about the city, to see what the place is like," he thinks, as he lights a cigar and saunters down the broad street.

Half an hour later, Barker has strayed farther from the hotel than he realizes and has unwittingly penetrated into the most disreputable quarter of Havana. For a brief rest he enters a cafe, and seating himself at a table in a corner of a room orders a light drink, absent-mindedly speaking in English.

Two dark-browed, yellow-skinned Cubans, who have been conversing earnestly in low tones at a table adjoining Barker's, glower at the newcomer, but as he gives his order to the waiter in English they resume their interrupted conversation. Barker idly sips his jerez and wonders what Jack Ashley will say on receiving the letter he left for him in New York.

Suddenly the word "Americano," hissed by one of the two Cubans, arrests his attention and he strains his ears to hear in what connection the word was used. The pair are talking in low tones, but the detective's trained sense is able to comprehend the tenor of the conversation.

The Cubans are discussing the assassination of some

person, an American, and presumably that American is John Barker!

The detective slips his hand around to his hip pocket, and as his fingers close over the butt of a 38-caliber pistol his pulse resumes its calm and even beat and he proceeds to make a mental inventory of the prospective assassins.

"Absolutely the most villainous-looking brace of cut-throats I ever saw," he sums up. "But why should they plot to lay me out? Do they take me for a New York millionaire in disguise, and think I carry a million or two around in my pocket? Ah, so you were not the distinguished individual picked out by the precious pair, Barker. It's some other American. But who? And how can I manage to warn him of his danger?"

Barker rapidly revolves the situation, while covertly watching the Cubans. He suddenly starts, as from words uttered by one of them, as they arise to leave the cafe, he becomes aware that the cold-blooded crime planned within his hearing is to be carried out within the next hour or so.

"There's nothing for me to do but to shadow the pair," he mutters, as he steps again into the now moonlit street.

It is a simple matter for the experienced detective to keep the Cubans in sight, especially as they never once take pains to glance backward. They have traversed several streets, when the detective observes that they have halted and are apparently loitering near a larger and rather more elaborate cafe than the majority.

"So the American is in that cafe," reflects Barker; "now, which is the better plan, to go in and endeavor to pick out my fellow-countryman and warn him, or keep in the rear of these chaps and swoop down on them at the proper moment? The latter I guess is the safer. We'll see what we will see."

The wait is not a long one. Evidently the Cubans are familiar with the habits of the person they are seeking, for within fifteen minutes a rather tall young man emerges from the cafe, stopping a moment to light a cigar, and then starts down the shadowy street. Barker, after the first glance, pays little heed to the newcomer, for his quick eye notes that he wears the undress uniform of a Spanish officer. To his surprise, however, he perceives that the two Cubans are stealthily following the man.

"So it is not an American after all," thinks Barker, as he steals silently along. "But I can't stand back and see a human killed in cold blood, whatever his nationality, and I won't!"

It is nearly 10 o'clock now and the street is deserted. As the form of the officer emerges into a clear patch of moonlight, Barker perceives that the Cubans have narrowed the distance that separates them from their prey, and he hastens to close up the gap between himself and the trio.

He is not too soon. When less than two rods from the Cubans he sees the flash of steel in the hand of the foremost of the pair.

"Look out!" Barker's voice rings out in English, loud and clear, and with the words he springs forward with a speed that rivals his sprinting in his football days.

"Tackle low!" The whimsical thought flashes through his brain as he clears the intervening space. And he does. The nearest Cuban goes down with a bone-breaking thud, the moonlight glitters for a second on something bright in Barker's hand, there is a sharp click, and the detective springs to his feet.

But there is no further need for his services. The other Cuban is speeding like the wind down the street.

"I owe you one for this, my friend," says the cause of the exciting episode in excellent English, as he strides up to Barker and warmly presses his hand. "But for your timely shout I should now be lying face downward there with the stiletto ornamenting my back. But what have you done to this scoundrel? He lies like a log."

"Oh, he'll be all right in a few moments," replies Barker, carelessly glancing down at the prostrate figure. "He went down so hard the wind was knocked out of him. Then I handcuffed him. Are there any policemen handy? If so, we can notify them and have him arrested."

"Never mind the police. The soldiers will take care of this cutthroat," returns the other. "But come to my quarters while I endeavor to express adequate thanks for your service to-night. They are near by and I will send a detail of men for this rascal."

"Oh, never mind the thanks," Barker replies carelessly. "It was nothing. I happened to overhear the pair planning to knife some one, and I followed to see the fun. Only I must admit I thought from their talk that their intended victim was one of my own countrymen, an American."

"So I am, or was, by birth. But I am now an officer in the Spanish army, Capt. Alvarez, of the staff of his excellency, the captain-general."

It is as well that a fleecy cloud at the moment dims the moonlight, for Barker, trained to control his emotions though he is, cannot avoid a sudden start.

Alvarez! the man beside him is Ralph Felton!

"Ah, here we are," continues the self-expatriated American, as he stops before a large mansion facing the plaza. 'Excuse me a moment while I send a man or two to look after your handcuffed friend."

Alvarez hurries to the rear of the building and returning shortly conducts Barker to a comfortably furnished room on the first floor. "My sleeping-room," he explains. "Now, tell me how you happened to overhear that precious pair planning to assassinate me."

Barker briefly details the events leading up to the attack on Alvarez, the latter listening with knitted brows, but without comment.

"Well, now of yourself," he says, when Barker has concluded.

Barker hesitates a moment, the while studying the face before him. "Cyrus Felton's son, or his double" he thinks. Then he takes a sudden resolution. "I am a soldier of fortune," he laughs. "I came down here to see the country and a little fighting maybe. My name is Parker; residence, the world. What are the chances for a commission in the Spanish army?"

"Hardly good for a commission. But"—Alvarez looks

Barker over shrewdly—"I should like to do you a service, and may. What do you say to becoming my orderly?"

Barker's eyes flash. He appears to deliberate for a moment, and finally says: "I would like nothing better."

"Good! To-morrow, then, will see you enrolled as a soldier of Spain!"

CHAPTER XXXIX .

ASHLEY TAKES THE FIELD.

The big, white moon that rolls through "heaven's ebon vault" and pales the glow of the southern cross looks down upon two young people on the veranda of El Quinta de Quesada. They have retired to the shadows for purely healthful reasons, of course, as a baleful influence is attributed to the direct rays of the tropic moon.

"You leave Santiago to-morrow?" asks Juanita, in tones of real regret.

"At the first streak of daylight," Ashley replies, lighting the inevitable Cuban cigar.

"And when shall we see you again?"

"Ah, quien sabe? I attack Spanish quite boldly now you see. As a matter of fact, I have no definite idea as to when I shall return. Sniffing the battle afar off has become monotonous. I am impatient to hear the rattle of musketry and the swish of the machete."

"You will not expose yourself!" cries the senorita.

Ashley laughs softly. "I shall not lead any desperate charges," he says. "For my position demands a show of neutrality, no matter how much I may sympathize at heart with the patriots. There is fighting all along the line between here and Havana, and I want a chance to describe a Cuban battle from personal observation. Besides, I like a good fight, and I shall probably itch to sail in and help the under dog, if said dog happens to be on the same side as my sympathies."

"But when such a chivalrous feeling seizes you,

restrain it; think of your friends, if not of yourself," adjures Juanita, gravely.

"Ah, well, they would be the only mourners if I stopped a Spanish bullet. I haven't a relative in the world except an amiable aunt in the western states, who threatens to some day turn over to me the squandering of her small fortune."

"No relative except an aunt?" repeats Juanita, sympathetically. "No one to weep for you?"

"Oh, the boys in the office would wear crepe for a week, and——"

"Don't talk so lightly on such a dreadful subject," reproves Juanita. "I am sure I should feel a great deal more distress than 'the boys in the office,' and I have known you only a fortnight."

"Thank you, senorita. You may feel sure that I shall studiously avoid being borne off a Cuban battleground upon my shield."

"You will keep on through to Havana?"

"Unless circumstances bar my way, I shall follow along the line of the railroad, stopping wherever night overtakes me, and resuming my journey whenever I feel like it. I have no definite plans. And, now, senorita, I believe I will say Adios. It is getting along toward 9 o'clock, and the proprietary genius of my hotel looks upon belated guests somewhat askance. I have made my adieus to Don Manuel and Don Carlos, and it only remains to express my regret at saying farewell to you, senorita."

Juanita watches him while he untethers his horse, and as he turns, bridle in hand, to lift his hat, she comes from the veranda and puts her hand in his.

"You will surely return?" she asks.

"As surely as a bad penny."

"Then I will not say farewell."

"Au revoir it is, then," says Jack. He lifts the little hand to his lips, and then with rather unnecessary abruptness he mounts his horse and rides away in the moonlight.

"Hang it!" he mutters, when out of sight of the quinta; "that makes at least half a dozen times that I have pulled myself together just in season to avoid making a fool of myself. Perhaps my vigilance would be relaxed if I could ascertain the precise relations existing between Juanita and Carlos. I never saw two persons more wrapped up in each other, and yet Juanita——" He stops and repeats the name, dwelling upon each syllable. "Pshaw! I believe I am getting soft in my head! G'lang, old nag, or we won't get to Santiago before midnight."

It is the 5th of April. Ashley has been in Santiago two weeks, and during the fortnight he has, in one way or another, kept his paper well supplied with news. He has also found many opportunities to run out to the quinta, and the welcome has always been so warm, and the adios so sincerely regretful, that he has begun to wonder whether his interest in the beautiful daughter of Don Manuel de Quesada is not lapping over the shadowy line that separates friendship from a sentiment which poets contend to be more powerful and philosophers regard as infinitely weaker.

Ashley has seen Murillo several times since his arrival, and between the Spanish general and the newspaper man something of friendship has grown. Murillo left for Havana two days before, to join the captain-general, who, it is reported, proposed to transfer his headquarters to Santiago.

When Jack reaches his hotel he is informed that a horse has been left for him at the stables.

"For me?" he inquires in surprise, as he goes out and looks upon a magnificent iron-gray beast fit for a king on coronation day.

For Senor Ashley, he is assured. It was brought during the afternoon. Jack looks the acquisition over, and then, turning to the trappings which hang near by, he discovers a bit of paper attached to the saddle. On it is written the single word "Navarro" and the mystery is cleared.

"By Jove! This is generous," he says. "But I'm blessed if I know where to send my thanks."

Dawn finds Ashley in the saddle and he makes quite a brave appearance as he rides away. He is clad in a suit of dark corduroy, with long riding boots and white-cloth helmet and as he looks his costume over complacently he remarks: "If my boots were a bit newer and shinier I'd make a good running mate for the war correspondent in 'Michael Strogoff.' It is a manifest libel to christen this horse Rozinante," patting affectionately the neck of his sleek charger, "but as he is a Spanish steed he must suffer from recollections of Cervantes. So Rozinante it is."

Before the sun has become too aggressive to admit of riding in comfort Ashley has covered some twenty miles and has passed through two villages, wretched little settlements that have ever existed in their present squalor for generation upon generation. At the second of these he stops for breakfast. The meal is no worse than he expected, and after he has finished his coffee he hunts up a shady spot on the outskirts of the town, and, hitching his horse, he smokes and dozes until the late afternoon breezes from the gulf suggest a resumption of his journey. At night he tarries at the house of a farmer. They call them "farmers" in Cuba. They burn charcoal, raise a few vegetables and peddle milk and eggs.

The next day is very much like the first, except that Ashley introduces the variation of sleeping all the afternoon and riding the greater part of the night. And when weariness finally overtakes him he camps on the edge of a vast canefield.

The third day is equally monotonous. He begins to think that his expedition is to be utterly devoid of adventure. He has seen no signs of either insurgents or Spanish soldiery, nor have the natives along his route. As evening approaches he rides into the decent-sized town of Jibana, on the line of the railway between Havana and Santiago.

Somewhat to his surprise he learns that the only hotel in the place is kept by an American. Landlord Carter proves to be a decent sort of chap and his hostelry is clean and inviting. After a really good supper Ashley turns in early; he is thoroughly tired, having ridden farther than on either of the previous days.

He wakes moderately early and has a brief ante-break-fast chat with Landlord Carter.

"Have I heard of any fighting around here?" repeats Carter, in response to Ashley's inquiry. "No, but I expect to see some most any day. There is a report that a large number of insurgents are encamped in the mountains within a score of miles of Jibana and the natives hereabout are becoming restless. A rebel victory or two would send the whole of this part of the province into the insurgent fold. By the way, a party of three Americans arrived last evening after you had gone to bed."

"So? What are they doing here and who are they?"

"They are going out to some sugar plantations near here to-day. I haven't learned their names yet, as ——"

At this moment the newspaper man hears a familiar feminine voice exclaim in tones of the utmost astonishment. "Why, Mr. Ashley!" and he turns to see Louise Hathaway standing in the hotel doorway.

Though somewhat dazed mentally, Jack lifts his hat and remarks, as if he had seen her but yesterday, "Good-morning, Miss Hathaway. You are an early riser."

"You don't appear a bit surprised to see me," says the young lady, as she gives him her hand; "while I am completely bewildered at meeting an American friend in the midst of this wilderness."

"Oh, this is a very small world," remarks Ashley.

"Now, do tell me how you happen to be in Cuba. I am dying with curiosity," declares Louise.

"Then I will explain in all haste. You should be able to guess from my military bearing and the fierce aspect which this helmet gives me that I am a war correspondent. I have been in Cuba a little over a fortnight. I arrived at Santiago three days after the Semiramis dropped anchor and was told that you had gone to Havana."

"But how did you know we sailed from New York on the Semiramis? My note, left at the St. James hotel, stated that we were going to Cuba on the steamship City of Havana."

"Exactly. And I supposed that you had, until I saw

you on the deck of the Semiramis when the yacht was running away from Uncle Sam's cruiser off Sandy Hook."

And now Miss Hathaway relates the effort which she and Mr. Felton made to reach the pier before the City of Havana sailed from New York. When she tells Ashley of the adventure of the blockade on West Broadway and of the subsequent appearance of Phillip Van Zandt and his offer to place the Vermonters on Cuban soil, Ashley twists his mustache reflectively.

Miss Hathaway's story is interrupted by the announcement of breakfast, and five minutes later Ashley makes one of a party of four at a table in the cozy dining-room.

Cyrus Felton greets the newspaper man with grave surprise, and Jack's keen eyes note that the ex-president of the Raymond national bank is looking bad. He is paler even than when he saw him last, in New York about a month ago, and in the gray eyes has settled an expression of vague unrest.

Phillip Van Zandt acknowledges the introduction with his accustomed reserve, and for an instant the eyes of the two young men meet in a searching gaze of mutual inquiry.

From the conversation that ensues, Ashley gathers that most of the time which the trio have spent in Cuba has been passed in and about Havana, and that they are now en route to Santiago, stopping off at Jibana to visit a sugar plantation in which Mr. Felton has an interest. And, what is more to the point, Ashley learns that the Semiramis is not to leave Santiago for at least another fortnight. This information comes from Van Zandt. Mr. Felton and Miss Hathaway do not appear to have any definite plans.

For his part, Ashley tells them that he intends to push on to Havana, and knows not when he will return to Santiago, if at all.

But as he watches Mr. Felton, Van Zandt and Miss Hathaway set forth, after breakfast, for the sugar plantation, which lies east of the town, he tells himself that he will return to Santiago before many days.

"I must keep my eye on those two gentlemen," he mutters, "and trust to Providence to throw Barker in my way, if indeed he has not already struck the trail. By the stars that shine, but there is a strangely assorted trio, unless I am clear off my reckoning. Nemesis is trailing his inevitable victim with said victim's father, and sooner or later they must meet. What is the town beyond here?" Ashley asks Landlord Carter.

"Cadoza," the innkeeper informs him.

"I believe I'll jog along to that point, anyhow," Jack decides; "and if nothing turns up in the line of excitement within twenty-four hours, then back to Santiago."

CHAPTER XL.

THE APPEARANCE OF THE SERPENT.

Half a dozen hours from the time that Jack Ashley mounts his newly acquired Rozinante and rides forth from Santiago on his journey into the west, a visitor arrives at Le Quinta de Quesada.

The Don and his daughter are seated on the veranda, the former dreaming of the day when Cuba shall be free, the latter of the blue-eyed young man who at the moment is many miles on his journey toward Havana and is expressing his opinion of Cuban roads in comical apostrophes, rivaling the natural extravagance of Spanish conversation.

"A visitor," remarks Quesada, as the crunching of carriage wheels sounds in the driveway, and Juanita's day dreams are abruptly terminated by the appearance of a vehicle, not a Cuban every-day volante, but a four-wheeled affair, the best that Santiago can provide.

The carriage draws up before the quinta, the driver opens the door with a profound obeisance, and out steps a lady whose radiant beauty rather dazzles the Cuban gentleman, who advances with easy grace to meet her.

For Don Quesada, though well past the meridian of life, is not without susceptibility to feminine charms.

"I have the pleasure of addressing Don Manuel de Quesada, I believe?" says the fair visitor in English.

"The pleasure is mine, madam."

"I am under the embarrassment of introducing myself," with a smile and a glance from a pair of liquid black eyes that instantly win for her the good-will of the master of the quinta. She tenders a bit of cardboard, and as the Don receives it with a bow, she explains: "When I left New York I had a letter of introduction from a gentleman who has the honor of your acquaintance"— she glances at the coachman standing near, and lowers her voice—"Don Rafael Manada."

"Ah!" murmurs Quesada, regarding his visitor with new interest.

"But I must have left it among my effects at Santiago. I certainly have not lost it, as I was too thoroughly instructed as to the importance of keeping its contents a secret," the lady finishes, with a meaning smile.

Quesada extends his hand and presses slightly the dainty palm laid therein. "Any of Don Manada's friends are welcome here," he says. "I am happy to place the quinta at your disposition, and its occupants are yours to command, madam."

Quesada leads the way into the house, whither Juanita has retired to add a few touches to her toilet.

"You are an American, Mrs. Harding," ventures the Don, as they pass through the long, wide corridor to the gallery at the rear of the quinta and the lady is provided with the easiest of chairs.

"My accent told you that immediately," is the smiling response. "Yes; I am the widow of an American ship-owner, who left to me, among other possessions, a sugar plantation somewhere in this fair isle. I had the pleasure of Don Manada's acquaintance in New York, and when he heard that I purposed visiting Cuba to view my possessions, he desired that I seek you, giving me at the same time the letter of introduction which, as I have said, I have unfortunately left at my hotel in Santiago.

But perhaps the password which he whispered to me, 'Cuba Libre,' will do as well. For the cause of Cuban liberty has no warmer sympathizer than myself, Don Quesada," she adds, earnestly, and the Don's countenance lights with pleasure.

"Don Manada could have conferred no greater pleasure," he replies, "and I trust that you will honor my daughter and myself by becoming our guest, for a few days at least."

Isabel's dark orbs snap with triumph not easily repressed, but she answers hesitatingly: "Thank you, but I do not see how I can trespass upon your kindness. I have not the pleasure of an acquaintance with the senorita, and——"

"Permit me to remove that objection at once," interposes Quesada, as Juanita at the moment stands in the doorway. "Juanita, mi querida, this is Mrs. Isabel Harding, an American lady and a friend of Don Manada, whom you met in New York. I have invited her to remain with us for a few days, or as long as our hospitality may prove attractive. Will you not add your request to mine?"

The more mature and voluptuous beauty of the older woman attracts the impulsive Cuban girl, and she seconds her father's invitation with a sincerity that would have won even a lady who had not come to the quinta with the deliberate purpose of securing such a proffer of hospitality.

And so the carriage is sent back to Santiago and Isabel Harding is installed at the quinta, the surroundings of which she finds much to her liking. Juanita is much charmed with her American friend, who fascinates the impressionable Cuban girl with her brilliant beauty, her wit and her knowledge of the great world amid whose pleasures and palaces Juanita lived for two years, and which she hopes some day to see again. The two women quickly become inseparable and naturally Juanita tells Mrs. Harding of her other recent New York friend, Jack Ashley. But Isabel, although she enjoys, or otherwise, an acquaintance with that industrious young man, does not know his name, and the adventuress has not even the fear of his reappearance to disturb her present serenity.

But if the Don and his daughter are charmed by their guest, not so Don Carlos, and it is with difficulty that that gentle youth conceals his dislike. An instinctive distrust of the beautiful American takes possession of him, and to avoid exhibiting this distrust, which he admits to himself is unfounded, he spends most of his time in solitary walks about the vast pueblo or in long rides upon the back of his favorite pony.

Late in the afternoon of the 7th of April, two days after the arrival of Mrs. Harding at the quinta, that lady, her elderly host and his daughter are seated on the veranda, enjoying the light breeze from the gulf which renders life in Cuba endurable and even attractive for a few hours.

An interruption to the conversation comes in the person of a courier, who rides up to the quinta, delivers to Quesada a small packet of papers, and, after a glass of wine, departs as hastily as he came.

The Don excuses himself and retires to his study. A few moments later he reappears and calls to Carlos, who is coming up the lawn. Young Navarro bows to Mrs. Harding and follows the Don into the study.

"I have just received important news," says the latter. "Capt. Guerra sends word that a big supply train was dispatched by the captain-general from Havana for Santiago this morning or last night. Is it not to-day or to-morrow that Navarro was to be at or near Jibana?"

Carlos nods. "He should certainly be there now."

Quesada paces the room, his brow knitted in thought. "If word could be got to him at once," he says, "Dios! The train might be captured. But how to send him word—there is the obstacle."

"How far is Jibana from Santiago?" asks Carlos, into whose mind has come a sudden thought that causes his cheeks to alternately flush and pale.

"A full day's journey by rail. No; I fear word could not be sent him in time." ·

"But if a courier were to leave on the early morning train, could he not reach Jibana in season to find Emilio?"

"Perhaps. It will take several days for the supply train to make the trip, but it will also take us too long to find a trustworthy messenger."

"Do you not consider me trustworthy?"

"You!" cries Quesada, looking at the slender youth in astonishment.

"Yes, Don Manuel; I will be the courier."

"No, no; I cannot permit it. What would Emilio say?"

"He will be too overjoyed to see me to think of scolding you. There is no danger. Simply the discomfort of the journey. I will start in the morning."

Against his better judgment, Quesada consents, and as Carlos throws open the study door the vision of Mrs. Harding flits by.

Over the teacups half an hour later Isabel tells Don Quesada that, if there is a conveyance to be easily procured at Santos, she believes she will run into Santiago for a day's shopping. And Quesada informs her smilingly that if she cares to arise with the sun she may find a conveyance in waiting, as Carlos is going to the city on business and will undoubtedly be charmed with her society on the short journey.

*   *   *   *   *   *   *

At Havana on the morning of the 8th of April.

With contracted brows and frowning face, the captain-general of Cuba scans a mass of official documents that lie upon his desk. Gen. Truenos is plainly displeased with the condition of affairs on the island. When he sailed from Cadiz it was to "put down the rebellion in three months," as the Spanish press boastfully asserted, but Truenos realizes that it is not now a matter of weeks or months, but of years, ere the red and yellow of Spain will wave again unchallenged over the gem of the Antilles.

In the meantime, Gen. Truenos gathers from the papers before him that some of the matured plans of the

Spanish have been checkmated through treachery in some quarter, and he is not enchanted with the glimpses he has obtained of the manner in which his subordinates conduct a campaign.

An officer enters the room with a dispatch and the captain-general reaches impatiently for the missive.

"Caspita!" he growls, as he glances over the contents. "Murillo at least is alive to what is transpiring under the very noses of my generals. I wish that I had more like him." Then to the officer: "Send Gen. Velasquez to me at once."

As the latter answers the summons, Truenos hands him the dispatch, with the query: "Has the supply train left for Santiago?"

"It left last night, your excellency."

"It must be stopped. As you will see by Murillo's dispatch, the rebels have learned of the train's departure and a courier is now en route from Santiago to notify that infernal El Terredo. If that courier is not intercepted, the supply train must be recalled or held. The dispatch contains a description of the rebel messenger. Now, then, to action."

Truenos unfolds a large map of the island, and as he runs his finger along the line which indicates the railroad, another dispatch is handed in. The captain-general tears it open and reads:

"Reported that El Terredo is encamped near Jibana, with a large force of insurgents.   Alvarez."

"Ah, remarks Truenos. "This is dated Cadoza. And Cadoza," he consults the map, "is less than a dozen miles from Jibana. Bueno! For once matters are dovetailing to my wishes. The courier cannot reach Jibana before nightfall, and when he does Alvarez shall arrest him. Let the supply train proceed, Velasquez, and immediately wire Alvarez to arrest the rebel messenger at or below Jibana. Send the description of the young man given in Murillo's dispatch and have Alvarez wire back that he understands. Quick! There is no time to be wasted."

It is to be an exciting night at Jibana.

CHAPTER XLI.

THE MEETING AT CADOZA.

It is something like ten miles to Cadoza, another and smaller railway town, and Ashley arrives about noon. There is no American hotel here. Instead, a lazy Cuban keeps a shiftless hostelry to which only necessity would drive a man. A party of soldiers are gathered at the inn and the yard is filled with their horses.

Ashley tethers his horse at a spot which he can overlook, as Rozinante is an animal that would tempt a man even more upright than a soldier in time of war. As he gives the bridle an extra hitch, a hand is dropped on his shoulder and a familiar voice whispers:

"Jack Ashley, by all that's holy!"

Ashley turns and cries out:

"Hello, Barker, old man! Where'd you get your uniform?" surveying the detective's distinctly military attire.

"Hist!" cautions Barker, glancing over his shoulder. "Buy a drink at the hotel and then ride up the road a piece. I'll join you there." Saying which the detective walks away and Ashley enters the hotel.

The drinking-room is filled with Spanish caballeria, who glance curiously at the American; after procuring a glass of wine and a cigar, Ashley mounts and rides leisurely up the road. A quarter of a mile from the hotel he finds Barker waiting, and he remarks, with a grin: "Barker, you're a fashion plate. Where on earth did you get those togs?"

"Hang it! Will you be serious ten minutes," growls Barker. "Let me tell you that the commanding officer of the gang at the hotel is Capt. Julio Alvarez, who is none other than our old friend Ralph Felton."

"So? And to trail him you turned trooper, eh?"

"Exactly. Through him I expect to find the other Felton, his father."

"I can tell you a quicker way."

"Ah!"

"Push along to Jibana, ten miles east of here. I left Cyrus Felton, Phillip Van Zandt and Louise Hathaway there this morning."

"Quick! Tell me all you know," demands the detective, aroused by the information imparted to him by his co-worker.

Ashley supplies the needed details, and Barker asks: "You are reasonably sure that Felton and Van Zandt will remain in Santiago for a fortnight?"

"I think you can depend on that."

Then affairs are shaping themselves advantageously for our purpose. Our command will go to Jibana this evening, but I don't want any collision there. See the position of the game. Van Zandt, is he is Stanley, is tracking the son through the father, and I am trailing the father through the son, intending to bag both of them, as I have an interesting bit of what may prove strong evidence against Ralph Felton. But I can't do anything with them at Jibana, and if Van Zandt runs afoul of young Felton to-day he is likely to kick over all my plans. Santiago is the place to play the last hand in this interesting game."

"I get the idea," remarks Ashley. "But what is this new evidence against young Fenton?"

"This: That I believe he is wearing about his neck at the present time the locket that was removed from Roger Hathaway's watch-chain the night of the murder and bank robbery."

Ashley whistles softly. "That's interesting," he says. "But how did you learn this? And while you are explaining kindly give an account of yourself from the time you jumped New York."

The detective complies, and when the interesting tale is completed, Ashley says earnestly: "Barker, old chap, my confidence in you has been increased tenfold in the last month."

"Thank you," responds the detective, though he suspects some raillery in the newspaper man's remark.

"Yes. There was a time when I doubted you a bit. And when you made arrangements to arrest Cyrus Felton I about concluded that the case was to prove after all an ordinary affair. But you have redeemed yourself, Barker. You have proved that the detective I have long admired in the pages of fiction is not a myth, but has his prototype in real life."

"Indeed?" grunts Barker. "Go on."

"Yes; just before you descended upon your victim with a triumphant swoop, said victim gave you the slip. Undaunted by such a trifling discouragement, you struck a bee line for Havana, and there——"

"Come, stow your chaff. I'd like to know whose tomfoolery prevented Felton's arrest in New York. By thunder, if I could have got your ear a moment after I discovered Felton's departure for Cuba, I'd have given you a dressing-down that would have knocked some of the self-sufficiency out of you."

"Well, you can consider yourself forgiven," says Ashley, soothingly. "What's up at Jibana? Anything special?"

"Yes; a rather important bit of work. This morning Capt. Alvarez, to give him the name he chooses to sail under, learned that a large force of insurgents under El Terredo were encamped somewhere between Cadoza and Jibana. He wired the fact to Havana and not ten minutes later received instructions to intercept a courier for the rebels who was on his way from Santiago to Jibana, presumably with dispatches to El Terredo. Although only his orderly, I am pretty close to Alvarez. The chap has taken quite a fancy to me, and to give him his due he is a devilishly clever fellow, with more pluck and fighting blood in him than a dozen Spaniards. American blood will tell, my boy."

"Well, what's the plan for the night?"

"This: We are to flag the train about a mile below Jibana and do the trick quietly, as the feeling about here is pretty strong against the Spanish; arrest the courier, secure the papers, and wire Havana that the road is clear, as I understand the dispatches relate to the big supply train which is on its way from the capital to Santiago. Truenos, you know, is shifting his headquarters to the latter city."

"Then the supply train has already left Havana?"

"Presumably. The rebels at the Santiago end of the line got wind of the shipment, and have sent Don Carlos to put El Terredo onto the fact."

"Don Carlos!" repeats Ashley, with a start that Barker does not notice; "and what disposition will you make of the prisoner?"

Barker shrugs his shoulders. "He will probably be honorably shot."

"Unhappy youth!" murmurs Ashley.

"It is rather tough," remarks Barker, coolly. "But it is the fortune of war."

Ashley's forehead is wrinkled in thought. "I'd like to take a hand in the fun to-night," he remarks carelessly. "I've been journeying through the desert for more than three days, with not a sign of adventure. I don't suppose it would do for me to show myself to Alvarez. How many men has he with him?"

"Twenty, including himself."

"Does he intend to take the entire command with him to hold up the train?"

"No; the affair is to be transacted in the quietest manner. Alvarez, myself and four more men are to leave the hotel about 9 o'clock—the train is due at Jibana at 10—and proceed down the track a mile or so. A few swings of the lantern and the train will stop, Don Carlos be removed and the train signaled to go ahead. If the arrest were made publicly, word might get to El Terredo, and the government's plans for a safe passage of the supply train would be frustrated."

"Your business completed at Jibana, I suppose you will push directly on to Santiago?"

"Yes, and you?" queries Barker.

"I shall probably follow at a respectful distance. I have been stopping at the Hotel Royal in Santiago, and you will probably find me there if I am in the city."

"How is Felton looking?" asks the detective.

"Badly; I shouldn't wonder if he had a presentiment that some sort of disaster was impending."

"And Miss Hathaway?"

"Superb as ever. There is apparently a tender regard existing between her and Van Zandt."

"Strange, strange are the workings of fate," philosophizes Barker, and with a sly grin he adds: "How are your studies in statuary progressing, Jack?"

"Suspended for the present, most sympathetic Barker. Just now I am interested in a study of the life."

"Ah; some dark-eyed Cuban senorita?"

"The most beautiful woman in the world," is Ashley's enthusiastic tribute.

Barker laughs good-humoredly, then suddenly exclaims: "Hello! There's the trumpet call. I must be off. By the way, I've changed my name to Parker."

"Parker! Why don't you get a name to match your clothes?"

"Go to thunder!" retorts the detective. "So long. I'll see you at Santiago." Barker plunges into the woods beside the road and returns to the hotel by a circuitous route.

"You'll see me again before you reach Santiago," soliloquizes Ashley, gazing after his friend's retreating form. "If Navarro is in these mountains I'll search him out, and we'll have a hand in the game at Jibana to-night that will remind Capt. Alvarez of a certain little straight flush he ran up against once upon a time. And if Navarro is not to be found, then, by George, I'll play the hand alone!"

CHAPTER XLII.

"EL TERREDO."

Ashley waits until he believes that Capt. Alvarez and his men have got fairly on their way toward Jibana; then he mounts Rozinante and rides back to the hotel.

Half a mile to the eastward, the landlord tells him, a trail leads off into the mountains. Ashley remembers passing it in the morning. Fortifying himself with a dinner, he sets forth.

After he strikes the mountain path, his progress is slow and painful. It is a dreary road, steep and treacherous. About him nothing but rocks, red clay, cactus and bog and a stunted growth of trees.

Ashley left the hotel in the vicinity of 1 o'clock, and by 3 he has hardly covered four miles. "If I do not secure reinforcements within the hour I must 'bout face and ride to Jibana," he reflects. "A man could never find his way out of this howling wilderness after nightfall! Jove! It must have been a matter of urgent importance that necessitated the dispatching of Don Carlos to Jibana. Poor little chap!" he mutters, and as he thinks of young Navarro lying under the stars with a bullet through his heart, he urges Rozinante at a dangerous pace.

Another half-hour goes by. Ashley is now in the mountains, and yet no living being has he seen to break the depressive solitude. Suddenly there rings out the command:

"Alto, ahi!"

Ashley checks his horse, looks about him and discovers that he is the center of a circle of leveled muskets, the owners of which are hidden from view.

"All right, gentlemen, I'm out," announces Jack, cheerfully, as he removes his eye-glasses and wipes the dust and moisture from them.

Forth from the bushes steps a gaunt Cuban, in a tattered uniform and with feet that have long since parted association with shoes. Throwing his musket across his arm, he hurls an inquiry at Ashley.

"You've got me there," states the correspondent, and smiling around the ominous fringe of musket barrels.

Finally, giving up all idea of a conversation with the dark-featured mountaineers, "El Terredo!" he cries, "El Terredo! Endonde El Terredo? I don't know whether that's right or not, but it's the best I have in stock."

The mountaineer appears to grasp the idea. He shouts something to the men in the bushes, and a dozen lusty fellows, white and black, come forth. The leader makes a sign to Ashley to go ahead, and the latter obeys.

For a mile or more the little cavalcade proceeds, when suddenly the leader of Ashley's silent escort emits a shrill whistle. An answering signal is faintly heard, and then the march is resumed. Five minutes later Jack rides into a clearing and hears a welcome voice ring out: "Welcome, Senor Ashley!"

"Glad to see you, Navarro," says Ashley, heartily, as he drops from his horse and grips the insurgent leader's hand. "Is this part of your army?"

"Yes; hardy fellows, every man of them," replies Navarro, signalling his followers to fall back. "What on earth brings you into the mountains?"

"Thought I'd drop round and return thanks for your generous gift."

"Ah, say nothing of that. I should have been glad to have sent you a stable of horses."

"One was enough. But this is incidental. You expect dispatches from Santiago to-night?"

"No; that is, no special ones."

"Some are on their way, nevertheless, in the keeping of Don Carlos."

"Don Carlos!" cries Navarro, turning pale.

"Ay; but that is not all. The errand of Don Carlos has become known at Havana and orders have been wired to Capt. Alvarez, who is now on his way from Cadoza to Jibana, if he is not already there, to intercept the courier, and secure the dispatches."

Navarro staggers as if dealt a blow. "My God! They will shoot him like a dog!" he groans, his face white as death. "When—where is Carlos to arrive?"

"At Jibana, at 10 to-night."

"Ho! Then all is not lost," flashes Navarro. "By heaven! I'll wipe Jibana and every Spaniard in it from the face of the earth!" ·

"Easy, my friend," counsels Ashley, grasping the infuriated man by the arm. "If Don Carlos is to be saved, and also the dispatches—keep those in mind—you will need your wits more than a thousand men. Now, listen to me a moment. There is time enough.

"Yesterday, or the day before, or sometime within the week, a big supply train left Havana for Santiago. Information of its dispatch must have been received by Don Quesada, and, knowing your whereabouts—did he know them?"—Navarro nods—"he has sent Don Carlos to notify you, that the train may be captured. This morning Capt. Alvarez was at Cadoza. He heard it rumored that a large force of insurgents were encamped in these mountains. He wired Havana to that effect, and ten minutes later received orders to intercept Don Carlos. I learned this while at Cadoza, and realizing the danger that threatened your brother, I set off for the mountains, trusting to Providence to run across you or some of your men. On my way hither I devised a plan by which you can outwit Alvarez and later capture the ammunition train—and I do not believe in doing things by halves. But first, how far is it to Jibana?"

"About six miles, as the crow flies."

"That means eight or ten by these awful bridal-paths, then. You have a score of men here at least. They will be more than enough. Now, I will outline my plan and we can perfect it on our way to Jibana."

Navarro listens without interruption while Ashley talks. When the programme for the night has been sketched, Navarro's dark eyes moisten and he seizes Jack's hands in a grip that makes the latter wince. "Ashley, you're a hero!" he cries.

"Nonsense," laughs Jack.

"I can never repay the debt of gratitude I owe you."

"Don't try. Suppose we push along to Jibana. We can talk matters over on the way."

"Good. We will start at once," says Navarro, and he communicates an order to his men.

"How many men have you back in the mountains?" Ashley inquires of Navarro as they ride side by side through the desert of rock and chaparral.

"Two thousand. Accessions have been coming every day. But they are not directly under my command. My part in the revolution has been a rather peculiar one. Up to a fortnight or so ago, when I parted with you on the Santos road, my identity was as much a mystery as that of the president of the provisional republic. Unsuspected as a leading factor in the struggle for independence, I mingled with the Spanish and listened with a smile to the stories told of the prowess of the cruiser Pearl of the Antilles and her mysterious commander, El Terredo. At the time the Mercedes was sunk I did command the Pearl and with my own hand aimed the dynamite gun that sent the Spanish battleship to the bottom. But most of my time has been spent on land. I have done more planning than fighting, and while I rejoice not in a single title except that of El Terredo, in a land where titles are cheap, my authority is unlimited, my orders are implicitly obeyed, and I could ruin Cuba Libre with a single command."

"Are you not fearful of being recognized during some of your trips into the camp of the enemy?" asked Ashley, looking at the young man with undisguised admiration.

Navarro smiles. "There will be no further exposure. When I left the quinta with you it was to take the field, not to leave it until Santiago falls. After the capture of the ammunition train, if luck favors us, I leave here for the coast," pointing westward. "In a harbor yonder rides the Pearl of the Antilles, and when I take command of her it will be the opening of a campaign that Spain's navy will long remember."

"Until Santiago falls?" repeats Ashley. "You look for the capitulation of that city?"

"Within a fortnight Gen. Masso will hurl 10,000 men upon it. The troops back in these mountains will form part of an army against which 20,000 Spanish will not avail. Unless you insist upon reporting the siege for your paper amid the bursting of shells and the roar of artillery, keep away from Santiago—at Santos, for instance. The Spanish squadron is already on its way to Santiago, and when the city falls into the hands of the patriots the battleships will open fire."

"Then I believe I will return to Santiago at once—or after our night's work is finished. Shall we reach the edge of Jibana before nightfall?"

"Probably not, but in season for the work in hand. It will be a night that Capt. Alvarez will long remember if memory lasts beyond this world."

"By Jove! That will never do," exclaims Ashley. Navarro looks at him inquiringly.

"Alvarez must not be injured," declares Jack. "I have particular reasons for keeping Alvarez alive for some time to come."

"Rather awkward," laughs Navarro. "I don't see but that you will have to overlook the job to-night, and sort out your friend, for I expect it will be necessary to kill one or two of the gang."

Ashley reflects a moment. "You should be able to identify the leader," he says, and he adds to himself: "As for Barker, I shall have to prevent his taking part in the affair. It's a ticklish job all round."

"Well, your wishes shall be respected," says Navarro. "Capt. Alvarez shall live. He is fortunate in having so influential a friend at court."

"Some of the most worthless of men are more valuable alive than dead. I have no friendship for Alvarez, but his demise just at present would complicate certain matters in which I have a large interest."

The moon is creeping up over a crest of the range, when, at a signal from the guide, Navarro calls a halt. After a whispered consultation, he tells Ashley that they are some little distance below the Jibana hotel and railway station.

"Two hundred rods beyond us lies the road," he says; "and fifty yards farther is the track. We will hitch here."

"Very good," declares Ashley. "Here, then, we separate. It is now nearly 8 o'clock," consulting his watch by the glow of his cigar. "Good luck, old man. The signal for my reappearance will be the old rallying cry of 'Santiago.'

The men exchanged a hearty handclasp. Then Ashley dismounts, and headed by the guide, leads Rozinante through the brush to the road. Here he vaults into the saddle again and canters toward the town.

<hr>

CHAPTER XLIII.

THE FIGHT IN THE MOONLIGHT.

"Didn't expect you back so soon," declares Landlord Carter, answering Ashley's halloa without the Hotel Americano at Jibana.

"I am a little ahead on my own calculations," is the reply. "Are the Americans still here?"

"No, sir; left this afternoon for Santiago."

"Full house, though, I judge, motioning toward the windows of the reading-room, from which emanate snatches of song and the clink of glasses.

"Yes; gang of Spanish troopers. Noisy devils. Stop overnight, I suppose?"

"Sure. I want some supper in a hurry and a room at your leisure."

The landlord shouts to the hostler, who leads Rozinante away to his well-earned grain, and Ashley follows Carter into the hotel, with the remark: "I do not care to have those chaps in there see me, or know who I am."

"All right, sir. This way. The troopers are all in the drinking-room and they haven't moved out of their chairs for an hour."

Supper over, Ashley is shown to his room and the

landlord is about to make his exit with a cheerful "good-night," when Ashley remarks:

"By the way, have you an old coat and hat of any description?"

Carter scratches his head reflectively. "I have an old Grand Army uniform that I brought with me from the states. I was a member of the 13th Massachusetts volunteers, and after the war joined the Chelsea post, when——"

"That will do very nicely," interrupts Ashley. "I want to borrow the uniform for a few hours."

"All right, sir. I'll get it out in the morning."

"But I want it to-night."

"Very good, sir. I've been too long in this business to ask questions. Used to run a small hotel in Boston," grins Carter, as he vanishes. He returns shortly with the clothes, and Ashley, after a glance, pronounces them satisfactory.

"One more request, Carter. You noticed, perhaps, among your guests a rather short, thick-set party, with a dark, closely cropped mustache."

"Smokes a short, black pipe and looks like an Englishman?"

"That's the chap. Send him up, but don't attract the attention of his companions."

Carter nods and disappears, and a few minutes later the good-natured countenance of John Barker is thrust into the room.

"Buenas tardes, Senor Parker," is Ashley's salutation. "Come in and shut the door."

"Where the devil did you come from?" demands the detective, dropping into a chair.

"Up the road a piece. I got tired of journeying through the desert, and concluded to take the back track. Fill up your pipe and make yourself sociable."

"Can't stop. It is nearly 9 o'clock and we start at that hour."

"Oh, yes; on the business you were telling me of this noon. You haven't changed your plans, then?"

"No; there was no occasion to."

"Well, it is not absolutely essential that you should accompany Alvarez, is it?"

"That was his wish. With the exception of Alvarez and myself and the four men who were to supplement our little party, the command knows nothing definite of the evening's work. Alvarez doesn't fraternize much with his followers."

"Why not send a man in your stead?"

"I am afraid it is too late to make any changes in the plans. Most of the men below are half-shot now."

Ashley takes a turn about the room and drops his hand on his friend's shoulder. "Barker," he says, "it was only this noon that you requested me to be serious for at least ten minutes on a stretch. I never was more serious than I am now, when I say to you, don't accompany Alvarez on his errand to-night."

"What the deuce are you so interested in the affair for all at once?" queries the detective.

"Well, remain here, and I will enlighten you."

At this moment the impatient shout, "Ho, Parker!" floats up from the hotel yard, and with the remark, "I'm off; see you later, Jack," Barker bounds from the room.

"Hang it! I ought to have told him at the outset how the land lay," mutters Ashley. "Now, I suppose I shall have to direct my undivided efforts to preventing his slaughter at the hands of Navarro's men."

Ashley slips off his coat and gets into the faded uniform of the landlord, dons the Grand Army hat and pulls it down over his eyes; examines his revolvers to make certain that they are in proper working order, and then, blowing out his lamp, seats himself by the open window, where he can command a view of the road.

Shortly after 9 o'clock he sees six forms cross the band of moonlight into the shadows beyond. He waits ten minutes and then glides softly down the stairway and out into the night.

Alvarez and his men leave the hotel afoot and instead of taking the railroad track, proceed down the highway. Alvarez rode over the ground during the afternoon and selected a point about a mile and a half below the village as the place for holding up the train. Here the road crosses the railway and beyond is a long stretch of straight track.

The six proceed silently to the appointed spot, and then, there being no further occasion for secrecy, they fall to smoking and chatting. The train is due at Jibana at 10 and there is yet half an hour to wait.

Twenty minutes of it go by, when Alvarez discovers that his party is short two men.

"Ho! Sancho! Francisco!" he calls, and repeats the shout, there being no response. "Whither went they, Parker?" he asks, turning to his orderly.

"They were here a few minutes ago, captain. I last noticed them strolling toward the road."

Alvarez utters an impatient growl. "Search them out, Pedro, and thou, too, Juan. The train will be here in five minutes."

As the two troopers addressed take themselves off in quest of their companions Alvarez lights a lantern and hands it to the orderly.

"By the way, what disposition is to be made of the prisoner?" asks the latter.

"We shall have to shoot him, I expect," is the cool response. "We can't very well take him with us, and we certainly cannot turn him loose."

"It seems a rather cold-blooded piece of business. It savors of murder."

At the word Alvarez shivers slightly. The nights in Cuba are damp and chilly.

"Ten o'clock," he mutters, holding his watch to the lantern. "Where the devil are my men? We shall likely have to go in search of the second pair. Ha, the train!"

The whistle of the Havana express is heard in the distance and the men leap to their feet.

"Down the track with you," orders Alvarez. "As for you," turning to four forms that are approaching from the shadows of the highway, "el diablo! What sort of men have I in my command?"

The troopers make no reply to the angry query of their leader.

The orderly swings his lantern and an answering blast comes from the train, which draws up upon the crossing.

"I have an order for the arrest of one of your passengers," Alvarez informs the conductor. "Watch the train and see that no one leaves it," he tells the four troopers, and, followed by the orderly, he boards the first coach.

Within this is the object of their search. Don Carlos Navarro is reclining wearily in a seat about midway of the car. He starts when the soldiers enter and the color flows from his cheeks when they stop before him.

Alvarez consults a paper, and, glancing from it to young Navarro, remarks: "The very chap. I have a warrant for your arrest, sir." Then to the orderly: "Remove the prisoner, Parker."

"By thunder, he's fainted," mutters the orderly, as he bears the limp form from the car.

"Search him," commands Alvarez, signaling to the conductor to go ahead.

As the train rumbles away the orderly goes through the coat pockets of the prisoner, but without finding any sign of papers, rebel dispatches or otherwise. Then he tears open the unconscious youth's shirt, and the next instant utters an exclamation of astonishment.

"By heaven! It's a woman!" he mutters, as he deposits his burden tenderly on the ground and straightens up to acquaint his chief of the surprising bit of intelligence.

* * * * * * *

The moon swings high above the range when Ashley leaves the hotel and proceeds down the railroad track, the route he naturally supposes Alvarez and his party have taken.

As the newspaper man, revolver in hand, moves slowly and cautiously along, his eyes on the alert for a glimpse of Alvarez' party, the danger of his situation suddenly occurs to him. If the Spaniards have already stationed themselves at some point along the rail he is likely to stumble upon them at any minute.

At last he sights the party of troopers. Then he remembers that the road is close by, and stealing through the brush, he proceeds softly along the highway until the hum of conversation greets his ear.

He crawls at a safe distance to a position beyond the group, not twenty feet distant from the spot where Alvarez and Barker are seated.

The brush is dense and he has nothing now to do but keep perfectly still. He has seen or heard nothing of El Torredo or his men, but he knows that secreted somewhere in the waste of chaparral around him are stout hearts and strong arms waiting for the cry of "Santiago!" to rouse them to swift action.

He watches Alvarez light the lantern, and, as the rays fall upon the orderly's features Ashley thinks: "If I could only get within whispering distance of the old man I'd give him a quiet tip to make himself exceeding scarce."

But at this instant the whistle of the express is heard and Ashley raises himself on his elbows. He sees Barker start down the track, and his impulse is to follow. But to do so he will have to cross a broad belt of moonlit open, and at this moment the four troopers come up.

The train comes to a standstill, Don Carlos is removed, the cars rumble away, and Ashley notes with satisfaction that the search for the papers is being conducted by the orderly. "He will not be harmed should Navarro's men open fire, if he keeps close to Carlos," he thinks.

But where is Navarro? The situation is becoming strained for the young man in the Grand Army uniform.

Jack is watching Barker. He hears him utter an ejaculation of astonishment as he lays the unconscious form of Carlos upon the ground. And then he hears a hoarse bellow of rage and sees one of Alvarez' troopers whip out his sword and spring upon the orderly.

Less than a dozen feet separate Ashley and Barker. With a cry of warning, Jack dashes forward and catches the descending arm just in time to avert the certain destruction of the detective, who is wholly off his guard. As it is, the edge of the falling blade catches Barker across the forehead, half-stunning him and cutting a gash that means a scar to recall this night in years to come. At the same instant Ashley recognizes El Terredo in the wielder of the sword, and he whispers, "Easy, Navarro," in time to check a slash at his own head.

Meanwhile the remaining three troopers have hurled themselves upon Alvarez and Barker. It all occurs in a flash and before Ashley recovers from his surprise at the unexpected turn of events a shrill whistle from Navarro has summoned nearly a score more of men from the surrounding shadows.

Navarro raises Don Carlos in his arms and the youth, who has recovered consciousness, clasps his arms about his brother's neck and bursts into tears of joy.

"There, be a man," soothes the latter. "Remain here a few minutes while I look after your Spanish friends."

Navarro picks up the lantern and flashes its rays into Alvarez' face.

"What's this?" he cries. "By heaven, Captain Alvarez, I think we have met before."

As the two men confront each other in the moonlight, there is no need of the lantern for each to see the other's countenance.

An exclamation of surprise and rage escapes Alvarez' lips, and he struggles in the grasp of the two men who pinion his arms.

"Curse you!" he grits, in a voice choked with passion; "I'd give half my life for five minutes of fair play now!"

"Fair play?" sneers Navarro. "You do not know the meaning of the phrase. You are a thief, a blackguard, and a traitor!"

Alvarez wrenches free by a mighty effort and with a fearful oath hurls himself upon Navarro.

CHAPTER XLIV.

THE METAMORPHOSIS OF DON CARLOS.

"Stand back!" commands Navarro, as his men start forward to the enraged Alvarez, whose fingers have twined about the insurgent leader's neck. "Back, I say! I can handle this gentleman without assistance."

Alvarez is as a child in the steely arms of El Terredo. The latter tears the clutching fingers from his throat, sweeps the Spanish captain off his feet and dashes him to the ground.

Half-stunned and crazed by passion, Alvarez struggles to his knees and whips out a pistol. It is knocked from his grasp before his arm straightens, as half a dozen watchful Cubans pounce upon him.

"Away with them!" orders Navarro, with a sweep of his arm, and as Alvarez and Barker are hustled off in the darkness he turns to Don Carlos, who has been a silent and trembling witness of the conflict.

"In heaven's name, my brother, what brings you on this errand? Don Manuel must be mad."

"Ah, Emilio, do not blame Don Manuel," gently protests Carlos, as he embraces Navarro. "The matter was urgent, a courier was required, and I myself suggested that I be that courier. To see you again I would have dared the perils of the journey, even were nothing more at stake."

"Brave heart," murmurs Navarro, brushing back the ringlets from his brother's brow. "But let this be your last commission, Carlos. I would not jeopardize your life for a thousand Cubas. But come, is the news you bring me verbal or written?"

For answer Carlos places a letter in Navarro's hands, and the latter reads it by the light of the lantern. It is brief, and as he thrusts it into his pocket Jack steps forward.

"Ah, Ashley," cries Navarro, grasping him by the hand;

the trick was quickly done, eh? Carlos, it is to our American friend that you owe your present safety and perhaps your life. It was he who warned me of the plot for your arrest."

"Spare me any praise," protests Ashley, as Carlos is about to express his gratitude. "By good fortune I became acquainted with Alvarez' design, and further luck cast me in your brother's way."

"After you rode for miles into the mountains in search of me," interposes Navarro.

"Yes," laughs Jack, "for I had a suspicion that, single-handed, I should not have been a match for the Spanish captain and his men. Now, will you tell me, my friend, how you circumvented Alvarez so cleverly?"   .

"It was an accident. The Spaniards came down the road instead of the railroad track. When they located themselves at the crossing we established our party about 200 yards from them, to wait the coming of the train. The watch growing irksome, I and two of my men set forth to reconnoiter. We had scarcely proceeded fifty yards, when we stood face to face in the moonlight with two of the troopers.

"Instantly we threw ourselves upon them and stifled their attempts to sound an alarm. They were dragged back to our ambush, bound hand and foot, and pistols placed to their heads with orders that they be instantly shot at the first outcry. I rightly assumed that their companions would institute search for them, and shortly after two more troopers came up the road. These we took from the rear and when all four were safely secured the idea of exchanging our dress for theirs and rejoining Alvarez naturally suggested itself. The rest you know."

"Yes, and I also know that only by a fraction of a second did I prevent your glittering sword blade from carving in twain the head of a very warm friend of mine."

"How? The fellow who was holding Carlos?"

"The same. He is an American, like myself, but it suits his purpose for the present to masquerade as a soldier of Castile. At the moment I interfered you were about to slaughter the man to whom Carlos primarily owes his escape to-night, for it was through him that I learned of the plan to arrest the messenger to El Terredo."

"San Pedro!" cries the impetuous Navarro, in tones of sincere regret. "I should never have forgiven myself. But I will at once set him at liberty and add the poor consolation of an honest apology."

"That is exactly what I do not wish you to do. It was to avoid recognition that I rigged out in this uniform, and I am confident that Alvarez did not recognize me. Barker, that is my friend's name, may or may not have discovered my identity when I cried out to you at the moment I clutched your arm. At any rate, I shall not attempt to ascertain. The principal point I wish to insist upon, if you will permit me, is that Alvarez and Barker shall not be separated; further, that they be permitted to proceed to Santiago within forty-eight hours."

"Your wishes shall be respected, my dear Ashley," says Navarro.

"Where have you had the prisoners taken?" asks Jack.

"To the ambush I spoke of, about 200 yards up the road."

"And your further plans?"

"I intended to have marched the Spaniards back to the mountains as prisoners of war. Within the hour I shall send a courier to the revolutionary camp with orders to forward two hundred men with which to capture the supply train. They should arrive early to-morrow forenoon."

"Good. That work successfully accomplished, you can then permit Alvarez and Barker to depart in peace."

"If you so desire. And now suppose we rejoin my men."

As the two move away Ashley's eye is caught by the glitter of a small object upon the ground. He picks it up and discovers that it is a locket attached to a broken bit of chain. As he turns it over in his hands and seeks to examine it in the pale light of the moon, Navarro calls to him from the road: "Still surveying the battlefield, Ashley?"

"Coming," says Jack. He drops his find into his hip pocket and proceeds to forget all about it.

"What is to be done with Carlos, now that he is here?" he inquires as he rejoins the Navarros.

"Carlos must return to Santiago at once," declares El Terredo. "If I might add to the already large debt of gratitude, I would ask that you accompany him."

"Gladly, Navarro. My intentions were to make Santiago at all speed. You will not have Carlos return by rail?"

"No; by horse."

"There is a possibility of running into trouble upon his arrival at the city."

"True; and to obviate that I have conceived a plan, not startlingly original. Carlos must disguise himself in feminine attire."

"Ah, then I pose in the role of a knight errant escorting a beautiful maiden over the desert sands to her ancestral halls."

Navarro laughs softly. "Is the part distasteful to you?" he asks.

"Nay. My only regret will be that Carlos is not the beauteous maid she will represent."

"But he will look the part to perfection, I promise you. Half a dozen of my men will act as escort and conduct Carlos to the quinta. But I want the assurance of your active head and arm the greater part of the journey."

"Thank you. And the female toggery—where is that to be procured?"

"That is a more difficult matter to adjust. Do you think the same wardrobe that fitted you out to-night could be called upon in this emergency?"

"It is possible," replies Ashley. "There are women folks about the Hotel Americano, else the house would not present its unusually neat appearance. And there being women some of them probably have a dress or two to spare. I will endeavor to negotiate with the land-lord for a suitable costume for your brother."

"Excellent. I will await you here."

The village is quiet as a churchyard when Ashley

reaches the hotel. Lights are visible, however, and a few raps upon the portals bring forth the landlord.

Carter receives back his Grand Army habiliments without comment, but his face is a study when Ashley broaches the idea of a feminine rig.

"By gum," he exclaims; "you're the funniest customer I've run up against in all my Cuban hotel business, and I have met some queer ones, too."

"My dear Carter," confides Ashley, "as a matter of fact, I am not altogether right in my head. I am seized at frequent periods with the most absurd notions. Fortunately, I always have money enough to gratify my freakish ideas."

"I am not so soft as I look," remarks Carter, dryly. "I'll see what I can do for you. How soon do you want the clothes?"

"As usual, at once. And while they are being hunted up I wish you would have my horse saddled, as I must take the road within the hour. It is getting along toward midnight. Where are the troopers—drunk or asleep?"

"Both, most of them," is the laconic response, as the boniface takes himself off to consult with his wife upon the subject of providing a costume for a slender young man about five feet in height, as Ashley describes the prospective wearer of the garments.

Landlord Carter has a daughter who rejoices in the possession of three dresses. This alone should constitute her the belle of Jibana. For a sum sufficient to double her wardrobe the young lady is induced to part with the best of her three outfits and a bargain is consummated.

Miss Carter is not at all pleased at being routed from her slumbers, but she is a rather pretty young woman, and after five minutes of Ashley's persuasive eloquence the landlord's daughter beams with good nature and laughingly inquires: "Do you want a complete costume?"

"To the last ribbon," declares Jack. "By Jove!" he adds, mentally, "if Carlos proposes to impersonate a young lady, he shall not lack verisimilitude through any neglect on my part."

"A thousand thanks, Miss Carter," says Ashley, when the clothes are finally tied in a big bundle and given into his possession.

"Isn't this too much?" demurs the young lady, glancing at the gold coin which he places in her hands.

"Not a bit," replies Jack. "If it is"—he glances around, sees that papa Carter has disappeared, and snatches a kiss from the young lady's red lips—"if it is, will you permit me to balance the debt?" he finishes. Miss Carter blushes furiously, but she does not reprove the audacity. Good-looking young men, alas, are few in Jibana.

Half an hour later Ashley turns the bundle of apparel over to Navarro and receives the latter's warmest thanks. "At what time do we start?" Jack inquires.

"At daybreak. You will need a few hours' rest before then."

"I can use them all right. But suppose Alvarez' men come nosing around after their absent leader?"

"They will not find him. Follow me and I will lead you to our camp for the night. I shall send with you as a guide a man who knows the country well."

With the dawn the little party is under way. Ashley stares in astonishment at the metamorphosis that has been effected in the person of Carlos. And as Carlos raises his veil and returns Jack's stare with a glance in which amusement is mingled with blushing diffidence, the newspaper man laughs outright.

"I told you he would look the part to perfection," remarks the elder Navarro, as he comes forward to say adios. "Take good care of him, Ashley, mi amigo. He is very dear to me."

"For your sake I will guard him with jealous care," replies Ashley. "Good-by, Navarro. I hope to see you again before many days."

"Most heartily do I echo the wish. But who can say what the future has in store?" murmurs the insurgent leader. He watches the little cavalcade until it disappears down the forest trail and then turns toward the mountains with a heavy sigh.

Ashley drops to the rear of the little procession, lights a cigar and relapses into a reverie. Suddenly he bethinks him of the locket which he picked up on the scene of last night's struggle.

Although his eyes never before rested upon it, as he looks at it now the locket has almost a familiar appearance. He is somewhat prepared for the surprise which follows his pressing of the spring.

The locket formerly contained two miniatures. One has been removed. That which yet remains is an exquisite portrait of Louise Hathaway.

As Ashley stares at the gold ornament with its broken bit of chain he realizes that he is looking upon the locket supposed to have been removed from the watch-chain of Roger Hathaway the night the aged cashier came to his death in the Raymond National Bank.

CHAPTER XLV.

THE DOVE AND THE SERPENT.

"Whoa, Rozinante! If thou art as weary of this road as I, good beast, a rest will not go against thy grain, or grass. What say you to a halt of half an hour within the shade of this royal palm?"

It is the afternoon of the third day since Ashley's return to Santiago, and, having parted with Don Carlos and the escorting party on the edge of Santos, this is the first opportunity Jack has had to ride out to La Quinta de Quesada and pay his respects to Don Manuel's beautiful daughter; for the last three days have been busy ones for the newspaper man. Truenos has arrived with his fleet from Havana, and the next week promises to be big with the fate of Cuba Libre.

Ashley left Santiago an hour ago, and at the rate he

has been traveling—the heat precludes a gait faster than a moderate amble—he judges that he has covered three of the four miles to Santos.

Hitching the amiable Rozinante, he throws himself upon the turf beneath the foliage-massed branches of the royal palm, and lights a cigar; as he smokes he grows thoughtful. And from rumination he drifts into moralizing, addressing himself to Rozinante.

"Look here, Rozinante; if you have any horse sense that you're not using you might assist your master to extricate himself from somewhat of a quandary. As you know, I came to Cuba principally on business for my paper, incidentally to trail down a murder mystery and again incidentally to follow a fair face belonging to the beautiful Louise Hathaway. A good many chaps in my place would have fallen hopelessly in love with Miss Hathaway at first sight, but I—well, that is not the cause of my quandary. If it were, I could easily dismiss it with a philosophical 'there is no accounting for the tastes of most women.' Ah, no, Rozinante; it is something far more serious; for what I want to ask you, Rozinante, is whether you believe that I, in my old age, have been so indiscreet as to fall in love?"

But Rozinante, being a well-bred equine, declines to poke his nose into young people's affairs and continues his grass-cropping.

"See how the case stands, Rozinante," continues Jack, tossing a pebble at his four-footed companion to enforce attention. "On the one hand is the Senorita Juanita de Quesada, the acknowledged Pearl of the Antilles, the adored of all the beaux in Santiago; Juanita, the beautiful, the accomplished, and the only child of the wealthy and elderly Don Manuel de Quesada, who is likely to become the president de facto of this cheerful country if the yellow fever continues to wilt the imported flower of the chivalry of Spain. On the other hand, Rozinante, look at me."

At this moment Rozinante lifts his head and blinks comically at Ashley, who grins back in the best of humors.

"Oh, I know what you are thinking about, Rozinante. You are saying to yourself: 'What a presumptuous fellow! But he is just like all Americans.' Well, you are not far from right, Rozzy. We Americans are a bit fresh. But that is a digression. To return to our subject, which is the always agreeable one of myself. Now, I am not a bad-looking chap. You can see that, Roz, with one eye. And I am fairly bright and all that. But hang it! I haven't a bank account bigger than three figures, and it will require nerve, my grass-eating friend, to step up to the wealthy Don Quesada and say: 'Don, old boy, I love your daughter. May I ask your blessing?' No one ever accused me of lacking in nerve, but have I enough to supply the demand of such an occasion? Of course, if Don Quesada becomes president of the republic of Cuba, and makes me his cabinet-premier, I might buy a sugar plantation and become enormously wealthy. But that, Rozinante, as you are probably aware, is a twenty-to-one shot.

"The most perplexing feature of the whole affair is the fact that I have no good reason to suppose that the dark-eyed Juanita returns in the slightest degree the deep interest which I feel in her personal welfare. I know that she likes me—why shouldn't she?—but her maidenly reserve I do not seem to be able to successfully penetrate. Again, my equine friend, I am not so certain that she is not hopelessly in love with that effeminate, downy-cheeked, pink-and-white and milk-and-water Don Carlos. And how any woman can—— But, pshaw! What is the use in quarreling with the chap? And what is the use of my lounging longer here, talking at an unappreciative audience? Ah, Juanita, if you would but encourage me a bit I would soon solve my perplexity. Just a draught from this spring back in the bushes, Rozinante, and then we will jog along toward Santos."

As Ashley bends over the spring the grating of carriage wheels sounds in the road.

A volante flashes by at what seems reckless speed; but the Cuban volante cannot upset. Two ladies are in the vehicle, and as they sweep by they glance curiously at the tethered horse. An instant later they are gone, and the young man who emerges hastily from the bushes and looks down the dust-veiled road emits a long, low whistle.

"Juanita! And unless my usually correct vision is deceived, her companion is my old friend Isabel Harding. The dove and the serpent! What the deuce is the meaning of this unholy intimacy? By heaven, Rozinante," mutters Ashley, as he untethers his horse and vaults into the saddle, "the presence of Isabel Harding at Santos augurs no good to the house of Quesada. Don Manuel must be warned at once." And kicking Rozinante's ample sides Ashley forces that amiable beast into a violent canter.

The remainder of the journey is quickly covered, and as Jack reins up at La Quinta de Quesada, Don Manuel comes out and greets him cordially.

"Welcome, Senor Ashley. You are quite a stranger. We had begun to fear that the Spanish press censors had suppressed you." Then, dropping his voice to a cautious undertone: "Any news from the field?"

"Yes, and rather good news. It is reported in Santiago that your yacht, the Pearl of the Antilles, engaged a Spanish ship of war yesterday, and that El Terredo, after lying alongside, fought a desperate and winning battle on the decks of the enemy's vessel."

"Bueno!" Don Quesada's eyes light up with pleasure. "Ah, Senor Ashley, there is a fighter after your own American heart. If we had a thousand such men we should drive the Spanish into the sea and off our loved island forever."

"I was passed on the road from Santiago by your daughter," remarks Jack, as he sits down in front of a brimming glass. "Will she be absent long?"

"For the entire evening. Surely you have not overlooked the grand ball to be given to-night by the new captain-general; a gathering of beauty and of chivalry, to express his supreme contempt of the insignificance of the Cuban cause," says Don Queseda, with faint irony.

"By Jove! I had overlooked it. The senorita was

accompanied by another lady. May I inquire her name?"

"Certainly. She is Mrs. Isabel Harding."

"I thought so," mutters Jack. Then:

"What is her business here?"

"Mrs. Harding is my guest," replies Don Quesada, rather curtly.

"She has been here long?"

"About ten days."

Jack stares and bites his cigar viciously. "You will pardon my questioning, Don Queseda. Believe me, I am not actuated by idle curiosity."

The Don bows and Jack leans over and asks, earnestly:

"During Mrs. Harding's stay here has she learned anything that would lead her to suspect that you are identified with the movement to free Cuba?"

"Naturally. She is one of us," replies the Don, dryly.

"One of us!" repeats Jack, in astonishment.

"Yes. An American, like yourself; she is an enthusiastic adherent of the Cuban cause and is enabled to do us much service."

"Then you have trusted her with some secrets?"

"She is at this moment the bearer of important dispatches to Captain Francisco Guerra."

"Great Scott!" Jack jumps to his feet. Don Quesada rises with him and demands:

"What do you mean?"

"I mean that I believe Mrs. Harding to be a spy in the employ of the Spanish government, and that you have signed and given into her hands your own death warrant and the utter ruin of your friends!"

It is a cruel blow. Don Quesada staggers under it and sinks helplessly into his chair. Jack pours him out a draught of wine and then paces to and fro on the veranda, his active mind intent on some path of escape from the desperate situation.

"At what hour does the ball begin?" he demands.

"At eight, I believe," replies Don Quesada, faintly. He is completely crushed.

"It is now nearly six," muses Jack, glancing at his

watch. "And Guerra? Where was he to receive the dispatches?"

"At the ball."

"Quick! Pen and paper," requests Jack. And as Don Quesada hurries away to comply the young man murmurs: "There is only one chance in a thousand, but I must take it."

When the stationery is brought Jack inquires: "In what form were the dispatches sent?"

"In a plain envelope, such as you have there."

"Good." Jack writes hurriedly a few moments, passes what he has written over to Don Quesada, and commanding simply, "Copy that," busies himself over another letter.

Don Quesada follows the directions without question, but as he writes a little of hope comes into his pale face, and he looks admiringly at Jack, with the remark: "Can you do it?"

"Quien sabe? It's a desperate chance." Jack glances approvingly at the letter which the Don has sealed, places it in his pocket and then addresses and seals the second letter, which he gives to the Cuban president.

"You must leave here at once. Where is Don Carlos?"

"He is here."

"He must accompany you. You must make your way with all haste as secretly as possible to Santiago and go aboard the United States cruiser America. This letter will explain all, and make you welcome. Once under the stars and stripes you will be safe when the storm breaks."

"But my daughter!" cries the Don, suddenly recollecting the beautiful Pearl of the Antilles. Jack's eyes grow tender, and, gripping the older man by the hand, he says proudly, as their eyes meet.

"Don Quesada, I love your daughter. I will answer for her safety with my life. And now, I'm off. Remember—to Santiago at once. Adios!"

And without waiting to ascertain how his declaration of love affects the father of his loved one, Jack springs into the saddle and clatters away.

CHAPTER XLVI.

PLAYING FOR HIGH STAKES.

Scarcely has a third of the distance to Santiago been covered when horse and rider realize that the pace set is no longer compatible with the Cuban climate. As Rozinante settles into a walk, Ashley pulls vigorously on a fresh cigar and revolves the situation in his mind.

"Credulous fool!" he grumbles, thinking of the betrayed Don Manuel de Quesada. "Played right into the enemy's hands. But wiser and greater men have been cozened by the smiles of a beautiful woman. Besides, he is Juanita's father. That covers a multitude of shortcomings. Ah, Juanita, I must indeed love thee when I would willingly risk my valuable life in thy behalf. I am not a hypocrite, and I confess that an absorbing interest in my personal welfare has ever been one of my glittering characteristics."

"Those papers must be recovered. But how? But I have a mighty big job on my hands, even if Truenos is not a Richelieu. Well, it is the pen against the sword, and may heaven maintain the vaunted mightiness of the pen."

It is something after seven o'clock when Ashley arrives at Santiago. The first acquaintance he meets, after he has put up his horse and proceeded toward his hotel, is General Murillo.

"Of course you are going to the ball?" remarks Ashley, as they shake hands.

Most assuredly General Murillo will be there. It will be a grand affair. Senor Ashley must attend, by all means.

Senor Ashley means to be there, and he thanks General Murillo for an offer to introduce him to a score of the prettiest maids in Cuba. And when the general insists upon his American friend dining with him, the latter quickly accepts. He has no time to waste, he tells himself, but he is much relieved when, in reply to his query, "And Truenos, is he at the palace?" General Murillo informs him that the captain-general has been called to Mentos, ten miles distant, on business of an important nature, and will probably be late in arriving at the festivities, which will not, however, be delayed.

The first flash of hope comes to Ashley at this intelligence, and he dines with a lighter heart. After half an hour of chat on commonplace topics, he manages to ask with well-played indifference:

"At what time did Truenos leave for Mentos, general?"

"Early this afternoon."

Ah, then it is not yet too late. Ashley breathes easier.

"Well, general, you are a loyal adherent of Spain and I am an out-and-out American. There is no chance for an argument between us. Let me fill your glass and we will drink a toast to all honest men and women, whether Spaniards or Cubans."

"With pleasure, Senor Ashley. To all honest men—and women."

"Which does not include your amiable friend, Mrs. Harding," thinks Ashley, as he raises the glass to his lips.

The dinner finished, the two men separate, while Ashley exchanges his travel-worn garments for an evening dress. Half an hour later he and General Murillo leave for the palace.

"I have a vague suspicion that I am booked for an exciting evening," muses Jack, as he enters the brilliantly lighted sala of the palace and is duly presented by Murillo.

The dancing has already begun, but Terpsichore is the last goddess he is desirous of wooing on this particular evening. His gaze wanders solicitously about the crowded room and rests at last upon her whom he seeks—Juanita.

"She is simply stunning to-night," he mutters, nervously tugging at his mustache.

And indeed Juanita is radiantly beautiful. Her dark

loveliness is set off by a bewitching gown of white; she is fanning herself with that lazily graceful motion which the Saxon cannot imitate successfully, and at the moment that Ashley discovers her she is telling Captain Ramon Huerta, who has requested with Spanish extravagance "the exquisite honor and incomparable delight of a figure with her," that she really does not care to dance this evening. At which Captain Huerta looks disappointed and scowls a trifle. But he continues to inflict upon her a presence which is palpably unwelcome.

Juanita's eyes light up with unfeigned pleasure when Ashley arrives upon the scene and she greets him with unreserved cordiality. She presents him to Captain Huerta, who bows as stiffly as he holds his revolver arm. Ashley returns the salute with a suspicion of exaggeration, and grins maliciously when the Spaniard takes himself off, after bestowing a glance of unmistakable enmity upon the American.

Juanita gazes after the retreating form with distinct aversion. "I have a strange fear of that man," she confides to Ashley, who smiles reassuringly and tells her that while she is in his vicinity there should be no such word as fear in her bright lexicon of youth.

Juanita rewards this gallant speech, which from anyone except Jack Ashley would sound boastful, with a glance that sets the American's blood tingling. But he has no time to-night for love-making, whether his suit be favored or hopeless, and as he drops into a chair beside the Pearl of the Antilles he asks casually: "Where is your friend, Mrs. Harding?"

"Ah, you know Isabel?

'You passed me this afternoon on the road to Santos, whither I was proceeding to pay my most humble respects."

"Then that horse by the big royal palm was yours?"

"Even so. I was close by, but your volante swept past at such a pace that I hardly recovered from my surprise at seeing you before you were gone."

"I am sorry we started away so early," Juanita says, regretfully.

"So am I," Ashley thinks, grimly, but he does not tell her why.

"I have seen nothing of Mrs. Harding since I arrived," he remarks.

Juanita's glance wanders about the room. "There she is," she indicates, "over by the staircase, the object of the devoted attentions of Count Gonzaga."

"Who the deuce is Count Gonzaga?" wonders Ashley, and he intimates as much to his companion.

"Have you not met the count? General Jacinto de Gonzaga is his military title. He is some sort of an assistant secretary of war and is representing the home government in Cuba for a short time. He seems desperately smitten with Isabel. She is very handsome, do you not think so, Senor Ashley?"

"Yes, very," replies Jack, absently. He is watching the pair by the staircase. and wondering what sort of a game Isabel Harding is now playing.

"She is coming this way," says Juanita. "Have you met her?"

"I have not had that pleasure," Ashley replies, unblushingly. "Not lately,' he mentally adds.

He turns away to admire some flowers and soon he hears Juanita's voice: "Isabel, allow me to present Mr. Ashley to you. Mr. Ashley, Mrs. Harding."

Ashley turns calmly and the two are face to face. She acknowledges the introduction with a composure equal to Ashley's own, and that young man permits a trace of admiration to mingle with the expression in his eyes which plainly says to the woman before him: "I know your game, my lady." And the answering flash from the midnight orbs is: "You have more than a match in me, Mr. Ashley. Beware!"

"We shall see," thinks Ashley, and then, led by Juanita, who sees nothing of the mutual recognition, the conversation drifts into the usual chatter of the ball-room.

"You remember, Isabel, that big horse we saw lunching so contentedly by the road this afternoon?" prattles Juanita.

"Yes, dear, and how we wondered whether its owner was enjoying a siesta in the bushes."

"Well, it was Mr. Ashley's horse."

"I saw you flit by," supplements Ashley, "but I was back drinking at a spring and your volante was out of sight before I had recovered from my surprise at seeing you." He is looking directly at Mrs. Harding and that lady smiles, a bit ironically.

"And I presume that when you saw the principal attraction of El Valle de Bosque Cillos being borne toward Santiago, you mounted your horse and sadly followed," ventures Isabel.

"No; I knew the senorita was in good company," Jack responds, dryly, "so I continued on to Santos and spent a profitable hour with Don Quesada."

"Ah!" Mrs. Harding regards him narrowly from between her half-dropped eyelids.

"I say profitable," continues Ashley, "as I did not know, until so informed, that Don Quesada numbered the charming Mrs. Harding in his list of acquaintances."

"Of course you congratulated him."

"Most assuredly."

The half-veiled contempt expressed in Isabel's face exasperates Ashley. Hidden somewhere in that corsage, against which beats the falsest heart in Cuba, are papers that mean the ruin of the innocent girl at his side.

He must have time to think, think, think. So he excuses himself and leaves the crowded ball-room for a walk in the cool air of the garden.

In one corner of the spacious inclosure he finds a little arbor, and in this nook Ashley sits and smokes and thinks, but no plan for the confusion of the adventuress suggests itself, unless, as he growls vindictively, he abducts or chloroforms her.

His meditations are disturbed by voices close at hand. Two gentlemen have, like himself, forsaken the heated ball-room for the outer air, and they pause in their stroll within a few feet of Ashley's retreat.

Jack pays no attention to them until by their voices and conversation he realizes that one of them is Captain

Julio Alvarez and the other is Count Gonzaga. "That's a happy combination," he laughs softly. "They ought to get a few more of Isabel's friends and hold a reunion."

"You are an excellent judge of beauty, Count Gonzaga," he hears Alvarez remark, with a faint sneer. "I have been noticing your devotion to the handsome Mrs. Harding, the widow of the enormously wealthy ship-owner."

"Ah, amigo, is she not beautiful?" the count replies, enthusiastically. He appears to be in rare spirits. "I must ask you to congratulate me, Captain Alvarez."

"I have—on your excellent taste."

"On more, amigo. The beautiful American has consented to become the Countess Gonzaga."

"The devil!"

"You are surprised."

"Rather. I am surprised that a gentleman of Count Gonzaga's position should think of linking his name with a lady of her character."

"Por Dios! Your meaning?" cries the count, with a flash of Castilian wrath that causes Captain Alvarez to curse his hasty words, which must have emanated from jealousy or something deeper. Ashley wonders what.

"Oh, nothing," Alvarez replies, carelessly. "You must pardon my unthinking remark, count. Believe me, I——"

"You will explain yourself to me, and at once, senor," declares Gonzaga, with frigid emphasis.

There is a silence, which Alvarez, who sees that he is in for it, finally breaks with: "Very well, count, but I warn you that you will regret your insistence. You will have to excuse me now, as I have promised to dance this next figure. Meet me at this place a quarter of an hour hence, and I will endeavor to satisfy you."

"Very good," grits Gonzaga. "I will be prompt," and the men separate.

"The fair Isabel is a star, surely," soliloquizes Ashley. "Who would have dreamed that she was playing her cards for the role of a countess? Alas! Gonzaga will be brutally undeceived by Alvarez. The latter has put his foot in it and there is only one way out. Jupiter!"

Ashley leaps to his feet, for the inspiration of his life has come to him.

"By George, I have it! But will she do it?" he cries. "She must do it. It is not her nature, still it's a chance, and if the fates are on the side of right Don Quesada and the senorita are saved!"

CHAPTER XLVII.

THE PEN WINS.

Upon his return to the ball-room Ashley is taken to task by General Murillo. "I have been searching for you for over half an hour," the general assures him. "Come over here while I introduce you to the prettiest girl in Cuba."

"Confound his kindness," grumbles Jack, mentally, who has no time to squander in talking nonsense with dark-eyed senoritas. There is work to be done. But he follows Murillo over the floor and is amused to find himself being introduced to Juanita de Quesada, who is the center of attraction of a group of young Santiago swells.

"Oh, Senor Ashley and I are old friends," cries Juanita, smiling at General Murillo.

"Are you, indeed?" remarks the general, favoring the American with a keen glance. "Well, I will leave you together with my blessing," and the warrior takes himself off.

"I have much to tell you to-night, senorita, but at another moment," Ashley says, as he makes his excuses for terminating a conversation that has hardly begun. "I have work to do, and it means much to you," he explains to the pouting young lady, and leaving her somewhat mystified and not at all pleased, he goes off to hunt up Isabel Harding.

He finds the latter alone. For excellent reasons Count Gonzaga is holding himself aloof. Captain Alvarez is not in sight.

"Don't you find the atmosphere of the room close?" he inquires, as he reaches Isabel's side.

"Not at all. I am entirely cool," she responds.

"But it is ever so much pleasanter in the garden," persists Ashley, as he twists his mustache and meets her curious glance with a smile that is amiability itself. Without another word she rises and accepts his extended arm.

"How delightful it is out here under the stars," rattles on Jack, as they emerge into the garden. "These glorious nights almost repay one for the sweltering days. Ah, here is an ideal summer house. You will find it as cozy as a society darling's boudoir. Won't you take a seat?"

Mrs. Harding laughs, a trifle ironically, as she sinks upon the wooden bench that runs around the interior.

"Now, Mr. Ashley," she remarks, "will you be good enough to inform me what you have brought me out here to tell me?"

"With pleasure, madam," responds Ashley, dropping back into his old deliberate self.

"If you will let your thoughts stray back about six weeks, Mrs. Harding, you will perhaps remember that on a certain evening I had the pleasure of relating to you a fairy tale, to assist you in dissipating the monotony of an attendance upon the French ball. The fairy tale lacked the closing and most interesting chapter, you will recall, and I requested that you supply it. 'Not to-night.' you protested, but you kindly promised me an interview upon the following forenoon.

"That promise, I regret to say, you broke with as little ceremony as one would——"

"I presume," interrupts Mrs. Harding, "that it will be unnecessary for me to assign my reason for failing to keep my promise."

"Quite. It would not mend matters. Now, suppose,

as the novelists say, we take up the thread of our narrative, which was broken when I left your box at the garden."

"Suppose we do? What do you desire of me?"

"I wish to possess myself of certain information in your keeping."

"Relative to that Vermont affair?"

"Precisely."

"I can tell you nothing."

"Excuse me. Perhaps you mean you will tell me nothing."

"As you please, sir."

"I think you will," Jack says, calmly. "Will you pardon a cigar, Mrs. Harding? Perhaps the smoke will keep these inquisitive mosquitoes at a distance."

Isabel laughs unpleasantly. "Do I understand you to intimate that you will resort to force?" she inquires, sarcastically.

"Assuredly; although I don't fancy the word 'force.' 'Induce' is the better term."

"A truce to your euphemism, Mr. Ashley. I am curious to learn what possible lever you can possess."

"I shall not delay the information. I have in mind a lever whose potency you can readily appreciate. I refer to the Count de Gonzaga."

"Good heavens! What do you mean?" In awed, whispered tones.

"I think you grasp my meaning," Jack returns, coolly. "Or will it be necessary for me to relate another fairy tale, concerning a beautiful woman who posed successfully for a time as the widow of an enormously wealthy American ship-owner?"

"You would not dare——"

"I would dare do several things, if the occasion for unusual trepidity seemed to arise. Besides, the vaunted brotherhood of man——"

"The vaunted brotherhood of man would lead you to betray a defenseless woman—one who never did you aught of harm, would it?" pants Isabel.

"My dear Mrs. Harding, consider how easily you may

avert such an unfortunate denouement. I don't care a rap about Count Gonzaga. Conceding your natural charms, which are legion, the count's affections are undoubtedly centered in your supposed fortune. That is usually the principal item in the matrimonial calculations of European nobility that seeks alliance with American beauty. As a matter of fact, I should rather enjoy seeing Gonzaga thrown down, if you will excuse the slang. Come. A bargain is a bargain!"

There is a silence. Isabel is presumably weighing the situation carefully, and she disappoints Ashley by rising and remarking: "I think I will return to the ball-room, Mr. Ashley, if you will kindly escort me."

"One moment," detains Jack. Isabel resumes her seat. "Have you carefully considered the probable result of your silence?"

"Perfectly."

"You must have some powerful reason for sealing your lips on that Raymond affair," comments Jack; and then he growls under his breath: "Why in thunder don't they come?"

"We may as well terminate this interview. Do your worst, Mr. Ashley."

"That is rather theatric, Mrs. Harding," banters Jack. "Clever woman, this," he thinks. "She knows I would not be such a beastly cad as to tell her story to Gonzaga. Ah!"

Footsteps are heard approaching. They stop just without the summer house.

"Stay!" Ashley whispers in Isabel's ear. "The count is here."

She starts to ask, "how do you know it is he?" but remains mute. An instant later the new arrival is joined by another.

"Captain Alvarez!" breathes Jack, gripping Isabel's arm. "Not a word!"

Isabel sinks into a seat. Ashley can feel her tremble. He tosses away his cigar and remains standing. The silence that broods over the garden nook is broken by

Captain Alvarez, who is so near the listeners that they could reach out and almost touch him.

"While I can find no objection, Count Gonzaga, to satisfying your unfortunate demand, I would advise that you drop this matter where it is. No good can come of wittingly injuring your amour propre. Believe me——"

"Captain Alvarez," interrupts the count, frigidly, "you made a distinct accusation against the character of the lady whom I have honored with an offer of my hand. I demand that you retract your statement and apologize for its utterance, or prove its truth."

"I am willing to recall my hasty words, count."

"Then you lied?"

There is a short but eloquent silence. "Very well," says Alvarez. "I perceive that you are determined to be wholly undeceived as to the imposition which has been put upon you. Know then that the wealthy American widow, Isabel Harding, is neither wealthy nor a widow."

"Not a widow?" repeats Count Gonzaga. "Caramba! What, then, is she?"

"What you will," replies Alvarez, indifferently. "What usually is an adventuress?"

"But the proof? Dios! The proof?" demands the count. Perchance Alvarez is lying to him.

A low, unpleasant laugh from the latter. "I had the honor of being at one time the very good friend of madam," he says.

"Scoundrel!" grits Ashley in Mrs. Harding's ear. The critical moment is at hand. "Victory!" murmurs Jack, as Mrs. Harding, who has risen and is twisting her lace handkerchief into shreds, gasps once or twice as Alvarez finishes his brutal story, and then faints in Ashley's arms.

"El Diablo!" the latter hears the count ejaculate, and with the mortification in his voice is mingled much of mental relief.

"Rather indelicate, but when a life is at stake delicacy must go by the board," mutters Ashley.

"Ah, the precious papers! Now, my lady, we will part company."

The fanfare of trumpets in the ball-room announces that the captain-general has at last arrived to grace the festivities with his presence.

"Have you quite recovered?" Ashley asks Isabel, with as much solicitude in his voice as he can command.

"Yes, thank you. You see I am yet a woman," she says bitterly. And she adds in tones of intense hatred: "The cur! The coward! But come, let us return to the ball——"

They have reached the entrance of the ball-room. Mrs. Harding stops and favors Ashley with the kindest look she has ever bestowed upon him.

"Mr. Ashley, you are no friend of mine. In fact, you are the only man I have ever feared. But I know you would not have been the coward that Capt. Alvarez has proved."

Ashley's response is an enigmatic smile. He remarks, lightly: "I have the honor of wishing you a very good evening, Mrs. Harding."

He watches her disappear in the crowd and sees her a few moments later in the long line that is passing the "reviewing stand." As she pauses an instant before the captain-general Ashley notes the latter incline his head slightly. Some words are spoken and Mrs. Harding continues on.

A triumphant smile flits over Ashley's face; he thinks exultingly:

"The pen wins this time! Now for Juanita!"

CHAPTER XLVIII.

THE SWORD TRIUMPHANT.

"You are in unusually good spirits this evening, Senor Ashley."

"I am always happy when I am near you, senorita," is Jack's fervent response. At which speech, the warmest she has ever heard from his lips, Juanita grows as rosy as the morn and does not appear displeased.

"Is that dreadfully important work which has occupied so much of your time this evening yet finished?"

"Very nearly."

"And you can devote a little time to your friends?"

"I am ready to devote the remainder of my existence to one of them, senorita."

"Oh, what unselfishness! When do you expect to begin?"

"Whenever I have reason to believe that such devotion will be rewarded by——"

"Reward? Then it is not a bit unselfish and does not deserve encouragement," interrupts the young lady, with a toss of her head.

"You are cruel, senorita," murmurs Ashley, but his voice does not betray a great deal of grief.

"I am just," declares Juanita. "While I have been sitting here at the mercy of a lot of frightfully stupid men, you have devoted your time to the entertainment of Mrs. Harding. Perhaps that was the devotion you alluded to a moment ago," ventures the young lady, with a pretty frown.

"Hardly," laughs Jack. "You do not know Mrs. Harding, senorita."

"Perhaps not as well as you, Senor Ashley. My opportunities have not been so good. I saw you come in from the garden. One would hardly judge that you had met her only half an hour ago."

"Oh, the fair Isabel and I are old friends," Ashley remarks, serenely.

"Indeed? Yet you told me——"

"I will tell you more, senorita."

"I don't want to hear any more," opposes Juanita crossly. "You have deceived me once and I——"

"Deceived thee? Ah, Juanita——" Jack checks himself as he notes the flush of annoyance in her cheeks.

"Hello! There's the chap I've been looking for," suddenly remarks Ashley, as he catches a glimpse of Capt. Guerra over by the big staircase. "Will you pardon me just a moment, senorita? That will complete my evening work, and then if a lifetime of devotion will——"

"Stop! I shan't hear another word," breaks in Juanita, imperiously. "And you need not hurry back," she adds irritably, provoked by Ashley's serenity.

Meanwhile Ashley is telling himself that he must be progressing in his wooing, since Juanita has betrayed symptoms of jealousy. "Devotion? She little knows how much need she has of a clear head and strong arm," he thinks. "Ah, Capt. Guerra," he remarks, pausing before a distinguished-appearing gentleman who is idling by the staircase, "will you be good enough to follow me into the garden?"

Ashley passes out and Guerra follows him curiously. When they are alone and unobserved Ashley takes an envelope from his pocket and presses it into the captain's hand.

"Read that and then destroy it," he directs.

"Your meaning, senor?"

"No explanation is necessary. I am ignorant of the contents of the documents further than that their publicity would be deuced awkward for you and incidentally for myself."

"Wonderful! How came you by them?"

"That is my affair, senor. Had I not rescued them they would now be in the hands of Truenos. Adios!" And Jack leaves the mystified Spaniard to his own devices.

Meantime a little scene that would afford Ashley the keenest delight to witness is taking place in one of the rooms of the palace. Gen. Truenos is seated at a table littered with maps and papers and Gen. Murillo and Isabel Harding have just been ushered into the apartment.

"You have succeeded?" Truenos asks as Mrs. Harding approaches.

"Beyond expectation. Quesada may not be the head and front of the offenders, but he is certainly one in whom there has been placed some authority."

"Quesada is now a fugitive," asserts Truenos.

"Indeed?" This is news to Isabel. "Ashley's warning," she thinks. "When did you learn this, general?"

"To-day. He has taken refuge on board the United States cruiser. I have strongly suspected Quesada, but have not particularly feared him. Quesada is a figure-head. What I want is proof of conspiracy on the part of men any one of whom is more troublesome than a dozen Quesadas—men I suspect to be conspiring against the government even while pretending to serve it."

"Would certain dispatches from Don Quesada addressed to Capt. Francisco Guerra furnish the necessary evidence?" asks Mrs. Harding.

"Ah! You have intercepted such?"

"Better. I am the bearer of them."

Truenos regards his spy admiringly. "Bueno! The papers at once!" he cries.

"And my reward?" suggests Isabel, as she takes from her bosom the precious envelope.

"Anything that you may ask—in reason," replies the captain-general, reaching impatiently for the documents. "Why, how is this? This letter is addressed to me.

"To you?" exclaims Isabel in astonishment. "Surely—why—there must be some mistake."

"Evidently," rejoins Truenos, as he breaks the seal.

Isabel watches him anxiously as he scans the document. A pale sickly light is beginning to break upon her bewilderment.

Ashley! The papers have been tampered with! It was for that he led her to the garden. How did he know, before they spoke, who were the two men whose meeting had interrupted their conversation in the summer house? And, oh, how weak she had been! She sees it all now and she swears she will be revenged. Aha! She knows where to wound him, to repay him in awful torture for the trick he has played upon her.

While these dark thoughts are flitting through her mind the captain-general has finished his brief examination of the letter, which he tosses over to her. She picks it up mechanically and reads:

"To His Excellency, Honorato de Truenos: Indisposition prevents my attending the grand ball to-night and offering my congratulations upon your safe arrival at Santiago. Under the directions of such a general there should be no difficulty in quickly subduing the insurrection, which I believe to be nearly at an end.   Manuel de Quesada."

"I have been tricked, Gen. Truenos," says Isabel, crushing the paper in her hand.

"It would seem so," remarks the captain-general. It is apparent that he is vastly disappointed. "Come, tell me of your stay at the quinta, all you know concerning Quesada and his movements."

There is much of importance to relate, and when Mrs. Harding has finished her story Truenos summons Capt. Huerta.

"Take a dozen of your men and repair at once to La Quinta de Quesada. You know where it is?" Capt. Huerta knows perfectly. "Ransack the house thoroughly and fetch me every scrap of writing upon the premises. Gen. Murillo, do you follow in the morning and look over the place. Go!" to Huerta.

The latter bows and leaves the room. Mrs. Harding follows. "One moment, Captain Huerta," she says.

A short but earnest conversation ensues. Isabel talks in rapid whispers, and the Spanish captain listens eagerly, while surprise, anger, hope and malicious joy are mirrored in succession upon his swarthy countenance.

"Within ten minutes," he breathes, and hurries away to execute the commands of the captain-general.

"I told you it would be better if you delivered the papers to me during the afternoon," General Murillo tells Mrs. Harding, after Truenos has gone. "Who has been the cause of your undoing?"

Isabel tells him of her suspicions, which she has come to regard as virtual facts, and Murillo is inclined to agree with her.

"The game is not yet played out, general," flashes Isabel.

"Well, take care, take care," admonishes Murillo, as they separate.

"Ah, here is the very man now," frowns the general,

as he re-enters the sala grande and is greeted by Ashley, who has just left Captain Guerra.

"My dear Senor Ashley," he observes dryly, "let me give you a piece of advice."

"With pleasure, general. I am always open to kindly counsel, although I do not always follow it."

"Do not let your interest in a young lady lead you into mixing with the affairs of a country toward which you are expected to maintain a strict neutrality," is Murillo's blunt remark.

"I don't think I catch your drift, general," drawls Jack. But he does, and the gleam of quiet triumph in his blue eyes irritates Murillo.

"I have warned you," says the latter, and turns on his heel.

"So I am suspected," thinks Ashley. "I imagined the fair Isabel would like to know to whom to ascribe her confusion. And now to undeceive Juanita."

But Juanita is not to be found. There are few guests remaining in the sala and she is not among them.

Ashley explores the garden, with like success. Then he questions the line of volante drivers drawn up before the entrance to the palace grounds. Have any of them seen Senorita de Quesada? None that he interrogates have had that pleasure, and the Pearl of the Antilles is known by sight to nearly all of them. Ashley is in despair.

"The Senorita de Quesada?" queries one of the Cuban jehus, who has just joined the group. "The senorita and another lady were driven away in a volante not ten minutes ago."

"In what direction?" demands Ashley.

"To Santos."

"To Santos? Heavens, man, they cannot go to Santos at this hour of night unescorted!"

Unescorted? Is not Captain Huerta and his men all the escort that one could desire?

This intelligence is a frightful strain upon Ashley's composure, as he thinks of Juanita, Isabel, Captain Huerta and the deserted La Quinta de Quesada.

"Quick! To Santos!" he cries, springing into a volante and tossing a handful of coin to the driver. "To Santos as fast as your horse will travel!"

The man leaps to his seat, cracks his whip and they are off.

As they clatter through the streets of Santiago and swing into the road which Ashley traversed only a few hours before, Jack shouts impatiently, "Faster! Faster! Great Scott! This is no funeral! Though it may be, before I'm through with it," he adds, savagely.

"But senor, we will dash the volante to pieces," protests his charioteer.

Inwardly chafing, but realizing the futility of impatience, Ashley forces himself to be calm. It seems an age before the distance to Santos is traversed, but finally the outlines of the few buildings which the hamlet boasts are seen against the starlit sky.

The driver reins up his steed for further directions.

"To La Quinta de Quesada," orders Ashley, and they rattle on.

Suddenly rings out the command, "Alto!" and the volante stops with a suddenness that nearly unseats its passenger, directly in front of El Calabozo de Infierno, the local carcel.

"What in the devil's name——" begins Ashley, but he is seized and dragged roughly from the volante, a pistol clapped to his head and the command hissed in his ear: "Callese!"

Lights appear about the entrance of the carcel, and as Ashley is hustled toward the gloom beyond he sees, standing near the passageway and watching the strange proceedings with a troubled face, the aged priest whom he noted at La Quinta de Quesada a few days before.

Ashley is hurried through the patio and along the ill-smelling corridor beyond to an open cell. Into this he is pushed and his ungentle captor tells him:

"En la manana muere V. sobre el garote!"

"Thank you," says Ashley. His stock of Spanish is just sufficient to enable him to comprehend the nature

of the cheerful intelligence, which is to the effect that he
is to die by the iron collar to-morrow.

"Will you leave the light?" he requests.

The smoky lantern is set upon the floor. Then the
door clangs to, there is a rattle of chains and the echo
of departing footsteps and he is alone.

CHAPTER XLIX.

EL CALABOZO DE INFIERNO.

An ordinary man, suddenly placed in the position in
which Jack Ashley finds himself, would perhaps exhaust
his strength in useless imprecations upon his oppressors,
and finish by sinking into utter hopelessness as to his
fate.

But, as was intimated when the reader first made his
acquaintance, Jack Ashley is not an ordinary man. The
practice of self-restraint has enabled him to retain to a
remarkable degree his self-possession at more than one
exciting moment, and his sublime confidence in himself
is never wanting.

Clearly his arrest has been arbitrary and unofficial.
He has not even been searched. His watch and money,
his papers, even his revolver, are upon his person.

"And best of all, they have not deprived me of this
incomparable solace," he says, as he draws a cigar from
his pocket and lights it at the smoky little lantern in the
cell. Then he throws himself on the wretched straw
couch, to think of some way out of the snare into which
he has stumbled.

Isabel Harding has undoubtedly imparted to Truenos
all she knows, all she suspects. But suspicion is not
proof. And the strongest suspicion would not have war-
ranted, much less likely have caused, such an outrage
upon a citizen of the United States,

Plainly there is some private villainy back of it all. Then a light flashes through his brain.

Juanita! In his selfish though natural consideration of his own unpleasant position he has forgotten for the nonce the Pearl of the Antilles, the one woman who has ever stirred his light heart to a love that, once given, means all of life to him.

He sees it all now. Don Quesada gone, his daughter unprotected, worse than unprotected as the companion of Isabel Harding, and at the mercy of Captain Raymon Huerta, who has haunted her for weeks and forced his unwelcome attentions upon her! The only man who could lend a defending arm locked fast in a Cuban jail, with the prospect of being garroted before another sun goes down!

It is infamous! Ashley leaps to his feet and paces the cell like a raging lion, and shakes the iron door with impotent energy.

"Pshaw!" he cries, and laughs recklessly. "What is the use in wasting my strength and nerves in this manner? Courage, Jack. If the senorita is to be saved, and yourself incidentally, you will need all of your strength and nerve. Let's take an account of stock." And he falls to meditating again.

How come Captain Huerta and his men to be at Santos at this hour of the night? Sent by Truenos, who perhaps has ordered Don Quesada's arrest, or, if he knows of the latter's flight, has ordered the quinta to be searched. How came Juanita to leave for home without bidding him adios? She could not have been so piqued by jealousy or by his good-natured banter that she would have left the palace without even a cold farewell. Isabel's work, without a doubt. Why has he been set upon by a horde of ruffians and thrust into a cell? Because his presence at Santos would interfere with some devilish plans afoot. Again Isabel's work, assisted by Captain Huerta.

But what vile plot is maturing outside the walls of El Calabozo de Infierno while he lies helpless here? As he thinks of Juanita he grits his teeth in suppressed fury and chews his cigar to a pulp.

As for his captor's gratuitous information, that he is to be executed in the morning, nonsense! That is what an American would term a cold bluff. They would not dare to proceed to such an extremity. They have gone to dangerous lengths already.

At this moment his meditations are broken in upon by a key being inserted in the cell door. The door swings open and closes behind Father Hilario, the venerable padre of the little church of San Pedro. At sight of the priest, Ashley's composure returns.

"Good-morning, father," is his salutation. "I noticed you at the entrance to my lodgings for the night, and I should have spoken, but my friends rather insisted on my maintaining a strict silence. I believe 'callese' means keep your mouth shut, or something of that sort, does it not?"

"I have but a short time to remain," says Father Hilario, surveying with some wonder the composed face of the young man before him.

"Well, whatever your errand may be, I am indebted to you for this visit," remarks Jack. "It's confoundedly lonesome here. I will not apologize for my apartment, as it is not of my own selection. Now, what can I do for you, father, or what can you do for me?"

"My son, you are not of the faith of Rome, but I have called to offer you the consolation which a clergyman can extend in your last hours."

"Is it as bad as that? Really, I don't take any stock in this garroting business. I believe that is thrown in for theatrical effect."

Father Hilario shakes his head. "Captain Huerta is a desperate man," he avows. "There is nothing to prevent his wreaking his enmity upon you."

"Oh, is there not? Thank you, father, for the offer of your ministrations, but really, I do not believe I shall need them. Do not misunderstand me," Ashley adds, quickly, as a pained expression passes over the kindly face of the priest. "What I mean is that I have too healthy an interest in life, liberty and the pursuit of happiness to pass many hours in such a stuffy, ill-smelling donjon as this."

Father Hilario holds up a warning finger. "There are listeners about," he says.

"Let them listen. If their stock of English is equal to my collection of Spanish they will be vastly entertained by my remarks."

"You will attempt to escape?" queries the priest, in a cautious whisper.

"At the first opportunity."

"The attempt will fail."

"It will succeed," retorts Ashley.

"No; it will fail," repeats Father Hilario. "The carcelero, always watchful, will be doubly vigilant to-night. He has probably been bribed."

"But a larger bribe——"

"Is out of the question. His life would pay the penalty."

"I don't believe it. But enough of that," says Ashley, impatiently. "Now tell me, father, of the Senorita de Quesada. Have you seen her to-night?"

The priest is silent. In his muteness, Ashley finds the confirmation of his worst fears.

"Speak, man!" he cries impatiently. "Do you know that the life and happiness of the senorita are more to me than my own existence? Speak!"

"She is in the church of San Pedro."

"In whose company?"

"She is alone."

"Alone in the church of San Pedro after midnight? What mean you?"

"She is a prisoner."

"A prisoner? Ten thousand devils!" rages Ashley, striding to and fro in his narrow cell.

"Calm yourself, my son," remonstrates Father Hilario. "Nothing can be accomplished by such wild outbursts."

"Oh, yes; I'll be calm!" grits Ashley. "By heaven, I'd give ten years of my life for ten minutes of liberty!"

"Come. Time flies, and the carcelero will soon be

here," admonishes Father Hilario. "Is there aught I can do for thee, my son?"

Ashley forces a tranquillity of mind that he little feels. "How came you to learn of the senorita's imprisonment?" he asks.

"I was returning from a midnight summons to a death-bed and had nearly reached my house when Captain Huerta and his men entered the town, escorting a volante. Suddenly the party were attacked in the darkness."

"By Huerta's own men?"

"That was doubtless part of the plot. The two women in the volante were separated. The senorita was borne fainting into the church and then quietness reigned again. I lingered about the scene, and was a witness of your arrest not many minutes afterward. I begged permission to see you, and the carcelero, in granting it, bade me roughly to tell you that you die on the morrow."

"A merry knave," remarks Ashley. "Well, father, you can be of great service to me. Will you not bear a message from me to General Truenos? Or, no; hang Truenos. To General Murillo, then. You know him. My detention here is without his knowledge, of that I am assured. It is a vile outrage that he would not brook."

The priest shakes his head. "It would be useless," he says. "From the instant I leave this place I shall be watched, shadowed every step of the way to my house. An attempt to leave Santos would be at once frustrated."

"You believe so?"

"I am positive of it."

"But the senorita. Can you communicate with her."

"Ay; and without the knowledge of Captain Huerta."

"You can?" cries Ashley, eagerly. "But you said you would be watched."

"Ah," says the priest, with a faint smile, "there is an entrance to the church that Captain Huerta knows not of—an entrance from my house through the little garden intervening."

"Good. Excellently good," remarks Ashley, into whose active brain has flashed an inspiration. "Father

Hilario, I have a plan. You must join the senorita and myself in marriage."

"Marry you? Impossible!" exclaims the astonished padre. Have the American's troubles driven him insane?

"Impossible nothing. Easiest thing in the world if the lady is willing," is Ashley's cheerful response. "Now, listen to me, father. Don Quesada is a fugitive, and his daughter, being a Cuban, is amenable to the laws of this country. From the Spanish government she would not likely receive much earnest protection or reparation for any wrongs she might suffer. But when she becomes 'Mrs. Jack Ashley," says Jack, dramatically, working up to a mild enthusiasm, "she is then an American citizen and as such she will be under the protection of a flag that the Spaniard dare not affront with impunity. You get the idea, eh?"

"Impossible, impossible, I tell you," repeats Father Hilario. "You are not a Catholic, Senor Ashley; the senorita is. Besides, the consent of her father——"

"This is no time for quibbling over technicalities. Would you see a woman, your friend's daughter, insulted, perhaps murdered, when a few words from your lips would save her?"

"I would do my duty," replies the priest, calmly. "The idea is madness. I cannot bring the senorita here, and you cannot reach the church."

"Oh, I'll be there in season," is the cool response. "Just leave the way from your house to the church open to me."

"If you have any message to send the senorita, you must make haste, adjures the priest. "The carcelero is approaching."

"It will be brief," replies Ashley. Then hurriedly: "Go to her at once. Comfort her. Pray with her. And tell her that I will be with her before the sun rises. Say nothing about the marriage. I prefer to do my own proposing. But, above all, remain with her until I come."

Then, in a different tone, as the cell door is swung open by the carcelero: "Many thanks, dear father, for your kindly visit and spiritual solace. I have made my peace with heaven, and to-morrow I will show these Spanish gentry how an American can die—when he gets ready," he adds, under his breath, as the iron door clangs to and he is once more alone.

CHAPTER L.

AT BAY IN THE CHURCH OF SAN PEDRO.

As the echo of Father Hilario's footsteps dies away adown the gloomy corridor Ashley glances at his watch. It lacks a quarter of two o'clock.

"The trick must be done within two hours, or all is lost," he mutters. Then he extinguishes the light and throws himself down upon the pallet of straw.

Ten, fifteen minutes pass. The tread of the carcelero on his rounds sounds from the corridor and a light is flashed into the cell. A counterfeit snore from Ashley greets him and he passes on with a muttered "Dios! He sleeps as if to-morrow were his wedding day." In five minutes, his round of inspection completed, he repasses the cell door and continues on, until silence again enshrouds the prison.

Then Ashley arises, takes out his jack-knife and opens one of the blades, a finely tempered steel saw.

"Thank heaven for that much Yankee inventiveness!" he murmurs, as he sinks on one knee beside the iron door of his cell and applies the saw blade to the lower end of one of the rusty bars.

As the steel slowly but surely eats its way into the corroded iron and finally slips entirely through, Ashley again, aided by a match, consults his watch. It is nearly three o'clock. Scarcely had he extinguished the lucifer than the approach of the carcelero is heard, and he retreats to his pallet, to again feign an audible slumber.

All still once more, and he attacks the upper end of the bar. When almost severed he seizes it with both hands and exerts all his strength. The iron snaps, and as Ashley falls back the bar slips from his hands and drops to the floor of the cell with a loud clang.

Jack inwardly curses his carelessness. Such a tremendous noise would alarm the sleepiest of guards. He must act, and act quickly.

To squeeze through the space made in the door is the work of some moments, and it is not accomplished an instant too soon. A light approaches.

Ashley remembers that opposite his cell is another, the door to which is ajar. With the iron bar in his hand he gropes his way across the corridor and into the open cell. A moment later the carcelero, lantern in hand, stands before the now tenantless pen, and stares stupidly at the wreck of the iron door.

Before he can utter an outcry the bar in Ashley's hand descends upon his head with crushing force and he drops like a log.

"I hope I didn't kill the poor devil," thinks Jack. He drags the unconscious man into the open cell, and, tearing and tying his handkerchief into a gag, he makes assured the silence of the carcelero. Then he extinguishes the lantern and is soon standing at the entrance of the prison.

To his left is life and liberty. To his right—ah, something dearer than life—Juanita de Quesada, locked in the little church of San Pedro, the outlines of which stand boldly against the star-gemmed heaven.

Within that little sanctuary the altar lamp sheds a soft light over a strange picture. Juanita is lying upon the steps of the altar, her head buried in her arms, and near by stands Father Hilario, his arms folded, gazing compassionately upon her.

"Why does he not come?" moans the girl, lifting her head and looking at the priest with tear-stained eyes from which hope has not yet fled.

Father Hilario is silent. The American does not come because, forsooth, he cannot leave his prison. But why undeceive the girl? Let her hope on to the end.

The opening of a door behind them causes both to start.

Jack Ashley stands upon the threshold, a smile upon his face.

With a glad cry Juanita runs to him and takes both his hands. "I was expecting you," she says, simply.

"Thank you.   And you?" asks Ashley, turning to Father Hilario.

"I bore your message. I did not expect you," replies the priest, regarding the young man with mingled wonder and admiration.

"Then you must have a more flattering opinion of the security of Cuban jails than I. And now, senorita, tell me how you come to be in this unhappy position."

The story is brief, but interesting.

"Five minutes after you left me in the ball-room at the palace," narrates Juanita, "Isabel came to me and declared that we should leave for Santos. She explained that Captain Huerta and his men were going to Santos at once, and would escort us, and that the ride would be enjoyable after the heat and excitement of the ball. At the mention of Captain Huerta I know I looked displeased, and Isabel remarked disagreeably: 'Perhaps you would prefer the escort of Mr. Ashley.' I replied that I should certainly prefer it to that of Captain Huerta, and she declared that you would not be likely to offer it, as——"

"As what?" asks Ashley, as Juanita pauses in confusion.

"She gave me to understand that you had proposed to her that night and that she had refused you."

"And you believed her?"

"I don't know what I believed. But I agreed to Isabel's proposition and we left for Santos at once. On our arrival there we were set upon by a party of men. All I remember is being lifted from the volante by Captain Huerta. Then I fainted, and when I recovered consciousness I was in the church, alone with Captain Huerta. He told me that he loved me. I replied that I hated him, and when he attempted to put his arm around me I struck him in the face. Then he swore frightfully and told me I would regret the blow. 'My father——' I began. 'Your father is a fugitive,' he sneered. 'You are wholly in my power.' 'Then I will kill myself,' I cried. 'Oh, no; you will come to your senses in a few hours,' he said, tauntingly. 'I shall expect to find you in a better humor when I return.' Then he went away, locking the church door behind him.

"When he had gone I piled all the furniture of the church against the door and then threw myself down before the altar and prayed. The opening of a door aroused me. I lifted my head, expecting to see again the hated face of Captain Huerta. Instead, to my great joy, I beheld Father Hilario. When he told me of your arrest I cried out in terror. Then he gave me your message and hope came to me."

"And Satan came also," quotes Ashley. "I fear your barricade would not withstand a very earnest assault," surveying the rude defense critically.

"It was all I could do. But tell me of yourself," urges Juanita. "What is the meaning of your violent arrest?"

As Ashley unfolds the black plot, beginning with the first appearance of the adventuress at La Quinta de Quesada, the Cuban girl grows very pale, and she realizes how much she owes to the blue-eyed young man who finishes his story with the smiling quotation: "And now, senorita, if a lifetime of devotion——"

"There, do not remind me of my folly," she protests, choking back a sob. "I will never doubt you again."

Thus encouraged, Ashley takes both of Juanita's hands and whispers very tenderly:

"In this darkest hour before the dawn I have found the courage to tell you what has been in my heart for— for nearly three weeks," he finishes with a smile. Even amid the dangers that surround them, the humor of his declaration impresses him.

A wave of crimson spreads over the girl's face, and in the big black eyes Ashley sees the light of a great love.

The young people's eyes meet in mutual understanding. He draws her to him, and the first kiss of love is exchanged. It must be followed by many others, for Father Hilario, after waiting what he considers a reasonable length of time, turns to the pair with an uneasy: "Well, what is all this leading up to?"

"A marriage, I should say," replies Jack, cheerfully. "That is usually the logical outcome of such a situation." Father Hilario bites his lips impatiently.

"The church and the pastor are here, and I think the bride is willing," continues Jack. The young girl gives the priest an anxious look.

"It is useless to argue that matter further," is the firm reply. "My duty to the church forbids." The priest's face convinces Ashley that the debate on the matrimonial question is closed.

"Then we must seek elsewhere for a clergyman," he remarks, coolly. "Come, Juanita." And he leads her toward the little door by which he entered the church.

"This is madness!" cries the priest, barring the way. "The town is overrun with your enemies. It is nearly day and the place is already astir. Hark! Do you not hear the tread of feet in the street?"

"Spanish or no Spanish, I don't propose to remain here and be trapped like a rat," declares Ashley. "We can at least make a break for liberty. I do not——"

The sound of a key being tried in the church door cuts short his words.

"It is Captain Huerta," whispers Juanita, and she trembles like a leaf in Jack's arms.

"Quick, father!" commands the latter. "You reconnoiter and see if the way through the garden and your house is clear." The venerable padre hurries away and Ashley improves the opportunity to shower kisses upon Juanita's cold and unresponsive lips.

"What a man you are!" she murmurs. "I believe you would make love on your way to execution."

"I should if the opportunity was offered," laughs Jack, softly. "What could more brightly illumine the last moments of a condemned man than to hold in his arms, if but for a few minutes, so much loveliness?"

At that moment Father Hilario reappears. "There is no hope," he reports. "Suspecting all was not right,

Captain Huerta has surrounded the church and grounds with his men."

"Then fasten that door," says Jack. "An attack at one end is all I care to look after."

The bolt is shot into place, and with the click comes the sound of muttered oaths from without, followed by a savage kick at the barricaded portal.

"Ho, there, within!" demands an impatient voice.

At the sound of the hateful tones Juanita shudders and throws her arms about Ashley's neck. "Save me from that man!' she whispers.

For answer Jack takes another reef in his confidence-restoring arm, and draws his revolver.

"Don't move, dear," he murmurs, solicitously. He rather enjoys the tight embrace of those soft arms, to which terror has lent a delightful fervency. "You need not fear Captain Huerta so long as there is light enough to shoot by."

It is a strange tableau that the altar lamp dimly shows. The three figures stand immovable, as if carved in stone. Ashley is calm, resolute, and his eyes are fixed upon the barricaded door. The resignation of despair is depicted in the beautiful face of the Cuban girl; her eyes seek those of her lover, her head upon his breast. They will at least die together. Near by stands the aged priest, his arms folded, his eyes turned heavenward and his lips moving as if in prayer. The tread of soldiery and the rattle of steel sound from the street.

The stillness within the church is broken only by a sharp click as Ashley's revolver is brought to half-cock.

The seconds drag by. Every one of them seems an hour.

Then there is the sound of a rush of feet without, followed by a loud crash, as the church door is hurled from its fastenings and piled upon the debris of the barricade.

The gap thus made throngs with Spanish soldiery, at their head, sword in hand, Captain Raymon Huerta. At sight of the picture within the church he starts back with a cry of surprise and a choice assortment of Castilian imprecations.

"You here, dog of an Americano? Who opened to thee the doors of the carcel?" And the Spanish captain glowers around upon his followers.

"I am indebted to no one except myself for my escape from your infernal den," replies Ashley; and he adds, sternly:

"Hark ye, Captain Raymon Huerta. I am here to protect this young woman from your deviltry, to protect her with my life. I warn you that any violence to her will cost you yours."

"Your life is already forfeited," sneers Huerta. Then to his followers:

"Ho, there, men! Seize the Americano and leave the girl to me!"

Ashley's arm comes up.

"Halt!" he thunders. "This woman is my wife and as such she is an American citizen. Another step, and, by the stars and stripes, I'll send your leader to perdition!"

The streak of dawn that struggles in through the little window above the altar glints upon the polished barrel of a revolver pointed straight at the heart of Captain Raymon Huerta.

CHAPTER LI.

UNDER THE RED, WHITE AND BLUE.

"You lie!" shouts Captain Raymon Huerta, white with rage.

Ashley retorts calmly. "I repeat, Captain Huerta, what I have asserted. As my wife, this woman is an American citizen. An order from you to your men to fire upon or seize us, will be the last words you will utter in this world!"

"The marriage? Impossible! The proof? The proof?" cries Huerta, foaming with passion.

Ashley points to Father Hilario. "The proof is the

word of yonder man of God, by whom we were wedded not an hour ago!"

Captain Huerta glowers upon the priest. "Speaks the Americano truly?" he fumes.

Father Hilario is silent. His eyes wander from the lovers to the rage-distorted countenance of the Spanish captain.

Ashley holds his breath. He has made a superb bluff. Will the priest fail him at this supreme moment?

"Speak, vile dog of a priest!" snarls Huerta, the padre's silence adding fuel to his rage.

At the brutal epithet Father Hilario's cheek flushes. Then he speaks, slowly and deliberately:

"It is true. They are man and wife in the sight of God, and around them are the protecting arms of the church of Rome." He raises his arms as if pronouncing a benediction, and murmurs under his breath a pious: "May God forgive me the deception!"

Captain Huerta bites his lip till the blood comes. One word to his men would mean the destruction of the heroic trio. But over the shining barrel of Ashley's revolver, pointed straight at his heart, the Spanish captain reads, in a pair of flashing eyes, a grim resolution that means his death if he but raises his sword.

The situation is critical. The strain is beginning to tell on even Ashley's steel nerves.

At this moment a commotion is noted in the throng of soldiery that bars the entrance to the church.

Pushing them right and left, a tall, distinguished-looking military man strides into the sanctuary.

Don Huerta dashes his sword back into its sheath and sullenly awaits developments.

General Murillo, for the arrival is he, glances from one of the party to the other, and then addresses himself to Ashley:

"Senor, may I ask the meaning of this warlike demonstration?"

Ashley lowers his revolver. "It means, general, that your arrival has averted an international episode."

General Murillo turns to Huerta. "Withdraw at once," he commands. "I will see you anon."

When Captain Huerta and his men have left the church Murillo asks:

"And now, Senor Ashley, will you be good enough to explain this peculiar affair?"

"Willingly. But first, general," says Jack, with a faint grin, "allow me to introduce you to the prettiest girl in Cuba." And for the first time since the storming of the church door he removes his arm from about the waist of the Pearl of the Antilles.

Murillo bows with Spanish profundity. "I have the honor of the acquaintance of the Senorita de Quesada," he remarks.

"Who is now plain Mrs. Jack Ashley," corrects the newspaper man. "Pardon me one moment, general," and he whispers to Juanita:

"Father Hilario looks very disconsolate; go and comfort him. And now, general," to Murillo, "I am at your service."

Ashley recounts briefly the exciting events that took place from the hour he left the ball-room until the arrival of his auditor. He says nothing of Mrs. Harding.

As the recital progresses Murillo's face darkens.

"I am convinced," declares Ashley, in conclusion, "that my arrest was wholly the work of that scoundrel Huerta."

"And what do you propose to do now?" asks Murillo.

"Well, I have no special plans beyond settling accounts with Captain Huerta."

"I will do the settling with Captain Huerta," observes the general, dryly. "As for you—you must leave Cuba."

"My duty to my paper will not permit me to leave at present. And even were I free, general, I should not desire to be understood as running away."

Murillo makes a gesture of impatience. "Just like you Americans. You would all want to fiddle like Caesar while Rome was burning."

"Your pardon; but I believe Nero was the soloist on that red-letter occasion."

The general frowns. "Come with me," he says; "I will furnish to you the necessary papers and you may proceed without interruption to Santiago. The cruiser America sails for Key West to-morrow. You must take passage on her. I do you a service, Senor Ashley, and I do it gladly, as I have a friendship for you. But I warn you that any delay in leaving Cuba may subject you to much annoyance, to use no harsher term. The government suspects you of secretly aiding the insurrection."

"The government is mistaken."

Murillo glances at Juanita, and smiles ironically. "Senor Ashley," he says, "I am not so easily deceived. The instrumentality that saved the senorita from annoyance is the same instrumentality that placed the traitor Quesada in his present safe retreat. But what I as a man might applaud, I cannot as a loyal adherent to Spain condone; nor would the government take a sentimental view of the matter. You will see the wisdom of my advice. Come." And Murillo leads the way from the church.

Before he leaves the scene of his new-found happiness Jack Ashley presses warmly the wrinkled hands of Father Hilario. "Father, you're a brick," he says, and adds solicitously: "Will not Captain Huerta seek to revenge himself upon you?"

"I fear him not," replies the priest, raising his head proudly. Then, placing the hand of Juanita within Ashley's, he lays a hand on the head of each, and in a voice choked with emotion says:

"My children, I have sinned for your sake, but I trust that God will condone the offense. Heaven bless and keep you and when you are happily sheltered in your northern home think sometimes of Father Hilario, of the little church of San Pedro."

Imprinting a kiss upon the brow of the Cuban girl, the aged priest turns away and sinks upon his knees before the crucifix over the altar.

It requires but a few minutes for General Murillo to make out the necessary passports and as he hands them to Ashley, he remarks: "You will follow my advice?"

"I will follow it to Santiago, at least, general."

The general shrugs his shoulders. "Do as you please. I have warned you," he says, and turns away.

Ten minutes later Ashley and Juanita are en route for Santiago in a volante.

The young lady is sad. The natural reaction has set in.

"I am thinking of my father," she replies to Jack's attempt to rally her.

"Your father is all right," he confidently assures her. "In an hour or two you will be in his arms, and I shall have the pleasure of asking him for the hand of the dearest girl in the world. Or, stay, I am progressing too rapidly," he muses, in mock concern. "It has occurred to me," he goes on, "that—oh, well, of course a proposal of marriage must naturally be regarded more conservatively now than——"

"Jack!"

"Yes, senorita."

"What are you talking about?"

"Of you, senorita. Ah, something in your eyes tells me that I may be presumptuous enough to hope."

"What nonsense! There, I knew you were joking," declares Juanita, as she catches a stray twinkle in Jack's eye. "You foolish boy, you know I love you. I have loved you ever since—I met you."

"Three whole weeks ago," muses Ashley, as he draws the blushing face to his and kisses it.

"Do you know, I have been insanely jealous of your friend Don Carlos all along," confesses Jack, after a long, happy silence, during which the pair quite forget the volante driver.

"Jealous of Don Carlos? Oh!" cries Juanita, bursting into merry laughter.

"I admit it is highly humorous, in the light of recent developments," says Jack, who sees nothing to laugh at in his remark. "What is there so amusing in it all?"

"Oh, you dear, foolish Jack," exclaims the girl, throwing her arms around his neck. "To be jealous of Don Carlos! Why, Don Carlos is a girl."

"I am aware that, to the public gaze, Don Carlos is at present a young lady," returns Ashley, loftily, "but you must remember that I knew Don Carlos before he exchanged his customary attire for his present feminine toggery."

"Oh, how superiorily wise you look," banters Juanita. "But I tell you that Don Carlos has always been, is now and always will be a girl!"

"What!"

"And you never suspected it—you who are so penetrating?" mocks the young lady.

But Jack makes no reply. His mind is attempting to digest this surprising bit of information. Then a light begins to break upon him.

"Her real name—what is it?" he asks, suddenly.

Juanita becomes serious again. "I must not divulge it, Jack, dear. I should not have told you what I have, but you looked so comical when you told me you had been jealous of Don Carlos. There, please don't catechise me further."

"I shall not," replies Ashley. "Besides, it will be unnecessary for you to betray her identity."

"Then you know——"

"I think I do. As I more than once remarked, I have an excellent memory for faces, although I am sometimes a dev—— a diablo of a while in recalling the names that go with them." And Ashley relapses into meditation.

"Well, here we are at Santiago," announces Jack. "In a short time you can bid a temporary adieu to the soil of Cuba; and the sooner the better."

And indeed, the streets of Santiago are in apparent possession of a riotous mob, swarming in and out of the cafes.

Ashley and Juanita find no obstacles in their path; half an hour later they are aboard the America, under the red, white and blue, and Juanita is in her father's arms, relating breathlessly the thrilling incidents of the last few hours.

Ashley leaves them to their exchange of confidence and affection, and goes off to talk with Captain Meade. When he sees Don Quesada again that gentleman takes his hand and assures him that he is honored by his prospective entrance into the family.

"As for Cuba," declares the Don, his eyes lighting with a trace of their old-time fire, "the cause of the patriots was never brighter. To be sure, I am a fugitive, and El Terredo yesterday suffered a severe defeat, the Pearl of the Antilles having been destroyed in an unequal engagement with three Spanish cruisers and gunboats. But General Masso is advancing upon Santiago, with 10,000 revolutionists, and the fall of the city is looked for within forty-eight hours. Already the Spanish warships are gathering preparatory to shelling the place should it come into the hands of the patriots, and foreign vessels are preparing to leave the harbor."

"I believe I will take Murillo's advice for the present," reflects Ashley, "but I shall return to-morrow with the cruiser and be in at the death." Then he goes in search of Juanita.

"Now," says that young lady, "if you have finished squeezing my hand before all these officers and seamen, come below and I will introduce you to—to 'Miss Carlos'."

"All right, sweetheart," replies Jack, gayly. "Let me see. I believe you remarked early this morning that you would never doubt me again."

"Yes?" responds the young lady, inquiringly.

"Then, after you have introduced me to 'Miss Carlos' will you leave us alone for a short time?"

"What a strange request! But it is granted."

"Good. And now let us go below."

The interview, whatever its nature, has a peculiar effect upon Ashley. Upon returning from it he is saying to himself, sotto voce.

"By Jove! This case has taken a turn that I little looked for. I'd give four dollars to see John Barker, detective, at this moment."

CHAPTER LII.

THE ENCOUNTER AT THE CAFE DE ALMENDRAS.

"You have settled your business interests in this country satisfactorily?"

"Perfectly so. Much more profitably, indeed, than I expected."

"Then there is nothing further to keep you here except sight-seeing?"

"Nothing—except sight-seeing."

Cyrus Felton, Phillip Van Zandt and Louise Hathaway are seated on the veranda of the little Cafe de Almendras, on the outskirts of Santiago. They have returned this morning from a short jaunt to the interior and are not impressed favorably with rural Cuba. So they gladly return to the contemplation of that view which is ever welcome, no matter where one may roam—old ocean.

"And you, Miss Hathaway—have you any Cuban ties that you will sever with regret?" inquires Van Zandt.

Miss Hathaway is more thoughtful than the occasion would seem to require. "None," she replies, slowly. "Unless," she adds quickly, "the pleasure of your society for the last month may be regarded as a Cuban tie."

"Thank you," rejoins Van Zandt, with a glance that brings a blush to the face of the Vermont maiden.

"No; I am utterly, uncompromisingly disappointed with Cuba," she says. "And the people! But I have been here but a few days, so I shall not place my opinion upon record."

"And yet your brief impression of Cuba, Miss Hathaway, would not be likely to change much for the better if you were to spend a dozen years here. The country is uninteresting. The Spaniard cannot be changed. The Cuban—that is, the Cuban we see about us—does not deserve freedom. He lets the blacks and his brothers of the chaparral do all the fighting, and hardly dares, except in private, to express his cordial hatred of his ancient enemy. Do you know, Mr. Felton, I rather fancied that you had relatives in Cuba."

"Relatives in Cuba?" The little color suddenly recedes from Mr. Felton's face.

"Yes," says Van Zandt. "The day before I had the pleasure of meeting you and Miss Hathaway I was reading in a New York paper an interview with a member of the Cuban revolutionary society. In speaking of the diversified character of the Spanish officers in Cuba, the gentleman mentioned that attached to the staff of General Truenos was a young American, a former sugar planter. His name was Felton, but he changed it to Alvarez. When I first discovered your name and learned that you were en route to Cuba I unconsciously associated you with this young sugar planter so friendly to the Spanish cause."

During Van Zandt's speech, delivered in apparently careless tones, Mr. Felton succeeds in mastering a strong emotion. Louise is regarding him somewhat nervously, but Van Zandt quickly refills Miss Hathaway's glass with jerez and passes it to her with a smiling comment on the quality of the wine.

The rather awkward silence is broken by Mr. Felton.

"Mr. Van Zandt, and to you, Louise, I may say that I believe I have a son in Cuba, and that he is the young man alluded to in that newspaper. One reason why I have come to Cuba is to find that son. I supposed he was operating the sugar plantation that we visited last week. I did not know that he had joined the Spanish service."

"I regret," remarks Van Zandt, "that my idle remark should have stirred you to speak of a matter on which you might have preferred to have remained silent."

"The subject is a painful one, it is true, but once started I may as well go on to the end. It is nearly a year ago —the 1st of June—that Ralph left home, and since then I have heard from him but twice, and vaguely each time."

Both Mr. Felton and Louise are gazing seaward, else they would note the swift look of surprise that passes across Van Zandt's face.

"The 1st of June," he repeats, as if attempting to recall some incident of the past. "Did not something peculiar occur in Raymond—that is the name of your town, is it not?—about that time?"

Mr. Felton shoots a quick, inquiring look at Van Zandt's face, but reads nothing there except disinterested curiosity.

"Something very peculiar occurred two days before that date," he replies, gravely. "On the night of Memorial day Roger Hathaway, Louise's father, the cashier of the Raymond National Bank, was found dead in his office at the bank, and the institution was discovered to have been robbed of a large amount of money. The murderer has never been discovered and presumably never will be."

An expression of self-reproach is visible in Van Zandt's face as he turns to Louise.

"Forgive me, Miss Hathaway; I was not aware——"

"There is nothing to forgive, Mr. Van Zandt," Louise replies. "But I do not share Mr. Felton's opinion that the veil of mystery enshrouding the tragedy will never be lifted. Something within me tells me that one day the slayer of my father will be brought to justice."

Miss Hathaway again turns her eyes, now wet with tears, toward the sea. Mr. Felton is very pale and it is apparent that he would welcome a change in the conversation. Van Zandt, however, continues:

"Now, that you speak of it," he says, knitting his brows, "I recall that I read something about the case in the papers at the time. Was no one suspected?"

"Three persons were suspected—two of them unjustly. Derrick Ames"—with a quick glance at Louise, who flushes scarlet and bites her lips—"was one and my son the other. You may be surprised at my stating this," in response to Van Zandt's questioning gaze, "but you will understand better why I am so anxious to find Ralph. He had some motive for leaving Raymond as he did, and until that motive is discovered and his name cleared I shall be one of the most unhappy of fathers."

"And the third party suspected? You have mentioned only two," says Van Zandt.

"The third? Oh, yes; the third was a young man named Ernest Stanley. He was the only stranger in Raymond, so far as known, on the day of the tragedy. This young man had been liberated from state prison on Memorial day, after serving two years of a three years' sentence for forgery."

"Then there was fairly good reason for suspecting him?" comments Van Zandt, with an enigmatic smile. "Give a dog a bad name, you know. But tell me about the fellow. I confess I am rather interested in him. Was his forgery a very serious affair?"

"A matter of $1,000. Mine was the name he forged."

"Indeed. How did you trace it?"

"That was a peculiar feature of the case. Stanley presented the check at the bank of which I was president."

"Rather a blundering piece of business, should you not say? But may he not have been innocent?"

"The forgery was proved."

"Ah! Stanley admitted it?"

"No; he told a fanciful story of the check having been given to him in New York, in payment of a gambling debt."

"Nothing impossible in that story, Mr. Felton. I will tell you why. A night or two before we left New York I was seated in Madison Square garden, listening to a concert, when a party of sporting men sat down at the next table, and one of them entertained his companions by relating a reminiscence of a game of draw poker in which he had played a part two or three years before. I will not repeat the story, but perhaps you will understand the point I am trying to make. Four men were playing and during the course of one hand the betting had narrowed to two of them. A held what he believed to be a well-nigh invincible hand. Flushed with confidence, and irritated by his opponent's insinuation that he had no more money to wager, A took a check-book from his pocket, wrote a check for $1,000 or some such sum, and tossed it upon the table. The bet was covered, the hands shown down, and A lost. Now," finishes Van

Zandt, "A might not have had a dollar in the bank. He might have put a worthless check upon the table, knowing, as he thought he knew, that there was not one chance in a thousand of a necessity for its payment arising. That being the case, what mattered it whose name was on the check, his own or—well, say his father's? I am only theorizing on what might naturally occur some time, you know."

Cyrus Felton's face has become ghastly and he appears to be on the verge of collapse. Miss Hathaway regards Van Zandt with wonder and apprehension. The latter seems unconscious of the effect his words have produced, and he remarks carelessly: "But I will not discuss the matter further, as I suspect it bores you."

At this instant the clatter of hoof-beats sounds from the road, as a detachment of Spanish caballeria ride up, tether their horses and hurry boisterously into the cafe. The Americans are established on a quiet veranda at the rear of the building, where they may be free from just such interruptions.

"Are you ready to depart?" says Van Zandt to his companions.

"I am anxious to return to Santiago as soon as possible," declares Mr. Felton.

Van Zandt raps upon the table for the waiter, but no response is made. Host and helpers are busily occupied with their noisy guests.

"Pardon me a moment. I will step within and settle the account," says Van Zandt, as he rises and enters the cafe.

The drinking-room is crowded with the boisterous soldiery, disporting themselves as if war were an amusement and the curtain nearly down on the farce of revolution.

The presumptive leader of the troopers is a tall, rather handsome young fellow, who sits with his back against the wall and a glass in his hand. There is no one within a dozen or twenty feet of him except one caballero, with a scar across his forehead, who sits by himself at a table.

As Van Zandt enters and closes the door behind him the Spanish captain glances up and their eyes meet.

"Great heavens! Am I dreaming," mutters Van Zandt. And then he stands with white face and clenched fists, staring at the man before him.

The latter returns the stare. "I trust you will know me again senor," he remarks, ungraciously, as he sets down his glass and strikes a match to ignite a cigarette.

"I believe I have had the misfortune of meeting you before," Van Zandt replies, folding his arms and regarding the other with blazing eyes.

The Spanish captain shrugs his shoulders. "May I ask where?" he inquires coolly.

"In the United States."

"The senor is mistaken. I have never been in the states."

"You lie!"

"Curse you! What d'ye mean?" demands the Spanish captain in the purest of English, as he drops his hand upon his sword hilt. The man at the table near by lays down his paper and turns a pair of interested eyes toward the young men.

"You lie!" repeats Van Zandt, moving not a step. Then he says in a voice passionate with hatred and ringing with the exultation of a Nemesis about to strike:

"So, Ralph Felton, I have found you at last!"

CHAPTER LIII.

A WOMAN'S VENGEANCE.

The cigarette falls from the Spanish captain's nerveless fingers and his face turns gray.

"Who are you?" he gasps.

"My name is Phillip Van Zandt. I don't wonder, Ralph Felton, that you fail to recognize me by that name, though it is my true one. But you will understand why

I have sought you and why I exult in now standing face to face with you, when I breathe the name of Ernest Stanley!"

"You are Ernest Stanley?"

"I was Ernest Stanley. Now, I am his avenger. Listen to me," commands Van Zandt, as Felton strives to speak. "When the doors of that New England prison closed upon me, nearly three years ago, I swore that I would be avenged upon the scoundrel who put me there. Until a month ago I did not know his name. Until to-day I was not sure that the father was an accomplice to the villainy of the son. But when I did learn who the coward was for whom I suffered I told myself that this world, vast as it is, was too small to hold him and me. Do you understand? You cur! Do you understand?"

Felton glances about the cafe. The soldier at the table near by has again picked up his newspaper and is absorbed in its columns. But any one who might take the pains to investigate would discover that he is not reading the paper. The score or more of others are occupied in their drink, jest and song.

Felton has regained his composure and lights a cigarette with a steady hand.

"Are you aware, Senor Van Zandt, that at one word from me my men would cut you to pieces?" he sneers.

"I know that one such word will mean your instant death," is the stern response.

"Well, I shall not utter it," says Felton, coolly. "I am competent to take care of myself. A moment ago you called me a coward. I will prove to you that I am not. You seek satisfaction?"

A bitter smile flits over Van Zandt's face. "Satisfaction!" he murmurs. "Ay, I demand satisfaction for two years of utter misery and, by heavens, I shall have it!"

"You shall! I swear it!"

"Ah! And when?"

"At once. This is my only opportunity to accommodate you at present, as I am ordered to Cienfuegos to-morrow. Come, I will wait for you without." So saying, Felton turns on his heel.

Van Zandt regards him with a look in which suspicion is mingled with a trace of admiration for his sang froid.

"You will attempt no treachery?" he says, sternly.

"I tell you, sir, I am not a coward," answers Felton, haughtily.

"That he is not," mutters the soldier with the scarred forehead, and he adds, as if addressing the newspaper in his hand: "This is a devilish unfortunate affair. I must have a hand in it. Hello! Was not that a woman's scream?" He rises and, throwing open the door leading to the rear of the cafe, steps out upon the veranda. An instant later he dashes the door shut with an ejaculation of amazement.

Standing at the further end of the veranda, terror depicted in her colorless cheeks, is Louise Hathaway. A dozen feet from her is one of the troopers, who has strolled out upon the veranda, and, while much the worse for liquor, has plainly insulted the American girl. When the new-comer arrives on the scene, he sees the caballero wiping the blood from a long, deep scratch across his rage-contorted face. Between insulter and insulted Cyrus Felton interposes a feeble barrier.

With a muttered malediction the baffled Spaniard turns and re-enters the cafe, followed by the scarred soldier, whose timely arrival has doubtless saved Miss Hathaway from further affront.

"Jove! I shall have my hands full for a few minutes," that individual soliloquizes. "Ah, one moment," as Van Zandt attempts to brush by him. "You have some friends out here, senor."

"Well?" demands Van Zandt, with a stare.

"Get them away at once, or these devils in here may make it hot for them."

"I do not understand."

"You have no time to listen to a lengthy explanation. Do as I direct. Send your friends to the consul's and have them avoid the main road. There is a path through the garden. and beyond that a trail down the hillside to the beach.   It is but a mile to the consul's residence by that route.   They'll be safe at the consul's."

All this is delivered in low, rapid tones and as Van Zandt moves away the soldier turns and sees the drunken cavalier standing within a few feet of him, a malicious smile upon his evil face.   "Hello!   What the devil are you playing the spy for?" cries he of the scar, and passes on with the muttered thought: "I wonder if the chap understands English."

When Van Zandt rejoins Mr. Felton and Louise he finds the old man as white as death and his head sunk upon his breast, while Miss Hathaway is in a semi-hysterical condition.

"I'm so glad you have returned," says the latter, as she comes forward to greet him and she tells him of the encounter with the Spaniard.

"The scoundrel!" grits Van Zandt, starting toward the cafe.   But he remembers that he has more serious business on hand than thrashing a drunken trooper, and he turns gravely to his companions:

"Miss Hathaway, and you, Mr. Felton, I must ask you to proceed immediately to the residence of the American consul.   I have a little matter that demands my presence here for another half-hour, and meanwhile it will not be safe for you to remain.   Nor will it be well to go by the main road.   The city is in the hands of a mob.   The scoundrel who insulted you is a fair example.   I was warned by one of the men within—an Englishman, I should judge from his voice and manner."

Mr. Felton and Miss Hathaway regard Van Zandt apprehensively, and Louise wonders at the pallor of his face and the strange look in his eyes.

"You know where the residence of the consul is.   You must follow yonder path through the garden, and strike the trail down the hillside to the sea; it is only a short walk.   I will rejoin you there within the hour—if I live," says Van Zandt, with a significance not understood by his auditors.

Without a word Cyrus Felton rises and, followed by

Miss Hathaway, starts off through the garden in the direction indicated by Van Zandt's outstretched arm.

While all this has taken place Ralph Felton has been leaning in the doorway at the front of the cafe. He looks up when Sanchez, the besotted sabaltern, comes in from his encounter with the American girl, and signals to him.

"Sanchez, I have a little affair of honor to settle within the hour, he says. "If I do not return, you are second in command. You understand?"

"Is it 'a la mort'?" inquires Sanchez.

Felton nods and turns away, and Sanchez goes back into the cafe in season to hear the last words of the warning extended to Van Zandt by the soldier with the scar.

Felton lights another cigarette and awaits indifferently the appearance of his implacable foe.

"I am ready, sir," says a stern voice at his elbow.

"And I have been ready for some minutes. Come." And Felton leads the way across the road and into a path to the woods.

The soldier with the scar walks out into the dooryard and watches the disappearing figures. "That duel must not take place," he says. "But how on earth am I to prevent it? Hello! What's this?"

His attention is attracted by an ejaculation within the cafe. Two men are whispering by the window next the entrance.

"What deviltry is this?" he scowls, bending his head. And as he listens the scowl deepens on his face, and his fingers clutch at his pistol stock. "By heavens! I must prevent that duel now," he mutters.

Simultaneous with a command given to the half-intoxicated Sanchez, he of the scar hears the sound of a shot over in the woods.

"Treachery!" he exclaims, and bounds away in the direction of the report.

*   *   *   *   *   *   *   *   *

Felton and Van Zandt proceed silently into the thicket. A short distance from the entrance to the woods is a cleared spot.

"This will probably suit our purpose," remarks Felton, and, coolly, he measures off ten paces.

"That will be distance enough, will it not?" he asks. Van Zandt nods.

"Will you give the word, Mr. Van Zandt?"

"As you please. We will fire at the word 'Three.'" Both men draw their revolvers.

"One moment," interrupts Felton. "In the event of a second fire?"

"There will be no second fire," is the grim rejoinder. "I shall kill you with the first."

"And I will endeavor not to waste mine. Well, sir, I am waiting."

"One!" Two arms are raised, and not a tremor in either.

"Two!" The pistols click.

The word "Three" is trembling on Van Zandt's lips, when a shot rings out from the thicket. Felton clasps his hand to his abdomen, with an exclamation of pain, sways a moment and pitches headlong to the earth.

The bushes part and a woman, heavily veiled, steps forth, smoking pistol in hand and walks to where Felton lies.

She looks upon the body for a moment in silence, and hisses:

"You cowardly hound! Your end is fitting!" Then, throwing back her veil, she reveals the face of Isabel Harding.

"I have saved you, Phillip," she says, with a calmness that is very near madness.

"You have cheated me of my vengeance," he replies, looking gloomily upon the body of her victim.

"My wrongs called for greater vengeance than yours," cries the woman, her eyes glittering feverishly and her voice breaking hysterically. "I followed him here. I saw through the cafe window your meeting with him, and I exulted that I was in time—in time to save the man I loved! Phillip! Phillip," sobs Isabel, sinking on one knee beside him, "I told you that some day you would realize how much I loved you!"

But Van Zandt, with a shudder and expression of utter aversion, turns away.

"Ah, I see I am too late," remarks a quiet voice, and Van Zandt looks up to see the friendly soldier with the scar.

"To the consul's if you would save the American girl," says the latter. "I'll look after these obsequies. Come, be off," as Van Zandt stares at him in surprise. "A plot is afoot, headed by that precious Lieut. Sanchez, and you have no time to lose."

"But the consul——"

"The consul was at his office in the city two hours ago, and is doubtless there yet. Ah, you are too late." The clatter of departing hoof-beats is borne upon their ears. "No; you can reach the consul's ahead of them, by the short-cut down the hillside. Here! Take my revolver! You may need more than one. And mind, don't waist any ammunition," shouts the soldier, as Van Zandt dashes off.

Then he turns to the scene of the tragedy. He kneels beside Felton's body and makes a brief examination. Then he straightens up.

"Go!" he says sternly, to Mrs. Harding. "Your work is done!"

She stares at him a moment, with her glittering eyes; then, with a little shudder, tosses the revolver into the bushes, turns and walks slowly away.

The caballero watches her out of sight and again turns to the body of the Spanish captain.

"Humph!" he grunts, as he lifts the limp form from the ground. "He is worth a dozen dead men, or my name isn't John Barker."

CHAPTER LIV.

AT BAY IN THE CONSUL'S HOUSE.

"There is something very odd in Mr. Van Zandt's actions," remarks Miss Hathaway, as she and Mr. Felton follow the winding trail down the hillside to the sea. The latter offers no explanation. He has aged fearfully in the last half-hour, and it is now a bowed, feeble, old man whom his companion more than once has to assist over the obstacles in their rough path.

"To the consul's. To the consul's," is all he says, and the journey is finished in silence.

The residence of William Atwood, United States consul, is situated about two hundred yards back from the shore, about a half a mile below the mole at Santiago. The nearest neighbor is a quarter of a mile away, toward the city. It is a plain, square, two-storied structure. A broad veranda fronts both stories and ivy very nearly conceals three of the walls of the building. An innovation, to the Cuban view absurd, is an electric door-bell, put in by the consul himself. It is this bell that Mr. Felton presses, with the remark: "I begin to feel at home already."

The summons are answered by a porter who tells them that the consul is gone.

"Gone? Gone where?" demands Mr. Felton, with a start of uneasiness that is inexplicable to Miss Hathaway.

The consul is at the city. Where, quien sabe? Probably at his office in the city.

"We can do nothing except await his return or the arrival of Mr. Van Zandt," Louise says, as they step into the hall.

At the right of the entrance is the library. On the desk is pen and paper, and here Cyrus Felton seats himself and writes, while Louise stands in the doorway and watches him with troubled eyes.

Suddenly she hears the sound of footsteps hurrying up the walk. The door is thrown open, and Van Zandt, breathing hard from the exertion of his run, stands before her.

"Thank God, you are safe!" he cries, fervently.

"What danger threatens?" asks Louise, laying one hand upon Van Zandt's arm.

For answer he leads the way out upon the veranda. "Look!" he says; and Miss Hathaway beholds the Semiramis, resting quietly upon the still bosom of the bay.

"We must reach that yacht, or I fear we may not leave Cuba alive!" he tells her.

Louise gazes at him in questioning dismay.

"Ah, there comes the enemy," says Van Zandt, pointing up the beach toward the city. A small troop of horsemen is approaching at a lively canter.

"What is all this mystery? Why do you fear those men?" asks Louise, as they re-enter the house.

"It is not for myself that I tremble," replies Van Zandt, who is critically examining his pistols.

"Then it is I whom they seek. Your silence answers yes," says Louise quietly. She is very white, but her voice does not tremble. Like a true heroine she has grown calm in the face of danger.

"By heaven!" Van Zandt bursts forth; "my life stands between you and those Spanish devils, and gladly do I place it there. As for you," turning to Cyrus Felton, who has risen from the library table and stands near them, "I would not lift a finger to save your worthless existence. For the wrongs which I have suffered, for the misery which you and your son have caused me, I meant to have exacted a bitter reparation, but fate has otherwise decreed. Ah, you know me!"

"Spare me your reproaches," says the old man, lifting his hand in protest. "I know you. You are Ernest Stanley. What I have dreaded, yet for nearly a year expected, has come at last. My sin has found me out."

"Ah, that it has. But you are safe from my hands now, and maybe from that of the law before this day is ended. Out of the way, unless you wish your miserable life cut short by a Spanish bullet. Miss Hathaway, I must ask you to step into the library, as our visitors have arrived." And, throwing open the door, Van Zandt stands upon the threshold, waiting.

Lieutenant Sanchez and his men rein their horses within a dozen paces of the house. The leader dismounts and comes leisurely up the walk, apparently oblivious of the presence of Van Zandt, whose watchful eyes are covering every movement of the scoundrelly band.

"One moment," commands the American, holding up his hand. But the Spaniard pays not the slightest attention.

"Halt!"

This time Sanchez pauses and strokes his mustachios with exasperating calmness. "I would advise the senor to make no opposition if he values his life," he says.

"What is your errand here?"

"The American senorita, to whom I am indebted for this token." Sanchez indicates the long, dull-red scratch upon his unamiable visage. "I have no time or inclination to parley with you, senor. Out of the way, or I shall order my men to fire upon you." The troopers half-raise their carbines.

Van Zandt tears down a worn edition of the stars and stripes that decks the wall above his head, and as he throws it across his breast and shoulder his voice rings out defiantly:

"Fire upon the American flag, if you dare!"

The answer is a volley that splinters the woodwork about him and brings down the glass above the door in a shower. Van Zandt feels a sharp twinge in his left arm, and with an exclamation of rage and pain he lifts his revolver and fires.

Lieutenant Sanchez falls dead in his tracks and there is an instant scattering out of range on the part of his followers.

As Van Zandt closes the door and slips the bolt he turns to see Cyrus Felton lying upon the floor, a stream of blood flowing from a wound in his side.

"Fool! I cautioned him to keep out of range," he exclaims, as he bends over the old man.

"Is he badly hurt?" asks the voice of Louise.

"I fear so.   We must retreat upstairs, as we may expect an assault at any instant. Quick!"

As Louise ascends to the floor above, Van Zandt follows with his unconscious burden. In the rear room is a sofa, and upon this Mr. Felton is laid.

"I have but a few minutes to live. Forgive me," he gasps.

"God may forgive you," replies Van Zandt, turning bitterly away. Louise takes his hand in hers.

"Surely, Mr. Van Zandt, you can forgive the past in this awful moment," she says, softly. "Remember, he was a father and he loved his son."

At the contact of that little hand Van Zandt feels a thrill creep over him.

"You know now who I am," he says, dully. The blue eyes meet the dark ones unwaveringly.

"I know that I believe in your innocence and that I trust you," is the quiet response. "Listen, he is speaking again." They bend their heads to catch the sinking man's last words.

"In my—coat—papers," gasps Mr. Felton, with his fast-glazing eyes fixed on Van Zandt. "They—will—clear—your—name," he finishes and sinks back, exhausted by his effort.

"Cyrus Felton," says Van Zandt, gravely, "if any forgiveness of mine will afford you an iota of comfort on your journey to the other world, it is yours."

The dying man acknowledges the absolution with a glance. An instant later his spirit passes to his Maker, to be judged by his deeds in this world of sorrow and sin, of hope and happiness.

*   *   *   *   *   *   *   *

Again the Cafe de Almendras. The boisterous troopers are gone and in their place a dozen or so quiet-appearing men in civilian dress are grouped about the tables, drinking little and talking less.

It has been a noisy day, the patron tells a tall man with black eyes and fierce mustachios, who lounges in the doorway and sweeps the street with his keen gaze.

But the tall man heeds not the chatter of the patron; his gaze is fixed curiously upon an approaching soldier, who bears across his shoulder the limp form of a man in the uniform of a Spanish captain. The face of the latter is hidden.

Barker brushes by into the cafe with the body of Ralph Felton, and meets the contemptuous glance of the tall man with a searching look that the latter does not fancy.

"Ho, there, patron! A room and a doctor at once!" orders the detective, and he gives the patron a handful of coin and effectually silences his grumbling protest about making a hospital of the place.

Having deposited his burden above stairs, Barker returns to the drinking-room and astonishes the tall man with the black eyes by tapping him on the shoulder and remarking:

"I think I have met you before."

"The mischief you have!" is the curt rejoinder.

"Now I am sure of it," grins Barker. "Your voice has not changed, but your mustachios do not fit you. Pardon me," he adds, just in season to prevent an outbreak, "I am indebted to you for this slash," indicating the scar across his forehead, "but I do not lay up any hard feelings. I'll call it quits if you will lend some friends of mine a helping hand. I have got my hands full upstairs. Listen." Barker briefly recounts the episodes narrated in the previous chapter.

As the tall man listens his brow grows black as night, and when the tale is finished his voice rings through the cafe in a sharp command:

"Haste, my comrades! To the American consul's to save my friends!"

The quiet-appearing civilians about the tables leap to their feet as one man, and, leaving the unpaid patron standing in hopeless astonishment amid the ruins of the glassware he has dropped, the little band sweeps out of the cafe.

"There will be music at the consul's this afternoon, unless I am greatly mistaken," mutters Barker, as he looks down the dust-veiled road. "And now for my patient. If he dies with his secret unrevealed I'll never forgive him!"

CHAPTER LV.

A SIGNAL FROM MACEDONIA.

Van Zandt and Louise stand, hand in hand, gazing sorrowfully upon all that is mortal of Cyrus Felton. A crash is heard below, as the front door is burst from its hinges.

Van Zandt leaps to the head of the staircase just as the feet of a brace of ruffians are on the lower step. Twice cracks his revolver and his aim is true. One of the Spaniards falls and the second drops back with a cry of pain. Then, as Van Zandt throws himself to one side, there is a flash of fire below, and the bullets whistle harmlessly by.

As he judges, there is no immediate second rush by the attacking party, so he proceeds to examine his surroundings and the result is far from satisfactory. There is no serious danger of the besiegers attempting to carry the staircase by storm. The Spaniard is not lacking in courage, but it requires a considerable amount of sand to lead the way to certain death. But the room to which they have retreated was not built for a fortress and he realizes that the end must come when the enemy will gain access to the second floor—by the veranda or by the rear entrance to the building.

Suddenly his eyes rest upon a ladder at the other end of the short hallway.

"Quick!" he whispers to Louise, as he points the way to temporary safety.

A minute later and they are on the roof of the building, the ladder pulled up, and the scuttle fastened down. Over them floats, from the flagstaff, the glorious banner of their native land, and above that bends a sky of heaven's deepest blue.

"Fairly outwitted!" says Van Zandt. Suddenly he feels a weakness come over him and he sinks upon the sun-baked roof. Then for the first time Louise notices that he is wounded, and she kneels beside him with a very white face.

"It is nothing," he reassures her. With her assistance he removes his coat, tears open the left sleeve of his shirt and discloses a bullet hole in the fleshy part of the arm. It looks more serious than it really is and Louise feels an inclination to faint. But she resists it and proceeds to bind up the still bleeding wound with strips torn from her own silken petticoat. The golden head is very close to the brown one, and as the fair surgeon bends to tie a knot, the soft sweep of her hair steals away all of Van Zandt's well-guarded reserve, and his right arm encircles her in a passionate embrace.

"I love you! I love you!" he whispers.

And Miss Hathaway, being a sensible young woman, who knows what she wants, does not remark upon the "suddenness" of the declaration of love, but presses her red lips to his and tells Phillip that she has loved him ever since she knew him.

But the lovers are brought back to earth by a chorus of yells and picturesque profanity sufficient to supply the captain of a whaling bark for an entire voyage.

"They have discovered our retreat," whispers Van Zandt, as he lifts the scuttle and listens to the tumult below. But he drops it as a bullet crashes through a few inches from his head, and moves out of such dangerous range. Then, as his eyes rest upon the flag above him an idea seizes him—a veritable inspiration. He steps to the flag-staff, detaches the halyards and the stars and stripes come fluttering down to his feet.

"What are you doing with the flag?" asks Louise.

"Giving utterance to the old Macedonian cry," he calls back, and up goes old glory again, this time with the union jack down. "Pray that my crew may see the signal," he adds, fervently. And Providence assists his effort, for a puff of wind streams the flag straight out upon the breeze.

Capt. Beals is on the bridge of the Semiramis at this moment, looking toward the shore, and his curiosity is excited.

He sweeps the roof top with one glance through his powerful glance and then issues a command that echoes to the farthest corners of the Semiramis.

A few moments later Van Zandt sees two boats cut shoreward through the blue waters of the bay as fast as muscle can send them.

"Thank heaven!" he exclaims, as his heart bounds within him, and he proceeds to hug Louise in a manner that vastly entertains Capt. Beals, who is still an inter-. ested though distant spectator. And if the bluff old sea dog could have made himself heard he would have shouted a warning, for he discerns what Van Zandt cannot see—a ladder placed against the side wall of the consul's house and three men ascending it, while back a short distance, with carbines raised, stand the rest of the scoundrelly horde.

The attack bids fair to be successful, but suddenly rings out the cry of "Santiago!" and the little band of patriots from the Cafe de Almendras dashes upon the scene.

The Spaniards now have all the fighting they can attend to. Van Zandt and Louise watch from the rooftop the progress of the battle royal. The fight is won. No quarter is given, and those of the Spaniards who have the ability to flee are in full retreat, and as they disappear down the beach they shout:

"El Terredo! El Terredo!"

Van Zandt sees a strange transformation in the appearance of the leader of the rescuing party. During a hand-to-hand struggle with one of the troopers his fierce mustachios have been knocked off, and it is a handsome, beardless youth, with flashing black eyes, who looks about him and remarks: "Well, my merry men, the victory is ours, but where are the Americans?"

"Coming," sings out Van Zandt, from the upper air. "We will be with you in a minute." And as he turns to Louise that young lady proceeds to faint in his arms. It is a logical reaction from the strain which she has borne with wonderful fortitude.

By this time the boats from the Semiramis have arrived, and in them enough fighting Yankees to handle twice their number of Spanish soldiery. A ladder is placed against the consul's house and the besieged are assisted to earth, one unconscious and the other with an arm tied up.

While revivifying operations are under way Van Zandt hears a startled exclamation at his elbow. It comes from El Terredo, who is gazing upon the marble countenance of Miss Hathaway with astonished and troubled eyes.

Without replying to Van Zandt's questioning look, El Terredo picks up his mustachios from the sand and again affixes them to his face. Then he turns calmly to Van Zandt.

"The third of your party? I was told there was an old gentleman."

"He is dead. Killed at the first fire," Van Zandt tells him, and he leads the way into the house.

As the two men look upon the body, which has not been disturbed by the troopers, El Terredo shudders, and murmurs: "My God, what does all this mean?"

"It means much to me," replies Van Zandt, gravely, as he takes from the dead man's person a packet of papers.

Without speaking El Terredo steps to the sofa and assists Van Zandt to bear the remains from the house.

The body is laid in the bow of one of the boats, reverently covered, and preparations are made for the return to the Semiramis. When all but himself and the rescuing party from the cafe have embarked Van Zandt turns to El Terredo, who, with folded arms, is gazing abstractedly toward the law-and-order deserted city. "You are going with us, are you not?" he asks.

"No; I shall remain here."

"Your safety lies with yonder yacht."

"Safety? Ah, senor, somewhere on this isle is one dearer to me than personal security." And the young man turns away to hide his emotion.

"But you can gain nothing by remaining here now. The survivors of the late scrimmage have recognized you and in half an hour the whole town will be at your heels. Aboard my yacht you will be safe and I will gladly land you at any point on the island you may designate. Besides, the papers——"

"Say no more, senor," exclaims El Terredo, extending his hand. "I accept your generous offer."

Dismissing his faithful followers, with the assurance that he will be with them again ere many days, the revolutionary leader steps into one of the waiting boats.

As they are about to push off a soldier whose horse is flecked with foam comes dashing down the beach, and as he leaps from his well-nigh broken steed, he calls out cheerily:

"Got room for one more?"

"Ah! My friend of the cafe," cries Van Zandt. "You are very welcome, senor."

"And just in time," remarks John Barker, detective, as with a hearty thwack he sends his horse riderless down the beach and clambers into the boat.

CHAPTER LVI.

THE FATE OF THE SEMIRAMIS.

"And now, what?"

The boats have reached the Semiramis. Louise Hathaway has been tenderly assisted to the deck by Van Zandt, followed by Navarro and Barker, and the dead form of Cyrus Felton has been reverently conveyed aboard.

A sort of council of war is being held on the quarter-deck of the yacht, participated in by Van Zandt, Navarro and Capt. Beals. The master of the Semiramis looks inquiringly at the insurgent leader as he utters the words quoted above.

"For me personally there is but one course," replies Navarro. "I must land somewhere in the night and make my way to Gen. Masso's camp. That will not be a difficult matter. It is your own situation that I am considering. The American man-of-war, is she still in the harbor?"

Capt. Beals shakes his head. "She sailed an hour ago for Key West, for supplies and instructions. She will not return for at least two days."

Navarro's face grows grave. "Then you are not safe from molestation even in this vessel and under that flag," he says, pointing to the red, white and blue floating from the masthead. "Without a man-of-war to protect you, the Spaniards, knowing that El Terredo is aboard, will search your yacht, possibly confiscate her and subject you to no end of annoyance, even though they should not find El Terredo. They respect no flag, no emblem, no rules of civilized nations, unless they are absolutely compelled to by superior force. You saw how they treated the American flag above the consul's own residence. There are now three Spanish gunboats in the harbor. Within the hour I fear your yacht will be surrounded."

"Then there is but one thing to do," promptly replies Van Zandt. "Capt. Beals, have steam got up at once and weigh anchor. We will follow the America to Key West."

There is silence on the quarter-deck for a few moments. Miss Hathaway has retired to her former stateroom immediately upon setting foot upon the yacht, and Barker is intently watching the shore from the bridge. For the time being Van Zandt and Navarro are alone. Suddenly the former breaks the silence.

"You are not a Cuban," he says. "Why are you enlisted with the nondescript army of the insurrectionists?"

Navarro flushes at the word nondescript, but does not reply at once. Finally he says quietly: "No, I am not a Cuban. I am, like yourself, an American. But my ancestors were Cuban, back more than six generations. Until ten months ago," continues Navarro, in a less-impassioned tone, "I was a careless, happy-go-lucky American youth, without any specific aim in life. But when the Cuban insurrection broke out, I was consumed with an overmastering desire to help free Cuba from the accursed yoke of Spain. I have sacrificed everything to that end, and now I am known to the Spaniards as 'El Terredo,' the terror. I believe I have been of some service to the struggling natives, and so I shall continue until Cuba is free, or——"

Navarro does not complete the sentence. While he was speaking the smoke has been pouring out of the chimneys of the yacht in steadily increasing volume, and now the clank of the steam windlass announces that the vessel is getting under way. Without replying to Navarro's words, Van Zandt hastens below to inform Miss Hathaway of the destination of the yacht. Capt. Beals has taken his station on the bridge and the graceful vessel steams slowly toward the narrow entrance to the harber of Santiago.

Navarro watches intently the three Spanish warships by which the Semiramis must pass within half a mile. As the yacht draws nearer, the watcher notes with anxiety a boat hastily putting out from the government wharf and evidently making for the flagship of the fleet, the Infanta Isabel. He communicates his discovery to Van Zandt, who has returned from below, with the comment: "They are evidently notifying the cruiser to have her stop this vessel. Rather than that she fire on the yacht and endanger the lives of those on board, including the young lady, you must surrender me. Then they may permit you to go unmolested."

"No man leaves this ship for a Spanish prison or the garrote," replies Van Zandt, his eyes burning with excitement, "as long as there is a timber of her afloat. It is less than six miles to the entrance to the harbor, and once outside we can snap our fingers at a whole fleet of Spanish cruisers. Besides, with all the various craft scattered about the harbor, they will not dare to fire on us."

Navarro shakes his head skeptically, but does not reply. The boat has reached the side of the war vessel. The Semiramis is now nearly abreast of the latter and distant less than half a mile. Suddenly a puff of smoke rises from the forward deck of the Spaniard, followed by the sharp crack of a rifle.

"There! She has signaled you to heave to," remarks Navarro. "As I told you, you must surrender me."

"This is my answer," replies the owner of the Semiramis, drawing his revolver and firing two shots in the air. Then to Capt. Beals on the bridge he sings out: "Full speed ahead!"

Smoke is now pouring from the stacks of the warship, and it is evident that she is preparing to pursue the American yacht, but she does not, as Navarro predicted, fire on the latter. Before the cruiser gets well under way the Semiramis is within four miles of the channel that marks the entrance to the harbor.

Van Zandt smiles at Navarro. "We will lead him a merry race if he thinks to catch the Semiramis," he remarks. "This yacht can go two miles to his one. And if he hasn't improved in his marksmanship I will risk his guns. Ah, there goes the first one!"

The Spaniard has succeeded in getting within range of the yacht without endangering any of the other craft, and the roar of his forward gun is heard as Van Zandt speaks.

"An eighth of a mile to windward," observes the latter, as he watches the solid shot skip over the water. "He can't race and shoot, too."

Evidently the pursuer has come to the same conclusion, for he fires no more guns, but doggedly plows the placid waters of the harbor after the great black yacht.

And now the latter is less than half a mile from the cleft in the precipitous coast line. Capt. Beals has slowed down the engines and the yacht is picking her way by the reefs that guard the channel.

"Ship ahoy!" suddenly rings out from the lookout forward. All eyes are turned ahead. A steamer, inward bound, has just come into view in the channel.

"Permit me," Navarro takes the glasses and focuses them upon the stranger. "It is the Spanish dispatch boat Pizarro," he says. "When the cruiser recognizes her she will doubtless signal her to intercept the yacht, and in the narrow channel she can make serious trouble, I fear."

The report of another cannon, followed by two more in quick succession, shows that the man-of-war has indeed recognized her compatriot almost as soon as the American. An answering gun from the dispatch boat also shows that she has heard and understands.

Capt. Beals looks inquiringly at Van Zandt. "We must continue straight on and take our chances in the channel with that craft," the latter says. Then to Navarro: "Do you know what her armament is?"

"Oh, she is not a fighting ship. She has no armament, merely one gun for saluting purposes, and her crew cannot number over fifty."

"Then we are all right. If she gets in our way she must take the consequences."

But the dispatch boat evidently does not intend that the American shall pass. She has taken a position in the narrowest part of the channel and lies stationary, presenting her broadside to the oncoming yacht.

"Signal that we propose to pass to port," Van Zandt says to Capt. Beals, "and if the Spaniard gets in our course run him down."

Capt. Beals nods and a second later the hoarse whistle of the Semiramis echoes over the waters. The signal is answered with a rifle shot from the Spaniard's forward deck and the dispatch boat moves forward two lengths, so that she lies fair and square in the announced course of the yacht.

But there are no signs of slackening on the part of the

latter, and her black hull looks threatening indeed to the officers of the dispatch boat.

Caramba! Surely she will not run down the royal vessel! Yet it looks very like it! But they will not dare! Still—the Spanish commander hesitates no longer. He signals his vessel to back at full speed.

Too late!

The Pizarro has moved less than half a length when the American yacht crashes into her. There is a grinding shock that brings Louise Hathaway in terror to the deck of the Semiramis, and then the yacht continues on her course, apparently unharmed. Van Zandt catches a glimpse of a great jagged hole in the bow of the Spaniard, into which the water is pouring in a cataract; of a panic-stricken crew rushing frantically for the boats; and then he turns to Miss Hathaway. It is nothing, he assures her tenderly; a slight collision, but the yacht is all right and perhaps she had better return to her state-room for the present. Later on—and Louise smiles, a little sadly, but permits Van Zandt to conduct her to the saloon.

Capt. Beals is awaiting Van Zandt as the latter bounds up the steps a minute later. "We are badly stove forward," he reports, "and are making water quite rapidly. With the steam pumps going, we may keep afloat three or four hours, but the yacht is doomed."

Van Zandt is so startled at the news that for a moment he is speechless. His eyes rove back to the Spanish warship, and then at the nearly perpendicular cliffs by which the Semiramis is steaming.

He looks for the dispatch boat, but it is not in sight. "The Spaniard?" he inquires, mechanically.

"Gone to the bottom," laconically replies the captain.

"Then there is no hope for us but to keep on and try to land by the boats somewhere on the coast," Van Zandt says. "The Spaniards will treat us all as enemies, now that we have sunk one of their boats. How long can we keep up this speed?"

"Perhaps an hour, perhaps more. The water will put out the fires."

"Well, have the boats quietly prepared and keep within reach of land. Do you think the Spaniards will continue the pursuit?"

"Undoubtedly. They will stop only to pick up the crew of the Pizarro, and then will keep on after us. If there was some little bay near here where we could beach the yacht, but there isn't."

The noble craft continues to plow the waves and her injured bow still tosses the foam on either side, but her speed is sensibly diminishing. All on board have recognized the fact that the yacht is doomed, but there is no confusion, no manifest anxiety. The boats have been prepared and each member of the crew has secured in a little package his most valued possessions. On the quarter-deck Van Zandt, Navarro, Barker and Louise Hathaway are silently watching the Spanish warship. The latter is gaining now, for the Semiramis is steadily settling.

Navarro, his hat drawn over his eyes and his coat wrapped about him so that his countenance is partially veiled, has carefully avoided Louise. When she returns to the deck he walks over to where John Barker is leaning against the rail and remarks in Spanish:

"If you do not desire to be shot as a deserter I should advise you to borrow a suit of clothes from our friend, the owner of the yacht."

The detective starts. "I guess you're right," he replies in English, and turns to Van Zandt. Five minutes later he emerges from the cabin attired in a fashionable suit of gray.

"The water is within two inches of the boilers," reports the engineer, and Van Zandt sighs heavily.

"Well," he says, "we may as well take to the boats. Come." He leads Louise to the steamer's launch.

"And he?" Louise points to where the body of Cyrus Felton lies, covered by its winding sheet of canvas.

"He will go down with the Semiramis. He could have no nobler tomb."

Boom! The roar of the Spanish gun is the salute the people of the Semiramis hear as the boats pull away from the doomed yacht. The cruiser is within range and though her commander must be aware that the American vessel is sinking he is firing on her.

"The coward!" grits Van Zandt. "But the Semiramis will not strike her flag. She sinks with the stars and stripes flying."

"Pull hard!" shouts Capt. Beals. "Pull hard! She's going down!"

CHAPTER LVII.

AN INTERNATIONAL EPISODE.

"Ashley, we will give you something to write about," remarks Capt. Meade, as the America steams out of the harbor of Santiago.

"What's that, captain? A thrilling description of a voyage from Santiago de Cuba to Key West?"

The commander of the cruiser smiles good-naturedly. "More excitement than that, and something that will cause the little senorita to cling frantically to your arm."

"Ah, then, you may open the ball at once."

"Not yet; not for an hour. In short, we are going to burn some powder by and by. A little target practice, and if you have never seen anything of the sort you will be rather interested."

"Confound his target practice," Jack mutters disgustedly, as Capt. Meade bustles away. "The only powder-burning I want to see is the shelling of the dingy old city of Santiago by the Spanish fleet."

But Ashley's temporary annoyance is soon forgotten in the pleasure of assisting Juanita up and down the steep ladders, of explaining the machinery, the guns, the great searchlight and the thousand and one interesting features of the cruiser.

The target practice, he also finds, is a decidedly interesting affair, after all, which conclusion may have been influenced by the manifest delight of his sweetheart over the novel experience.

But the last gun is fired, the buoy mark is demolished, and, within forty-eight hours, Capt. Meade tells Jack, the America will be lying at anchor in the harbor of Key West.

"And she will return to Santiago, when?" the correspondent inquires. "I must be back at the finish, if the insurgents capture the city and it is shelled by the Spanish fleet."

Capt. Meade shakes his head. "That depends on instructions received at Key West. I suppose though, that the cruiser would be ordered directly back to Santiago after coaling."

Just then the captain is summoned to the bridge, where it is evident that some unusual occurrence is engrossing the attention of the officers.

Jack observes that the captain has his glass turned toward the northwest, and he also looks in that direction. Trails of black smoke low down on the horizon, evidently from two steamers, are all that reward his gaze, but he notices that the course of the America has been changed and that her speed has been materially accelerated.

"What is in the wind?" he inquires, casually, of the youthful ensign.

"That's just what we're going to find out," is the reply, and Ashley follows Capt. Meade to the bridge.

"Nothing special that we know of," is that official's response to Jack's query as to the cause of the change of course. "Some stranger, probably a Spanish gunboat, is in pursuit of another steamer, and as it is not much out of our course I concluded to run up nearer the scene."

The white cruiser is now rushing along at a speed that reminds Jack of his first memorable trip upon her, and is rapidly reducing the cloud of smoke on the horizon to the outlines of a formidable man-of-war.

"The Spanish cruiser Infanta Isabel," is the conclusion of Capt. Meade, after a long and careful study of the distant steamer. "But the craft she is in pursuit of I cannot quite make out. She is a large steamship of some sort and the Don is overhauling her hand over fist. We shall be there just in time to see the fun."

The America's course is converging toward that of pursuer and pursued. Capt. Meade's keen eyes are alternately riveted on the Spanish warship and the unknown vessel.

"If that steamship did not set so low in the water," he remarks, thoughtfully, "and was going about two-thirds faster, I should say that she was our old friend, the big black yacht Semiramis. But—great heaven! The steamer is sinking! That's what's the matter with her! She is steadily settling!"

All eyes on the cruiser are now directed toward the crippled stranger. She is, as Capt. Meade says, slowly sinking while yet the waters are dashing on either side of her bow like mountain streams.

"A game struggle, but all in vain," is the comment of the captain, shaking his head. "Probably the Spaniard hulled him below the water line early in the struggle, and he has been slowly making water ever since. He can't last much·longer. The water must be near the fires now. Ah! I thought so!"

For the strange steamer has apparently lost headway. The black smoke that a moment before poured from her chimneys now mingles with a white cloud of steam.

"Her fires are out," Capt. Meade explains to Ashley. "She will go down in twenty minutes, if she doesn't blow up before."

The boom of a heavy cannon startles the watchers and they turn quickly to the Spanish man-of-war. A curling wreath of smoke from her forward deck tells the origin of the report, and their eyes return to the sinking vessel. A puff of wind lifts for a moment the flag hanging limp at her masthead, as if in mute defiance of the Spanish shot. Capt. Meade starts as if he had received an electric shock.

"The American flag!" he thunders, "and fired on by the Spaniard!" Then to the executive officer: "Signal for the forced draught and bear down on the steamer. We will pick up her boats and then investigate the outrage on the flag."

Another shot, and still another, comes echoing over the water from the Infanta Isabel, her target the fast-filling steamer.

Suddenly Ashley is electrified by the command in the stentorian tones of Capt. Meade:

"Clear the ship for action!"

A second later the trumpet's harsh notes and the sharp rattle of drum, mingling with the shrill whistles and rough voices of the boatswain, mates and the noisy clanging of the electric gongs, call the sturdy crew of the America to "general quarters."

Then, indeed, is the blood of the newspaper man stirred by the scenes about him. The decks throb with the rush of hurrying feet as the men hasten to their stations. The gun crews are casting loose the great guns, the murderous rapid-fire cannon and the secondary batteries. Some are hastily donning equipments, others filling sponge-buckets and still others stripping themselves of all superfluous clothing, laying bare their brawny forms.

Hatches are covered, hose laid and pumps rigged, ladders torn away, and decks turned topsy-turvy, in the twinkling of an eye. Rifles, cutlasses and revolvers come out from the armory in quantities that amaze Ashley. The marine guard falls in and topmen are scrambling nimbly aloft to secure anything movable there.

Down come the rails, out come davits and awning stanchions—everything movable is stowed away or secured. The magazines are opened and the tackle rigged over the ammunition hatches ready to hoist shot and shell for the guns.

"The grim panoply of war," Jack thinks, as he hastens to conduct the wondering Juanita below. Even here, he observes to his great surprise, the captain's sacred cabin has been invaded "on the jump" by the crews of the after guns.

As Ashley returns to the quarter-deck he notes that the America is bearing hard down almost at right angles on the Spanish warship, now distant less than a mile.

"Evidently here is an excellent opportunity for an international episode," he thinks, as he glances at the stern face of "Fighting Dave" Meade on the bridge. Then his hand involuntarily goes to his ears and he catches at the rail for support, as the forward gun of the American cruiser thunders forth and an eight-pound solid shot skims over the waves across the bow of the Spanish cruiser.

Before he recovers from the shock of the concussion there is a murmured, "She's going!" from the officers on the quarter-deck and Jack looks quickly in the direction of the sinking steamer. But the black hull has already disappeared beneath the waves and he sees only the fluttering red, white and blue ere the whirling eddies reach their eager arms for the beautiful emblem.

The gun from the America does not have the anticipated effect on the Spaniard, for he continues full speed toward the spot where the steamer sunk. But it has evidently had effect in another direction. With the aid of his marine glasses Ashley observes four boats, which had hitherto escaped his notice, pulling toward the white cruiser. The purpose of the Spanish vessel is thus apparent. She designs to cut off the fleeing boats before they may reach the America.

Again the white cruiser careens to one side and a second deafening report, this time the gun from amidship, roars out in language not to be misunderstood by the on-rushing Spanish man-of-war.

It is not misunderstood.

There is a rapid gush of escaping steam, the stacks cease to vomit forth their black clouds and the Infanta Isabel turns her course and steams slowly toward the America.

Ashley watches curiously the flashing oars of the coming boats, and when the forward one is almost within hail he lifts the glasses to his eyes and scans her passengers.

"Thunder and Mars!" he exclaims, "if there isn't John Barker in the bow and—yes, it must be Louise Hathaway, Van Zandt, and—who the devil is that chap with the ferocious mustachios? El Terredo, or I'm a sinner!"

CHAPTER LVIII.

THE END OF THE TRAIL.

When the first boat is alongside the America, Barker is the first man to clamber to the deck, and the first individual he gets his eye on is Jack Ashley.

"Hello! Well met," remarks that young man, extending his hand. "I was expecting you any minute."

Barker gives Jack's hand a perfunctory clasp and passes on with a gruff "Hello!"

"I am not yet forgiven. I see," thinks Ashley, as he turns to the rest of the party coming aboard. He greets Miss Hathaway warmly and Van Zandt genially, and grips Navarro's hand with a pressure of strong friendship.

There is no present opportunity for mutual explanations, as a serious interruption is apparent in the shape of a boat that has put out from the Spanish man-of-war and is rapidly approaching the America.

With a shade of anxiety the people of the Semiramis await the arrival of the boat. They note the preparations to receive with due honor the representative of the Infanta Isabel, the marines drawn up in double file beside the gangway, the officers of the America in position on the quarter-deck. But there is no time for speculation or conjecture. Eight pairs of dripping oars are simultaneously raised, the boat glides softly to the side of the cruiser, and a moment later the Spanish officer is bowing profoundly to the commander of the America.

His excellency, Admiral Sanchez of his majesty's man-of-war Infanta Isabel, presents his compliments to the commander of the United States cruiser America and begs to say that the passengers, officers and crew of the steamer just sunk, who have sought asylum on the American vessel, are rebels, in arms against his majesty the king of Spain; that their vessel, just sunk, has within the last three hours destroyed the royal Spanish dispatch boat Pizarro. Wherefore his excellency respectfully asks that the said officers, passengers and crew of the rebel ship be delivered to the representative of her majesty's ship Infanta Isabel as prisoners of war.

Captain Meade listens patiently while the Spanish officer delivers his message, his brow knitting slightly at the reference to the destruction of the dispatch boat. Then he turns to Captain Beals:

"What have you to say to this statement and why were you flying the American flag, if you were in command of an insurgent vessel?"

"We are not insurgents and we did not destroy the dispatch boat," is the reply. "The pleasure yacht Semiramis of New York, Van Zandt owner, was in collision with the Pizarro in the harbor of Santiago. The Pizarro stood directly in our course, notwithstanding our signals that we proposed to pass to port. We should have gone aground if we had not fouled her. We did not stop, as the Semiramis was badly stove and subsequently sunk, as you have seen. Further, our officers and crew and the passengers are without exception American citizens. As such, I appeal to the commander of an American vessel for protection."

"And you shall have it," murmurs Captain Meade under his breath. To the Spaniard he says: "Present my compliments to his excellency, Admiral Sanchez, and say that the commander of the America finds upon investigation that the officers and crew of the late steamer Semiramis are American citizens, who claim the protection of the American flag; that her captain and officers maintain that the destruction of the Pizarro was an accident for which they are in no wise responsible. Therefore I am constrained to decline to grant the courteous request of his excellency."

The Spanish officer bows respectfully and continues: "His excellency also desired to convey to the commander of the United States cruiser America the information that among the persons lately on board the sunken steamer was one Cuban rebel, denominated El Terredo, whom his excellency has every reason to believe has sought refuge on board this ship. He respectfully requests that said El Terredo be delivered to the representative of his majesty's ship."

Captain Meade's eye strays over the little group, but before he can speak Navarro steps forward and says in English: "I have been designated as El Terredo, but I am an American citizen."

"I can testify to that statement," supplements Ashley.

Captain Meade waves his hand. "That is sufficient. Inform his excellency that all of the persons picked up in the boats from the lost steamer are American citizens. As such, I cannot surrender them."

Again the officer bows, and his errand performed, he salutes and returns to the boat. What will be the effect of his report? Will Admiral Sanchez resent with force Captain Meade's decision, or will he gracefully bow to the inevitable? The latter apparently, for a few moments after the officer ascends the side of the man-of-war the Spanish flag is dipped in salute to the America and the Infanta Isabel steams slowly back in the direction of Santiago.

"Again is Providence on the side of the heaviest guns," murmurs Ashley, as he walks over to where Barker is leaning against the rail, and claps him on the back. "John, I am powerful glad to see you," he declares heartily.

"I don't know whether I can say the same or not," rejoins the detective, sulkily. "For a man whose infernal meddling with affairs that did not concern him nearly cost me my life, you appear pretty cool and unconcerned."

"My dear friend," says Ashley, "if I had not been at Jibana half a dozen days ago you would never have forgiven yourself for the part you played as a soldier of Castile. Do you know who Don Carlos was?"

"I know he, or she, was a woman."

"Oh, you do?"

"Yes; and if you had shown yourself after the scrimmage, instead of sneaking off to Santiago, I might have told you of my discovery."

"Ungrateful wretch!" cries Ashley in mock reproach. "I admit that I got you into the scrape, but I also got you out of it. The fiery El Terredo would have strung you to a telegraph pole had I not begged for your life and liberty. Yes; Don Carlos was a woman, and she was Helen Hathaway."

"Then El Terredo?" marvels the detective, who is beginning to see daylight.

"Was Derrick Ames, of course. Anyone except a detective would have discovered that long ago."

"Indeed," retorts Barker. "When did you find it out?"

"Early this morning," laughs Ashley. "But let us be serious. Where are the Feltons, father and son?"

"One dead, and the other perhaps so," replies Barker, and he tells Ashley the story of an exciting day at Santiago.

"It must be done," the detective is saying, concluding his narrative. "Your sympathies naturally stand in the way, so I will relieve you of all active participation in the affair. All you will have to do is to be a silent witness. One thing you must do, though. You must see Mrs. Ames and have her pledge that she will not let her husband know that she has told you her story. I must handle the affair gently, as Ames is as flashy as gunpowder. You will see Helen, then?"

"Yes; I will fix it immediately. When do you occupy the center of the stage?"

"To-morrow. I will let you know in due season."

"All right, old chap. I will be glad when it is all over. So long."

There are many happy hearts on the America this night. The meeting between the sisters, Helen and Louise, was a dramatic one, and after affectionate confidences had been exchanged each sought the man she loved best.

But a shadow of sadness hovers about the four as they sit on the quarter-deck and watch the big white moon rise out of the sea. Now that all the excitement is over Van Zandt has dropped back into his old reserve, and the consciousness of his odd relations to Louise Hathaway reverts to him with unpleasant keenness. Ames is moody and abstracted and only the incessant flow of spirits of Jack Ashley, who joins the group with Juanita, keeps the little party alive.

But bedtime comes early, for everyone is thoroughly tired, and the party disperses with many a fervent "Good-night, and pleasant dreams."

And as Van Zandt prepares to go below he feels a touch on his arm and turns to see John Barker. "Mr. Van Zandt, will you grant me a few minutes before you retire?" requests the detective.

"Certainly," is the reply. "Come to my stateroom."

Ashley rises early the next morning and as he smokes his after-breakfast cigar Barker joins him.

"I shall want you at ten o'clock, promptly," says the detective. "Meet me in the private cabin, or whatever it is called on shipboard. I have secured exclusive use of it for an hour."

"Very well," replies Jack, abstractedly.

Promptly at ten, Ashley repairs below, and as he enters the cabin he finds Ames and Van Zandt there. They look at him questioningly, but before he has opportunity to say more than "Good-morning," Barker enters, closes the door and locks it.

Ames flushes angrily. "So," he says, "it is at your request that I am here?"

"It is," replies the detective, calmly.

"What do you mean, sir, by inviting me to this place and locking the door upon me?"

"I simply do not wish to be disturbed," is Barker's unruffled response. "The cruiser America is now United States territory. I have business with you, Mr. Ames. Gentlemen, will you not be seated?"

CHAPTER LIX.

"WRITTEN BY THE HAND OF FATE."

"You are a detective," murmurs Derrick Ames, as he drops back into his chair.

"I am," answers Barker. "For nearly a year I have been on the track of the murderer of Roger Hathaway, being ably seconded in my quest by my friend Jack Ashley. The trail has been a tangled one, and has wound under the flags of three countries, but for the past fortnight the end has been clearly in view. By a remarkable combination of circumstances affairs have been so precipitated that to-day nearly all the living characters in the Raymond drama are upon this vessel, the United States cruiser America. My work is done. I have only my story to tell. I shall begin, Mr. Ames, by asking you a few questions," resumes Barker.

"Well?" queries the object of his remarks.

"At what hour did you enter the Raymond National Bank on the evening of Memorial Day of last year?"

"I cannot say exactly. I judge that it was in the vicinity of 7:45."

"Will you be good enough to state what took place there between you and Roger Hathaway?"

Ames scans the detective's face keenly for a moment, then replies to Barker in deliberate tones:

"I went to the bank to ask Mr. Hathaway's consent that his daughter Helen might become my wife. I was confident that my errand was useless, as he had twice before scorned my suit. Helen and I had been idling all the afternoon on the hillside below the town. As evening drew on I left her at the bars and went to the bank, as she stated that she had understood her father to say that he should spend the evening at work upon his books. It being Memorial Day the streets were deserted, and, barring one acquaintance, a chap named Sam Brockway, I did not meet a person on my walk up the main thoroughfare. As I crossed the bridge I saw Mr. Hathaway standing on the steps of the bank, delivering a note to a boy, and when he re-entered the building I followed him.

" 'What do you want?' he demanded, almost fiercely. I told him, and he broke into a torrent of abuse. Naturally hot-tempered, I answered his railings in kind, and I know not what might have happened had not Mr. Hathaway suddenly ended the dispute by seizing me by the shoulder and pushing me through the bank door to the street, threatening, as he did so, to have the law on me if I continued my attentions to his daughter. Through the glass panel in the door I watched him walk rapidly away in the darkness of the interior; saw him as for an instant his form passed into the lighted office in the rear of the bank. Then the door to that room closed. I never saw Roger Hathaway again."

"That is sufficient," says Barker, as Ames pauses. "Your further progress up to to-day is known to me."

"Indeed?"

"Yes. And I may say that from the outset neither Mr. Ashley nor myself believed you guilty of the murder of Roger Hathaway. At the most, we considered that you might have been a witness to the tragedy. But your testimony is the last link in the chain. I am now prepared, gentlemen, to relate what in all human probability happened in Raymond on the evening of Memorial Day last year."

"Pardon me, Mr. Barker," Van Zandt breaks in, abruptly. "I regret to tell you that the trail which you have so patiently followed has led you to what I should judge, from your preliminary remarks, to be a false conclusion."

"What!" cries the detective, starting from his chair.

"You think Cyrus Felton killed Roger Hathaway. So did I once. We were wrong. If Cyrus Felton was responsible for Hathaway's death it was only indirectly, and the Raymond tragedy was the cause of more misery to him than any human being should be compelled to bear."

Barker is too astounded to reply for an instant, and Ames and Ashley stare questioningly at Van Zandt.

"Let me relate briefly that much of my story which bears directly upon the tragic events in Raymond," says Van Zandt, quietly.

"On the afternoon of Memorial day of last year I was released from the State prison at Windsor, Vermont, after serving two of a three years' sentence for forgery, which, in reality, was committed by Ralph Felton.   I took the afternoon train for Raymond, arriving there at 7:45.   I went directly to Cyrus Felton's residence, and reached it at 7:55.   As I was about to ascend the porch I heard footsteps behind me, and, thinking they might be those of the man I sought, I stepped into the shadow of the porch.   The new arrival had apparently called to see Felton on business.   I heard the housemaid tell the visitor that Felton was not at home; that he might be at his office in the bank building.   As the man walked away I followed leisurely.

"When I reached the entrance of the bank building a man, presumably the caller at Felton's, came down the stairs and walked down the street.   Then I went up the stairs and proceeded down the corridor until I reached a door with Felton's name upon it.   But the door was locked and the office was dark.   As I retraced my steps and stood again at the entrance of the block a man passed by hurriedly, ascended the steps to the bank, opened the door and went in.

"I remained where I was for five minutes, and then walked to the bank door and glanced through the glass panel.   The interior was dark, save for a ray of light that issued through the partly opened door to the cashier's private office.   Perhaps Felton is within, I thought, and pushing open the front door, which was ajar, I walked softly toward the shaft of light that slanted across the bank floor.

"What my errand to Felton was, gentlemen, it is not necessary for me to now state.   Enough to say that when I threw open the door to the cashier's office I looked upon a sight that froze the blood in my veins.

"Lying upon the polished floor, which was stained with his life-blood, was the body of Roger Hathaway, and standing over him was Cyrus Felton, a revolver clenched in his right hand.

"When I made my appearance upon the threshold of the office Felton turned his head and our eyes met for an instant that must to each have seemed an age. Then I closed the door, and a moment later stood at the entrance of the bank, gasping for air. Can you not imagine the horror in my soul? My one impulse was to flee from the fearful scene. I had looked, as I thought, into the face of Roger Hathaway's slayer, and that was the man to whom, incidentally at least, I owed the two past years of misery. Falsely imprisoned for one crime, might I not be accused of another and greater one? All this and more flashed through my brain, and I hurried to the railway station. There I learned that no train was due for hours. I staggered away from the station and plunged down the track into the night.

"How I made my way over mountain and through forest to southeastern Vermont and rode to New York on the trucks of a freight car; how I read in a New York paper of the crime that startled Vermont and of my supposed connection with the affair; how in that same paper I saw a personal advertising that if Phillip Van Zandt, who left Montana over two years ago, would communicate with Ezra Smith, lawyer of Butte, Montana, he would learn of something to his advantage; how I, being the much wanted Van Zandt, proceeded to Montana and discovered that I was sole heir to the immense fortune of my uncle, a silver king in that State, from whom I had foolishly parted in anger two years before—all this and more I will relate at another time, gentlemen, if you care to listen.

"Not until late last night," continues Van Zandt, "did I have the opportunity of examining the papers given in my possession by Cyrus Felton just before he died in the consul's residence at Santiago."

As he speaks Van Zandt takes from his pocket a packet of papers, selects one of them and tosses it across the table to Barker. "Read that," he says. "Read it aloud."

The detective unfolds the document and reads:

"Santiago de Cuba, April 15.—This is written by the hand of fate. I shall not live to see to-morrow's sun rise. I know it. The presentiment of my end is so irresistible that no effort of will can shake it off. And I am glad that it is so. I could not endure another day such as this has been. I should go mad.

"To-day I saw the detective. I have felt that for months he has been pursuing me. And I have looked again into the eyes, the glittering, pitiless eyes, that stared at me nearly a year ago across the corpse of Roger Hathaway—the eyes of the man whom, to shield my son, I cruelly wronged. From the hour, a month or more ago, that I met Phillip Van Zandt I feared him. A nameless dread took possession of me. To-day I recognized him and I read hatred, contempt and menace in his eyes. He thinks I killed Roger Hathaway, and what manner of vengeance he has in store I know not.

"But Roger Hathaway killed himself. Together we wrecked the Raymond National Bank. It was the old story of unfortunate investments, and the blame was chiefly mine. But when the crash was imminent Hathaway proved the hero and I the coward. He killed himself and saved both his name and mine. And yet with that bullet he put an end to all his troubles, while I—I have suffered for months the tortures of the damned.

"With this I inclose his letter, which he left on his desk for me the evening of Memorial Day. It has been on my person since that fatal night, and it has seared my very soul. I have not dared to destroy it or to leave it where it might be found, for it is at once the proof of my guilt and of my innocence. If it becomes necessary to clear——

"Ah, he is coming.   Cyrus Felton."

Barker mechanically unfolds the inclosure, three sheets of letter paper crumpled and worn. The stillness within the cabin is deathlike as the detective reads:

"Before your eyes rest upon these lines the hand that pens them will be cold in death. I have taken the only alternative. For myself I care not, but that the finger of scorn should be pointed at my defenseless children; that their young lives should be blighted and they shunned and avoided as lepers because their father betrayed his trust and cruelly wronged his friends and neighbors, I cannot bear it. The banks, both of them, are irretrievably involved. The funds deposited by the county to pay the bonds have been used to meet pressing obligations. The crash would come to-morrow. It cannot be staved off another day. I have thought it all out. For the sake of my children and the name they bear I am about to take my own life. But they nor any other living person save you must ever know that I did not die by the hand of the assassin. I have arranged that it will appear as if the bank has been robbed and the cashier murdered. As I write this room bears evidence of a fearful struggle. The vault is open and the securities in confusion. Thus will our crime be hidden from the eyes of all save God. Your personal account over-drawn I have fixed by the removal of pages from the ledger, so that when the examination of the bank's affairs is made there may be no suspicion of irregularity on your part or mine. You will be the first to find my lifeless body. The weapon by which I die you must secure and secrete.

"And now, farewell. That the sacrifice I am about to make may not be in vain I adjure you guard well the secret of my death. Care for my children. Watch over them, cherish them. By our hope of heaven and forgiveness, by our life-long friendship, by the bitter sacrifice to which duty points the way, by all these things I charge you, Cyrus Felton, fail not at the peril of your good name   Roger Hathaway."

As Barker concludes the reading of the remarkable epistle each of the four men is busy with his thoughts. No one offers any comment on the message from the dead. Finally Ames breaks the silence.

"And Ralph Felton?" he queries, turning to Barker.

"He had nothing whatever to do with the death of Roger Hathaway," returns the detective. "He refused to answer the coroner's question at the inquest as to where he had spent his time between 7:45 o'clock and 8:30 on the evening of Memorial Day because he did not wish his association with Isabel Winthrop, or Harding, to become known when he had been a suitor for the hand of Helen Hathaway. But that was not his principal reason for leaving Raymond as suddenly as he did. As bookkeeper of the savings bank he had embezzled a portion of the funds—not a sensational peculation, only sufficient to keep pace with his expenditures, which were in excess of his income. Fearing that his offense would be made public when the bank's affairs were overhauled, he fled. It was with difficulty that I extracted from him yesterday afternoon a confession of his reason for leaving Raymond.

"As to the locket supposed to have been removed from Hathaway's watch chain the night of the tragedy, and which Mr. Ashley picked up a few nights ago, I supposed until yesterday that it had been dropped by Ralph Felton. But it seems that it was torn from Mr. Ames' neck when Felton hurled himself upon him on that memorable evening at Jibana. Mr. Hathaway had detached it from his chain the morning of Memorial Day, as the spring was broken, and had given it to Helen to convey to the jeweler's to be repaired. It left Raymond with her, and when she and her husband took up their Cuban life the miniature of the younger sister was removed, for obvious reasons, and Mr. Ames wore the locket about his neck, attached to a long gold chain."

Another silence, which this time Van Zandt breaks.

"Now that the facts in the case are in your possession, Mr. Barker, I presume you will feel it your duty to report them to the proper authorities."

The detective does not reply. He glances curiously at Ashley, and the latter passes over a cigar, which the detective bites in meditative fashion.

"And you?" Van Zandt queries, turning to Ashley.

"It would make a capital story," drawls Jack, who has already told himself that the big bunch of "copy" in the pigeonhole of his desk in the Hemisphere office will never greet a compositor's eye.

"No doubt," says Van Zandt, gravely. "But, like many capital stories, it would be a source of endless pain to two estimable young ladies. It would render nil the sacrifice which Roger Hathaway made to preserve his family name from disgrace, and would make a hollow mockery of the simple epitaph which you tell me marks the marble shaft above his grave—'Faithful Unto Death.'"

The detective lights his cigar.

"Is there any likelihood, Mr. Barker, of the state of Vermont paying the $1,000 reward which was offered?" continues Van Zandt.

"None," replies Barker. "The reward was for the arrest and conviction of Roger Hathaway's murderer."

"And the additional $4,000 offered by the bank?"
Barker smiles sardonically.

Van Zandt takes from his pocket a folded slip of paper and passes it across the table to the detective.

"There is a check for $5,000," he says. "It is not a bribe. It is only your just dues for the labors that you have expended on the case. Personally, I am under deep obligations to you. As to whether the Raymond mystery shall remain a mystery, I leave it to your own sense of duty."

Barker folds the check slowly, and, as he slips it into his vest pocket, he remarks, with a glance toward Ashley:

"If my partner consents, the Hathaway case may as well remain as now fixed in the coroner's records in Raymond, Vermont."

"Your partner came to that decision some time ago," is Ashley's quiet response.

"Thank you, gentlemen," says Van Zandt, as he rises. "And now, my friends, suppose we rejoin the ladies. They will begin to think that we have deserted them."

THE END.